Valerie Wood was born in Yorkshire and now lives in a village near the east coast. She is the author of *The Hungry Tide*, winner of the Catherine Cookson Prize for Fiction, *Annie, Children of the Tide, The Romany Girl, Emily, Going Home, Rosa's Island, The Doorstep Girls* and *Far From Home*, all available in Corgi paperback.

Find out more about Valerie Wood's novels by visiting her website on www.valeriewood.co.uk

Also by Valerie Wood

and published by Corgi Books

ANNIE

Valerie Wood

CORGI BOOKS

ANNIE
A CORGI BOOK : 0 552 14263 8

First publication in Great Britain

PRINTING HISTORY
Corgi edition published 1994

3 5 7 9 10 8 6 4

Set in Linotype Plantin 10/11pt by
Hewer Text Ltd, Edinburgh

Corgi Books are published by Transworld Publishers,
61–63 Uxbridge Road, London W5 5SA,
a division of The Random House Group Ltd,
in Australia by Random House Australia (Pty) Ltd,
20 Alfred Street, Milsons Point, Sydney, NSW 2061, Australia,
in New Zealand by Random House New Zealand Ltd,
18 Poland Road, Glenfield, Auckland 10, New Zealand
and in South Africa by Random House (Pty) Ltd,
Endulini, 5a Jubilee Road, Parktown 2193, South Africa

Printed and bound in Great Britain by
Cox & Wyman Ltd, Reading, Berkshire

Papers used by Transworld Publishers are natural, recyclable
products made from wood grown in sustainable forests
The manufacturing processes conform to the environmental
regulations of the country of origin.

Special thanks to Catherine for her assistance, for Peter and Ruth and all my family for their constant support and encouragement

Acknowledgements

Sources of general information.

The Country Life Book of Nautical Terms Under Sail

The British Seaman. 1200–1860 A Social Survey
Christopher Lloyd

Dress in 18th-Century England
Anne Buck

Jane Austen's Town and Country Style
Susan Watkins.

Smuggling on the Yorkshire Coast
Jack Dykes

Library Services, H.M. Customs and Excise. New
King's Beam House, 22 Upper Ground, London,
SE1 9PJ

My thanks to Patrick Howlett, Hessle, for loan of maps
and information on Hessle.

Prologue

Did other rivers, streams and creeks fall into these mighty waters, cascading down hills and surging through valleys to swell the rushing waters of the mighty Humber? Annie wrapped her shawls around her. A wind was rising, cold and sharp, coming in from the sea. It disturbed the water's dull surface, agitating it into frothy white crests and she saw by the increasing undercurrent that the tide was on the turn. The river was on a journey and she was compelled to follow it.

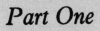

Part One

1

They're coming. They're coming. They're coming. Gibbet.
Gibbet. Gibbet. Tha'll swing. Tha'll swing. Tha'll swing.

At each detaining suck and slurp of the mud around her
boots, Annie thought she could hear the menacing warning
echoing in her ears.

She glanced over her shoulder. The fog was eddying
around the middle of the river, hiding the banks of
Lincolnshire on the other side. But as the grey dawn
broke, the vaporous mantle started to lift, rising to reveal
the muddy brown waters lying just below the footpath
where she was so desperately running, away from the
town of Hull and the consequences of her wrongdoing.

'Oo – oh, who'll help me?' She wailed, and then in fright
put her hand over her mouth and looked again over her
shoulder to see if the constables were following her and
listened for a hue and cry.

A painful stitch in her side slowed her down, and as she
gasped short, dry, rasping breaths to relieve it, she became
aware of a melancholy moaning. She stopped and listened,
but the sound also stopped. She hurried on and it started
again. A whimpering lament of distress. She closed her
open mouth. It was there again; inside her head, filling
her mouth, her ears, her throat, shaking her body with its
intensity so that she could no longer stand. Her trembling
legs gave way beneath her and deposited her onto the
muddy path.

'Oh dear God, what have I done?' On her knees she
rocked and cried. 'I'll get found out. They'll come for me.'

Wide-eyed with terror she hunched into herself and
listened again, this time the only sound was the familiar

lap of the river, the heavy-winged flight of cormorants as they swooped low over the water, and the thud of her own laboured breathing.

They won't have found him yet. She took deep shuddering breaths. 'Course they won't. 'Tide will have covered him. They might never find him. Francis Morton's face swam in front of her and she screwed up her eyes to stop the tears and obliterate the vision.

'I'm that tired,' she mumbled. 'Dare I stop?'

She hadn't slept all night. She had gathered together her meagre possessions, her last few coins, her boots and shawls and morsel of bread, and left the dark damp room which she and her children had called home. She had kept to the narrow alleys until she reached the edge of the town, then with a brief backward glance, had slipped out of the broken, decayed walls and headed for the river.

In that dark hour before morning she'd hesitated on the Humber bank and surveyed the deep waters as she had done every day of her life; from her childhood on the wharves to her wifehood in the mean house in the rat-infested alley on its banks, and contemplated that all she knew was that beyond the spit of Spurn the river emptied itself into the yawning mouth of the German Ocean; but up river, of that she knew nothing. Having no patient mother or wise father who might have explained the river's direction, she had only hearsay that the river split into two, dividing itself and going separate ways.

And what then? Did other rivers, streams and creeks fall into these mighty waters, cascading down hills and rushing through valleys to swell the rushing waters of the Humber? She'd wrapped her shawls around her. A wind was rising, cold and sharp, coming in from the sea. It disturbed the water's dull surface, agitating it into frothy white crests, and she saw by the increasing undercurrent that the tide was on the turn. The river was on a journey and she was compelled to follow it.

* * *

The sun was breaking through the clouds. Lying low on the skyline it transformed the dark water to a pale mirror of gold and shimmered through the gossamer strands of dispersing mist, and she realized that shipping, schooners and cutters, colliers and trading luggers, would soon be moving up river, and that the footpath by the bank, and the old road just beyond it, would start to become busy with travellers making their way between the towns of Hessle and Hull.

I'll have to hide, she thought, glancing along the narrow shore. Maybe I can sleep for a bit, and then move on again tonight. It wasn't far, she had heard, to the town of Hessle, only five or six miles, though she had never been. But she knew of the town, where they built ships, and a ferry since ancient times had run a passage across the shortest stretch of the Humber to Barton in Lincolnshire.

She could see the banks of that country now as it appeared through the fog, and wondered if she could get there. Nobody would know me there, she considered; but she started to tremble at the prospect of someone remarking on the sight of a strange woman travelling alone across the water, and asking questions.

The sound of voices and the jangle of a harness startled her and she jumped down onto the pebbled foreshore and pressed herself into the side of the bank. She didn't look up until she judged that the travellers had passed, then peered over the top to see the retreating figure of a man holding the reins of a mare, which pulled a small cart in which a woman was sitting.

'They're off to 'market,' she mouthed. 'I'd best be sharp and find somewhere safe.'

She hauled herself up the grassy bank onto the road and scurried along it, afraid of being seen. Beyond the road lay fields and meadowland and between the grassy areas were strips of scrub, common balk, overgrown with hawthorn and bramble, which marked the boundary and divided up the ownership of land.

Into the thick of this she scrambled, sliding down into

the ditch at the road side and into the undergrowth, not heeding the thorns which tore her hands and pulled the threads of her shawl and skirt. She scrabbled on her hands and knees as far into the thicket as she could, pulling aside the prickly stems of dog rose and blackthorn and noting the red hips and blue-black, plum-like fruits which hung there.

I wonder if I can eat them? Her stomach was beginning to gnaw with hunger. She fished from beneath her skirts for the parcel of bread which she had hidden there, and chewing slowly to make it last longer, she ate half of it. Then, rewrapping the remaining piece, she pinned it carefully back beneath her skirt, placing it next to a small bag of coins.

As she lay in her small dark cave, her shawls pulled about her and her head resting on her hands, she heard voices from time to time, the sound of laughter and the measured clip of donkeys' and horses' hooves, and she shrank further into the undergrowth, praying that she wouldn't be seen from the road. The day drew on and towards midday as the warmth of the sun reached her, she dropped off into intermittent sleep.

Her body twitched as she dreamed and she moaned softly. 'Me poor bairns. Me poor bairns. What'll become of us? Lizzie, I did it for thee.'

In her dreams she saw again the smiling face of Francis Morton. Then his smile became rigid as the knife in her hand struck, his teeth turning black as blood oozed from his mouth and covered his shirt, and his eyes stared accusingly at her.

She sat up with a cry. 'Oh, dear God. They'll hang me. I'll swing from 'gibbet.' Her hands touched her throat as if feeling the rope, and then locking her thin arms around her knees, she rocked, moaning softly. 'What'll happen to me bairns? Their ma a murderess!'

Tiredness took hold of her again, and brushing a pile of dead leaves into a pillow, she lay down and gazed up into the canopy of branches and shrubs above her, watching the patterns of sunlight as it filtered through.

Lizzie will be all right, she thought. Maria and Will will take care of her. They promised when I asked them. They've been good friends to me. 'Onny ones I've ever had. They said they'd take care of her, even though they've bairns of their own to feed, and Maria expecting another.

Happen I shouldn't have been so hasty, but I was that angry. I thought Francis loved me. When I asked him, he said he did. But when I caught him in 'house—, and our Lizzie, poor bairn, being so frighted, well me blood was up. I couldn't help myself. In God's name, I couldn't.

She touched her cheekbone and felt the tender swelling and the cut which still oozed blood from the blow Francis had given her and cried softly. I seem to have spent my whole life weeping. I've had no happy times that I can think of. None that lasted anyway. Alan never made me happy. I thought he would, when he married me, but he was nowt but a bully when he was at home. I was allus glad when he went back to sea, glad of those long voyages to 'Arctic, and I can't say that I was sorry, not really sorry, when he died.

She sat up and wiped her eyes with the end of her shawl, and thought of the day when she was called to the office of the ship-owner, Isaac Masterson. 'Mrs Swinburn,' he'd said gently. 'I'm sorry to have to tell you of your husband's death.'

Maria's husband too, Will Foster, had suffered terrible injuries on the ill-fated voyage of the whaler, the *Polar Star*, but he had been a hero, while Alan had died because of his own drunkenness.

She sniffed. Makes me wonder why we're here at all, when there's only misery and pain.

And me two lads. What of them? Will they make out without me? I've never been a good ma, even though I loved them. I never knew how. She nodded as she sat in her damp hollow. They'll be better off without me.

Seamen's Hospital will look after them. Ted, he's not well, poor bairn, and Jimmy, why, I could do nowt with him, but he'll look after himself will Jimmy, when he's big enough; he'll grow just like his fayther.

Convincing herself that her children would manage at least as well without her as with her, she waited, sometimes dozing, sometimes peering through the branches towards the narrow road and listening to the slap of the water on the pebbled shore.

As the sun started to sink she brought out the remaining piece of bread and nibbled half of it. She was very hungry, yet dare not eat more, and once more she carefully wrapped it and put it down beside her. She leaned forward and pulled a handful of hips and the small blue fruit which hung so temptingly above her.

'These is hips, I know, and I don't think they'll harm, but these plums, if they are plums, dare I try them?'

She ran her finger over the waxy skin, disturbing the bloom, and on impulse sank her teeth into the flesh.

'Aagh. Aagh. I'm poisoned. I'm poisoned. I'm done for. God forgive me for me sins.'

She spat and retched as the bitter juices stung her tongue and scorched her throat and she reached for the lump of bread and tore off a piece, chewing furiously.

'Tha's lucky. Tha could be lying dead. How stupid thou art, Annie. Never did have any gumption. That's why tha's in such a fix.' She muttered and grumbled, hunger making her lightheaded, and she eyed the remaining piece of bread. 'Shall I eat it now? Or shall I wait until I really need it? It's not 'first time I've felt hunger.'

She lay down again and waited for darkness. There had been many times in her life when she had felt the pangs of hunger. When she was a child living beneath the river wharves she had had many days without food, when the other children had not had enough to share with her – until she had learned how to scavenge and beg for her own bread, she had known how to exist on very little sustenance.

I wonder what happened to me own ma? Who was

she? Will my bairns forget who I am? No. No. They're older. They'll remember me. I was only a babby when she went.

Instilled in her mind was an image of a woman who suckled her, who sat with her beneath the wharves, and who laughed and smelled of warm milk and liquor, and who one day, when she reached for her, had gone and left only emptiness in her place.

Other hands had taken her and fed her on watery pap until she was old enough to fend for herself. The 'River Rats', people used to call them, and named them as thieves and ruffians. They lived on the refuse that others had discarded, searching in the mud when the tide had turned for anything that they could find and sell and turn into food.

And as for her father: the man who appeared from time to time claiming her as his own, demanding what little she owned as his, and giving her a beating when she objected; he too had disappeared, and she wasn't sorry.

As dusk fell, she roused herself and prepared to leave her leafy shelter. She could hear the wind blowing strongly and she wrapped her shawls tightly around her head, tucking her lank fair hair inside. She reached for her bread. It was dark in the hollow and she couldn't see it. She searched the ground where she had been lying.

'It's not here! It's gone. Me bread. Where's me bread?'

Her fingers touched some dry crumbly fragments and she peered at them. 'Me bread! Summat's eaten me bread!'

Furiously she banged the ground with her fists. All that was left of her precious bread was a small pile of crumbs. She heard scurryings beneath the branches, of mice or birds, of cats or rats. Whatever it was, had she been able to catch the offending creature she would without any compunction have strangled it with her bare hands.

There was a heavy swell on the river, white flecked waves spilling over onto the shore as she climbed down. I'll walk here until dark, she thought, and then go back onto 'road.

She felt nervous. She wasn't afraid of the dark, but this was unfamiliar territory, a new country, an open space full of strange sounds, and the further she travelled, the higher the white cliffs which edged the shore became, intimidating her by their loftiness.

Even the Humber, her own river, which she had always lived alongside, seemed like a stranger, showing her a different face from the one which she had known from the confines of the town walls, longer and lonelier, and somehow threatening. While the vessels running for their home port before darkness fell, seemed to turn their surging sails accusingly towards her.

She remembered the old tales she had heard long ago from superstitious old women. Stories of the ghosts who roamed the river bank. Ghosts of the dead who had been carried in their coffins towards the churchyard in Hessle, in the time long before there was a place to bury them in Hull, and who were swept away by the turbulent waves, along with the grieving mourners who carried them, down into a watery grave. They waited, in the darkness, so it was said, their skeletal fingers dripping with slimy strands of river weed, stretched out to waylay travellers along the riverside path.

'I don't believe it. It's just an old tale.' She picked up her skirts and ran along the deep shingle, stumbling in her fright over the scrubby bushes and wild shrubs which reached out to trip her. But the shadows seemed to dance menacingly about her, and as the smudgy darkness fell, fiendish spooks and demons whispered in her ear, and with them, she thought she could hear the intimidating laughter of Francis Morton.

With relief she watched the moon emerge, sailing high above the water, lighting up the Lincolnshire coast and pointing the way with Neptune's Path across the river, and it lit also the path on the shore, shining white on the pebbles beneath her feet. As she neared the Hessle creek, she could make out by its light the silhouette of boatsheds and the masts of boats which lay anchored in the water.

She crept silently towards the inlet and looked over. There was the ferry, held at anchor, its mast and rigging traced black in the moonlight, gently swaying on the water. It was a busy harbour, packed tight with boats, and on the bankside masts and canvas rigging were laid and crates stacked high one on top of another. She froze as she heard the sound of a man cough and then spit, and then saw the swinging beam of a lantern.

''Watchman,' she breathed, and sank low behind a crate. It would be off to the magistrate if she was found and then all would be finished, she'd be sent back to Hull to a fate she didn't dare contemplate.

As she watched, another figure emerged only yards from where she was crouched. She followed his progress as he dodged behind crates and boxes as if he was stalking the figure of the nightwatchman. He dashed across towards a boat which was lying beached on the quay, and hid behind it. She saw his face quite clearly in the moonlight. He was young, younger than her, she thought, his face unshaven, and merry as if he was having great sport. His dark hair was long and curly, and she saw a glint of an earring in his right ear.

She shifted her position, standing on tiptoe and peering above the crate, to be able to see him more clearly and he looked up, alerted by the slight sound, and saw her. For a moment alarm showed on his face, and then a grin appeared and he put a finger warningly to his lips.

Something told her that she should go, that things were happening here that could embroil her. Tha's in enough trouble of thine own, she told herself. Tha doesn't need any more.

Silently she edged backwards until she reached the riverside path again. She retraced her steps until she came to the stone bridge which crossed the haven and took another path climbing higher and leading away from the river, and up across a grassy sward to a small wood. Here she rested again. Her legs ached from walking on the deep shingle and she leant back against a tree and contemplated what she should do next.

Sleep must have overtaken her for she opened her eyes to the beginning of day. The sun was not yet fully up but a pale flush filtered through the trees and touched her cold cheeks with warmth. She looked around at her surroundings and found that she was on the edge of a copse, smaller and thinner than she had thought the night before, when the trees seemed blacker and denser than they were.

The copse edged a paddock where a stringy horse and an old goat were tethered and beyond the paddock was a cottage with a hedge of hawthorn around it. Annie dropped to her stomach and slithered along the ground until she came to the hedge, and lay in the damp grass peering through a gap.

A glimmer of light burned in the cottage window, and above the thatch the chimney-pot discharged a thick gush of spiralling wood smoke, whilst through the half open door drifted the tantalizing smell of something cooking.

She wasn't so much hungry now, for she was well beyond the stomach rolling pangs of emptiness, but had the pinched and stabbing muscular cramps of an unfed belly which cried out for sustenance.

She wrinkled her nose. Could it be mussel and onion stew like we used to make down by 'river when I was a bairn? 'Mussels that were big and tender and salty, and if anybody had managed to pinch bread, we used to dip it into 'stew and it would be soft and pappy, and even them without teeth could chew it.

Or a drop of fish broth would be tasty. I used to make that for me bairns when Alan left me without money, and I'd bring home some fish heads from 'dock side and boil them with 'taties. Or eel pie like Maria's ma used to make. She had 'knack with paste had Maria's ma, all golden and crusty it was, not heavy and lumpen like mine.

She licked her dry lips as she hallucinated over the sweet white fleshy strands of eel, and its dark succulent skin which she used to draw through her teeth, and she lifted her head and sniffed, drawing in a deep breath to catch the aroma which floated towards her.

It was getting much lighter, the sun was rising with its pale light suffusing the sky with pastel streaks of rose and yellow and lighting up the house in front of her. She saw now that it was a low dwelling, a mere hovel, and she felt relief because of it. Perhaps the residents of this abode had also known hunger and would therefore be glad to share their morning meal with her. Or, she sank down again in despair, more likely they would turn her away as a beggar because there wasn't enough for another mouth.

A shadow moved across the grass in front of the window and a donkey lifted its head and ambled forward. She envied it for its ability to eat grass, she had tried that too, but there was no nourishment in it.

Painfully she got to her feet and stumbled round the hedge. She wiped her face with the end of her shawl and smoothed her matted hair, and with weak and listless knuckles knocked timidly on the door.

2

'What does tha want?'

A scrawny old woman in a bonnet and apron over her black dress stood in the doorway, one hand held up against the door frame, the other on her hip.

'Can tha spare me a bit o' bread, or a drop o' soup? I've had nowt to eat for—.'

'No. Clear off. We've nowt to spare for beggars.' The woman made to shut the door.

'Oh, please. I'm no beggar. Just down on me luck.'

'Tha's beggin', so that makes thee a beggar. Be off with thee.'

There was no mistaking her meaning and Annie turned away, then looked back; behind the woman she could see a man about to put on his coat.

'A drink o' water then?'

The woman pointed down the garden. ''Well's over yonder. Get a sup and then go.'

'Who is it, Mrs Trott?' The man came to the door and peered over the woman's shoulder. He was tall and stopped and as gaunt as the woman, but he looked kinder, Annie thought.

'Just a beggar woman. We've nowt to spare for likes o' them.'

'Oh, come now. She's onny a lass. Give her summat. We've enough.'

Annie hesitated. She didn't want to cross the woman by appearing too eager, but she was so hungry. She closed her eyes as a dizzy spell came over her and she felt herself sway.

'She's badly, poor lass. Fetch her inside, Mrs Trott.'

'Tha's daft. Tha allus was. Taking in beggars and ne'er-do-wells. We'll never sleep safe in our beds.'

The woman grumbled and muttered, but roughly took Annie's arm and pushed her through the door into the cottage.

'Tha'll sit there and not move while I dish thee some soup. I'm not having me home ransacked while me back's turned.'

Annie sank down onto a wooden stool by the fire where the woman indicated. The old woman could say what she wanted, call her every name she could think of, she wouldn't care. Just so long as she gave her some of the soup that was bubbling in the pan over the fire.

Mrs Trott ladled some into a bowl and then cut a hunk of bread and handed them to Annie.

'Think thy self lucky that he was at home.' She cast a thumb towards the old man who was hovering at the door. 'Tha'd have got nowt if it had been left to me.'

'I'm very grateful.' Annie's eyes and nose watered as she dipped the bread into the hot soup. 'Fish stew. It's 'best food in 'kingdom.'

Mollified the woman shrugged, then turning to the table cut another piece of bread and handed it to Annie.

The man smiled and turned away. 'I'll be off.'

'Tha's leavin' me alone wi' beggar then?' Mrs Trott folded her arms about her and called him back. 'And tha'll be surprised if tha finds me dead wi' a knife in me back when tha comes home.'

With a cry Annie rose to her feet, slopping the soup down her skirt and onto the floor. 'No, please. Please, don't say that, I'll not harm thee. I've got no knife. I've got no knife.'

She collapsed back onto the stool, racked with sobs. 'I've got no knife. Honest to God.'

'Now look what tha's done, woman. Tha's frightened poor lass to death. Have some pity. Enough's enough.' His voice, which had been slow with the wide-vowelled

25

words of the district, grew sharp. 'There's some wi' short memories.'

'Take no notice.' He bent over Annie and patted her arm. 'She's nervous of strangers, that's all. Eat up tha soup. We can't afford waste.'

Annie obediently ate whilst the man stood over her, her tears salting her lips as they flowed unchecked. The woman's words had unleashed terror into her heart and she could see with infinite clarity the flash of a thin blade as it penetrated flesh.

The man left, casting a severe look at Mrs Trott who sat stony-faced at the table, not looking at Annie but staring at the door.

'Can I do summat for thee, to repay thee for tha kindness? Fetch water, or bring in wood?'

Annie didn't want to leave the warmth of the fireside, she'd do anything to stay longer. Her belly was full with bread and soup and she just wished that she could curl up on the bed at the other side of the fireplace and sleep.

The woman watched her closely as Annie's gaze fell on the feather bed. 'Aye, tha can shake 'bed for me. Feathers get up me nose and I sneeze all day, and when tha's done that tha can fetch me in a bucket o' water.'

Annie heaved the bedding outside and shook it so hard that feathers flew and dust filled the air. The old woman obviously hadn't shaken it in a long time.

Next she took a pail to the draw well, and as directed, wound the handle of the windlass, lowering it down and drawing up a bucket of sparkling spring water. She cupped her hand and took a drink.

'By. That's best water I've ever drunk. Better than river water by far.' Annie spoke freely.

'Tha'll be from Hull, then?' Mrs Trott gazed suspiciously at her.

'Wha—, what makes thee think that, mistress?'

'They drink river water in Hull. I know, I, – I had a relation once from there. She's dead now.'

'Aye. I worked there for a bit. Now I'm on me way back to me own country.'

'And where would that be?'

Annie swallowed hard. 'York. I come from York.'

'I know of it,' Mrs Trott nodded. 'It's a goodly way from here, and a long way to walk, if that's what tha intends? And wi' no food either?' she added.

'I was robbed,' Annie responded swiftly. 'There's a lot of ruffians in Hull. They took me money. All I had. That's why I had no food or owt. They took it all.'

She followed the woman inside, carrying the brimming bucket of water and splashing it over her boots. She noticed as she entered that there were clumps of mud on the floor, mud from the river bank that must have dropped from her boots when she came in.

She bent to scoop it up. 'I'm sorry, – on tha clean floor an' all. I'll clean it up if tha'll give me a floor clout.'

Mrs Trott fetched a cloth and handed it to her. Annie rubbed enthusiastically at the wide wooden boards, spreading the mud and leaving a brown stain.

'Give it here.' Mrs Trott snatched back the cloth. 'I can see tha never kept a tidy house. Brought up to be a lady, was tha? Why, it's worse now than it was afore tha started.'

Annie stood shamefaced. She never had been housewifely, and as she glanced from under her lowered lashes, she saw that Mrs Trott was, that the room, though poor, was clean. The floorboards, wide enough for a ship's deck, and the table top, were scrubbed to paleness and the hearth swept free of ash.

'Aye,' she answered with a sorrowing sigh. 'Me ma would never learn me. She said as she wanted better things for me, 'wanted me to be a lady's maid, or summat like it.' She hid her red, roughened hands beneath her shawl as she spoke and hoped that Mrs Trott hadn't noticed them. 'She'd turn in her grave if she thought I'd come to this.'

Mrs Trott humphed and gazed with narrowed lids. 'And did tha ma give thee 'fancy petty, or did tha get it by some other means?'

Annie looked down to the hem of her skirt. It was muddy and torn and where the torn flap dangled, a glimpse of yellow satin showed. It was her only piece of luxury. When she had gathered her belongings before her swift departure, she had dressed in all the clothing she possessed; her cotton shift and flannel petticoat, her black woollen skirt, a grey woollen shirt that had been Alan's, two shawls and her old, worn boots.

She had almost left behind the shiny petticoat with its edging of lace, not wanting to be reminded of him who had given it to her. But the habit of acquisition, acquired at an early age, when something unwanted could be sold for food, had never left her, and she had reluctantly drawn it on beneath her skirt.

'It was me ma's,' she began, and then saw the hankering gleam in the old woman's eyes. 'Onny thing I've left to remind me. I'll never part with it, never.'

Disappointment showed in Mrs Trott's face. 'Tha can stay 'till after supper. I can't be fairer than that.'

Annie stayed silent, then sighing turned as if to leave.

'Tha can sleep one night. Then tha must be off.'

'Can I sleep in 'feather bed?'

'Nay.' Mrs Trott looked shocked. 'That's Mr Trott's bed.'

Annie considered. 'Can I have a sleep now, while he's out? Then tonight I'll sleep anywhere tha says.'

A frown creased the woman's forehead, but Annie lifted the hem of her skirt. 'It's best satin tha can buy. Feel it. Go on, feel how shiny and slippery it is.' She shook her head. 'I don't think I can part with it. What would me poor ma think?'

'All right.' Mrs Trott gave in. 'Tha can sleep in 'bed 'till he comes home. But tonight tha'll sleep on 'floor. I'll not share my bed wi' strangers.'

Annie slipped off her top skirt and then slowly as if unwilling, whilst Mrs Trott waited anxiously, she stepped out of the petticoat and handed it over to her eager hands. She unfastened her boots and the cloth which bound her feet to avoid blisters, and sank into the softness of the feather bed.

'Them's us own ducks.' Mrs Trott nodded, at the mattress, stroking the petticoat lovingly. 'Tha'll not sleep on better, even if tha got to be a lady, which tha won't.'

Annie didn't answer. Sleep was stealing over her as the warmth of the bed claimed her, and within seconds she drifted away. Then some innate alarm woke her and she felt urgently about her waist for her bag of money. It was there, beneath her flannel petticoat. Reassured, she clasped it in her hand and fell fast asleep.

It was whispering which woke her, and begrudgingly she lifted heavy eyelids. The room was gloomy as the light outside had faded, but by the glow of the fire, she saw Mrs Trott sitting on the stool by the fireside, and opposite her, with his back to the bed where Annie lay, was a man. His hair lay in curls on his shoulders, so it wasn't Mr Trott, whose hair on his head was sparse and grey, though he had an abundance of beard; the man turned his head as he was speaking and she saw the glint of gold in his ear.

She closed her eyes quickly and listened, but they were speaking with such low voices that she couldn't catch their words. She was certain that it was the man she had seen last night skulking about the haven. Should she pretend that she had never seen him? He may wish that she hadn't, for he could only have been up to mischief. From her life by the river, she knew enough about shipping and its cargo to know that there could be valuable goods lying in the crates by the waterside. Then too, he may wish to know why she had been there, alone, in the darkness.

There was the scraping of a chair as someone stood up, and the fall of footsteps near the bed, she opened her eyes and gazed into a round, dimpled face and a smiling mouth with a gap between the front teeth.

Brown eyes looked down at her. 'Don't be afraid. I'm a friend of the Trotts'. Are you well rested?'

29

'Aye,' she said, and reached for her skirt which was lying at the end of the bed.

He moved away and turned his back. A gentleman? She slipped on the skirt and stood up. Nay. Why would there be a gentleman here, chatting so intimately with Mrs Trott?

'Mrs Trott tells me that you are travelling to York.' He smiled amiably and lit the lamp which Mrs Trott had brought to the table.

Annie nodded. She felt uneasy. This man wouldn't be so easy to mislead. Behind his charm was an intelligence superior to hers.

'Aye, that was my intent.'

'It's a very fair town. One that I know quite well.'

She was dismayed. Now she was caught. If he should question her of the whereabouts of the place she had claimed as her home, she couldn't tell him. She knew not a street or alley by name.

'You'll know the Shambles of course? Petergate? Whip-Ma-Whop-Ma-Gate? Jubbergate? Yes of course, you will,' he added, as dumbly she nodded in agreement. 'And no doubt you'll be familiar with the snickets and ginnels which are buried in the heart of the town? Yes indeed, who wouldn't know those familiar streets who had lived their lives there?'

She stared as he drew a chair to the table. What was he talking about? What language was he using? He indicated that she should be seated and then pulled a stool towards her and sat down.

Mrs Trott removed the steaming kettle from the fire and made a dish of tea, bringing it to the table and putting a cup in front of him.

'Why, Mrs Trott, how absent-minded you are becoming,' he joked. 'Where is a cup for Mrs er—?'

Annie gave a small gasp. 'Annie. Annie, – er, Hope.' Alan had been well known in Hull. He frequented all the inns and taverns, and the cock and dog fights. This man might well know his name.

'Hope! What an excellent name, for it is all we have left in these hard times, is it not, Mrs Hope?' Smiling, he looked steadily at her.

'Forgive me,' he said, standing up. 'My name is Tobias Linton, Toby to my friends.'

Mrs Trott begrudgingly brought a dish of tea to Annie and as she placed it on the table, Mr Trott came through the door.

''House is full o' gossipers as soon as me back's turned,' he said dryly. 'Tha's back early Toby. I thought tha was in York.'

'Indeed I was, all of yesterday and night. I rode out at midday today. I thought if I was lucky I might catch a bit of supper with the Trotts.' He glanced towards Annie as he spoke and in his eyes was a question.

He knows it was me, she thought. He's wondering if I'll give him away. Well, it's nowt to do with me what he was doing on 'quayside, or why he should lie to Mr Trott.

'Ah. I almost forgot. I've brought you a gift.' He rose from his stool and went to fetch a bag that was lying near the door. 'Pheasant,' he said triumphantly, bringing out a brace. 'The best of the shoot.'

Mrs Trott's eyes gleamed greedily, but the old man frowned. 'Are they 'Squire's bods?'

'They are,' grinned Toby. 'And he sent them with his compliments. At least, he would have done, had he known about them. You know well how generous he is.'

A flicker of a smile touched Mr Trott's mouth, but he shook his head. 'There'll be 'devil to pay if tha gets caught.'

'Nonsense, Henry,' Toby replied airily. 'What could he possibly do? Put me in gaol like a common thief?'

'Somebody's been hanging about 'haven.' Mr Trott ignored Toby's comment. 'Last night's watchman told me that summat's been shifted about – crates and that.'

'It's as well tha wasn't there then, Mr Trott. Happen tha might have been blamed if owt was missing.' Mrs Trott busied herself by the fire, putting on extra wood and lifting a cauldron on to a hook above it.

'Nowt was missing, that were funny part of it. He said it was as if they was onny looking. Well, if I find anybody mooching about when I'm on tomorrow night, they'll feel 'strength o' my truncheon, make no mistake about it.'

'The villains won't dare come if they know you're on duty, Henry,' Toby stretched lazily. 'Everybody knows what a law-abiding citizen you are, *and* that you wouldn't think twice about defending your master's property! Well, Mrs Trott, are you going to offer me some bread and cheese, or do I go on my way with a hungry belly? I must be off. I have business to attend to.'

Annie watched as Mrs Trott fussed over him, scooping out the soft middle from a crusty cheese onto a plate, and plying him with extra bread, and cajoling him to stay longer for a sup of stew.

'Mrs Hope will stay and help you eat it. I hear that you are staying the night, good lady? The Trotts' will look after you well, have no doubt.' He rose to leave and bent towards Annie. 'Sleep well. I may see you tomorrow before you set off on your journey. It's a long way to York, you must take great care on the road.'

Annie helped Mrs Trott to clear away the dishes after supper. She belched appreciatively. 'Thank thee for taking me in. I can travel well now on a full stomach.'

Mrs Trott opened up a wooden chest and brought out two blankets and handed one of them to her. 'Aye, well tha can sleep in front o' 'fire tonight. Mr Trott will want his own bed.'

She caught Annie's questioning gaze. 'I sleep on 'floor yonder. Allus have done.'

Annie looked at the bundle of bedding at the back of the room where Mrs Trott had thrown the other blanket. She nodded. 'Shall I keep 'fire going?'

'Course tha'll keep 'fire 'going,' she snorted. 'What sort o' dowly wife is it who lets 'fire out?'

Annie sat crosslegged, gazing into the flames while the old woman settled herself onto the floor and wrapped her blanket around her. Mr Trott sat on a bench at the side of the hearth, sucking on a clay pipe.

Presently a gentle whistling and snoring flowed from Mrs Trott's side of the room and Mr Trott tapped out his pipe on the hearth and commented. 'She's away. Like a kettle o' steam she is once she gets going, huffing and puffing all 'night long.'

'Wouldn't she rest better on 'bed?' Annie ventured.

'Aye, she would, but she'd rather act 'martyr on 'floor than have a bit o' comfort.' A note of bitterness had crept into his voice and she looked up wonderingly.

'I'm going to have a tankard o' ale,' he said, rousing himself. 'Would tha like a drop? Help thee sleep.'

She refused. 'I'll not need any rocking, even though I had a sleep during 'day.' She wrapped the blanket around her shoulders. She wished he would go to bed so that she could lie down and rest.

'Go on, get into 'bed,' he said. 'I don't need much sleep, I can doze here by 'fire just as well.'

'Nay,' she protested. 'I'll not take thy bed. Has tha a job o' work to do tomorrow?'

'Not in 'morning. I'm on nightwatch tomorrow night down at 'shipyard. I'll not need to be up ower early. Go on,' he persuaded. 'We'll not tell Mrs Trott.'

She needed no further bidding and in the dimness of the room she slipped out of her top clothes and into the comforting softness of the feather bed.

Sleep must have come almost immediately for when she awoke with a start some time later, she felt alert and fully rested. For a moment she wondered where she was, and then remembered. Mrs Trott was still snoring, the pitch having changed from a shrill, rousing, clarion call to a full-throated snort. But it wasn't Mrs Trott's snoring which had so rudely awakened her, but the shaking of the bed as someone crept in beside her.

3

She edged away to the other side of the bed and felt the roughness of the cold wall against her nose. She lay perfectly still, not daring even to breathe. It wasn't the old woman beside her, she was still snoring, and she'd said that she wouldn't share her bed with strangers, and Mr Trott had verified that she preferred the floor.

It had to be Mr Trott. Perhaps, she thought, he had forgotten that she was there and had routinely climbed into his bed. Or – the other possibilities crossed her mind, and she involuntarily shuddered.

A hand touched her shoulder. 'Mrs Hope, art thou awake?'

She didn't answer but feigned sleep. Then she felt a pair of bony knees clad in flannel come close to her.

'I'll not harm thee.' Mr Trott's voice was soft and quavery. 'I just felt 'need, 'need of some comfort, that's all, and tha seemed lonely like me. I've not felt 'warmth of a woman next to me in a long time.'

She turned her head towards him. She could smell the ale on his breath. 'Mrs Trott?'

'Nay, she's a cold woman. She's never shared my bed. Never in fifteen years.'

She suddenly felt sorry for Mr Trott, sharing his life with a disagreeable, mean old woman. She knew what it felt like, knew only too well what misery life was without the warmth of loving arms. Alan had never been loving, always demanding when drunk, and indifferent when sober.

Gently she put her hand over his, which lay still on her shoulder, and patted it. 'Stay then,' she whispered. 'It's all right. Onny, keep still. Go to sleep.'

Sleep didn't come back to her. She lay quietly, not moving, feeling his presence next to her and hearing his breathing becoming regular as he dropped into slumber. Soon, he too started to snore and his resonant rasp and gurgle swelled into a fanfare, and joined in a discordant serenade with Mrs Trott's sibilant wheeze.

There's no wonder they don't sleep in 'same bed, Annie brooded, they'd blow each other out. Tha could set sail down 'Humber with 'power of these two.

She saw daylight easing its way through the cracks of the shutters, and with sudden forethought, removed Mr Trott's arm from about her waist and slid out of bed. She built up the fire with the kindling by the hearth and put the kettle on to boil. Then she wrapped the blanket around her and sat watching the flames catch hold of the dry wood and kindle into crackling life.

'Humph.' A snort aroused Mrs Trott and she sat upright. 'Hast put 'kettle on?'

'Aye. It's almost on 'boil.'

Mrs Trott blinked as if she had forgotten why Annie was there. She gazed at her through narrowed accusing eyes. 'Tha didn't let 'fire out then? Tha's been stoking up all 'night by 'look of it. Tha'll have to fetch more wood in afore tha goes.'

Annie nodded. She'd be glad to be away from this parsimonious woman. 'I'll go now and collect a bundle.'

Mrs Trott folded her blanket. 'Mr Trott still sleeping? It's not like him, he's generally up afore me.'

Annie smiled thinly. 'He's resting well. Happen we should leave him to his dreams.'

She wrapped her shawls around her as she went outside. Rain-clouds were gathering and the river looked dark and unfriendly. I'm going to get very wet if I set off today, she pondered. But I'm not sure if I could spend another day in that house, even if I was asked.

She wandered down to the riverside path. Pieces of timber and driftwood were lying on the shoreline and she jumped down on to the narrow strip of shingle to gather them into her skirt.

'Good day, Mrs Hope.'

She turned to see Toby Linton leaning against the bank, shallower here than on the other side of the haven, and idly tossing a pebble in his hand. She smiled. It was good to see a friendly face, even though she was wary of him.

'G'day, sir.'

'Has the old woman sent you out for fuel?'

'Aye. She thinks I've been building up 'fire all night and using up all her kindling.'

He laughed. 'She's had a hard life. She doesn't like to think she'll ever be without the essentials, not even kindling. Here, let me help you.'

'They're a strange couple,' she said as she handed him some pieces of wood. 'Not like a proper wedded pair.'

'Why do you say that?'

'Well, she sleeps on 'floor for one thing, and he sleeps in 'feather bed on his own.'

He kept hold of her hand. 'And what of your husband, Mrs Hope. Does he sleep alone in a feather bed, whilst you're roaming the river bank?'

The sudden question startled her and she pulled her hand away, dropping the wood. 'Me husband's dead. I'm a widow.'

'I'm sorry. You're young to be widowed. You must be only my age, twenty-two – three?'

She shrugged. 'Where I come from, 'life we lead, widowhood is common. And my age? I'm more'n that I think.'

How could she know when life had begun. She had little memory of childhood. Life had always been the same, searching for vittals and scrounging for money. Only when she had met Maria and her mother, had she realized that there was another type of life, different from her own. Maria's mother's house had seemed like a king's palace, with a proper bed, a table and a chair and a fire in the hearth.

She gazed out across the river seeing again the compassion on the lined face of her friend's mother and feeling the touch of her fingers as she'd stroked her cheek.

'I didn't mean to upset you.' Contrition showed in his eyes, he had obviously mistaken her pensiveness for sorrow. 'Curiosity overcame me. I'm sorry.'

She bent her head and sighed. 'Aye. I'm all alone in 'world. There's nobody to care what happens to me.'

'No children from your marriage to comfort you?'

She hesitated. Could she deny her bairns? 'They're gone from me. I don't want to talk about it.'

I suppose I was very young, she reflected. I'd just started my flux when I met Alan by 'river bank. He'd come looking for a woman and saw me. He kept coming back all that summer and I didn't know why. Then Maria's mother saw him and told him that he ought to marry me if he wanted me, and give me a home. She wasn't often wrong, but she was wrong about him.

'And so now you go to York? Back to your own town?'

There he goes again with his questioning. I haven't asked *him* anything, yet I could. Why is he living here, looking like a beggar in his shabby clothes, but with 'talk of a gentleman? There's summat not right.

'But why, Mrs Hope?' He didn't wait for her reply. 'Why do you come this way? Surely you know that there's a better way to York from Hull? The turnpike road is safer, and you could, no doubt, get a lift much easier along there, than on the deserted lanes across country from here!'

She bit her lip. She didn't even know where York was. She only knew that it stood well back from the sea, and that travellers and merchants from Hull took their goods there to sell.

''Cos of river,' she muttered. 'I feel safer by 'river. I was going to follow it as far as I could.'

A smile turned up his lips and she knew he wasn't persuaded. 'You know the river well? Its moods, its tides?'

She nodded, looking at him warily. 'Well enough.'

'And the sea, do you know the sea?' He laughed at her, dimples creasing his cheeks.

'Nay.' Anger suddenly flared as she realized he was having a game with her. 'I don't know 'sea, only that it flows beyond Spurn, and it's to be treated wi' caution. Why's tha asking me all these questions?'

'Oh, I have my reasons.' He didn't appear at all offended by her outburst. 'You may think it idle curiosity on my part, but I can assure you it is not.'

She eyed him suspiciously. 'Tha's nowt to do wi' 'law?'

He gave a great laugh. 'Not I!'

She remembered the pheasants. 'Tha's not above 'law?'

He shook his head. 'No-one is. Though it might seem so, to some who receive unwarranted discipline from others more corruptible than they.

'But, Mrs Hope – Annie? Surely you've nothing to fear from the law?'

Her face paled but she shook her head. 'Nay. Not me. Never. But, but I had a f– friend. Then I found out that he had a wife, and he thought that I would tell or ask for money, and he's sending his cronies to look for me.' Her imagination ran on, but she spoke truthfully as she added. 'I'm fearful for me life.'

He stared unblinkingly at her as if he was weighing the implications. Then he smiled. 'And that's why you came this way? You didn't think they'd search on this road?'

She hid a sigh of relief. 'Aye, that's 'reason.' She nodded. 'That's it.'

He came towards her and took hold of both her elbows. 'I don't believe a word you're saying, Annie Hope, if that's your name. But it doesn't matter. Why should it? We all have our secrets, and if you choose not to tell, why, that's perfectly all right by me.'

She stared back at him. He had such a smiling face, full of mischief, full of life, and she felt she could trust him. Yet fear held her back. I can tell nobody, she considered. Never in my lifetime. I'm sentenced to carry 'burden until 'final roll-call at doomsday.

He was still talking. 'And, we must make the most of this life, Annie. I can call you Annie? Life is such fun if we make it so, and we must, for we get only one. So why don't you?'

'Why don't I what?' She was bewildered. Life had never been fun for her; and she hadn't caught all that he was saying.

'You were not listening! I said, why don't you stay a little longer? I could put some work your way. Why, I believe we could be a good team, you and I. I knew it when I first saw you.'

'What sort of work?' She eyed him suspiciously.

'Oh!' He gazed out at the river in contemplation. The rainclouds were hovering, black and menacing above them and a few drops of rain started to fall. 'Just selling a few things.'

'Hawkin' tha means? A common hawker?'

'Not exactly. I need someone to deliver goods to my regular customers whilst I get on with other business. Of course, if you could sell them other goods too, then you would make some extra money.'

It was tempting. If I could make some money, she thought, then I could pay to go over on 'ferry. She forgot for a moment why she was running, then she remembered.

'Nay. I can't. I have to be off. If them folks should come looking for me!'

'No-one will find you,' he said persuasively. 'We won't give you away. No-one knows you're here. Only the Trotts', and I'll talk to them.'

'Will I have to stay wi' them?'

He grinned. 'Unless you stay with me. And you may.'

I could become fond of him, she thought. He's got a happy nature. I could laugh with him and forget me troubles. But nay, I'll not be tempted again.

'I'll stay wi' Trotts', I'm not promising I'll stay long, mind, but just 'till it suits me.'

Mrs Trott grumbled, as Annie thought she would. Mr

Trott agreed, quite eagerly, – too eagerly, she contemplated. He said, speaking for Mrs Trott also, he emphasized, that they would be glad of the company. They didn't see many people, being just off the river path. It wasn't like living in the town of Hessle itself, where there was always something lively going on.

'Only time we see's folk to have a chat, is when we go up to common wi' pigs and sheep. Tha can maybe help me wi' them, Mrs Hope. Mrs Trott doesn't like to go, and my back is playing me up.'

'I know nowt about animals,' she said, horrified at the thought. 'I've onny ever seen them in 'market.'

The Hull market was littered with crates of live hens and ducks, squawking and cackling and feathers flying, and pigs snuffling on the end of a rope, or sometimes escaping and causing chaos as they upset the market stalls.

'Tha'll have to do summat to earn tha keep,' Mrs Trott began, but an admonishing glance from Toby stopped her.

'Annie will be helping me,' he said. 'I'll arrange for her keep. You'll not be out of pocket.'

Mrs Trott's face became red and flustered and she protested that it wouldn't be necessary, but Annie felt antagonism, and something more, maybe jealousy, directed towards her.

After Toby had left, Mrs Trott gave her a bucket of corn and told her to feed the poultry round the back of the house. 'But don't collect 'eggs. I'll not have anybody upsetting 'henhouse.' She glanced at Annie. 'I've got a sick hen, I don't want her disturbing.'

Annie took the bucket. She had no desire whatsoever to go into the henhouse. She'd seen it already, it was dark and smelled of warm damp hay and was full of feathers.

'I don't allow anybody in there,' Mrs Trott insisted. 'Not even Mr Trott.'

'I won't go in,' she answered; but wondered why if feathers made Mrs Trott sneeze, didn't she let someone else gather the eggs?

She didn't care for the hens clucking and scuttling around her feet as she threw the corn, nor the messy white splodges that she stood in. The ducks were even worse. They had turned the muddy pool where they dipped their heads, into a quagmire. They thrashed their wings as she approached and waddled away complaining with squawking vigour. She found a clutch of large, pale-green eggs hidden in a clump of grass and took them to Mrs Trott, who was locking the creaking henhouse door with an iron key, which she then put in her pocket.

'Them's no good.' She took them from Annie and threw them to the hens. 'They've been there all 'summer. They're daft, ducks are, allus hiding eggs and then forgetting where they've put 'em.'

'Who is Toby Linton?' Annie asked later as she sat with the Trotts and ate bread and cheese and drank a cup of ale. 'Is he a gentleman?'

'Aye, he is.' Mrs Trott was sharp. 'So mind thy manners.'

'But a friend, all 'same.' Mr Trott answered more mildly. 'A squire's son who chose a different sort o' life from his fayther.'

'Chose!' Mrs Trott's voice rose. 'Nay, he never did. It was that flinty faced, strait-laced old fayther who chose for him, and for Matthias. Turned them both out he did!'

Mr Trott shook his head. 'Mrs Trott won't hear a word said against either of 'em. But it can't have been easy for 'Squire to bring up two lads without a wife. He did 'best he could, I'm sure.'

'He could have had help, 'best there was, but he refused it.' Mrs Trott's lips drew into a thin line and she got up from the table. 'He's a mean old man. He was mean when he was young and he got meaner as he got older. Thank 'good Lord his sons took after their poor mother and not him.'

'But it's no life for a gentleman,' Mr Trott insisted. 'If his brother should choose a life at sea, so be it; but Toby does nowt worthwhile. He had a choice, he could have been a soldier, or he could have taken 'cloth, but he wanted neither, and now he's nobbut a tradesman selling goods. And he's worth better'n that.'

He too got up from the table and unhooked his coat from behind the door and put it on. He put on thick socks and pulled on his boots and Mrs Trott fetched him a scarf and fastened it around his neck.

She seemed unfeeling at first, Annie thought, as she watched them. But perhaps I was mistaken. Mrs Trott wrapped up the remaining bread and cheese and put it into his coat pocket, and taking the pan from the fire poured soup into a jug.

'There now, will that do thee?'

'Aye, don't fuss, woman. There's enough vittals to last a week.' He picked up a stout stick. 'I'll be off. I'll see thee in 'morning.'

The light was only just fading from the day and Annie stood in the doorway and called to him. 'Tha's lucky to be in regular work!'

'Aye, that's what I tell myself in 'middle of 'night, when wind is blowing off 'river and there's nobody on quayside but me.' He stood with his stick in his hand and his shoulders bent. 'That's what I allus say – tha's very lucky, Henry Trott, very lucky indeed.'

The evening dragged on. Mrs Trott didn't seem disposed to talk and Annie had nothing to do but gaze into the fire and wonder about Lizzie and Ted and Jimmy, and if Mrs Trott noticed the tears which coursed down her cheeks, she made no comment as she sat on the opposite side of the hearth mending a tear in a pair of Mr Trott's breeches.

Presently she got up and went to the blanket chest and brought out Annie's blanket. 'Here, tha might as well be in bed as sitting doing nowt. Tomorrow Master Toby will want thee to start work.' She pointed to the feather bed. 'Tha can have 'bed seeing as Mr Trott's out all night.'

Annie was curious as to why Mrs Trott should be so well informed of Toby's intentions, but she took the blanket and made no comment, except to ask if Mrs Trott wasn't tired too, for she sat down again by the fire and made no attempt to go to bed.

'Nay, I'll sit for a bit,' she muttered, 'and finish my mending. But don't tha mind me. Go off to sleep. Tomorrow'll be a long day.'

She lay quietly, but she wasn't in the least tired. Shifting barrels of fish makes thee tired, running from 'law makes thee tired, she mused, not scattering corn to hens or gathering kindling. She lay silently, just thinking, and wondering what life had in store for her, or if in fact she had any life to look forward to, when she became aware as the evening drew on, that once or twice Mrs Trott put down her mending and surreptitiously glanced across her way.

Sleep was about to close over her. The bed was warm and she had disposed of her melancholy thoughts, trusting that the morning would bring her better fortune, when she heard the door creak open and then quietly close. She kept still, the old lady had probably stepped outside to relieve herself; but after several minutes elapsed and she hadn't returned, Annie threw back the blanket and tiptoed to the door.

She opened it a crack and listened. Could she hear whispered voices, or was it only the trees shedding their rustling leaves? She opened it wider and wondered whether to call to Mrs Trott, to ask if she was all right; but as she peered around the door she saw the swing of a light and heard the creak of the henhouse door.

Thieves. She was aghast. Stealing an old woman's hens. Then she heard again the hum of voices. One of them was Mrs Trott's. The other was Toby Linton's.

4

She stepped back inside and picked up one of her shawls and wrapped it around her bare shoulders. Her boots she left beside the bed. Being barefoot held no qualms for her, her feet were hard and calloused. She had worn no boots until she'd married, and not always then, sometimes she had had to sell them to buy food, buying them back when Alan came home and gave her money.

She slipped outside, keeping to the house wall and creeping round the back until the henhouse was in view. Mrs Trott was standing by the open door next to some bales of hay and holding a lantern, and every now and again the light shook as she suppressed a sneeze. Annie could see two other figures, one, she guessed by his build to be Toby, the other, man or boy, was small and his voice husky.

They were manhandling sacks and boxes from a donkey cart and under Mrs Trott's direction were putting them into the henhouse. When they had done this, apparently to her satisfaction, they finally lifted from the cart two casks which they rolled into the henhouse throwing the bales of hay in after.

'Geneva!' Annie breathed. 'So that's what they're up to. And what's in them sacks? As if I couldn't guess!'

As they started to close and lock the henhouse door, Annie ran back inside, her bare feet making no sound on the damp grass. She dropped her shawl onto the floor beside her boots and climbed back into bed and closed her eyes.

So, Master Toby Linton. Now we know what tha's up to. There's no wonder thy father wanted thee out of his house. Who'd want a smuggler for a son? Two sons! For

I'll bet my bag o' money that thy brother Matthias is in it too.

She huddled beneath the blanket as she heard the door creak open and Mrs Trott's feet shuffle across the room. She opened one eye as she heard the lid of the blanket-chest open and saw her take out her blanket, then she feigned sleep again as Mrs Trott turned towards her. When she looked again from beneath her lashes, Mrs Trott was knelt beside the chest busily emptying it of its contents and replacing them with several parcels wrapped in calico.

The old woman's head and shoulders were buried within the box and as Annie peered above her blanket she could hear her muttering and gasping to herself. In the dying embers of the fire there was a flash of something shiny, something yellow, and Annie smiled as she recognized the petticoat which she had given to Mrs Trott.

It seemed as if she had only just fallen asleep again when she felt someone's hand on her shoulder roughly shaking her awake.

'Come on. Tha can't stay in bed all day, there's work to be done. And besides Mr Trott will be home afore long and will want his bed back.'

Mrs Trott was fully dressed, and Annie wondered if indeed she had been to bed at all. The room was tidy, her bedding put away and the fire was blazing.

Annie stretched her arms above her head and yawned. 'By, I've had a grand night's sleep, never woke up once.' She put her feet to the floor. 'Mr Trott's got a nice warm bed to get into.'

Mrs Trott's mouth turned down; she made no comment but simply pointed to the table where a dish of gruel lay waiting.

'Eat that. Master Toby'll be on his way to fetch thee. Don't keep him waiting.'

'Where am I going?' Annie dressed quickly and spooned the gruel into her mouth. It was thin but warming and smelt of goat.

'Up onto 'Wolds, I expect. He'll tell thee.'

45

Annie stared open-mouthed, her spoon held loosely between her fingers. It slipped and clattered into the bowl, splashing the gruel onto the table. Mrs Trott tutted and fetched a cloth to wipe up the mess.

'Where's that? How can I? I don't know 'way. How will I know where to go?'

Panic enveloped her. She might get lost and not find her way back to the river.

'Somebody'll tek thee and show thee. Hush, here's Mr Trott.'

Mr Trott wearily hung his coat behind the door and held his hands towards the fire. 'It's been a cold night, but a quiet one. Nowt much happening on 'river.'

'Why, what might be happening?' Annie slyly put the question and watched Mrs Trott.

'Why, tha should know, if tha's worked in Hull.' Mr Trott pursed his lips. 'There's allus somebody up to no good, in shipping and that.'

Annie shook her head. 'I onny worked wi' fish, I know nowt about shipping.'

She saw Mrs Trott's face relax and she put down a dish of gruel for Mr Trott.

'Get that down thee, and then away to tha bed. Me and Mrs Hope are off to 'village, so tha'll not be disturbed. Get tha shawl, Mrs Hope, if tha's finished, we haven't got all day.'

The old woman swept out of the house, draping a black shawl about her head and shoulders and grasping a large umbrella. Annie hurriedly finished the last mouthful of gruel, and hopping first on one foot and then the other, she fastened on her boots. She turned back from the door and in a loud whisper called to Mr Trott. 'Bed's still warm, Mr Trott!'

Mrs Trott marched across the grass in front of the cottage and out of the gate, and turned right up a narrow lane which ran away from the river. The lane sloped uphill and had a high grassy bank on one side, and a hedge of dog rose and hawthorn on the other, the red hips and berries festooned with lace curtains of fragile cobwebs. Studded at intervals in the hedgerow, tall trees and slender young saplings sprouted, which dripped droplets of moisture down onto them, so that Annie once or twice put out her hand and looked up, thinking that it was raining.

'Where 'we going, Mrs Trott?' she panted as they reached the top of the hill. This was the first hill she had climbed. Hull was a very flat town. So flat that the streets and houses often flooded when the river was high.

She turned to look back the way they had come and saw the Humber stretched below, its surface flat and gleaming as the morning light touched it. She narrowed her eyes. Across on the far side of the river she could see dark hills rising, and trees. She cupped her eyes with her hands, she could see habitation, and thin spirals of smoke as if from cottage chimneys.

'Is that Lincolnshire, Mrs Trott? I've never seen it so clear afore.' From the walls of Hull that country had seemed far away, a mere thin smudge on the other side of the river.

'Tha doesn't know owt, does tha? Did nobody larn thee owt?' Mrs Trott seemed to take pleasure in reproaching her ignorance.

'And is that where 'ferry goes to? Is that Barton?'

'Hush wi' tha questions. I've not time to be thy teacher, I'm off to 'village. Wait here. Don't go wandering off. Master Toby'll be here afore long.' She shook her umbrella at Annie, turned a corner and disappeared from view.

Annie waited for a moment, then, curious to know where she was going, ran along the lane after her, but the lane forked and each path was overhanging with low branches and looked dark and gloomy, so she wandered back again to where she had been told to wait. She paced up and down, wishing that Toby would hurry; doubts and fears were starting to crowd in now that she was alone. When she had company she put her fears to one side, pretending to herself that nothing bad could happen.

She cupped her hands again around her eyes and looked down towards the river. There was a cutter, she could see

47

its long bow-sprit and tall mast, its vast sails billowing. It was lying low in the water and moving swiftly up river, while landward, nearer the northern banks were two cobbles, plying a more leisurely pace.

'Good day, Mrs Hope.'

She jumped at the sound of Toby's voice above her. He was standing on the top of the bank, his arms folded, smiling down at her.

'Tha startled me. Where did tha come from? I didn't hear thee.'

He grinned. 'I have my own secret passage way. I don't like to use the public paths.'

'Why? Hast tha got summat to hide?'

'I might have. But nothing that harms anyone.' He put his hand out with an invitation for her to take it and he hauled her up the bank. 'What about you? What are you hiding, Annie?'

'I've told thee already, so don't keep asking.'

'But if I'm to be your friend, we must trust each other. I need to trust you if you are to work for me.'

A friend? She had never had a man friend before. Husband and lover, yes. But not a friend. She'd better put the matter to the test.

'Tha might as well know now, Toby, then we know where we stand. I'm finished wi' men. I want no truck wi' any man again. I've been ill used by 'em, and I'm never going to be caught again. I'll work for thee and I'll not thieve thee, be sure of that, but there'll be nowt more, so don't expect it.'

His face was solemn though she thought she caught a flash of humour in his eyes, but as she looked sharply at him, it was gone and he was serious again.

'I'm sorry that you've such a poor opinion of men, Annie. It's true that there are a lot of wicked fellows, but I venture to suggest that there are also many wicked women. But I wouldn't be so arrogant as to suggest anything more than friendship. I said before, we could have great larks you and I, if you are willing. We could be like brother and sister!'

'Why?' She eyed him suspiciously. 'Why would likes of thee, tek up wi' me? I'm not thy class. And tha has a brother, why should tha want a sister?'

His eyebrows rose. 'You've heard of my brother? Ah, of course, the Trotts' will have told you.'

'Aye. And that tha's a squire's son. So what does tha want wi' me?'

They had been walking as they were talking. There was no proper path where he led her, but they stooped through thickets whose branches he pushed back after they went through them, so that there was no sign of their entry, and they scrambled over rough chalky terrain until she was quite out of breath, and insisted that they sat down for a moment.

He stretched out on the ground beside her and plucked a piece of grass and placed it between his teeth. He pointed. A formation of ducks were flying swiftly up river, their long necks stretched and their wings moving rapidly. The air was clear and sharp and though there was a smell of frost, it wasn't cold, there was a touch of warmth from the sun as it lifted higher in the sky. Below them was a curl of woodsmoke, which she guessed came from the Trotts' cottage.

'What do I want with you, you ask?' He rolled the stalk of grass idly between his fingers. 'Well, to be honest, Annie, I'm bored with the company I'm keeping. Oh, don't misunderstand me, Henry and Mrs Trott are a fine pair, but they're old and no fun, and Mrs Trott still treats me like a three-year-old. As for my brother, well, I see him for only a brief time, even though we meet quite often. We have no time for pleasantries.'

She wasn't convinced. 'Tha must have other friends, from thy youth?'

He shook his head. 'My mother died when I was five, Mrs Trott was her maid, you know. She idolized my mother, worshipped the ground she walked on and she was devastated when she died. But she hated my father and though she looked after Matt and me as if we were her

49

own, she couldn't do right for him. We were sent away to my aunt's house, Mrs Trott too, but she complained that my aunt didn't know how to look after children, and she didn't of course, being a maiden lady, which Mrs Trott was too – her name in those days was Agnes Whittle – then my aunt wrote to Father that Mrs Trott was getting above herself, and she was given notice.'

He sat up and watched as a flotilla of ships sailed by, heading for the port of Hull. Then he leaned back again on one elbow and she saw a shadow cross his face.

'We didn't know then, we were too young to know what was happening, but they wouldn't give her a reference. They just gave her what she was owed and no more. She had been with my mother since before my mother had married, and yet she was cast out with nothing.'

'So how did she come to be here? How did she meet Mr Trott?'

'Dear old Henry. He found her, so he told me, in Hull. She was practically at death's door and about to throw herself in the river. She couldn't find work without references, and she had only ever looked after ladies, and children. Anyway, he brought her back here and fed her, and made her well, and here she has been ever since.'

'And then he married her.' Annie murmured.

He shook his head. 'No. She wouldn't marry him. She just took his name. Come on,' he said, rising to his feet. 'Not much further.'

'But I don't understand,' Annie panted, the last bit of incline was taxing, though she was encouraged to see the thatch of a dwelling just above her. 'How did tha find her again?'

'Pure coincidence. It was about five years ago and I'd left my father's house – I'd decided to join my brother. I was rowing down the river when my boat struck a sandbank. I knew I couldn't get it off until the tide turned and I decided to swim for shore. Well, I nearly drowned. I hadn't realized just how treacherous the Humber was, but as luck would have it, old Henry was on the river bank and saw me struggling. He ran for a boat from the haven and hauled me in.'

He smiled at the memory. 'And when he took me home to dry off, there was my old nurse. She didn't recognize me straight away, but I would have known that old sour face anywhere,' he said affectionately.

He led her towards a cottage which was almost hidden by an overhang of chalk cliff and a tumble of bramble and hawthorn scrub. He opened the door which was unlocked and invited her in.

She hesitated. 'What is this place?'

'It's mine. It's where I live. My very own.'

It was small, smaller even than the Trotts' cottage, but where the Trotts' room was neat but barely furnished, here was a jumble of boxes and crates, and rugs on the walls as well as the floor, and two handsome wooden chairs and a heavy table.

He waved to her to take a seat and then disappeared outside, returning in only a moment with an armful of dry kindling which he threw into the hearth, where it instantly caught alight from the warm ashes.

'Would you take tea, Mrs Hope?' he said, giving a small bow. 'It isn't often I have company; please do.'

She stared wide-eyed at him. What manner of man was this? What game was he playing with her? Then she laughed. She saw the mischievous look in his eyes and realized that he wasn't playing a game *with* her, but was inviting her to play the game.

'I thought I was starting work today?' She sipped the hot tea and wished she could stay here forever. 'I'm not used to sitting about drinking tea mid-morning.'

'*Taking* tea, Annie. Not drinking it,' he advised, and she pulled a face and giggled.

'You are, – starting work. I want to show you what you have to do, what you have to sell.' He went across to one of the many boxes and opened it.

I wonder? she thought. I wonder if he thinks I'm that dim that I don't know a sack of illicit tea or 'baccy when I

51

see it? But she was just a little surprised when he pulled out a bundle, not a waxed bag containing tea or sweet smelling tobacco, but a cotton bundle holding an assortment of linen and lace and ribbons, such as ladies or housewives might buy in any draper's shop.

He pulled out another, this one containing lengths of muslin and nets and he held them up to her. 'What do you think, Annie? Will the women of the Wolds be pleased with these? They can't get out, you know, to buy from shops in the way townspeople can. They rely on traders like me to bring them what they want. And if there's nothing here that they fancy, then they only have to say, and I'll get them what they require the next time round.'

She handled a piece of muslin. She had never owned anything as lovely as this. The only thing she had ever had that was pretty was her satin petticoat, and she'd given that away to Mrs Trott.

'Where does tha get it, this stuff?'

'Why I buy it, of course, from the manufacturers. Where else?'

She shrugged. 'I don't know. How would I know?'

But she'd like to sell it. She'd like to bring it out and drape it over herself, like the draper in his shop in Hull did.

'What is 'Wolds? Is it a town? How will I know where to go? Will tha come wi' me?'

'No. The Wolds is an area. It's country, beautiful country, full of hills and valleys, sheep and birds, trees and flowers, and it stretches from the Humber to the sea. And no, I won't be coming with you. That's why I need you, so that I can get on with other things. But I have a companion for you, and if I'm not mistaken I can hear him coming.'

Annie had heard nothing, but as Toby finished speaking she heard someone cheerfully whistling, and then a sharp rattle on the door.

5

A round, weather-rosy face appeared at the door. 'G' day, Master Toby.'

'Good morning, young Robert. Come in. There's someone here I wish you to meet.'

A youth of about thirteen shuffled in through the door. His light brown hair hung in a queue at the back of his neck and a shaggy fringe about his forehead, his eyes were bright and eager and he had a short turned up nose. 'Aw, Master Toby, tha knaws I don't like me Sunday name. Robin. Call me Robin, *please.*'

Toby laughed. 'All right, you know I only tease. Mrs Hope, this is Robin, my right-hand man.'

She watched the boy's face flush with pleasure at the compliment, and he touched his forehead. 'Pleased to have your acquaintance, Mrs Hope.'

'It'll be more than acquaintance, Robin. Mrs Hope is going to be your travelling companion.'

Robin looked questioningly at Annie, and then frowning, back to Toby. 'Dost tha mean instead o' Mrs Trott – or as well as? 'Cos I don't think I could stand two women lashin' me wi' their tongues. Honest, Master Toby. I couldn't. Me skin'd be stripped to ribbons.'

Annie smiled. He could be an older version of her son, Jimmy. But would he be as difficult? He was a young varmint, was Jimmy. A lump came to her throat at the reminder of her children and she wondered where they were, and if she would ever see them again.

'No,' Toby said. 'Mrs Trott won't be going travelling again. She's getting too old. It's time she took a rest.'

Robin grinned with delight. 'Puttin' her out to grass,

53

is tha? By, I can't say I'm sorry.' He put his hand out to shake Annie's. 'I hope's as we get on well, Mrs Hope.' He laughed. 'Here, that's a good name for anybody to have.'

'Tha can call me Annie.' She warmed to this cheerful youth. 'It's 'name I'm most used to.'

'I'll expect you to show Annie what to do, and where to go,' Toby said. 'Introduce her to the farmers' wives and the housekeepers, and the innkeepers' daughters and so on. You know the score. She's not from these parts, so she'll want a little guiding.'

The boy's small stature seemed to grow with the importance of the task in front of him. 'Don't thee worry, Master Toby, or thee Mrs Hope – er, Annie. Tha'll be safe enough wi' me. I'll show thee where 'best customers live. Mrs Trott, sir, I have to say, was a bit sharp wi' her comments if wimmin didn't like her goods. She wasn't cut out for this kind of business, no tact, tha knaws – but thee and me, Annie, why I can see, we'll mek our fortune yet.'

Toby filled a pack with linen and cotton, and Robin shouldered it onto his back and left, saying he would meet her the next morning just after daybreak.

'Help me, Annie,' Toby started to empty the crates. 'Put these muslins into bundles, and tell me, if you will, what you think they are worth.'

'I can't.' She sat on the floor beside him. 'I've never bought such stuff. I've onny ever seen it in 'draper's shop.'

'Then try to remember what he charged, for we must charge a little less. Not too much less, for the ladies have to pay us for bringing these goods to them. But we must still let them think they are getting a bargain. Then when you've sold something, you must enter the name of the customer and the amount in this pocket book.'

Her lip trembled and she bit it, and tried to quell the tears that were forming. I might have known it wouldn't be so easy, she thought. Now I've lost 'job afore I've started.

He looked at her as he held the book towards her, and when she didn't take it from him, he sighed.

'You can't read or write, Annie?'

She shook her head and huge tears brimmed over and down her cheeks. 'No. I never learnt. I'm sorry.'

'Don't cry.' He patted her hand. 'It's not your fault. We'll get round it somehow. But Robin can't either, I relied on Mrs Trott to mark up the book.'

I must have been mistaken about him. Annie wiped her tears. It's a proper business after all, and I thought he was running smuggled goods.

'I can add up,' she sniffed. 'In me head. And I've a good memory for names. Tha could write up what I tell thee when I get back.'

'Yes.' He nodded thoughtfully. 'But you must make some sort of mark in the book. The customers would prefer it. Could you do that?'

She said that she could, and would think of something to represent each person. Then he stood up and told her he would take her back to the Trotts' house.

'Before we go, Annie.' He looked uneasy. 'You won't take offence?'

'How do I know? What's tha going to say?'

She watched him curiously as he went across to a chest of drawers on which there was a mirror. He picked up a hairbrush and handed it to her. She turned it over in her hand. It was baleen bristle, she knew that, made from the whale, but the back was silver and beautifully embossed with flowers and trailing stems.

'I'm not giving it to you, because it was my mother's – but will you use it to brush your hair?'

She stared at him and then turned and walked across to the mirror, and for the first time saw herself through someone else's eyes. The face staring back at her wasn't one she knew. The eyes were large in the thin and pinched face, the fair hair matted and lank.

She turned appealingly towards Toby. 'I look like a

55

drab. A slatternly drab. How can I visit folks looking like this?'

'You need feeding up. I'll ask Mrs Trott to give you extra food. And you can borrow the hairbrush to tidy your hair.'

'Tha'll trust me to give it back?'

He smiled. 'Oh, yes, Annie. I'll trust you. Like my own sister!'

She slung a large bundle over her arm as they went out of the door and Toby took two more. 'How am I to carry all of this,' she asked. 'Will we be walking far tomorrow?'

'Didn't I tell you?' he said, as he strode off down the hill. 'You're riding in style, in Henry Trott's donkey-cart. There's too much to carry, and it's too far to walk. You'll have to stay out overnight. But don't worry. Robin will look after you.'

Robin had also brought his dog to look after her. 'He'll guard thee wi' his life, if I tell him,' he said, as he loaded the bundles into the cart the next day. Mrs Trott looked on, her nose wrinkled in distaste at the sight of the dog, who was, Annie thought, the oddest, ugliest-looking dog she had ever seen. He had a flat face and a pair of torn and battered ears, a short body and extremely long legs. His coat was brindled and he wagged a long white tail.

'I'd never have him in 'cart wi' me,' Mrs Trott complained. 'Stinking dog.'

'Nay. He never does.' Robin protested. 'I chucked him in 'river 'specially last night, just so's he'd be sweet smelling for 'journey. But he'd never travel in 'cart wi' thee, Mrs Trott.' He touched his forehead in esteem. 'He'd be after running alongside. Aye, he knaws his place, does Charlie.'

Annie turned away to hide a smile. She was going to enjoy young Robin's company, and Charlie wasn't the only one who had had a bathe in preparation for the journey; for she had drawn a bucket of water from the well when she had got back to the Trotts', and taking it round to the side of the house, she had stripped down to her shift and washed her hair, and rinsed her face and arms and body with the clean, cool water, and with a fustian sheet she had borrowed from Mrs Trott, she dried herself, then dressed and ran up and down the riverside path until she was warm and glowing and her hair had dried.

She'd sat by the fire in the evening and as she'd brushed her hair, teasing out the tangles, Mrs Trott had snatched the brush from her.

'Where did tha get this? This isn't thine.'

'Toby's lent it 'me, Mrs Trott. I never stole it. It was his ma's.'

'Aye. I know.'

Annie thought she had seen a softening of the old woman's face and a tremble on her lips, but then the instant was gone and she'd said tersely. 'Tha'll never have hair like she did, no matter how often tha brushes it. Like gold it was, and soft as silk.'

But she'd told her to sit down and she'd do it for her, and brushed it gently enough, and cut out the tangles that wouldn't be brushed out, until it was sleek and straight again; and Annie was disappointed that Toby wasn't there to see them off this morning and see how fine she looked.

Robin cracked the whip, but the donkey put his head down and started to graze. He cracked it again and shouted, and still the animal wouldn't budge.

Mrs Trott took a carrot from her apron pocket. 'Here, give it this, it's onny way to move him.'

Annie climbed out of the cart and took the carrot and tentatively held it out towards the donkey. It opened its mouth, showing large yellow teeth and brayed long and loud at her. She dropped the carrot in fright and ran back behind the cart.

'Give it here.' Robin got down from the cart and went to pick up the carrot, and the donkey was off, careering madly across the paddock, the bundles in the back of the cart bouncing, and falling out onto the grass.

When they eventually caught him and reloaded the cart, with Annie cracking the whip, and Robin leading the donkey and with the carrot held coaxingly just out of reach, the sun was almost up, and Robin was anxious that they should get to their first call before midday.

They drove up a wide lane into the town of Hessle and Annie looked curiously about her. The town was formed in a square with two principal roads, and at the intersection of the road stood the ancient parish church with long low cottages clustered around it. There was a bakery and a dairy and cheesemaker, two fine inns, and east of the town through the gated road lay the marshy common where the townspeople grazed their cows and pigs and poultry or grew strips of corn and barley.

'This is a fine town, Robin,' she remarked as they bowled along, the donkey trotting in a sparky rhythm.

'Aye, it is.' He raised his whip to a man at the other side of the road who was driving a pig towards the butcher's in Cow Lane. 'Bankers and merchants from Hull are coming out here to live, they're building handsome houses big enough for servants as well as themselves. They've got to hear about 'pretty meadows and sylvan glades and have come to join us. This is me home town, me ma and da were both raised here, but they're both dead and buried now.'

'So who does tha live with, or does tha fend for thissen?'

'Me sister. She gives me a bed, and feeds me. But she'd dearly like me out of 'house. She's enough wi five bairns of her own. Though I pay her, when I can.'

They reached the Beverley turnpike and had turned to cross it by the wicket gate so that they didn't have to pay the toll, when Robin gave a shout. 'There he is. I knew he'd come to see us off.'

Annie looked expectantly along the road, but all she saw was a man on a horse. A gentleman by the look of him, for it was a fine horse and the man was wearing a tricorn hat held by a silver pin. But he was also wearing an earring.

She felt shy as Toby cantered over to speak to them. He touched his hat with his whip. He didn't look like the merry young gentleman from yesterday, or the roguish rascal she had first seen on the quayside. But he bent over and smiled at her, the smile reaching his eyes.

'What is it, Mrs Hope? Not feeling nervous are you? I told you that Robin would look after you.'

Dumbly she shook her head. He looked very handsome in his velvet coat and grey breeches as he sat astride the chestnut stallion, and she wondered where he was going.

'I shall be back in three days,' he said. 'Perhaps even before you. Take care on the road, Robin.' He nodded to Annie and flicked his whip on the horse's flank and started to canter away. Then he reined in and wheeled around.

'I almost forgot. I have a present for you, Mrs Hope.'

'For me?' What can he be giving to me? Annie was astonished. Will he want summat in return?

He took a scarf from around his neck and leaning over fastened it around hers. It was soft and silky, and pale blue.

'I meant to give it to you yesterday. I thought it would match your eyes.' He grinned, and she saw again the same Toby as before.

She fingered the scarf. 'Is it mine to keep?'

'Yes, of course. I said, it's a present.'

'He's taken a shine to thee all right, Annie.' Robin nodded sagely as they trotted away. 'He's very generous to his friends, is Master Toby. That's real silk, that is. If ever tha gets to 'bottom o' barrel, tha'll knaw tha can buy several crusts wi' that.'

'I'll never sell it, Robin, never.' She fingered the silky texture and felt the warmth of friendship. 'Not if I'm at death's door.'

'He'll be off to see his fayther, I expect.' Robin got

down from the cart to lead the donkey through a narrow, rising, woodland path. 'He goes to see him every now and again, to try and heal 'breach between 'em. But 'old man's stubborn as this donkey, so I hear.'

'Where does he live, his fayther?'

Robin pointed upwards to beyond the wooded dell. 'Big house, next village but three.' He started to pant as the path became steeper. 'This first bit allus gets me, 'til I gets me second wind.'

Annie jumped down to join him. If Robin was panting, then the donkey must be labouring with her in the cart. But she too was soon wheezing as the unaccustomed hill climbing tore at her calf muscles and made her heart race.

'Is these 'Wolds, then? Is that what these hills is called?'

'This is onny foot of 'Wolds,' Robin gasped. 'It's all up and down from now on. But it's best scenery I know, and if tha should be here in summer – why it smells that sweet, tha could almost eat it. Honeysuckle and bluebell, and May blossom; and 'air is that full o' birdsong tha can't hear thyself think.'

Even now, in autumn, Annie could hear the call of birds; the throaty call of wood pigeons, the chattering of finches and something loud and crotchety that flew up above them as they disturbed its privacy.

'Pheasant!' Robin took imaginary aim. 'That would be good in 'pot.'

'Are we nearly there?' Annie felt she had been walking for days. 'We haven't seen any houses yet. How can we sell our stuff out here?'

'We're a couple o' miles off next village. But we'll stop in a minute and have a bite o' bread. There's a stream just along here where we can tek a drink.'

They'd come out of the wooded area and entered a clearing. Annie paused to look around her and saw the gently rolling hills dotted with grazing sheep, the dip and sweep of the steep-sided valleys. She saw the hawthorn hedges which trembled with hidden wrens and chaffinches, and the wild crab apple trees heavy with fruit. Above her hovered a silent kestrel seeking its prey of voles and field mice, while down below, down, down, down, and she couldn't believe how far they had come, lay the Humber, stretched like a silver ribbon at their feet.

'This is 'last we'll see of 'Humber for a bit.' Robin stood at her side. 'Next valley will take us out of sight.'

'Oh. I've never been out of its reach afore.' She felt uneasy. The river had always been there; comforting, familiar. Safe, even at its most threatening, when it broke its banks and deposited mud and silt on her doorstep. She knew what to expect from it and was never surprised. She had even anticipated, that when life had no more to offer her, she would end her days beneath its enveloping waters.

Robin unpacked bread and cheese and a jug of ale, given to him, he said, by Mrs Trott. Annie hadn't given a thought to food and was glad that the old woman had considerately provided it. The walking and the clear air had made her ravenously hungry. She took a drink from the stream and then swilled her face. She felt a curious uplifting of spirits, something she was quite unused to.

She stretched out on the grass when her appetite was satisfied and closed her eyes, but as sleep was about to claim her, she heard the dog give a low warning growl, and felt Robin's hand touch hers.

'Ssh. Don't make a sound,' he whispered, and she cautiously opened her eyes and saw him take the dog by his scruff. She lay still and beneath her body she could feel the drum of hooves.

Robin lay down beside her, his hand still on Charlie's neck. 'Keep still, pretend to be asleep.'

How can I pretend to be asleep with that racket going on, she thought, as the sound of men's voices and the jingle of harness carried through the air.

'Blast that donkey.' Robin cursed softly, as the donkey, unhitched from the cart and tied loosely to stop him wandering, uttered a loud bray as he heard the sound of horses.

They sat up as the shout came down to them. 'Hey. You down there. Where are you heading?'

A red-coated, heavy-booted troop of soldiers sat astride their mounts on the path above them. The sergeant who had called to them, shouted again. 'Didn't you hear what I said?' He had a thick Scots brogue.

'Aye, I heard thee allreet.' Robin put on his broadest accent. 'But I didn't understand thee.'

'What did he say?' The sergeant turned to his men. 'Did anybody understand what he said?'

The soldiers shuffled about in their saddles, but shook their heads.

Annie got to her feet. 'What's tha trouble, sergeant?' She smiled and put her hands on her hips. She'd dealt with soldiers before. 'Has tha lost thy way?' She spoke slowly, so that the Scotsman would understand her.

He smiled down at her, relief showing on his leathery face. 'Aye. I canna find the road to Weighton. Are we going the right way.'

'Tell him yes,' Robin muttered. 'He means Market Weighton, tell him to follow 'road to 'Caves, he'll find it then.'

She repeated the instructions and the soldier shouted his thanks and moved off, the other soldiers turning round in their saddles to throw admiring glances at Annie, to which she responded by waving her hand.

'I never talk to 'em,' Robin grumbled. 'Doesn't do.'

'But tha shouldn't antagonize them.' Annie cautioned the boy. 'It's best to be pleasant. They'll remember thee if tha's awkward. I wonder what they're doing up here?'

'They're all over 'place. They're allus watching 'river, and they're often in villages. Not that they ever find owt.'

'What are they looking for?' Annie watched the boy's face.

He shrugged. 'Trouble. That's all I know.'

He didn't know, she could tell that from his honest face. He's just a lad, she thought, trying to earn a living. But then, who was it who had been with Toby and Mrs Trott near the henhouse? She'd previously been sure that it was Robin.

They came to the outskirts of a village just after midday, and entered a farmyard gate. Robin tied Charlie to a tree and told him to stay. 'Tha doesn't like Sam, tha knaws tha doesn't,' he told the sulking dog. 'Tha fights wi' him every time we come, and we'll nivver sell owt while tha's scrapping.'

He led the way to the back door and hammered on it. 'She's a mite deaf is Mrs Corner, but she makes a nice bit o' sweet cake.'

A voice hollered from within. 'If that's thee, Mary, come on in.'

'It's not Mary, Mrs Corner,' he shouted. 'Tha'll see that when tha sets eyes on me. It's Robin Deane, come on a bit o' business for Master Toby.'

A plump, grey-haired woman, with flour on her face, and a wooden spoon in her hand appeared at an inner door.

'Come in, come in.' She beckoned him in. 'I'm just stirring 'puddings, and sweet cake is just out on 'table. Tha's got good timing, I've noticed afore.'

'Why I can smell thy baking down in next valley, Mrs Corner.' Robin inhaled appreciatively. 'I fair flew up side o' hill when I got 'drift of it. Why, I was just commenting to Mrs Hope here – oh begging tha pardon, ma'am. This is Mrs Hope. She's travelling along wi' me, 'stead o' Mrs Trott—.'

'Tha means that ol' misery face hasn't come wi' thee? Well that calls for a bit o' celebration. We'll have a drop o' apple wine on strength o' that. But,' she dropped her voice to a whisper. 'Can we have same arrangement?'

'Mrs Hope's in charge o' accounts, Mrs Corner. Tha'll have to talk to her, but I'm sure she'll be more than willing to come to a satisfactory arrangement.'

'Aye,' Mrs Corner's eyes flicked from one to another. 'Weren't 'accounts I were thinking on—,'

'Mrs Corner.' Annie interrupted and reached for a bundle, and as she did so, managed to give the woman a conspirational glance, excluding Robin. Mrs Corner looked relieved and Annie wondered just what arrangements Mrs Trott had made. 'I thought tha might be interested in seeing these.'

'Nay, this is pack tha wants, Mrs Hope. This is real good quality cotton, wear for ever it will, as Mrs Corner'll appreciate. She'll not be wanting that fancy stuff.'

The bundle which Annie had reached for and which Robin had disdained, contained muslins and fine cloth. His was packed with strong cottons, linen and calico.

'Aye, it's true.' Mrs Corner sighed. 'I can't be buying fancy stuff every year if it won't last, mayster'd soon give me my marching orders. Tha'd better measure me out three lengths o' that fustian, and one 'o calico.' She leaned towards Annie. 'That's a right bonny kerchief tha's wearing. I remember well, when I was a lass, I had such a piece. Not so soft and fine as this,' she said, fingering the scarf at Annie's neck, 'but colour was as blue.'

Annie pointed to the door. 'Can I hear thy dog barking, Robin? Happen tha should dash out and see. He might have wrapped hisself around 'tree.'

Robin jumped to his feet. 'By, but tha's got sharp ears, Mrs Hope, and I never heard a thing. He's that daft, that dog, he's probably strangled hisself.'

He dashed for the door and Annie opened the other bundle. She winked at Mrs Corner. 'Just take a look in here, ma'am. This'll make thy mouth water.' She brought out a length of muslin and draped it over her shoulder and let it hang in folds about her front.

'And this.' Another, in cream. 'Feel how fine.'

'Oh. It's grand,' Mrs Corner breathed. 'Why, our Mary would dee for this. That's me granddaughter,' she added, seeing the question on Annie's face. 'She lives over 'hill in 'next village. But she's got no money for such fripperies.'

'Why doesn't tha treat her?' Annie persuaded. 'Go on, what wouldn't tha give to see her in this? And—.' She took out a small length of pale-blue soft cotton, which she had noticed when she and Toby had been packing the bundle the day before. 'There's enough here to make thee a neckchief. Go on, I'll let thee have this at half 'asking price. Colour'll suit thee no end.'

Mrs Corner was tempted and fell. This kind of bargain was too much to resist. Her face beamed with generosity of spirit as she assured Annie of her Mary's certain delight on receiving the length of muslin.

'But other matter I mentioned,' she whispered as they heard Robin's whistling return. 'Mrs Trott and me had an arrangement.' She watched Annie's face. 'I'd offer thee a dish o' tay, but tha knaws price it is.' She nodded her head significantly.

Annie nodded back. 'Arrangements have to be made, Mrs Corner. It'll be next trip afore I can do owt, does tha understand? It's 'cos of it being my first trip.' She tapped the side of her nose. 'They think I don't know what's what!'

Mrs Corner came to the door to see them off. 'And don't forget a bit o' summat for Mr Corner when tha comes next time,' she called. 'He'll want a sweetener if he finds out how much I've spent.'

6

'Tha did well, Annie,' Robin was full of admiration. 'I'd never o' thought of showing her them muslins.'

'What tha must realize, Robin,' they were trotting towards the next village, 'is that just 'cos a woman's old and toothless, it doesn't mean she can't appreciate summat nice. And Mrs Corner back there, I reckon, has a bit o' money put by.'

And next time we come, I've got to bring her tea and 'baccy. Annie pondered on this and wondered if the arrangement was wholly between Mrs Trott and Mrs Corner, or if Toby was involved in the deal?

The third village they reached just before nightfall and were given a space to sleep by the fire in the home of a shepherd's wife. They had sold cottons and ribbons, and been given a dozen eggs by a farmer's wife.

'We'll stop night at 'hostelry,' Robin said at the end of the next day as they trotted alongside a beck which ran towards the next hamlet. 'We'll get a good night's lodgings here.'

'How much'll it cost?' Annie felt for her bag of money beneath her skirt. She hadn't spent anything since being with the Trotts. She'd offered to pay her board, but Mrs Trott had said that it had been taken care of.

'We can pay out of our takings, if we're asked. But usually, Master Toby has made arrangements.'

More arrangements, Annie thought. I wonder what the innkeeper will want in exchange.

'Annie?' Robin led the donkey into the inn yard. 'Tha knaws what tha was saying about women still liking nice things, even when they're old?'

She nodded and looked about her. The inn was small, not much bigger than a cottage, quite unlike the inns in Hull which accommodated foreign seamen and travellers.

'Well.' He shuffled about in embarrassment. 'Well – I wondered. Do old folk still feel 'fire in their belly, same as when they're young?'

She gazed at him in astonishment and though it was almost dark, saw, by the lantern swinging on a nail above the stable door, that his face had turned crimson.

'Maybe not to 'same degree,' she said, hiding the laughter that bubbled up inside her. 'But I'm not old enough to know yet, even though I might look as if I am.'

'Aw, no. I didn't mean that tha was. I just thought tha might knaw.'

'Why does tha ask?'

He took his time over the donkey's harness. 'It's just – it's just – well I wondered how long it took afore 'fire died down, 'cos, sometimes,' his words came out with a rush. 'Sometimes I wish I was already old so that 'flame'd dampen down a bit.'

She smiled in the darkness. 'Hast tha got a lass, Robin?'

He shook his head.

'And never had one, I'll be bound?'

'Nay, who'd look at me? I've got nowt.'

'Tha's got plenty. Tha's not been in 'front row when good looks were being handed out, but tha's got a cheeky grin, and tha's got good temper and humour, and there's many a lass wouldn't turn away if tha stole a kiss.'

'Does tha think so, Annie?' His face brightened as they went through the low doorway into the hostelry. 'I hope tha's right.'

The innkeeper greeted Robin cordially. 'I'd hoped tha would be along soon. Hasn't tha brought Mrs Trott?' He looked enquiringly at Annie and then towards the door.

'Mrs Trott's giving up 'business, as tha might say. She's getting past it, all this travelling – so this is Mrs Hope, she's taking her place. This is Mr Sutcliff, Annie. He's got 'best bed and board for miles.'

'We aim to please, Mrs Hope, we aim to please.' He was a small round man, with a belly that protruded from his waistcoat and over the top of his breeches. His hair was dark and he wore a neat pointed beard.

'Come in, tha must be weary.' He led them into a room where there was a large table set for supper, and a bright fire burning in the hearth. 'Have a sup of ale, and tha'll have a taste o' rabbit pie? Lily, my eldest, makes best pastry in the valley.'

Two young women entered the room as he spoke. Both were tall, taller than Mr Sutcliff, and dark like him. Both were dressed in grey woollen skirts and white aprons, and Lily, for Annie guessed it was she, was wearing a cotton cap, while the other, Joan, had her hair tied back in a knot and fastened with a red ribbon.

Lily nodded to Annie and Robin, and without speaking placed a large crusty pie in the middle of the table. A vent in the crust had steam escaping from it, which carried the most delectable smell of rabbit and onions. Annie licked her lips and watched as Joan opened up a white cloth she was carrying and brought out a batch of brown loaves, still hot from the oven.

Next, Lily returned with dishes of floury potatoes, carrots and cabbage, and a boiled suet pudding, flavoured with herbs. She stood back from the table, her hands folded in front of her and waited for her father to speak.

'Sit down please.' He indicated the places where Annie and Robin should sit and then shouted into the back room. 'Meg! Rose! Look sharp, we're ready and waiting.'

Two younger girls appeared, their faces flushed from the heat of the kitchen. Meg was about fifteen, dark like her sisters, with huge blue eyes; she wiped her hands on her apron and grinned at Robin, who blushed; the other, Rose, about thirteen years of age, was just blossoming into womanhood, her skin with an unblemished bloom and her hair as black as night.

Robin bent his head, his neck was as red as fire and Annie saw as he lifted his head, as Lily heaped his plate with rabbit pie, that his eyes were wet with emotion.

Ah, ha, so here's 'reason for 'fire in his belly. Poor lad's smitten all right, and that Meg's leading him on, I'll bet – and nowt at end of it.

When the four daughters had seen that the guests and their father had been served, they too sat down at the table to eat with them, all keeping silent while their father talked, of the weather, and crops and grain – which Annie found incomprehensible – and how bad business was, and likely to get worse as the winter drew on.

'We'll get no travellers passing this way come December, save the military that is, and they don't stay over, they onny have a bite to eat and a sup, and they're on their way. Not that I'd have 'em to stay. Can't take 'risk with four daughters at home.'

It was the daughters' turn to blush, even the two eldest and Annie saw them exchange covert glances.

Lily's mouth turned down. 'It's onny company we get, Father. Why should tha want to deprive us? There's no other male company around here.'

'I'll not have sodgers dallying with daughters of mine. There's no future in it. They're here a month or two, and then they're off to another garrison and that's last we'd see of 'em. Beside's they're in cahoots with magistrates and they'd be watching every move. Not that I've owt to hide,' he added, wiping his mouth of gravy. 'But some of my neighbours wouldn't be too pleased. No, I'll be pleasant enough and welcome them to my table, for it's not their fault they're so far from home, but I'm allus glad to see 'back of them.'

When the pie dish was empty, Lily removed it and brought in its place an enormous plum pudding and a dish of sweet white sauce.

'I'm stuffed.' Robin belched. 'I don't think I can manage any more.'

'Come lad, 'course tha can.' Mr Sutcliff signalled to Lily to heap more on to Robin's plate. 'It'll go to 'swine otherwise.' He laughed. 'Then tha'll be eating it next year instead.'

Annie felt her bloated stomach. The band around her skirt was cutting into her waist. Mrs Trott was a good cook, but her portions were nowhere near as large as the ones she had just eaten. She had never, in her life, she thought, eaten as much as she had at this table.

Mr Sutcliff, when he had scraped his plate clean, pushed it from him and rose from the table. 'Well, if tha'll excuse me. I've a few jobs to do afore I lock up for 'night. Hast tha locked up geese, Meg?'

Meg nodded. 'Aye Father. I did.'

'Rose?'

'Pig pen's locked and henhouse fastened, Father.'

'Good. Our Lily will show thee to thy bed, Mrs Hope, when tha's ready. I'll say goodnight, but no hurry, take tha time.'

As soon as he had disappeared from the room there was a flurry of activity. Meg and Rose whipped away the dirty dishes and plates, Joan wiped down the table with a wet cloth, and Lily built up the fire with logs.

'Now,' said Lily, turning towards them and dusting her hands together to remove the ash. 'Come on, Robin, lets see what tha's got in them packs.'

Robin grinned and went to fetch the packs from a corner of the room where he had left them.

'Why there's nowt much left, Miss Lily. Mrs Hope here is a right good trader. We're practically out o' cotton, onny fancy stuff left, nowt that thy would want, muslins and nets and such.' He winked at Annie as he leaned past her to place the packs in front of Lily.

'Wait. Wait for us.' Meg and Rose squealed from the other room where there was a clatter of pots and pans.

'Leave them,' Joan called. 'Tha can do them later when Mrs Hope's gone to bed.'

'Tha can call me Annie.' Annie said shyly. She wasn't used to formality, and Lily and Joan, she thought were probably of her age, if not older.

'Has tha got a husband, Annie?' Joan asked curiously.

'Me husband's dead. I'm a widow.' Annie bent her head as if in sorrow.

'Does tha like working for Master Linton?' Meg came into the room and stood by Annie's chair. 'Doesn't tha think he's handsome?' She closed her eyes and puckered her lips.

'That's enough, Meg.' Lily was sharp. 'Mrs Hope's just said she's a widow.'

'Oh, I beg thy pardon, I didn't hear. How long has tha been a widow?'

It feels like years, Annie thought. Scrimping and saving on Seaman's Sixpence. Still, without it we'd have starved.

'Less then six months,' she said softly, trying to put sadness in her voice. 'Now I've to make me own living.'

'Tha must be heartbroken.' Meg's eyes were full of sympathy. 'Why Lily, can tha imagine? Mrs Hope must be onny same age as thee, imagine losing 'man tha loves, when tha's onny young.'

'Aye.' Annie sighed. 'I wanted for nowt, and now I'm penniless and driven to working as a hawker. Not that Master Linton isn't kind,' she added hastily, in case she had gone too far. 'He's a very fair employer – more than patient to somebody not used to working for a living.'

'I heard that he's vowed never to marry.' Meg's voice dropped to a whisper. 'Mrs Morpeth's niece has a friend who's cousin works for his father in his kitchen, and *she* said that he's been crossed in love and has pledged *celibacy*, even though there's another lady willing to have him.'

'Don't talk such nonsense.' Lily reached out to slap her. 'If tha doesn't shut up tha can take tha self off to bed.'

Chastened, Meg sat on the floor while Annie, vaguely

thinking that there was no smoke without fire, opened up the parcels of muslins and nets, and began deftly draping them about Meg and Rose, softly folding the lengths of cloth about their hair and shoulders, while Robin, his eyes misty and lips apart, gazed dreamily at them.

'Wilt tha have a dish of tay, Annie, afore tha goes to bed?' Lily having decided on the household purchases and a length of fine cotton for herself, stood up, while her sisters hummed and hawed over which colour and fabric suited them the best.

'Aye. I'd appreciate that no end. I allus used to *take tea* about this time,' she emphasized sorrowfully. 'In 'old days I mean.'

Lily nodded sympathetically and hung the kettle which was standing at the side of the hearth, on to the hook over the fire. 'Fetch me 'tay caddy, Rose. Look sharp now, 'kettle's almost on boil.'

Rose returned with the caddy and Lily took a key from her pocket and opened it.

'Oh. Would tha look at that. Here am I offering our visitors tay, and 'box is near empty. There's onny enough for a mashing either tonight or in 'morning. Which would tha prefer, Annie?'

She held the caddy towards Annie and she peered in. There was very little tea in the bottom; as Lily had said, only enough for one brewing. As she tipped the box towards her, Annie saw the glint of coins beneath the leaves; she looked up and caught an enquiring glance in Lily's eyes.

'Tomorrow, Lily,' she said. 'Let's keep it 'till 'morning.'

Robin was given a palliasse by the fire, and there was a truckle bed made ready for Annie in a corner of the girls' room. She fell into it just as soon as she could make her escape from the excited chatter of Joan, Meg and Rose who talked and giggled about the designs they would make for their new dresses.

'Who'll see thee in them?' Lily had asked, as she'd

grudgingly agreed to their purchases. 'Nobody, that's who. Onny chapel folk, and they'll have plenty to say about it.'

'I hope tha fayther won't be angry about thee buying fancy stuff?' Annie sat up in bed as Lily came into the room; she'd been worrying in case they got into trouble.

'Nay, he won't. We all twist him round our fingers. We get most of what we want.' Her solemn face brightened as she smiled but then became dismal again. 'Except for what we really want – men's company. We're all doomed to be old maids.'

'Nowt wrong wi' that.' Annie yawned and stretched. 'Not everybody makes a good match. Happen tha's better off without a man. Tha might get somebody who beats thee and doesn't treat thee right.' She sat up and leaned on one elbow. 'That's what I've heard anyroad. I wouldn't know of course. I never had owt to complain about.'

Lily came and sat on her bed. 'I had an arrangement wi' Mrs Trott,' she whispered. 'She used to get me—'

'Tea. Aye. I know. But there wasn't a shipment this time round. I'll have to bring it next time. But what about tha fayther? What did she bring him?'

Lily looked blank. She shook her head. 'Nowt, as far as I know. A bit o' baccy maybe. Though – Master Linton comes himself sometimes, on his way to see his father, does tha think he brings summat?'

'Nay. I must have been mistaken. Master Linton doesn't travel wi' goods himself.'

'That's what I thought.' Lily started to undress. 'Tha won't mention to me father about 'tay, wilt tha? He'd be that mad if he knew what I was up to.'

Robin banged on her door the next morning to waken her. All the Sutcliff girls were up and about their tasks, and from the kitchen came the smell of bacon, kidneys and thick pork sausage, and on the table as she went down were hot wheaten cakes, split and running with butter. Tea was made and a jug of ale was on the table.

'Do we settle up wi' thee or tha fayther,' Annie asked as she finished her breakfast. 'For our bed and board, I mean.'

Lily hesitated. 'Mrs Trott and me had—,'

'An arrangement, aye, I know.' Annie shouldered her almost empty pack. 'But I've brought thee nowt.'

'I don't like to charge thee, not when tha's on such hard times.'

Annie stared. This was genuine compassion. She felt ashamed. She'd played on the sympathy of this kindhearted woman with her makebelieve of sorrowing widowhood.

'Tha's bought plenty from us,' she said. 'I'll get paid from Master Linton, be sure of that. He'll be generous, make no mistake.'

'But,' Lily looked down. 'I've enjoyed thy company. Tha's a lot livelier than Mrs Trott,' she laughed.

'I can't make thee pay for me company.' Annie reached beneath her skirt for her money bag. 'I'll give thee that for nowt, gladly.' She handed over some money. 'Take this for our food and lodgings, for Robin and me. It's best I've ever had, and tha'll be sure I'll be back again.'

Robin was talking to Mr Sutcliff as she went into the yard. The donkey was harnessed into the cart and it lifted its head and brayed as she approached.

'He thinks we're off home.' Robin scratched the donkey's back. 'He's allus a lot livelier going back.'

'Tha'll give Master Linton my regards, Mrs Hope? Tell him I look forward to a visit soon.' Mr Sutcliff stood watching them as they put the depleted packs into the cart. 'He, er, he didn't send owt? A parcel or such?'

Annie shook her head. 'He didn't. Probably next time.'

He waved them off from the gate and they turned towards the next dale. The donkey brayed and rammed all four legs to a halt.

'Come on tha daft brute.' Robin cracked the whip above the animal's head. 'We've another day yet.'

'Dost think it's worth it, Robin?'

'What?' Robin took hold of the donkey's snaffle and pulled, but it obstinately stood its ground.

'Well we've hardly any cloth left. A few odd lengths o' calico, not enough to make much. Some bits o' net, and buttons and bootlaces. What's women going to think if that's all we've got to offer 'em? They might buy from 'next hawker that comes round. But if we don't go, then they might wait for our next visit. They'll know that tha usually has plenty o' good stuff?'

'Aye. Tha could be right, Annie. They'll be disappointed I expect, if we haven't got what they want.'

'Let's get back then. If we crack on a bit we'll be back in Hessle by nightfall.'

Annie set off in the opposite direction and Charlie with an eager bark, jumped down from the cart to follow her. The donkey pricked up his ears and set off at a trot after them which set Robin running.

'Jump in Annie, if tha's a mind.'

She shook her head. 'I'll walk for a bit, I'm enjoying this.'

It was a fresh cool morning and she took in a deep breath of country air. By, this is grand, she thought. I can feel it doing me good. I don't know if I could live here though, even though 'scenery is lovely. She looked down beyond the sheep studded banks into the dry valley bottom and saw ploughmen and their teams ploughing up the springy pasture, making ready for crops. What would I do for company? Those poor Sutcliff lasses. Nobody lively to talk to. They'll get snowed in every winter I bet, and then no visitors at all. Onny pigs and geese for company.

Towards midday they turned into the next valley and trotting along the narrow winding road towards them was a company of red-coated soldiers.

'It's 'same lot as before,' Robin muttered. 'What 'they after?'

'Good day.' The Scots sergeant was pleasant enough, though he didn't smile. 'We meet again!'

'Aye.' Annie nodded to him but noticed that he was looking in the back of the cart.

'Have you done good business?'

'Not bad.'

He got down from his horse and gave the reins to one of his men. 'Have you got anything interesting in your packs?' Idly he picked one up and shook it, as if testing the weight.

She smiled and lowered her lashes. 'A few ribbons and fripperies. Would tha like to look, hast tha a lady to buy for?'

There was a ripple of amusement from the men and the sergeant looked annoyed. 'Open it,' he demanded sharply.

Annie took it from him, brushing her hand against his and smiling a shy apology. 'There, sergeant,' she breathed. 'Pink or blue, or a pretty yellow, which colour would suit her? Or—.' She leaned over him to reach for another pack. 'If she's not partial to colour, I've a piece o' plain linen?'

He shook his hand for her to fasten them up. 'That's not what I'm after.'

'Well maybe next time. We'll be getting fresh supplies. We'll have good linen, nice muslins and such. Stop us if tha sees us and tha can have tha pick.'

He swung back on to his horse. He looked tired and dusty, as all the men did, as if they had been riding all night.

'Sergeant?' She called him back as they prepared to ride away. 'Could tha eat a good dinner?'

'Oh, couldn't I?' he said wearily. 'I'd be glad to get off this damned hoss's back for an hour or two.'

'I can tell thee where tha can get 'best food in 'Wolds, if there's a mind for it. Good ale, and pleasant company.' She shaped a female form with her hands.

His face brightened, and his men turned eagerly towards her. 'Will we be welcome? Not all folks round here will have us over the threshold.'

'I can promise thee tha'll be welcome, just be mindful o' thy manners and treat 'daughters of 'house wi' respect. Tell 'em Mrs Hope sent thee.'

Robin gave them instructions for finding the Sutcliff inn and Annie translated slowly for them, for they still couldn't understand him.

'We'll have to learn to talk proper, thee and me, Robin, if we wants to make our way in life.' She watched them ride away up the hill.

'I hope we've done right, Annie, sending them there. What if Mr Sutcliff won't have 'em in?'

'He'll not turn them away. They'll spend money with him. He'll be glad to make on, with winter coming. And Sutcliff lasses will be thrilled to bits.' She smiled and climbed into the cart. 'I reckon we've done everybody a favour, including ourselves.'

7

'Does tha want to go straight home, Robin?'

They had reached Hessle as dusk and a light rain were falling.

'Tha might as well, no sense in coming back to 'Trotts, Toby won't be there, and 'donkey will find his way home.'

'If tha's sure? Aye I will then. I'm dead beat.'

They were both tired, the journey had seemed longer coming back, and they had had to walk up most of the hills, urging on the donkey who refused to carry their weight, and jumping in the cart as he gathered speed on the downward slopes.

But Annie had delighted in the selling. Once she had got over her diffidence of talking to people, when she knew that she had something that they wanted, she began to feel the confidence of success. Her enthusiasm in the quality of the goods, and the way in which she handled the material as if it was something precious, influenced the women, whether cottagers, or cooks, housekeepers or farmers' wives, and they had all bought from her.

The pocket book which Toby had given her in which to record her sales she'd filled with pictures. For Mrs Corner she drew two circles, one on top of another to denote her roundness and she counted on her fingers the items she had bought, and drew short straight lines to mark how many. For another customer she drew a figure with a man's hat on and a pipe in its mouth and a cloud of smoke issuing from the bowl, for the old woman had puffed constantly as they had shown her their goods, and Annie had thought that she would die of coughing. Four stick figures represented the innkeeper's daughters, two taller than the others; and for the innkeeper, again, two fat circles – and she knew she would remember who had asked for the special arrangements.

She took the reins from Robin and cracked the whip. She'd been wanting to do this since the start of their journey, only hadn't liked to ask. To her surprise the animal moved off immediately, heading for home.

She mused on another time when she had ridden in a cart. Francis had been driving it, and she had felt like a lady until he had ordered her out in no uncertain manner. She shivered as she thought about him and fear descended now that she was alone. Nobody knows him here, she told herself, or me. How could they? But she glanced nervously at passersby and pulled her shawl about her head.

Mrs Trott had locked up for the night and Annie had to hammer on the door to be let in. The old woman grumbled at her and told her that she was back too early, that they should have stayed away another day.

'We've sold out,' Annie explained. 'There was nowt left to sell. We've come back for fresh supplies.'

'What? All muslins and that? Never!'

'Aye. 'Whole lot, except for a few ribbons and bits of stuff. I kept getting asked for extras,' she added slyly. 'I wasn't sure what they meant.'

Mrs Trott looked sour. 'Aye well, I used to take a few bits o' this and that, for special customers. I never reckoned on somebody else taking me place.'

No wonder she's got the hump, Annie thought. She must think Toby's ditched her because of me. 'Well maybe we can come to some *arrangement*, Mrs Trott. Think about it if tha wants.'

Henry Trott arrived back from his night shift the next morning and Mrs Trott took herself off to the village to buy cheese from the dairy and meat from the butcher.

'Tha can bring in wood and draw water and wash 'vegetables, and I'll bring back a bit o' shin for stew.

79

Then tha can scrub 'table and sweep 'floor. Don't sit about doing nowt and don't disturb Mr Trott.'

There's not much chance of doing that, Annie thought, looking at him already in his bed with his nightcap askew, and his lips quivering. We're going to have a performance any minute now.

After stacking the wood at the side of the hearth she took a broom and swept up all the dust. She looked round. It looks clean enough to me. She'd never know if it was done or not. Annie brought in the water and then looked glumly at the pile of potatoes and turnips which she'd been told to scrub. She sighed and wandered to the door. The morning was damp and misty, winter was on its way.

She closed the door to keep in the heat but the fire began to smoke, so she opened it a crack and then walked idly around the room. Mrs Trott had left out her bedding. Usually she folded it and put it into the chest, but today she had straightened it and left it on top of the lid.

Annie took the blanket to the door, shook it and folded it and lifted the lid of the chest. She knelt down beside it and placed the blanket on top of the sheets and linens that were there. Idly she ran the material through her fingers. It was good stuff, quite fine, not ordinary fustian like most people used. Mrs Trott obviously treated herself to the best, although it looked unused.

She lifted up the top layer, there was her own satin petticoat, washed and folded, and next to it another piece of coloured silk, underneath that was a fold of lace. 'Why, she's nowt but a squirrel,' she muttered. 'When's she going to use these?'

Curiously she delved further into the chest, Mr Trott was still whistling and rattling in fine form and she knew that he would sleep for hours. There was another blanket stretched across the length of the chest and she lifted a corner. Beneath it were two parcels wrapped in calico, she opened them and inside were waxed bags. She pulled one out and sniffed it. 'Baccy, she grinned. I knew it. 'Old lass has got a bit o' business going. She pulled up the other

80

one. The smell wasn't so strong so she tore a corner with her finger nail and put her nose to it. Tea! She breathed in the aroma and sat back on her heels.

Her back was to the door and she didn't hear it being pushed further open, but she saw the shaft of light against the floor and then the shadow as Toby stepped into the room.

'What are you doing? I didn't think you'd be back yet.' He stood over her as she quickly pushed back the bags and straightened the blanket on top of them.

'Nowt,' she stammered. 'I'm just putting Mrs Trott's blanket away. She forgot,' she added lamely, 'I'm just tidying up for her.'

He put his hand over his mouth to hide a laugh and glanced towards the bed. 'You? Tidying up? Come outside.' He grabbed her by the arm and dragged her to the door.

'Now tell me what you were really doing, Annie? You were searching in Mrs Trott's chest. What for?'

She hung her head and scuffed the ground with the toe of her boot. He didn't sound cross, just stern and disappointed.

'When we went to some of 'customers, they asked if Mrs Trott had sent them owt, I told them I'd bring what they wanted next time. Only I wasn't sure what it was they were after, well, only partly sure – I guessed it was tea and 'baccy.' She lifted her head defiantly and stared him in the face. 'So I thought I'd look. I knew she put things in 'chest, cos I've seen her do it. One night when she thought I was asleep, I saw her. It was 'night she opened 'henhouse door for thee.'

He gasped and she knew that now they were on an equal footing.

'I'll not tell on thee, Toby. Tha's been good to me and I'll not forget it, but if I'm to work for thee, I want to know 'risks.'

He shook his head. 'You don't understand, Annie. The selling that you and Robin do, has nothing to do with the other. Mrs Trott must have been selling for herself, and I didn't realize – no really,' he added as Annie pulled a cynical face.

'I wondered why she was so against you going in her place.' He leaned against the wall and stared blankly into space. 'She's helped me, I have to say, with hiding stuff, and I've paid her in kind, with tea and tobacco, or linen. I thought she was keeping it for herself. She's a hoarder, she always was. And all the time she's been taking such a tremendous risk.' He put his hands to his head. 'If she'd been stopped and searched!'

Annie laughed. 'Nobody would have stopped her. She'd have given 'em 'sharp end of her tongue if they had. But what about thee? What about risk thy's taking?'

He grinned, his eyes merry. 'I told you before Annie. Life can be fun. It's also exciting. I get a tremendous thrill inside when I'm pitting myself against authority, when the chase is on and it's them or me. And,' he said in mitigation. 'I'm not hurting anybody, I'm helping those who can't help themselves. These are hard times and the people can't afford to pay taxes on tea and tobacco; it's only his Majesty and his Government who are losing out, and they can well afford it.'

There was silence between them, then he reached towards her and pulled her towards him. She gasped as he put his arms around her and spoke with his mouth against hers.

'So. What do I do about you, Annie? You could tell the authorities about me and collect a reward. Or you can join me and live dangerously.'

She struggled free from his arms and pushed him away. 'I telled thee afore. I'm finished wi' men, so don't try owt.' She flushed, his arms had felt strong and safe. 'Tha said afore we could be like brother and sister.'

'And so we can, Annie.' His face told her he was teasing. 'I was only giving you a brotherly hug.'

'And – and besides, I heard that tha was finished wi' all that.'

'Finished with all what?' He looked puzzled.

'Women and that.' She felt embarrassed. She had never come across a man who was ever finished with it.

'Has someone been saying something?' He looked angry.

'Somebody said that tha'd been crossed in love, and had vowed to be er—,' she searched for the word.

'What?' His voice was sharp, devoid of humour and she knew that here was a different man.

'Celibate,' she whispered. 'Though I'd never believe that of any man, none that I've ever known anyroad.'

They both turned as they heard the creak of the paddock gate and Mrs Trott came into view. As she tussled with the catch and her umbrella, Toby took Annie's hand and hurried her around the corner of the house.

'Quickly. Don't let her see us.' They ran up the slope at the back of the house and into the shelter of a belt of trees.

'She'll come looking for me. I haven't done 'vegetables like she said.'

He peered out from behind a bush. 'She won't come up here; and anyway it will give her some satisfaction if she has to do the work herself. She told me that you wouldn't be any good in the house.'

Annie bridled and then laughed. 'She'd be right.' She thought that his good humour had returned, but she was mistaken for he pulled her down onto the ground beside him and pinned her down.

'Now, tell me what's been said,' he demanded. His eyes were cold and bore into her.

'Don't look at me like that, Toby.' She started to cry. 'I should have known tha's just like all 'rest. And I'd thought tha was a proper gentleman – all this talk of being brother and sister,' she sniffed away her tears as he still had hold of her hands. 'And it means nowt.'

He let go of her hands and taking a handkerchief from his pocket, he gently wiped her face. 'Have you been ill-used, Annie? Your husband?'

'Was a bully to me and me bairns, and I wished him dead many times, God forgive me.'

'And it's him who's searching for you, not someone else's husband, as you said?'

She sat up and wiped her nose on her skirt and shook her head. 'Nay, he's dead all right. He died at sea. It's somebody else who's chasing me, but I daren't tell thee who.' The tears started to fall again as she thought of the punishment due to her. 'I've to live wi' this for 'rest of me days.'

'I didn't mean to frighten you, Annie. I'm sorry. It's just that there have been so many rumours about me. Mostly I don't mind for it stops people wondering what I really do. But sometimes I get angry at the insinuations.'

Annie looked at him and saw a childlike, lonely sorrow on his face and impulsively she leant forward and kissed his cheek. 'Let's be friends, thee and me, Toby. I think I can trust thee and I'll do nowt to harm thee, if tha wants to confide.'

They sat within the shelter of the trees and smiled as they heard the sound of Mrs Trott calling Annie's name. Ahead of them down the slope and beyond the cottage was the glint of the river, dark today and murky.

'I fell in love,' he began. 'There was a young lady visiting a family near to our home. I was introduced to her and we fell in love. Foolishly, I told my father that I wanted to marry her when I came of age. He laughed at me and said that I'd better get some experience first. I was sixteen; my brother who was two years older had already left home, and I had no-one that I could turn to for advice. My father had always had women, cheap women, and even so-called *ladies*; they used to visit him at our home or he would go to theirs. He was quite blatant about his excesses: I suspect that my mother had been forced into marriage with him, she could never have chosen him of her own free will.'

He shuddered and Annie looked at him curiously. She had always imagined that people of class, with money and nice houses, lived happy lives; that only those in poverty, like herself and of her ilk, had suffered abject misery. Yet Toby, in spite of his merry manner, had had an unhappy childhood and an unloving father.

'My father had a regular woman visitor called Hetty and of all the women she was quite pleasant towards me. I decided to confide in her. I told her of the young lady and my feelings towards her, and what my father had said. She said that she would make plans for me, that I should leave it all to her.'

He looked so unhappy that Annie took hold of his hand and kept it clasped in her own while he went on talking.

'She took me to York. We went in my father's carriage so he was obviously a party to it, and she introduced me to a woman who kept a house there. It was a fine house, small, yet clean and well furnished, and there by the charms of a particular young woman I came into manhood.'

Annie stifled a yawn. What was he coming to. Wasn't that what all men did, one way or another?

'She gave me the clap.'

He shook his hand away from Annie as if he might contaminate her, and glared at her, defying her to judge him.

She nodded. 'Aye, she would.'

He stared at her. 'Aren't you horrified? Isn't it so degrading?'

'Tha'd get over it. Everybody gets it at some time, unless tha's a monk and I wouldn't put it past them to get a dose now and then.'

He got to his feet and looked down at her. 'Don't you understand Annie? I was infected with this terrible disease, and my father and Hetty laughed. They thought it was a huge joke that it should happen on my first encounter with a woman. But what was worse, was that they told the father of the lady I loved. He too thought it was a great joke, until he heard that I had planned to marry his daughter, and then that was a different matter entirely. He said that if I was such a dissipated rake at sixteen, then there was no hope for me and he banned me from seeing her.'

'Oh, that was daft. Tha'd have got over it eventually, she probably wouldn't have caught it from thee.'

She knew that was true. Her husband had got it from some whore, but he hadn't passed it on to her. But then, she'd managed to get him so drunk every night until he went back to sea, that he didn't come near her.

Toby sat down and put his head in his hands. 'I loved her so much. Her father told her why he wouldn't let me marry her and she was repulsed by the thought of it and said that she would never marry me anyway, even if her father said that she could. I vowed then that I'd never touch a woman again, never in my life.'

What a lot of fuss about nowt, Annie mused. It seems a waste though, a handsome man like Toby. I suppose that's what folks might call principles. Principles. She turned the word over in her mind. She liked the sound of it. She didn't think that she had ever had any; she shook her head as she pondered. Nay, not me, principles are not for 'likes of me.

Toby had begun talking again. 'So you see, Annie. This is why I play a dangerous game.' His eyes glittered. 'I revel in defying authority. I pay back society for the way I've been treated. And one day,' he said bitterly. 'I'll get even with my father.'

'Tha might get found out. What if 'military catch thee?' She told him of her meeting with the soldiers.

He shrugged. 'I've nothing to lose but my life, and no one who would care.'

Shocked, she said, 'I'd care, and 'Trotts 'd care, and what about thy brother?'

'Ah, my brother. Yes, you must meet my brother, Annie. Are you with me? Will you join me in this mad game? Will you put some excitement into your dull life?'

He was merry again, she thought. It was as if he had locked away all the cares that had previously troubled him. As if he had not even spoken about them. Perhaps she should do the same.

'Aye, Toby. Happen I will. Like thee I've nowt to lose.'

8

When Toby called the next day and told Mrs Trott that
Annie was to join the team she could barely keep her
anger under control. She's fair spitting, Annie thought
as she watched her wrinkled neck and then her face turn
scarlet.

''Rest of 'team'll not be happy about it. We know nowt
about her. She could be spying on us and then we'll be
done for.'

'What rubbish. And anyway,' Toby's voice rose and he
stared long and hard at Mrs Trott. 'I run this team and I
make the decisions. If anyone doesn't like what I choose
to do, then they don't have to stay.'

Mrs Trott squirmed and spluttered but Toby stood his
ground. 'We need someone else, you know that. We need
someone to watch the river. It's too cold for you to be
doing it now that winter is coming.'

He patted her arm and said in a gentler tone. 'I'm
thinking of you, Mrs Trott. You should be tucked up in
your bed at night, not wandering along the river-bank.'

She thinks of him as hers. Annie watched as Mrs Trott
had a change of mood and fussed over Toby, cutting up
bread for him and slicing cheese. He's like a son she never
had. That's why she doesn't like me. She's jealous. She
thinks I'm going to take him away from her.

'Who's 'rest of 'team?' Annie asked and unbidden
helped herself to cheese, whilst Mrs Trott glared at
her. 'I thought it was just thee and Robin and Mr
and Mrs Trott.' And whoever it was with thee by
'henhouse, she mused, and Mrs Trott doesn't know yet
what I saw there.

'No!' A harsh whispered duet came from Toby and Mrs Trott.

'Mr Trott knows nowt, and don't thee dare tell him.' The old woman pushed her face close to Annie's. 'He knows nowt. Does tha hear?'

Annie backed away. 'I hear thee. I hear thee. And Robin?' She turned to Toby.

'He knows nothing. He simply sells my legitimate goods. He's a good cover for me. It gives me a reason for travelling the countryside, to visit my customers. But I wouldn't want to involve the lad. The rest of the team? Well, you might meet them, and then again you might not.'

He leaned his elbows on the table and looked into Annie's eyes. 'We don't go in for names. Some of the men wouldn't be happy to give them, though I suspect that they all know each other, but under cover of darkness they make believe that they don't. This is a dangerous game, Annie, we won't pretend that it's otherwise. If the revenue men get wind of a run taking place we have to watch our backs, and if they bring in the military, then we're doubly careful, for they're armed. But,' he said cheerfully as he rose to leave, 'we're lucky along this river, there are numerous creeks that they can't reach and tall reeds to hide us, and we've had Lady Luck on our side up to now.'

He said he would collect Annie later that evening. 'Henry's at work tonight, isn't he?' he asked.

Mrs Trott nodded. 'Aye. He'll not be around to notice she's not here.'

After Toby had left, Annie did her best to ingratiate herself with Mrs Trott. She fetched in wood and drew water, and then swept and washed the floor of the cottage while Mrs Trott sat outside on a stool and sewed a piece of linen.

'I was never any good at sewing.' Annie sat down on the doorstep when she'd finished. 'Me ma never learned me.'

'Hah. It seems to me tha ma learned thee nowt.' Mrs Trott smiled complacently. 'I had a good teacher. 'Best ever.' She rested her sewing on her knee and gazed out towards the river. She didn't speak for sometime and Annie peered towards her, wondering if she had fallen asleep.

'Aye, she was a good teacher, in spite of her being so young. She was not much more'n a bairn when I met her. Master Toby's mother, I'm talking about.' She turned towards Annie, speaking slowly and carefully; as if I'm slow in 'head, Annie thought.

'Aye. I guessed that's who tha meant. Tha was fond of her, I can tell.'

The old woman nodded. 'I was onny kitchen maid to begin with, but mistress took a fancy to me.' She gave a cackling laugh, 'and she would have me upstairs wi' her. Her mother and father weren't too pleased I can tell thee, but she could get anything she wanted from them. She was that sweet and pretty, they just ate out of her hand. She told them she'd teach me, and she did. I learnt to read and write, and I can talk proper. I haven't forgotten.'

She stared at Annie and her voice took on a lighter, haughtier tone. 'I didn't say *thee* and *thine*, but *you* and *yours*, and I learned how to serve tea and dress her hair. She was such a lovely lady and when she married, I went with her and helped her with her babbies.'

Mrs Trott rubbed her eyes and sighed and picked up her sewing. 'Still, all that's done wi' now.'

'But tha's lucky. Tha's found Master Toby again, and he's fond of thee, and tha's got Mr Trott. Tha's luckier then me who's got nobody.' She sniffed loudly. 'And I made a promise.' Annie crossed her fingers behind her back. 'When me husband died I vowed I'd never know another man.' She nodded her head meaningfully. 'Tha knows. In that way.'

It was a lie, but only a small one, for after Alan had died, Francis Morton had swept her off her feet with his promises, promises which everyone else knew to be

89

false. I was so stupid not to see, she thought, I should have known. But never again.

She thought she saw a softening of Mrs Trott's face at her words and when she added. 'I've found a real good friend in Toby. He wants nowt more than friendship, and as we both know, Mrs Trott, there are'nt too many men around who'd be satisfied wi' just that,' the old woman almost gave her a smile as she rose and said she would make them a dish of tea.

Mr Trott had been left for work only five minutes when they heard the creak of the gate. 'That'll be Toby,' Annie said, picking up her shawl. 'I'd best be off.'

'Wait.' Mrs Trott reached to the peg behind the door. 'Take this. It'll keep thee warmer than what tha's wearing,' and handed Annie a long black woollen cloak.

Annie put it on and felt the warmth. 'Oh, it's grand, Mrs Trott.' She whirled around. 'I feel like a lady.'

'Aye. Well it was once a lady's, many years ago. My lady's. She gave it to me one winter when she got a new 'un. But it's as good as new. Cloth like that doesn't wear out.' She sighed, 'and tha might as well have use of it now, it's cold down by 'river at night.'

Annie thanked her profusely. She guessed that Mrs Trott's pride and antagonism had softened considerably since their talk earlier in the day.

Toby opened the door. 'Come on, Annie. Let's go.' He nodded to Mrs Trott. 'We'll only explore the river bank tonight. Nothing more. A reconnoitre only, to make sure all is ready.'

He took Annie's hand as they crossed the paddock. 'I don't go near the haven when Mr Trott is on duty. I wouldn't want him to become involved. He's as honest as the day is long, but who would believe him if I should be caught, knowing as everyone does, that he is a friend of mine?'

'But I saw thee,' Annie began. 'That first day.'

'Yes.' He stopped close to the hedge. 'But that was just

a game that night, to find out if the watchman was aware of us. There were two of us but you only saw me. And the watchman didn't see either of us.'

He put two fingers to his lips and gave a low piercing whistle and Annie heard a muffled clomp. She gasped as in the darkness a large shape appeared in front of them and she smelt the warm breath of an animal close to her face.

'Aagh.' In fright she clung to Toby. 'What devil's this?'

'No devil. This is my faithful Sorrel. Have you ridden before, Annie?'

'Ridden? On a horse? No never. I can't. I'd be afeeard to.' The animal snuffled up to her and whinnied softly and she backed away.

'Well you're going to have to learn because we haven't the time to walk.' He put his foot in the stirrup and heaved himself up. 'Come on, give me your hand.'

'I can't. I can't. He's too big, I'll tummel off.' She flinched and fell against the hedge.

He loosened his foot from the stirrup and leant down towards her. He seemed to be at a great height above her. 'Put your foot in the stirrup and give me your hand,' he demanded. 'We can't stay here all night. Just do as I say.'

Awkwardly she lifted her leg and tried to put her foot in as he commanded, but she hopped and hopped and finally fell on her back onto the path and she was glad of the darkness as her skirt flew up over her knees.

'*Please*, Annie. Show a little sense. Put your foot in the stirrup. Take hold of the saddle with one hand, and give me the other. That's it. Now *jump*.'

She felt herself fly through the air and somehow or other land on the horse's back behind Toby. She clung to him desperately. 'Tha won't let him gallop, will tha? Not 'till I get used to 'feel of it.'

Beneath her arms as she clung to him, she felt his body shake with suppressed laughter. Finally he could contain himself no longer and gave a great guffaw. 'Oh Annie, what a tonic you are. You make me laugh so.'

She grunted. She felt as if the breath was being shaken out of her body as the horse at a soft command moved forward in a firm trot. 'I'm glad I'm making somebody happy,' she gasped. 'It'll be 'first time ever.'

With her eyes shut tight and her head hunched down, she hung on for dear life as they moved swiftly over rough terrain. Then as the hooves made a different crunching sound, she cautiously opened her eyes and saw that they were riding along the foreshore of the river with the water breaking over the horse's hooves.

'Where 'we going? Is it far? All me bones is breaking.'

'Ssh. Speak in whispers. Voices carry out here. They'll hear you over in Lincolnshire.' He turned in the saddle towards her. 'Are you all right? Try to get the feel of him. Ride with him, not against him. We're going up to Ferriby and maybe beyond. We'll ride on the shore as far as we can, then turn across country again.'

'Tha'll have to watch 'tide,' she whispered. 'We could get swept away. Hast tha seen 'strength of 'waves?'

'Yes, I have, but don't worry, it's low water tonight.'

The sky was light though there was no moon showing and in the distance she could see the shadowy spire of a church. As they drew nearer towards it, Toby suddenly wheeled the horse's head to the right and with a swift leap they took the bank.

'Hold on,' he said in a hoarse whisper, and again a leap and another, and they cleared a hedge and a ditch and cantered into pasture land.

He reined in after a while. 'We'll have to walk for a bit. We're going to head back towards the river but it's too muddy to ride, and with two of us on his back the prints will be deep.'

Annie thought she would never walk again. The muscles in her stomach and buttocks were stretched with pain and her thighs were burning as if they were on fire. She stumbled after Toby. 'Wait. Wait. Don't leave me. I'm crippled.' She could barely talk, all the breath had been pummelled from her.

But if she was expecting sympathy there was none forthcoming. Toby put his hand up in warning. 'Be quiet.'

She put her hand to her mouth. She suddenly felt frightened. She shivered. She also felt wet. Her boots were squelching. She shuffled her feet and felt the mud oozing beneath them.

'Toby,' she whispered. 'Me feet are wet. Are we—?'

He put his hand over her mouth. 'I said be quiet. There's someone down there.'

He'd been leading the horse by its reins but now he put them into Annie's hands. 'Don't move,' he said. 'Stay right there until I come back.'

She was terrified. Not of the unseen presence somewhere below the bushes where Toby had disappeared, but of the snuffling horse who kept nudging her with his big head, his warm breath on the back of her neck, and his great hooves trampling on her feet. She tried to move away, to hold him at a long rein's length, but each time she moved he followed her, his large teeth nuzzling her hair.

'Oh, Toby, hurry up,' she muttered. 'What's tha doing?' She strained her ears to catch any sound. She could hear the ripple of water and a rustle in the reeds as the breeze ran through them, and guessed that they were near a creek or a stream; she didn't think that they were yet on the river-bank, as the rush of tidal waters would have been stronger, more vibrant in its impetuous flow.

She ducked her head as a snipe suddenly flew into zigzag flight above her, a dark shadow that flew high and then dived, the wind vibrating through its stiff tail feathers as it circled its invaded territory.

Sorrel pricked his ears and whinnied softly as he caught his master's voice. There was a murmur and a drift of laughter, and then a low whistle. Sorrel moved off at the command, pulling Annie in his wake slipping and slithering on the wet grass as she tried to keep tight hold of his reins.

Toby's head and shoulders appeared at her feet out of the darkness of the bank and he jumped up to join her. He took the reins from her and fastened them to a scrubby bush and patted Sorrel on his neck, speaking softly into his ear.

'Toby?'

'Ssh. Don't speak. Pull your hood over your head, and then follow me. Don't say a word unless you really have to.'

He took hold of her hand and helped her down the bank to a narrow path, a mere foothold only, and they held on to the reeds as they made their way along the side of an overflowing creek. He put his fingers to his lips in warning and she saw in the darkness a shadow of a man. Someone whose height was no more than hers and who spoke to Toby in a husky whisper as they approached. The same person she assumed, who had been at the henhouse and whom she had mistakenly thought was Robin.

As her eyes became accustomed to the darkness she saw the square stern of a coggy boat tied to a spar which protruded from the water.

Toby nudged her. 'Get in,' he said in a low voice, and to the man, 'thanks, tomorrow then, as arranged.'

Annie thought that the man looked towards her, but she put her head down so that the hood of the cloak dropped over her face as she stepped into the boat.

She smiled to herself. It had been a long time since she had been in such a boat. She felt the sway and roll of the water beneath her and thought of the times when she and the other children used to watch from beneath the piers of the Horse Staithe on market days, and wait for a boat to come in. When the occupants had unloaded themselves and their baskets and taken themselves off to market, they would climb into the boat and unfasten the painter, and row off down the river. They'd return after an hour and fasten it up again so that the owners never knew that their boat had been away on a very precarious voyage.

Then they would wait again for the next victim. Sometimes they would be lucky and find the owner's dinner, maybe a hunk of bread or some fruit and they would sit in the middle of the river watching the town, seeing the hubbub of life from a different angle as they gorged themselves on stolen vittals.

'Are you all right?' Toby took an oar and pushed away from the bank. 'I didn't want the fellow back there to hear your voice. As you're wearing Mrs Trott's cloak, I'm hoping he thought you were her. The fewer people who know about you the better.'

'Who was he?'

'I told you, we don't go in for names, though he knows mine, and Mrs Trott's.'

'So he could tell 'law of thee, but tha couldn't tell of him? It seems a bit one-sided to me.'

'He won't tell of me. His supply would dry up and he has a nice little business going with a regular tub of geneva and a half anchor of rum, not to mention a parcel or two of tea and tobacco. No, he won't give me away.'

'So they can't do 'run without thee?'

They slipped out of the creek into the river. Annie felt the swell dipping beneath her and watched as Toby now took both oars and rowed up river.

'Me or my brother,' Toby answered, pulling with long strong strokes. 'And Matt wouldn't risk a run with anyone else, he just wouldn't trust anybody else. His life and liberty depends on me.'

'Does he have his own ship? How is it he hasn't been pressed?' Annie was curious. The press-men were notorious on the seas, even going as far as boarding whalers, and with the threat of firearms they would try to press the crew, even those with exemption tickets, to join the navy.

Toby laughed. 'He's captain of his own ship and he's had many a battle with the press-men, he's even lost some of his crew, but so far he's escaped them.'

'He keeps weapons, then?'

'Of course.' Toby manouvered into another creek, so narrow and covered by reeds that Annie ducked as the tall reeds closed about her. 'What seaman doesn't these days?'

He shipped the oars and pulled on the reeds and Annie followed suit, feeling the sharpness of the stems cutting into her palms as she pulled.

'There, that's far enough. We're well hidden, we'll not be seen here.' He pulled in and fastening the mooring rope securely to a tree stump, he climbed out. There was a nervous croak of a disturbed marsh hen somewhere in the reed bed.

'Now what do we do?' Annie asked as she stepped on to the bank. 'How do we get back to thy hoss.'

'We walk,' Toby grinned. 'How else?'

'But we've come miles,' she gasped. 'Why did tha have to move 'boat?'

'Questions, questions,' he complained, grabbing hold of her hand and pulling her along. 'You never stop asking questions.'

'How else can I find out,' she retorted, shaking him off. 'Tha's just brought me out on a wild-goose chase, and never explained owt.'

He smiled. 'You're right, of course. But I didn't know when we came out, that we would have to move the boat. Not until we met the fellow back there. He told me that the soldiers have been patrolling that part of the river-bank. That's why he was there, waiting for me. I've moved the boat up river to this creek because they can't come down here on horseback; it's too wet and marshy. They'll only patrol the top road.'

'Well that's all right then, just so long as I know.'

She bent down and started to unfasten her bootlaces.

'Annie! What are you doing?'

'I'm taking me boots off,' she said as she knotted the laces together and hung them around her neck. 'This is onny pair I've got, and I'm not having 'em ruined wi' all this walking.'

9

Toby called the next morning and said he was going to ride into Hull. 'Do you want to come? See some of your old haunts?'

She felt sick at the thought. What if she saw her bairns? How could she not rush to them and hug them? How could she explain to them why she had run away, and why she couldn't come back? And what if she saw Mrs Morton, Francis's mother, that scheming, blaspheming, rough and raucous woman, who would whistle for the law if she as much as set eyes on her?

'No. No. I can't. I told thee. If them folks should see me—'

'I'd protect you Annie.'

'Aye, I'm sure tha would and I'm grateful. But they'd mark thee, Toby, and tha doesn't want trouble wi' likes o' them. Not when tha needs to keep tha head down over this other business.'

Toby pursed his lips and considered. 'You're right of course. Who knows, they might be in a similar line of business, and they might try to get back at you through me. Some of them wouldn't think twice about tipping off the Customs about someone else, if it meant immunity for themselves.'

She nodded. She didn't like to lie to him about these fictitious villains, but she dare not, could not even think of, going back into Hull. 'There's a good deal of smuggling going on,' she said. 'Ships is coming in all 'time with stuff. Aye and taking it out. I heard tell of a ship bound for Denmark getting caught wi' three tons of wool on board. So tha's best sticking wi' folks tha can trust out here, Toby, not dealing wi' riff-raff in Hull.'

To her relief he agreed and set off, telling her that he would be back before dark and that she should be ready to move off as soon as he arrived.

Mr Trott caught her as she was feeding the hens. 'Tha can come wi' me up to common if tha wants,' he said. 'I just want to check on 'sheep, make sure they're not taffled up in 'hedge bottom.'

Fortunately Mrs Trott came out as he was talking, and before Annie could think of a suitable reason why she shouldn't go – for she had no wish at all to look at his sheep or grunting pigs – Mrs Trott shouted to him not to be taking Mrs Hope anywhere.

'I need her here wi' me. She might as well earn her keep while she's here, not wasting her time out on marsh and waste.'

Mr Trott moved off glumly. 'I just thought she might like to have a chat with some of 'other folk on 'common,' he said. 'There's nobody to talk to down here.'

Annie heaved a sigh and followed Mrs Trott into the house, another invitation and she couldn't accept either of them.

'It's best that nobody knows tha's here. Folks' talk and they might wonder why tha's hanging around.'

She's only concerned about Toby, Annie thought. She's not really bothered about me.

The day hung long and dreary. She helped Mrs Trott and then wandered outside and down to the river. She felt restless and uneasy. Tha's a fool, Annie, she told herself. Why *is* tha hanging around here? Tha could have been halfway to York by now, or even over in Lincolnshire if tha'd been brave enough.

Onny I'm not brave enough. She sat down on the shingle and stared at the water. Long-legged waders, redshanks and curlews, searched in the shallows, dipping deep in the mud with their long pointed bills for crustaceans and insects. I've got caught up with a fellow, that's 'trouble.

Why is it that I have? Even though there's nowt in it, no love or passion or owt, it's just as if I can't manage on me own. But I will. Just as soon as I've had enough of this caper, then I'll be off.

She looked up into the sky as a large flock of widgeon flew over. I'll be as free as them birds flying up there. I'll be behodden to nobody. But as she defiantly thought the words, she knew in her soul that it wasn't true. She knew that she needed the presence of others, that she hated being alone and that more than anything else, the things that she wanted most had always been denied her, to be loved and to be needed, and to belong.

When she put on the heavy cloak that night Mr Trott looked up curiously.

'Where's tha off to this time o' night, Mrs Hope?'

'I'm, – I'm just off to help Toby wi' sorting his linens and stuff, so's we're ready for 'next trip. Don't bother to wait up,' she added. 'I might be late.'

Mrs Trott nodded approvingly at the excuse and whispered that the door would be left unlocked for her return.

Her stomach churned with excitement and fear. I don't know why I'm going. What use will I be? I wonder if I'll meet Toby's brother?

Toby was riding Sorrel and as Annie, this time, took only two attempts to clamber on the horse's back, she mused that the bumpy ride would at least be preferable to walking all the way to the hidden creek.

'We'll make a horsewoman of you yet, Annie. Don't you love the feel of it? The power and strength beneath you?'

She had to admit that the sensation was quite exhilarating as the wind rushed through her hair and the cloak billowed out behind her like a black sail, but she felt hampered by her long skirt and petticoats, and her bare legs and thighs were still sore from the last ride.

'It must be easier wearing breeches,' she panted into Toby's ear.

'But not the thing for a lady,' he laughed, turning his head towards her. 'You should really be riding side-saddle wearing an elegant riding habit and a feather in your hat.'

When they were half a mile off the creek, they halted, tied Sorrel to a tree hidden from the road, and traversed the remaining distance on foot. Annie had again come barefoot. She felt more comfortable without her boots, even though the marshy ground squelched between her toes.

'Hull was very lively today,' Toby whispered as they walked. 'The soldiers from the garrison were patrolling the town. It seems they were expecting trouble. The price of flour has gone up yet again and the townspeople are in a terrible mood.'

'Aye, well, I daresay there'll be trouble, but it won't make price go down,' Annie said, with the philosophical air of someone who had seen it before.

'Oh, yes, and I was just in time to see them pull some poor soul out of the river.'

Annie stopped dead in her tracks and Toby turned in surprise.

'Who was it?' she asked in a barely audible whisper.

Toby shrugged. 'I don't know. Just some poor beggar.'

'Was he—? Did tha see his body? Did he just drown, or tired of life, was he? Or was he killed or what? There's been a lot o' murders. Fights and that. I know, I've seen 'em. Fighting over women or a wager on dog fights. Drunks and that.'

She started to shake. 'I've seen 'em fished out – all swollen they are. Had he been in 'river long – could tha tell?' Her voice got tighter and tighter as she fought the fear inside her.

'Annie! What morbid curiosity.' Toby put his arms around her as if he feared she would take flight. 'Annie! It was a woman. It was some poor old beggar woman that

100

they pulled out of the water. She'd been there for days by the look of her. It wasn't a man!'

She pulled away from him and retched violently onto the grass. 'I'm sorry,' she said, straightening up and wiping her mouth. 'It allus makes me sick when I hear of it. It makes me that afeard. I allus think that's how I'll end me days.'

She made her excuses but she knew he didn't believe her. Still, she didn't mind, for he took her arm solicitously as they walked on, and he didn't question and he didn't probe, and she was comforted for she knew that if he ever should find out, that it wouldn't matter, he would still be her friend.

A low whistle and croak greeted their arrival at the creek and Toby responded with a similar cry. A dim light from a lantern showed and from out of the reeds appeared the short figure of the man they had met previously. He handed the lantern to Toby and then helped Annie down the bank and into the boat which was just below. She kept her head averted but she sensed his curiosity.

To her surprise he too climbed in after Toby and each took an oar as they cast off.

'Take the lantern, but keep the light low until I tell you.' Toby handed the light to Annie and she noticed that he didn't speak her name. 'Don't let the light out, but keep it hidden.'

They came to the end of the creek and waited at the edge of the reed-bed, dipping softly on the gentle tide. Annie's eyes adjusted to the darkness and as they waited she saw the dark shape of a ship coming silently up river, looming large against the backdrop of the sky.

She wanted to ask. Is this it? Is this thy brother's ship? But she dare not risk Toby's anger or let the unknown man hear her voice, not until Toby told her that she could.

Suddenly the ship was abreast of them, her sails trimmed as she was brought up.

'Come on,' Toby muttered. 'Here she is.'

'Nay, wait. Wait for 'signal,' whispered the other man, and Toby stayed his hand, grasping the oar tightly.

'There it is!' A light flashed, then another.

'Show a light, show a light,' Toby uttered urgently and Annie held up the lantern and opened the shutter wide.

'Now close it. Now open it.'

She did as she was bid, her heart hammering painfully against her ribs and her throat constricted with fright.

'That's it, come on.' An answering light on the ship showed them that this was the vessel they were waiting for and Toby and his partner pulled hard towards it.

Annie turned her head as she heard sounds from the reed-bed, a lapping of water as wooden oars made contact with the water, and behind them she saw a fleet of small boats emerging from hidden anchorages along the side of the river.

'Toby,' she breathed. 'Look. Behind us.' She tried to keep her voice low. 'Are they with us, or against us?'

Toby glanced over his shoulder and she saw him smile in the darkness. 'They're with us. It's the rest of the team.'

Damn thee Toby Linton, she thought. Why didn't tha tell me there'd be others. I'm nearly sick with fright. I thought it was 'customs after us.

She was still fuming when they lay alongside the ship and she heard the sound of a whispered greeting and soft laughter as a jack ladder was thrown over.

The other man in their boat scrambled up first and as Toby made the boat fast, he whispered to Annie. 'Go on then, up you go.'

'What! Tha must be mad. I can't climb up there.'

'Course you can. You've just learnt to ride a horse, haven't you? Now you're going to climb aboard a ship.'

'But, I can't!' She looked up at the dark wall of the ship towering above her and the ladder swinging from side to side. 'I'll get stuck. It's too high. If I fall, I'll drown.'

Her voice started to rise in protest and Toby hushed

her. 'Get up that ladder or else I'll put you over my shoulder and carry you up.'

'Why can't I stay here and look after 'boat?' she began, but she saw an obstinate look on Toby's face as he took a step towards her and she hurriedly turned away and reached her hand for the ladder.

She felt it sway as she put first one foot and then the other on the wooden rung and she clung desperately with both hands.

'Move up a step, then I'll steady it from the bottom,' urged Toby. 'Go on, you'll find it easier as you get higher. Push your weight towards the hull.'

She was glad of the cloak which covered her as she climbed higher, for she was aware of her bare legs and the gaze of the men in the other boats staring upwards as she climbed. Mrs Trott never did this, she thought grimly. *They'll think you're Mrs Trott*, she mimicked, recalling Toby's previous remark. I'll give him *Mrs Trott* when I'm down from here.

Somehow she reached the top and hands reached out to pull her aboard. Hands which were more than willing as they made contact with her body and lingered as they felt the shape of a woman.

She lashed out with her hands and feet. 'Don't touch me,' she hissed. 'Keep tha hands to thyself,' and they took her sharp words so literally that they dropped their hold of her and she fell in a heap onto the deck.

'Who have we here?' A lantern was held up above her and she squinted to see the face in shadow behind it. She caught a glimpse of a gold earring and a silk scarf knotted casually around a muscular neck.

'A new team member, Matt,' Toby came up the ladder behind her and jumped on board. He put his hands beneath her armpits and hauled her to her feet. 'Let's do the introductions below, shall we?'

He gave out instructions to the men who were following him on board and then turned to the stern, taking Annie's arm, to follow his brother to his cabin below decks.

Annie looked on silently as she watched the brothers open their arms wide, and with a great guffaw, embrace each other with genuine affection. Curiously she gazed at Matthias Linton. He was taller and slimmer than his brother, his body hard and lean. His hair was as fair as Toby's was dark, his beard short and curly, and even in the dim light of the timbered cabin she saw that his face was tanned and his eyes a brilliant blue, much bluer than hers and bigger and wider than Toby's brown ones. But the facial differences ended there, for they both had a straight nose and Matt had the same gapped teeth, which smiled now as he looked at her.

He's laughing at me. She ran her fingers through her tangled hair which had become windswept, despite the hood, as the breeze had run through it as she'd sat in the coggy boat and climbed the swaying ladder.

'What waif have we here, Toby?'

'No waif, Matt,' Toby answered with a lazy smile. 'This is my friend, Mrs Hope, though I think she might let you call her Annie, when we're out of earshot of the men.'

'Mrs Hope!' Matt took hold of her hands, stretched her arms wide and perused her, turning her this way and that. 'Annie! Are you sure she's not a stray whom you found wandering along the river-bank? Though, indeed, – no, I can see by her borrowed finery, that she could well be a lady.'

She snatched her hands away, she was suddenly aware of her torn and tattered skirt which she still hadn't mended. 'Mrs Trott let me borrow her cloak. And I'm no waif or stray. I was on a journey until thy brother persuaded me to join him in this prank. And,' she said, lifting her chin. 'I'll not allow thee to call me Annie, 'til it suits me.'

'Well said, Annie.' Toby was idly watching them spar. 'Don't let him bully you.'

'I'll not do that, sir.' She gazed intently into Matt's blue eyes and saw a mocking challenge. He put his hand to his heart and gave a taunting bow. 'I'm used to bullies,' she sneered. 'They come in all shapes and sizes, and seemingly in every class, though I'm surprised to find thy brother's one.'

'It's just a game with him,' Toby said, as if his brother wasn't there, and sat down on a leather bench seat which ran around one side of the cabin. He put his arms behind his head and stretched out his legs. 'Don't take any notice of him.'

He's not used to being answered back, Annie thought. That must come of being captain of his ship, of giving orders and being obeyed. Well, he's not giving me orders, so he needn't think he is. I don't have to come on this lark if I don't want to.

Matt turned away with a shrug and reaching into a locker, took out a glass decanter. With an exaggerated show of respect he invited Annie to sit down. He placed the decanter and three glasses on the table, pushing aside a pile of charts and nautical instruments and poured a measure of brandy in each.

'To a successful run,' he raised his glass, 'and the good ship *Breeze*. God bless her.'

'And those who sail her,' Toby replied, clinking his glass against his brother's. 'You must take care though, Matt. The military are out this way, so I hear, and today I saw two strangers riding towards Hessle, they could well be customs men.'

'If you get this run away safely, then if they board us they'll only find an empty ship.' Matt tossed his brandy back and poured another. 'We got all the other stuff away off Spurn, the fishing smacks were waiting to trade and we slipped past the revenue cruiser without them even knowing.'

He threw his head back and laughed. By, he's handsome, Annie thought begrudgingly as she saw his eyes light up in merriment.

'They'll be hopping mad when they realize we've gone and they have to wait until the next trip.'

Annie took a sip of brandy. The strength seared her throat. It was fiercer and more potent than any she had tried before and she coughed as it slid down her throat. Her eyes watered as she spluttered and caught her breath.

'Mrs Hope! I do declare I had forgotten you were there.' Matt leant to pat her back. 'The liquor is stronger than a lady of your sensibilities is used to, I fear?'

'No,' she gasped, and took another sip. 'It's fine,' she said. 'But I generally take a drop o' water with it.'

'But of course, how forgetful of me. Do forgive me.' Again he gave her a mock bow and she wanted to throw the brandy at him.

He moved across to an alcove lined with books and took a jug of water from the lower shelf and brought it to her.

She lifted her glass but abruptly drew it back and placed her hand over the rim. There was a dead fly floating in the water. 'Beggin' tha pardon, Captain Linton,' she said, trying to sound squeamish. 'But I onny ever drink fresh water.' She had many times drunk muddy water from the Humber without ill effect, but she intended to score from this hectoring adventurer. 'I fear thy jug of water has seen much company.'

He flushed and taking the jug, opened the cabin door and threw the water out onto the deck, calling as he did so for the cabin boy.

Annie rose to her feet. 'Don't bother on my account Captain Linton. If tha'll excuse me, I'll wait on deck 'till tha's finished tha business. I'm in need of some fresh air.' She gave him a small curtsey and passed in front of him looking defiantly into his eyes. A small shudder passed through her at the silent mettlesome response. He made her feel very strange. A deep piercing sensation stirred her blood; some kind of agitated passion stung her, as if she had been scorched by fire or touched by fever.

She shivered as she waited outside the door. Tha's bitten off more than tha can chew, Annie. Tha's meddling wi' fire. Yet though she felt she was in dangerous waters by antagonizing Captain Linton, a small smile touched her lips. Here was an emotion she hadn't tasted before, and she felt lightheaded and giddy as if she had drunk several bottles of wine and not just a few sips of stolen brandy.

She leant her head against the closed cabin door, ahead of her was the companionway leading to the upper deck, but she decided she would wait here for Toby rather than brave the winks and nods of the seamen above.

The sound of raised voices reached her from within the cabin. She heard Toby answering some question of Matt's. 'I want her to join us, Matt. She'll be useful. She's sharp and clear-headed, and,' he added in an obstinate tone. 'I like her.'

Then Matt's voice came clear and strong.

'I know I've trusted your judgement before. I'm not denying that. But this is not a game we're playing, Toby, and you're forever finding strays; so tell me, which scrap heap did you find this rag-bag on?'

She caught her breath. He's talking about me. Anger flooded her. I'll show thee, Captain bleedin' Linton, just see if I don't.

10

'Heave ho, my lads. Make ready. Make ready.' Matt called the order as he took her arm to help her over the bulwark to climb down the perilous ladder, and she heard the pad of running feet hitting the deck as the men rushed to obey. Toby had gone down first and the men from the other boats had already cast off and were rowing swiftly back to shore. There was a shallow swell with only a slight roll but she stumbled slightly as she prepared to climb over and he steadied her with the pressure of his hand against her shoulders.

She felt a shock run through her as his fingers clasped her. She looked up and for a second, thought that he had felt it too, for there was a sudden uncertainty in his eyes, which disappeared as quickly as it had come, replaced by a cool taunting stare. He gave a small bow and raised her hand, touching her fingers with his lips. 'Farewell, Mrs Hope. 'Till we meet again.'

She nodded. 'God speed.' It was a phrase she had often used when her husband had set sail for arctic waters. It was almost a superstition to say it, but this time she meant it. It would be a pity if this fine captain should meet disaster just because she failed to utter the words.

He looked taken aback for a moment, the derision fading from his eyes. 'Thank you,' he said. 'You're very kind.'

'No, I'm not,' she said softly. 'I'm not kind at all. No more than thee.'

They watched from the reed-beds as the ship weighed anchor, their coggy boat low in the water from the extra weight of bags and barrels which had been loaded into her. Dawn was breaking in the east, streaking the horizon with white and rose, a soft halo lighting the grey canopy of sky. As the flush of day progressed and the wind freshened, the schooner, full rigged, seemed to take a deep breath, filling her sails with the breeze. She heeled smoothly windward and began to make headway in perfect harmony with the elements.

'She's beautiful isn't she?' Annie breathed, forgetting for the moment her animosity towards the captain of this graceful vessel which sailed swiftly up the estuary towards the Trent Falls. 'There's wicked mudbanks in 'river, so I hear tell.'

'So there are, but he's a good seaman, and so are his men.' Toby shaded his eyes as the ship sailed further into the distance.

'Can we get off Master Toby? We'd best get this stuff moved afore it's light.'

Annie looked at the man in the boat. She could see him quite clearly now, as indeed he could see her, as the day lightened. He was a cheerful pug-faced individual and he reminded her of someone.

'Sorry, Josh.' Toby spoke absentmindedly, reluctantly drawing his eyes away from the schooner as it faded from view, then realizing his error glanced at Annie.

'It's daft, us not having a name,' she said. 'We've got to be called summat, even if we don't use our own.'

Josh grinned at her. 'Well I knew tha wasn't Mrs Trott as soon as I saw thee, even before I saw thee climb 'ladder,' he added impudently.

'How?' Toby and Annie spoke together.

'Why, Mrs Trott's never got such a nice turn of ankle,' he said, his grin turning up his cheeks so that his eyes almost disappeared. 'And I ain't never seen her without her boots.'

'Annie!' Toby said reproachfully. 'You gave the game away.'

They emptied the cargo, hiding some of it, the barrels of

brandy and half ankers of geneva, in the bushes and long grass at the side of the creek, until such time as they could come back with donkeys-and-traps to retrieve it. Some of the waxed bags of tea and tobacco they concealed within sacks which they carried over their shoulders.

As Toby and Annie made their way back towards where they had tied Sorrel, Josh waved his hand, climbed a bank and disappeared into a wood.

'Now that we're on our own I want to talk to thee,' Annie began.

'Ssh, keep your voice down, there might be soldiers about, or the revenue men. Those men that I saw earlier in the day, I'm pretty sure were customs officials. They had a look about them, a smell of the law.'

Annie found it difficult to convey her annoyance and anger when she could only do it in a whisper. Nevertheless she told Toby what she thought of him for not telling her to expect the other men in the boats.

'If I'm going to come in with thee, tha's got to trust me, tell me the plan. If I don't know 'rules, how am I expected to obey them.'

'I'm sorry Annie. But I had to know how you would react, you might have gone into a blind panic, refused to go on board, which you nearly did,' he added, giving weight to his argument, '—anything, and then it would have been too late if I'd told you all we were doing.'

'Aye, well, all right. But another thing – thy brother, he's a—'

He put up his hand. 'I'm not answerable for Matt. He's my brother and I love him dearly, but we do things differently and I don't always agree with what he does, but for all that I won't hear anything detrimental about him. I wanted you both to meet, but if the two of you want to spar then do so, but don't expect me to take sides.'

'But – he said I was a rag-bag! I heard him.'

'Eavesdroppers never hear good of themselves.' He shook a finger at her. 'Anyway, it's true. You are. You look as if you've just climbed out of the hedge bottom.'

He gave a sudden grin. 'Come on, Annie, don't look so glum. I like you just the way you are.'

They were trotting along a path overhung by leafless branches of ash, the sacks slung across the horse's saddle with Annie's cloak covering them, when they heard the jingle of harness. Toby wheeled about and cantered towards a copse where they waited, hidden deep in the undergrowth.

A small troop of soldiers came riding along the same path they had been using, travelling in the opposite direction and accompanied by two men dressed in dark clothing.

'Those are the men I was telling you about,' Toby whispered.

'And those are 'same soldiers Robin and I saw up on 'Wolds. I recognize 'sergeant. He owes me a favour,' she whispered back.

'Well don't be too surprised if you don't receive it,' he said hoarsely. 'They're not in the habit of giving. Unless it's a ride to the gaol house.'

They waited until the soldiers had ridden out of view and then cautiously rode back onto the path. 'It's too late to take this stuff to the henhouse,' Toby said, glancing up at the sky. 'Old Henry will be about now and will hear us. We'd better go to my place and hide it there.'

Annie nodded behind him. She was very tired and the movement of the horse was lulling her to sleep. She put her head against Toby's back and her arms around his waist and closed her eyes. When she opened them again they were in the meadow below Toby's cottage and he was urging her to wake up.

'I don't know how you stayed on,' he said as she slid off the horse's back and he swung down. 'Come on, help me with this and then you can have a sleep.'

They unfastened the sacks and as they finished, Josh appeared, appearing as if from nowhere.

'How did tha get here so quickly when tha was walking? Did tha see soldiers?'

'I know all 'shortcuts,' he winked at her, 'and I did see 'sodgers.' He turned to Toby. 'I heard 'em an' all. They're expecting ship tomorrow. They've been given 'wrong information. They'll be waiting down by 'river all tomorrow night and they'll catch her coming back from Goole.'

'And if they try to board her they'll find a ship going back to Flushing with legitimate cargo, and my brother with wounded pride that they should accuse him of illegal running!'

'By heck,' said Josh gleefully. 'I hope it rains.'

Toby turned Sorrel over to Josh. 'Feed him well and water him,' he said. 'He's had a long night, just as we have.'

Josh swung into the saddle. He pulled the stirrups up high and sat forward with his knees almost up to his chest. 'Will do, Master Toby, I'll look after him.'

'Are all the goods away.'

'Aye, sir. 'Men have done a good night's work. Arrangements are as usual.'

He rode off and they made their way up the hill and through the bushes and hidden paths which led to Toby's cottage.

'Does Josh know where tha lives? He seems to know his way around.'

'I suspect he does, though he's never been. His brother, Robin, is the only one who's been here, apart from you.'

Annie felt privileged as she walked in the door, as if she had been given a special secret. 'I'll never tell, Toby. Never.'

He put down the sacks and smiled at her. Then he pulled her towards him and placing both his hands on her cheeks kissed the tip of her nose. 'I know that, Annie. I know that very well.'

She was confused. It was an ordinary kiss, yet tender, and she had seen some hidden depths in his brown eyes which she hadn't seen before when he had teased and joked with her. Playfully she punched him on the cheek. 'Never mind all this monkey business, let's get unpacked and then we can get some sleep.'

They packed the tea and tobacco in separate pine chests and draped rugs over them, then Toby took embroidered cushions from his bed and piled them on top.

'It looks grand, Toby.' Annie looked round admiringly. 'I wish I lived here. It's so comfortable.'

'I like it,' he said. 'It reminds me of home. These are my mother's things. I stole them from my father's house.'

Annie breathed open-mouthed. 'Oh. Is tha sure nobody got 'blame? A servant or anybody?'

He shook his head. 'He's never even noticed that they're gone. Oh, my mother's silver brush and mirror I asked him for, and he said I could take them in remembrance of her, but the rugs and hangings and cushions I took bit by bit; the servants know, but they won't tell.' He smiled. 'Their supply of tea and 'baccy would dry up if they did.'

'Tha's a rascal,' she said. 'Tha looks so innocent, but tha's a real villain!'

He brought out a truckle bed for her to sleep on and some soft warm blankets, and he lay fully clothed on his own bed, his arms behind his head, staring open-eyed at the boarded and beamed ceiling.

She dozed for a while, but she could hear the call of wood pigeons from the copse behind the cottage and the cry of wild ducks as they flew over towards the river, and the sun was shining, creeping bright pencils of light under the door.

Presently Toby got up and kindled the fire, putting on curls of straw to coax it to burn. He took a pan and went outside, leaving the door ajar and letting the light flood into the room.

He came back a few minutes later with the pan and a jug full of water and placed the pan on a trivet on the low fire. He glanced towards Annie, but she was hidden beneath the blankets and didn't speak, but watched him from half-open eyes as he went back outside the door and standing on the grass, stripped off his shirt and started to wash.

His shoulders were broad, broader than they appeared in his shirt and coat, the muscles in his upper arms, powerful and sinewed. She saw him dip his head in a bucket of water, then gasping, throw back his head, shaking his dark hair like a dog, scattering a shower of water droplets which sparkled in the sun.

For some reason as she watched him, she thought of his brother, Matt, who would now be well up river if the wind held – and she could hear it blowing gently in the trees – and she wondered if he was like Toby in build. They were unlike in temperament, but, she thought, he would have the same strength. She'd felt it when he'd grasped her when she'd almost fallen on the deck, and seen the width of his shoulders as he'd bowed so mockingly.

She felt a hot flush running through her and she screwed up her eyes and clasped her hands up tight, and nipped her knees together beneath the blankets as she tried to shake away the image of the arrogant, disdainful sea captain.

How dare he say I'm a rag-bag, she fumed. Who does he think he is? He's nowt but a criminal. He could hang if he was caught. She shivered as a small still voice of conscience said, and so could you.

'Annie? Annie? Are you awake?'

Toby stood over her, buttoning up his shirt, his hair looking black in its dampness. 'I've put a pan of water on the fire, it should be warm now if you want to wash.'

'Warm water? What a treat. Tha's spoiling me, Toby.' She smiled up at him.

'Well!' He sat on the end of the bed. 'I think you deserve some spoiling after last night. I shouldn't have been so hard on you, making you climb up the ladder; not many women would have done it, especially in the dark.'

She sat up and stretched. 'Tha did right to make me. I'd never have done it otherwise. I'd have sat there shivering in 'boat if tha hadn't insisted.'

He fiddled with his shirt buttons. 'And – and I'm sorry

about my brother, he was extremely rude. I should have stopped him – said something. I don't know why he took against you so.'

'But tha agreed with him,' she said slowly. 'When he said I was a rag-bag, tha said that I was.'

'I'm sorry.'

She hadn't seen him like this before. He was usually so cheerful.

'But, Annie, look at you. You don't care about yourself. You go to bed in all your clothes!'

It was true, she had, but that was modesty, she thought. I didn't want to embarrass him, with him being celibate an' all.

'You wear torn clothes and you never brush your hair, even though I lent you a brush.' He shook his head in admonishment. 'What are we to do with you?'

'Tha said tha liked me as I was!'

'So I do, because I've got used to you as you are. But I'm looking at you afresh since my brother said what he did. Now he's pointed it out,' he grinned ruefully, 'I have to admit, you are a bit of a scarecrow!'

'All right.' She pushed the blankets to one side and put her feet on the floor, her toes were black with mud. 'All right. Go outside while I wash, and I'll mend me skirt if tha'll lend me needle and thread. But I'll onny change me ways on one condition.'

'And what's that?' His humour had changed. She saw the old Toby appearing.

'That tha'll let me stop here.'

He stared at her. 'Is that a good idea, Annie? What about the Trotts? Aren't you bothered about what they think?'

She shook her head. 'No. It doesn't matter to me what they think. Anyway, *they* share 'same roof, but not 'same bed, so it's just 'same. And Mrs Trott will be pleased to have me out of 'house.' She smiled. 'Mr Trott will miss me though. He likes me to warm his bed.'

'What?'

She laughed at his horrorstruck expression. 'I sleep in his bed when he's on nightshift, so that it's warm for him to get in to next morning.'

He flushed. 'I thought you meant—!'

'Aye, well, he's not too old, so don't think he is. So if I can stay here, I'd rather. Tha can say I'm housekeeper if tha wants.'

She stripped naked after he'd gone outside and washed her body. The water was soft as silk. Toby hadn't a well and had gathered the water from a stream which ran above the cottage. When she'd finished she poured the remaining water from the jug over her hair, catching it in a bowl.

She rubbed her hair dry with her shift and picked up the other clothes she had taken off. Toby was right. They were just a heap of rags. She sat on the bed. Her skin felt cool and clean. She sniffed at her armpits, she smelt nice, it was a pity to put the dirty clothes back on again. She picked up her money bag and looked inside. She had sufficient money to buy something else to wear. Toby had paid her for selling his goods; she'd never been so rich.

Toby's shirt that he'd worn yesterday was lying across his bed. She picked it up and held it against herself. It would do until she had washed her own petticoats and shirt. She put it on and it just covered her buttocks.

'Mm. That's hardly decent. What else?'

She glanced around the room. There were no curtains that she could borrow and drape around herself, only rugs and they were hiding the chests, and besides would be too heavy to pin around her waist.

A pair of breeches were folded neatly across the back of a chair and she eyed them thoughtfully.

'Annie. Haven't you finished yet? We've things to do.'

'I won't be long,' she called back. 'I'm just dressing.'

When she opened the door wide to admit him, she laughed aloud at his astonished exclamation and gave him a bow.

The breeches were long on her and came almost down to her ankles, but for all that they were not a bad fit and she had tightened the waist with a leather belt. Her hair she had tidied with Toby's brush and comb, and tied it back with a scrap of linen.

'Why, Annie, I wouldn't know you. How lovely your face is.' He ran his fingers over her cheekbones and eyebrows, shaping them. 'You've never shown your face before, you've always had it covered by your hair.'

I do look different, she thought. When I looked in Toby's mirror last time, I was haggard, my eyes were heavy with great bags under them, but I was tired and frightened then. Now she saw that her skin was clearer and with her hair tied back, her eyes looked bigger and brighter.

'Mrs Trott's food has done you good,' he said admiringly. 'You've put on weight. Are you sure you want to come and live here? The diet's much simpler.'

'Yes please.' She saw a look of pleasure in his eyes and for a fleeting moment, remembering her vow that she'd never again become entangled with a man, wondered if she was making a big mistake.

11

The next run wasn't for another six weeks, and in the meantime Annie bought woollen cloth from Toby and asked Mrs Trott if she would have it made up into a skirt for her by the seamstress in Hessle. Mrs Trott had tutted when she'd seen her in Toby's breeches and said it wasn't seemly to be wearing men's clothes. She'd fished about in her box and brought out an old skirt of her own. The colour was faded but it was clean, though patched, and Annie agreed to wear it until the new one was ready. Her old clothes she put onto a bonfire and watched them burn.

'There's 'old life going up in smoke,' she'd said, as the sparks rose.

'But what of your children, Annie?' Toby had been silently watching her and the question was sudden and direct.

'I said I don't want to talk about them.' She'd turned away and went indoors, slamming the door behind her as if shutting out a memory.

She and Robin made another trip into the Wolds, she'd persuaded Toby to let her carry some tea and tobacco for Mrs Corner and Lily Sutcliff as well as the new stock of linens and muslins.

''Weather will be bad soon, and we don't know how many more trips we'll be able to make. We don't want to disappoint them.'

'I'm bothered about the military,' he'd said. 'The revenue men have gone back up the coast, but the soldiers will still be on the lookout.'

But they hadn't seen any soldiers and the trip had been

profitable. They made visits to the customers that they had missed the last time and were met with open arms by the Sutcliff sisters who were full of excitement about the soldiers' visit to the inn.

'They were very polite and well behaved,' Joan said, 'and even father was impressed and said they could call again.' She'd cast a coy glance at her sister. 'Sergeant Collins was very taken with Lily.'

Lily had blushed but didn't deny it and Annie was pleased that her ruse had worked so well.

Toby explained the system they employed on the run. Matt brought in a consignment of French brandy, Dutch geneva, tea and tobacco from the shores of Holland. Not all of it came down the Humber, some of it was despatched to the waiting fishermen off the coasts of Whitby, Scarborough and Bridlington. The revenue men and militia were thwarted once the goods had safely reached the shore for they fast disappeared into the warren of streets and narrow alleyways, by donkey-cart or horse panniers, and no amount of persuasion or offer of reward could persuade the taciturn residents of these towns to give information on their brothers, cousins, neighbours and friends, to the despised King's men.

'It's much more dangerous when the ships are out at sea,' Toby explained. 'The revenue cutters are fast and armed and the customs men are determined to rake in their prize money for seizure of contraband.' He gave a grim exclamation, 'but not as determined as the smugglers are to stop them.'

'But what about Matt—?' she began.

'Oh, he can look after himself. Besides his ship is faster than anything the revenue men sail and he knows the coastal waters and the estuary better than they do. Money from various sources is pooled to buy goods abroad,' he continued. 'Matt furnishes a list of goods supplied which he gives to me, and then I arrange distribution amongst the men, who in turn supply others; people like Sutcliff – innkeepers, farmers and so on; then I collect the money from them at a later date. Most of the trade is done on trust, but no-one has let us down yet.'

On the next run Annie was employed as lookout. She roamed the river-bank keeping a sharp eye open for soldiers and those people who were not about their everyday tasks, and watching for the *Breeze* to put in an appearance, while Toby went once more into Hull to listen for reliable information of the whereabouts of the customs men.

'Bernard Roxton is the revenue officer to watch out for,' he reported on his return. 'And he's snooping around in Hessle already. He's staying at the Admiral Hawke Inn. He's tall and thin and wears a black hat to cover his lack of hair. It's rumoured that he's out to make a catch of every smuggling craft that comes up river. He's in trouble from his superiors for missing the contraband on the coast and he's working closely with your Scottish sergeant and his men.'

'Sergeant Collins is his name,' Annie said. 'He's the one I sent up to 'Sutcliff's for a good feed. I hope he remembers if we should chance to meet.'

'I've told you Annie. Don't depend on it.'

The next evening a rider came in from Hull and left a message with Josh. The *Breeze* had been seen at the tip of Spurn. 'It'll take a few hours even with a favourable wind to come round 'headland, avoiding 'sandbanks,' he reported to Toby. 'She'll come up on flood tide. Tha'd best be having a bit of rest. It'll be a long night.'

Toby took his advice and lay on his bed, but Annie said she wasn't tired and sat in a chair by the fire, sewing a length of goldd woollen cloth. She felt strangely jumpy and tense and she kept pricking her finger with the needle. She sighed, she was no seamstress and was beginning to wish she hadn't started this project.

Presently Toby sat up and sat staring at her. 'What is it Annie? Why do you keep sighing? Are you nervous?'

She shook her head. 'No. I mean – aye, a bit. No, I'm sighing 'cos of this sewing. Mrs Trott cut it for me and I daren't make a mess of it or she'll have summat to say.'

He smiled and got off the bed and came over to her. He picked up the material and fingered it. 'I wondered if you could manage it when you asked me if you could have it.'

'I just fancied it that's all. I thought how nice it would look inside that black cloak, and it'll be that much warmer.'

She'd thought of lining the cloak when Mrs Trott had said that she could keep it, that she didn't want it back, and Annie had wondered if the old woman had had a qualm of conscience about taking her satin petticoat and was trying to make amends.

But that wasn't the reason that she was restless. Toby had said that she could stay on the river-bank to act as lookout. That she didn't have to climb the ladder and go on board the *Breeze*, that she didn't have to face his brother. And the annoying thing was that she wanted to.

It was cold by the side of the creek and she wrapped her cloak tightly about her. Toby and Josh had moved off towards the *Breeze* as soon as they received the signal, and as before, other boats appeared, coggy boats and cobbles slipping silently out from the reed-beds, rowing swiftly towards the waiting schooner. She had to keep a keen ear for the sound of hooves on the road above the boggy meadow, and a sharp eye on the shingle beaches of Hessle and North Ferriby in case the revenue men were watching and waiting to cast off in their cobbles as soon as the *Breeze* was discharged.

'You must also watch the river,' Toby had said. 'The revenue cutters can move fast and be on top of us before we realize. Be ready to give a warning signal.'

She shivered, a fog was starting to descend, it clung to her hair and she pulled the hood of the cloak about her head. She listened intently. What was that? Some sound. She was unfamiliar with the sounds of the country and the rustling and croaking in the reed-beds and long grasses made her uneasy. She wanted to lift the lantern to frighten away the nocturnal creatures, but dared not show even a glimmer of light.

Ducks, she hoped, or those little black creatures with the red beaks that swim so fast. Or, she cringed, maybe water rats. I've seen plenty of them, and land rats, and the more I see of them the less fond of 'em I become.

Land rats and water rats. Land rats and water rats. River Rats. That's name we were given, them as lived beneath the wharves. Scavengers all, dredging up a living. And here I am still, earning me crust by 'river bank with me feet wet and watching out for 'law.

She drew further towards the edge of the creek, holding on to the reeds so that she didn't fall into the water and peered out down river. If the revenue ships were coming then they'd sail from the direction of Hull where they were based, she was almost sure.

The mist was thickening, shrouding the *Breeze* in a ghostly curtain so that only the skeleton of the ship, her masts and rails, stood superimposed, black and stark, against the grey background.

The tide was high and it washed against her feet. Tentatively she stretched her foot into the icy water feeling for the shingle. She reached bottom and gingerly put her foot down. It was firm and held her. She put down the other one, still holding on to the reeds. The water was almost to her knees but from this position she could see better, both up and down river.

She blinked. Were her eyes playing her tricks? She thought she could see in the distance a ghostly veil of sails. She listened, her head on one side and her hood thrown off. Did she hear the rush of water against a bow? She narrowed her eyes. Yes! The tall masts and square sails of a cutter were bearing fast up river towards the *Breeze*.

She let go of the reeds and prayed that the rush of water wouldn't knock her off her feet as her fingers fumbled incompetently with the shutter of the lantern. What was the signal? For a second she forgot, then remembered. Two long, two short, then repeat in quick succession. She held her breath as she waited for an answering light. Two short. A query. Again she repeated the first signal and then, oh blessed relief as they signalled that they had understood.

Her relief was shortlived. From further up river she heard the muffled creaking of oars and as she leaned perilously out and strained to see through the fog she saw a flotilla of small boats appear from the banks, heading towards the schooner. She gasped. Revenue men! They'll catch Toby and 'others as they come ashore, and 'cutter will catch 'Breeze. We're done for! We'll go to gaol!

But Toby's men were already on their way. She could hear the heavy breathing of the oarsmen as they raced to beat the revenue men ashore, and they had a shorter distance to cover as they headed across from the middle of the river towards the banks, while the customs men were well up river, close to the North Ferriby shore.

'Come on. Come on,' she breathed. 'Pull. Pull.' She urged on these unknown men, willing them to find an extra ounce of energy to pull them to safety. Some of them veered away, going back down river towards Hessle where they could beach their square stern cobbles, stern first on to the shingle shore. Others headed for the hidden creeks and inlets which they knew of and the revenue men didn't, being strangers to this area.

A shot rang out overhead. She jumped. It came from the cutter which was now sailing ever closer to the Breeze. Then came a warning shout and a volley of small arms fire; she saw the spark and crack from the deck. Immediately came an answering shot from the Breeze and the rattle of the capstan as the ship weighed anchor and prepared to sail. The sails were unfurled, they filled and she moved, her pointed bow cutting through the water.

Tide'll be on 'turn any time. If onny he can bring her round, she'll lose 'cutter. Her thoughts were on Toby's brother and his ship, and she was startled when Toby suddenly appeared at her side, like her up to his knees in water as he waded towards her.

'Where did tha come from, where's 'boat?' she whispered.

He put his finger to his lips and drew her back to the cover of the reeds. Then he pointed to the river. Three small boats were rowing towards the *Breeze*, the angry shouts of the men on board them clearly heard.

'They lost us. We've stowed the coggy further down,' he breathed. 'Now they're trying to catch the *Breeze* and they don't stand a chance, and if they're not careful they'll get run down by the cutter.'

Another volley of gunfire rang out followed by answering shots from the *Breeze*. They held their breath, and Annie didn't even notice the freezing water which was washing over her skirt and cloak, as they watched the sparks and flashes of the ammunition as the two ships exchanged fire.

'Ready about.'

The muffled command carried across the water.

'She's turning. The cobbles will get struck if they don't move.'

The revenue men in the small boats suddenly became aware of their danger as the *Breeze*, with its shallow draught and its fore and aft manoevrable rig, heeled towards them. They shouted in alarm and started to row in the direction of the Lincolnshire shore to escape being run down, but now they were in the way of the revenue cutter which was gaining fast on the *Breeze*.

The frenzied shouts of the cutter captain urged them in no uncertain language to get out of the way. His was a fast ship, but it was long and old, and hadn't the turning power of the *Breeze*.

'Heave to! Heave to!'

They heard the command, and watched as the captain tamed the power of the sails to avoid crashing into the cobbles, and listened with amusement as he cursed and swore at them from the deck, and heard too the laughter of the seamen on board the *Breeze* as it sailed swiftly past the cutter towards Hull on the ebb tide.

Annie lifted her head and put out her hand. ''Wind is rising. They'll make it safely back to port.'

Toby nodded. 'There might well be another customs ship waiting for her.' He smiled. 'But it won't matter. We got everything off. You did well, Annie. You warned us just in time.'

'But what about 'goods? We can't risk carrying it.'

'No. We'll have to leave it for a while. The men have gone to ground and they'll come back when they think it's safe. The soldiers will be searching inland and the customs will bring their boats out in daylight to see what they can find. So we shall just have to keep our heads down for a few days until they get tired of searching.'

They tramped wearily back across country, both shivering with the cold and feeling the cling of their wet clothes against their legs. They climbed uphill so that they could approach Toby's cottage from above, rather than keep to the river where they might bump into a stray revenue man making his way back from an unsuccessful night's work.

Annie stopped. 'Ow,' she said. 'I've just trodden on summat sharp.' She leaned on Toby and lifted her foot to look, when without warning he grabbed her. He put his arms around her and kissed her hard on the mouth, pressing the weight of his body against her and pushing her hard against a tree.

For a moment she was too shocked and surprised to do anything. Then she caught her breath and pushed him away. 'What do—?'

He put his hand over her mouth and pressed his head against her breast. 'Ssh,' he whispered. 'Don't say anything. Just kiss me as if I'm the best thing that's ever happened to you.'

Again he pressed his mouth to hers and it wasn't unpleasant, she thought, though it doesn't set me on fire.

She kissed him back and as she opened her eyes wide saw the shape of a man standing in the shadows behind Toby. She gasped and pulled away. ''ere,' she shouted. 'What's tha staring at? Paul Pry! Get off home. Peeping on decent folk.'

The man stepped forward. His head was covered by a black hat and he stood with his collar turned up, so that there was very little of his face to be seen.

'I assure you I didn't intend to pry. My business here is legitimate. I'm an officer of His Majesty's Customs, and I would ask you what you are doing here so late at night?'

Toby opened his mouth to speak but Annie squeezed his hand to silence him. 'Well, I'd say it was nowt to do wi' thee or His Majesty, God bless him, but what does it look like? Can't a lad and lass have a bit of privacy when they want it?'

The man remained unperturbed and folded his arms in front of him. 'You.' He nodded towards Toby. 'What have you got to say for yourself. Does she always do all the talking?'

Toby swallowed. 'Aye.' His voice came out deep and husky. 'She does.'

The man gave an impatient shrug. 'I suppose it's no use asking if you've seen anyone else about? Men carrying things?'

Annie sighed and put her arms around Toby's waist and drew him closer. 'We've been pretty busy, we wouldn't have noticed; and now *if* tha doesn't mind, we've got to get back home afore we're missed.'

'And where is home?' asked Bernard Roxton.

'Hessle.' Toby answered quickly before Annie could answer. 'We come from Hessle.'

Annie took off her cloak and wet skirt as Toby tried to coax the dead fire into life. 'He's horrible. I thought it was some ghoul coming out of 'wood. Then I realized who it was. I remembered what tha'd said about Roxton's hat.'

'I heard him, just as you stopped. I guessed there might be someone about but I thought it would be the militia. I thought Bernard Roxton would be down on the shore.'

'Huh, maybe he doesn't like getting his feet wet. Why don't you leave that,' she yawned. 'We might as well go straight to bed. We'll find dry kindling in 'morning.'

'But you're wet through to the skin. You'll get a chill.'

She laughed. 'No, I won't. You might, but not me. I'll soon warm up when I'm in bed. Them blankets are that soft and warm. I've never slept so comfortable as I have here.'

Toby's blankets were of the softest 'thickest wool, nothing like the thin fabric she was used to. 'Aye,' she said as she climbed into the truckle. 'I'm getting really spoiled.'

Toby came across to her. 'You were really brave tonight, Annie. I was very proud of you.' He knelt by the bed and leaning forward he kissed her forehead. 'I wish—'

'What does tha wish, Toby?' she whispered with a trace of suspicion in her voice, though from the look in his eyes she thought she could guess, and she trembled. It was a pity. She had felt safe with him, unthreatened, living with him as a sister. But he was a man, after all, with bodily needs; and though she felt that he wouldn't be brutal, for he had so far been very kind to her, she had been happy to live without the threat of a demanding body thrusting roughly into hers.

'Oh, it's nothing. It doesn't matter.' He got up and went to his own bed and blew out the lamp. She heard the soft sigh of the feathers as he climbed in.

'Toby?' she asked in the darkness. 'How was thy brother?'

'He's well,' he answered.

'Good,' she said in a still small voice.

'He asked about you.'

She didn't answer but smiled to herself as she snuggled down.

'Yes,' he said softly. 'He asked if the ragamuffin was still with me.'

12

'Just this one last trip. Then no more until spring. 'Weather's good, I don't know why tha's worrying.'

'You don't know the weather up there,' Toby answered her. 'The snow can come down so suddenly the villages get cut off. You wouldn't be able to get back.'

'Then I'll stop there 'till it thaws,' she said. 'Look, we've all this stuff to sell. Let me go. Me and Robin will make just one quick trip.'

The weather had been mild, fog by the river and some rain, but no snow so far and they couldn't see any snowline up on the Wolds, not even looking through Toby's glass.

Reluctantly he agreed. He'd bought a considerable amount of ends of range from the manufacturers. Lengths of linens with a slight flaw, which with judicious cutting could be made perfect. Muslins of last year's shades and patterns, and coarse fustian cotton which the thrifty Wolds women favoured for its hard-wearing qualities, which had been lying on the dusty floor of the mill and needed only washing to bring it to pristine condition. All of these Toby would sell at low costs to satisfy his customers and still make a profit for himself.

'Shall I come with you into Hessle?' They loaded up the cart and Annie climbed into the cart and took up the donkey's reins.

She shook her head. 'I can manage. Ned's getting used to me. I think he likes me better than he does Robin.'

'Don't forget what I said if you meet the revenue men. Be polite and for heaven's sake don't let them look under the blankets!'

She set off towards Hessle to pick up Robin. He had said, when he called to make the arrangements a few days ago, that he would come to meet her, but she'd told him there wasn't any need for him to make the journey. She knew the way now and she would pick him up at his sister's house.

The cart lumbered over the rutted lanes. It had rained steadily during the night and the ruts had filled with muddy water which splashed up the sides of the cart, and though the rain had stopped the trees dripped a heavy shower onto her. Annie pulled up her hood. She was glad that she had at last finished the lining to her cloak. It was warm and cosy and she was wearing her new skirt and a thick shirt belonging to Toby.

Her money bag beneath her petticoat had only a few coins in it, sufficient for her needs, for she had asked Toby to look after her money which had accumulated to an astonishing amount, comparable to the wages which Alan gave her when he came home from a whaling trip, but which, unlike this money, was always spoken for by the moneylender, the landlord, the butcher and various vendors who gave her credit when she was completely without a copper coin to her name.

Aye, I'm almost rich, she thought. I could buy me bairns new clothes and boots, good food to fatten 'em. And yet I daren't go back to fetch 'em. If 'law should be waiting for me! What shame they'd have. A criminal for a mother. Hanged at that. How would they ever live with that disgrace? Nay. Better they live without me. Forget I ever was, rather than live with knowledge of what I did.

Morbid thoughts always swamped her mind when she was alone. The fear of being found out and brought to justice filled her with dread and made her shake as if afflicted with ague.

She rattled into Hessle and thought what a prosperous town it seemed to be, though a little dusty from the chalk which was worked and processed from the quarries on the cliff. Ship-building, too, was a major industry in the town, and the ferry brought in trade from across the estuary on the main route from London and Lincoln through to York.

'Come on Robin,' she urged under her breath as she waited by the cottage door. 'Tha's never still in bed.' She knocked again. It was nearly six o'clock, surely someone must be up. The doorbolt rattled and a sleepy-eyed child opened the door. 'Is Robin here?' She smiled down at the girl. She must be about eight, same as our Lizzie, she thought.

The little girl opened the door wider for Annie to enter and she caught the sound of a woman's voice calling from behind a curtain which divided the room. 'Is that Mrs Hope?'

'Aye, it is. I'm looking for Robin.'

A weary-looking young woman who, Annie guessed, was Robin's sister, pushed aside the curtain and came into the room brushing a tangle of hair from her face. 'He's sick. He's got 'fever. He'll not be fit to go travelling. I've been up all night with him and one of my bairns.'

'Oh,' said Annie, at a loss to know now what to do. 'Can I see him? Is it owt catching?'

The woman pursed her lips and then shrugged. 'I don't know. One of my other bairns had it a week ago, so he's maybe passed it on. But it's not deadly,' she added encouragingly, 'he's all right now and back at work.'

Annie followed her behind the curtain and found Robin, red and sweating beneath a pile of blankets and next to him a small boy, pale and languid and obviously most unwell. At the bottom of the bed were two other small boys, hale and hearty with wide grins on their dirty faces.

'Get out, both of thee,' said their mother and aimed a slap across their heads. 'This lady wants to talk to Robin and she can't with thee in bed. Go on, out, saucy jackanapes.'

Annie smiled at the harassed woman. She knew how

hard it was to deal with a handful of children, especially when one of them was sick. But these youngsters, except for the sick one looked happy enough. Not cowed and frightened as hers had often been when Alan had been at home.

'Is tha husband away?' she asked.

The woman shook her head, puzzled by the question. 'No, thank God, he's in regular work just now and earning money, and I'm onny sorry that Robin is sick and can't go out, for I badly need some proper sleep in my bed instead of on 'floor.'

'Sorry, Jinny.' Robin stretched his hand out to his sister. 'I'm feeling much better. Tha can have thy bed back tonight, honest.'

Jinny patted his hand, and picking up her shawl wrapped it around her shoulders. 'I'm off to get a jug o' milk,' she said. 'I won't be long,' and nodded to Annie as she went out of the door, scooping up the children with her as she went.

'I'm sorry, Annie. We can't make 'trip this time, I can't hardly stand. Maybe next week if 'weather holds.' Robin gazed at her from watery, bloodshot eyes and whispered, 'tell Master Toby how sorry I am.'

Annie sat on the edge of the bed, not too close as to risk catching anything, but already feeling the heat from the fire which was blazing in the hearth. She fanned her face with her hand. 'There's no wonder tha's sweating,' she said. 'It's like a furnace in here.'

'Doctor said to keep 'fire built up and 'blankets piled on so as to sweat out 'fever,' Robin wheezed. 'I feel like I'm lying in 'middle of a lake; I'm soaked through, but if that's what's to be done!'

Annie nodded. That was the cure, she knew, and if you were strong enough to stand the sweating then the fever would subside, but, she looked anxiously at the child beside Robin, this recklin doesn't look strong at all. A sudden anxiety hit her. Her own bairn Ted, wasn't healthy. Would he be looked after properly at the

Seaman's Hospital. Would they sit with him and hold his hand as she did?

Tears came to her eyes and she held back a sudden emotion. What if he'd died and she hadn't been there to comfort him?

'Annie? Is tha crying?' Robin spoke huskily. 'Don't cry over me. I'll soon be up and about.'

She sniffed away her tears. 'No, I'm not,' she said. 'I was just thinking that I'd go on my own. Up to 'Wolds I mean.'

Robin hoisted himself onto one elbow. 'Tha can't.' He was scandalized. 'What would Master Toby say? He'd be that mad. It's far too dangerous for thee on tha own.'

Annie put her chin in her hand and pondered, patting her fingers against her cheek. 'He wouldn't know until I was well gone and then it would be too late. We've loads of stuff to sell. If tha'd let me have Charlie, I'd pay thee for loan of him, and then tha won't be too much out of pocket.'

She suddenly remembered the donkey tied up outside and all the goods in the cart, to say nothing of the items hidden beneath the blankets, and stood up.

'Wait, Annie. I don't know. Tha can have Charlie gladly and I want nowt for him, he'll look after thee, same as I would, but tha can't go alone.'

'Pooh, course I can. I'll be back in three days and Toby won't even know I'm gone. Don't tell him unless tha has to. Don't worry him if tha can help it.' She knew that Toby wouldn't let her go. That he was doubtful about her even going with Robin when bad weather was imminent. He would certainly put his foot down about going alone, but she wanted to. She wanted to know if she could be independent, to know if she could manage without a man to protect her.

She remembered her fear when she'd heard that Alan had died. How she'd wailed and cried to her friend Maria that she was finished, that she and her children would starve with no man to protect them. But they didn't starve for she had found Francis, who had fed them and given her money, but oh, she shuddered, at what price.

'Take care, Annie. I can't say I'm happy about this, but take Charlie, he's tied up round 'back.'

Annie turned to him from the door. 'Tha sister called me a lady.'

'Aye, that's what I told her tha was. She's a proper lady, is Mrs Hope, that's what I said.' Robin sank back into the bed. 'And I meant it, tha's a real brave lady, Annie.'

A grin turned up her lips. A lady. She'd never been called that before. Many other names, but not that one.

Charlie greeted her enthusiastically, leaping into the air with all four legs off the ground and his tail wagging fit to drop off. Then seeing the cart waiting with one of Robin's nephews patiently guarding it, he leapt in with a bound and sat eagerly waiting, his tongue lolling from his panting mouth.

The going was harder than she'd imagined, for the tracks up the hillside were muddy and slippery and she had to take the donkey by the reins and pull when he sometimes refused to move. She fell several times and soon her boots and cloak were caked with mud. As she reached the summit of the hills it became easier, the chalky ground was harder and less muddy and the air was drier, the fog disappeared and she could smell the sharpness of winter.

She allowed the donkey to graze for a few minutes and Charlie to run and sniff, he caught the scent of rabbits and chased round and round searching eagerly and she let her gaze wander at the landscape around her. The sky was bright with no sign of snow, though the sharpness of the cold pure air pierced her nostrils, and the brightness reflected on the chalk-white track in front of her. It stretched onwards through an expanse of open, gently undulating country, without a sign of habitation, not a cottage or farmstead could she see, but merely a coppice of trees standing dark against the sky in the distance.

'Come on, Charlie,' she shouted. 'Let's be off. We can maybe reach them trees by midday and tha can have a fine time lifting thy leg at all of them.' The dog looked up at her voice and then set off after her as she urged on the donkey with a crack of the whip.

She looked down into a shallow vale from the coppice as she sat and ate a hunk of bread and cheese. She had learned now to pack some food for her midday meal and she had brought plenty for she had packed for Robin too. Water she had brought also, for though the water in the Wolds was sweet and pure, streams were infrequent in the dry valleys.

At the western end of the valley she could see a farmstead, a cluster of barns and low buildings. We haven't called at that place, she thought. We skirted 'top of this vale and went down 'other side. I'll maybe give them a call this time.

The farmer's wife was eager to buy. 'Nobody comes down here, we're onny farmstead in this valley and it's a long pull uphill to get out, so they allus miss us. Next vale has more folks in it.'

'Well, I'll call on thee, missus, though maybe not every time, and I might not get here again until spring on account of 'weather. They say it gets bad out here.'

The woman looked at her in surprise. 'Dossn't tha know about our weather? By, Mrs Hope, if tha's not prepared for it tha'd better be getting off home. Another couple o' days and snow will be here.'

Annie looked out of the low window at the blue sky and smiled. 'Doesn't look much like snow to me. It's a beautiful day.'

'Take notice on what I say,' the woman assured her. 'It'll snow! Now, let's see what tha's got.'

As Annie puffed and panted up the hill out of the valley she realized why the woman was so glad to see her. Poor soul won't see anybody save her husband and a few pigs and sheep. I'll have to think twice afore I tackle this hill again. Her heart hammered against her chest, her ears

135

pounded and her vision was filled with floating stars. Still, she bought plenty, and some tea, she thought gleefully. How her eyes lit up when I offered her that.

She reached the top of the ridge and caught her breath. The wind was much sharper up here and a few clouds were rolling in. She cracked the whip again and headed off, this time in the direction of the Sutcliff's inn. She had asked directions of the farmer's wife and she had said that it was no more than a three hour walk, less by donkey or mule.

The road curved and undulated through shallow valley bottoms and gentle hills, and here and there she found a farmstead nestling within a dip, or an isolated hamlet, and in each she stopped and offered her wares. She sold mostly fustian and strong linen and a large quantity of buttons and thread, needles and knitting pins, but she didn't offer tea or tobacco, for though these people invited her in, they were reserved and uncommunicative and she was afraid of being rebuffed.

She recognized the next valley as being the last one before reaching the Sutcliff's and she heaved a sigh of relief. She was so weary and it was almost dusk. She looked up. Coming out of the darkness down the hill towards her was a company of soldiers and she drew in a breath of dismay.

'Jump in Charlie. Come on.' She ordered the dog into the cart where he curled up on the blankets and she stepped down and walked alongside the donkey.

'Good evening to ye, Mrs Hope.'

Thank goodness it's Sergeant Collins, she thought. I hope he remembers what I did for him.

'You're out late tonight, and alone! That's hardly wise. Where's your brother?'

'My brother? Oh. Robin. He's sick, and all these good folk out here are waiting for their warm wool cloth ready to make up for winter. I couldn't let them down so I came by myself.'

'How very commendable.' He gave her a wry look as he sat above her on his bay stallion.

'Has tha been to Sutcliff's?' she asked cheekily. 'I'm just on me way there now. I'm ready for a good supper.'

'No.' He shifted uneasily in his saddle. 'We've had to miss them this time.'

She thought that one or two of the men muttered to each other and Sergeant Collins spoke sharply to them.

'We've called several times and they've been most hospitable. However,' he hesitated as if debating what to say, then said quietly, 'it doesn't do, I'm afraid, to become too friendly. We have a job to do out here – questions to ask which might impose a strain on friendship.'

'I'm sorry. I didn't realize.' She suddenly felt afraid. Did he suspect Mr Sutcliff of receiving smuggled goods? Was he trying to warn her? And yet, she felt a pang of sympathy for these soldiers so far from home, who were trying to assist the customs officers in endorsing the King's regulations amongst lonely farmsteads in open country, or on windswept river-banks and hostile coastal villages.

Sergeant Collins signalled to his troop to ride on and they continued along the valley. He swung down from his mount and her sympathy disappeared. What if he should want to search the cart? Charlie growled but stayed on the blanket as he approached.

'Can I offer thee a pretty ribbon? I said last time I saw thee I would have more goods.' She made as if to open a pack.

He shook his head and she saw his lips turn down.

'I think I know someone who would appreciate it,' she was flippant and yet still he remained serious.

'Mrs Hope, can I speak with ye?'

He gazed at her so gravely that she was quite sure he was about to tell her that he knew exactly what was in the cart and that he was about to take her into custody. She was sure he was only saving her the embarrassment of arresting her in front of his men, because she had previously been kind enough to direct them towards a warm fire and good food and ale.

Her legs started to tremble, her stomach churned and

she tasted half digested food in her throat. Oh, I hope I'm not sick. Oh, don't let me retch. Not here in front of him. Will I hang? But I can't hang twice. Would I rather swing for a few ankers of brandy and a sack of tea than for—?

'Mrs Hope?' He touched her arm. 'Can I confide in ye?'

She clutched the side of the cart. 'What? Oh – aye, 'course tha can.' Her sickness started to subside as she realized that he was more concerned over some trouble of his own, than he was over any misdemeanor of hers.

'It's about Miss Sutcliff – Lily.'

Annie started to smile, weakly at first at her own deliverance, then with more gaiety as she thought that Sergeant Collins was about to tell her of his warm feelings for Lily.

'I want ye to do me a favour. Will ye tell Lily that I've had to go away? Tell her that I've been transferred.'

'But why? Is it true?'

'Not strictly, though we shall be moving on soon. No. It's just that it's better if I don't visit again.'

Annie eyed him suspiciously. 'Tha's not got her into trouble and trying to slide out of it?'

He looked shocked. 'Nay. I was brought up to be a strict Calvinist. There's been nothing of that sort.'

She was unsure what a Calvinist was, but by the look on his face it appeared there was not much merrymaking, which was probably a pity. But poor Lily. Was her only chance of meeting a worthy man about to slip away?

'Then why? I reckon she could get fond of thee, given 'chance.'

'That's the trouble you see. I could get very fond of her, I am already.' He twined long strands of his horse's mane around his fingers and looked down the darkness of the valley towards where his men were merging into the landscape, merely a blur of red uniform standing out from the shadows.

'I already have a wife.'

The statement came out terse and blunt and Annie stared at him open-mouthed. Poor Lily.

'I was married at seventeen and joined the regiment six months later. I've seen my wife no more than six times in fourteen years. I can't even remember what she looks like, yet we're tied together for life. And as for Lily. What can I tell her? That my marriage was a mistake? That I can offer her nothing? I could love her, I know that, and I think she could love me.'

Annie nodded. 'Aye,' she said quietly. 'I think she probably could.'

'So will ye tell her? Tell her that I've been called away, and that I'm sorry. You'll know what to say – being a woman. You'll have the right words.'

Her lips trembled as she watched him ride away. He cantered swiftly down the valley until he was barely to be seen, then she narrowed her eyes as she saw him rein in and turn towards her and canter back again.

'I'm so troubled by my own thoughts that I almost forgot. Be careful, Mrs Hope.'

'What? Nay, I'm perfectly safe. There's nobody who'd harm me out here.'

He shook his head. 'That's not what I mean and well ye know it. Take care. There's a revenue man who's running a vendetta against particular smugglers. Make sure you're not involved.'

He turned and cantered away again before she could make any reply to his warning and with a shiver which ran down her spine she climbed back into the cart and drove up the hill.

There was a lantern hanging on the gate of the Sutcliff's inn and she stopped and opened up a pack by its light. She took out a length of dark blue ribbon and carefully cut it with her scissors, and tied the piece into a bow. Then she placed it back onto the top of the pack and refastened it.

'Come on then, Ned. Tha'll be glad of some oats. Tha's worked hard today.' She stroked the donkey's ears and led him into the yard. Charlie jumped down from the back of the cart and stretched himself and then went to the door of the inn and barked.

She put her hand up to knock but the door opened and Lily stood there, her face smiling with pleasure at seeing Annie.

'It's so good to see thee, Annie. Come in, do.'

Aye, she'll not think so in a minute, Annie thought as she entered the inn. There's no amount of tea or pretty muslins that'll make up for what I've got to tell her.

13

Mr Sutcliff helped her unload the cart. She pulled back the blankets and he lifted out two half ankers of geneva and one of brandy. She kept the bag of tea for Lily well hidden.

'Tha did well,' he whispered and lifted the spirits into a wooden barrow. She followed him down the yard and into the vegetable garden and held a lantern high as he lifted up some heavy boards which were lying on the ground. Beneath the boards was a deep pit and into this he stored the spirits.

He wiped his brow. 'Thanks. Let's get into supper before those wenches wonder what we're up to.'

'I just wanted to tell thee,' she said urgently. 'Be careful. I've had a tip off. Revenue men are about, so watch out for strangers.'

'And what about 'sodgers? I've not seen them about.'

'They're moving on, so I hear. They'll not be up here again for a bit.'

Supper was already on the table as they went in and Rose manoeuvred the places so that she could sit down next to Annie. 'I'm sorry that Robin is ill,' she whispered as she helped her to floury potatoes. 'Will tha tell him I was asking about him and hope he'll soon be well.' She blushed as she spoke and Annie glanced across at Meg who was sucking enthusiastically on pigs' trotters, and realized that she had been mistaken, it was sweet Rose who Robin hankered for, not merry Meg, and the desire appeared to be reciprocated.

She wasn't able to speak to Lily alone until they went

up to bed, and Joan, Meg and Rose were finishing off their chores in the kitchen.

'Has tha seen Sergeant Collins?' Lily asked shyly. 'He hasn't been here for a week or two. He's a very pleasant man, a man I can talk to.'

Annie sighed and sat on the bed. 'Come and sit here,' she said and patted the patchwork coverlet. 'I want to talk to thee.'

Lily did as she was bid. 'Tha's seen him,' she smiled. 'Is he coming?'

'No.' Annie shook her head and grasped Lily's hand. 'He's not. I've seen him, it's true, and I've a message for thee. But it's not a message tha'll want to hear. At least not entirely, though tha's lucky to have such a fine man think of thee so well.'

'Whatever does tha mean, Annie?' Lily blushed.

Annie reached into the pack which she had brought upstairs and opening it brought out the bow of ribbon. 'He sent this for thee. Ordered it 'specially he did and chose 'colour himself, 'said how much it would suit thee.'

Lily took the ribbon and smoothed it with her hands. 'I've never had a present from a man before.' She looked up at Annie, a slight frown puckering her eyebrows. 'But there's something else? What is the message?'

'His unit has been ordered to move on. He rode over from 'garrison at Hull just as soon as he heard. I had to promise to tell thee as soon as I could.'

'But where has he gone? Isn't he coming back?' Lily spoke in barely a whisper.

'Oh, right up north. He's that upset, Lily. I've never seen a man so miserable. But he has to go. He'd get 'lash if he didn't. He'd even thought of absconding on account of thee, but I told him that tha wasn't that sort of a woman who'd want a man to destroy himself for her. Why, if they found him he might even be shot!'

Lily put her hands to her face. 'Oh no, I wouldn't want that. But is that what he was willing to do, Annie? To risk his life for me?'

'Aye. He took some persuading to go back I can tell thee. I told him that tha would take some comfort in knowing that he cared for thee.'

'Oh, I do, Annie, I do.' Lily started to sob and Annie put her arms around her.

'Then tha's luckier than most women. When he gave me this ribbon for thee, he said, tell her I'll allus remember her and when she wears this, maybe she'll think on me.'

Well, that's what he would have said, she thought, as she lay in bed and listened to the soft snuffling noises coming from Lily's bed across the room. He would have said it if he could have found 'right words. I just wish somebody would say it to me. She turned over and gazed up at the small square window. The sky was clear and bright with stars and she thought of a ship sailing beneath them and a buccaneer with blue eyes and a fair beard.

She moved off after breakfast. Mr Sutcliff had been in a very jovial mood and bought his daughters lengths of wool cloth to make into new skirts. Lily said she didn't want any more but he insisted. She was quiet, but, Annie thought, she didn't look desperately unhappy. The knowledge that she was cared for seemed to be sustaining her.

''Weather's going to change.' Mr Sutcliff saw her off at the gate. 'Don't spend too long up here, it'll snow maybe tonight, maybe tomorrow. If it comes down heavy, 'roads will be covered and tha'll lose tha way. One valley looks like any other when it's covered wi' snow.'

She said she would take heed but nevertheless turned up the dale towards the next village. She still had plenty of linens and muslins to sell and thought she would call at some of the big houses rather than the farms.

As she drove down the winding drive towards a stone built mansion she remembered what Robin had told her. 'Allus go to 'back door,' he'd said. 'Tha'll get a boot up tha backside if tha goes to 'front and tha won't sell owt.' So she turned Ned towards the back door and got out and knocked.

The housekeeper was pleased to see her and bought

fustian for sheets for the maids, and cottons and pins for sewing. Then she asked her if she had anything else.

'Muslins and fine cotton,' Annie said. 'Fit for a lady they are. Lovely quality and cheap at 'price.'

'Have some curd pie and a drop o' barley wine while I nip and see 'mistress. She's not averse to a bargain and she has some young ladies staying with her who might buy.'

She came back in ten minutes and said Annie had to go with her. 'Mrs Burnby will see thee. Better wash thy hands and straighten thy hair,' she added. 'She's very particular.'

Annie did as she said. She readjusted the silk scarf which Toby had given her, and leaving her cloak in the kitchen she followed the woman upstairs.

She was quite unprepared for the splendour of the room which she was ushered into. The floor had patterned rugs upon its polished surface, and elegant gilt furniture, too dainty and fragile, she thought, for sitting on, was placed around the outside of the room. A large gilt mirror was over the marble fireplace, and a pair of tapestry face screens placed at either side of a warm fire. In the centre of the room were several sofas and chairs and relaxing gracefully in them were three ladies, two young and one older, who looked towards her as she entered.

'This is 'woman I was telling you of, ma'am. She has some good cloth that you might like to see.'

Annie was glad that she was wearing her new skirt and the shirt of Toby's that she was wearing, she knew was a good one. She bobbed her knee. 'It's good of thee to see me, ma'am.' She'd heard the housekeeper call her mistress, *ma'am*, and so followed suit. 'I have some pretty muslins that might interest thee or 'young ladies.'

One of the young women, fair haired with rosy lips, glanced at her companion and put her hand to her mouth to hide a sniggering smile, and Annie felt an irritation. Never done a day's work in her life, I bet. Sitting around all day gossiping or doing a bit of sewing and looking down on them as has to work for a living.

'Let me see what you have,' said Mrs Burnby. 'I'm not saying I will buy, but I'll look.'

Annie opened up one of her packs which contained fine linen and some pretty ribbons.

The young woman who had laughed, picked up some of the ribbons. 'These are quite pretty, don't you think, Jane?' she said airily. 'I'll have one of each.' She glanced at Annie's neckerchief. 'That's very pretty too. I'll have one of those, but in yellow.'

'I'm sorry to have to disappoint thee, miss. But this is very special. It's 'only one there is.'

'And so you keep it for yourself! How very odd!'

'No, miss. It was a present from a friend. I didn't buy it.'

'Perhaps the woman will sell it to you then, Clara,' remarked Jane. 'The blue would suit you.'

'I'm sorry. I couldn't possibly sell it,' Annie said quickly. 'It was given to me in friendship. It's not for sale, I have other silks and muslins that I can show thee.'

Clara sat back in a sulk and Mrs Burnby turned to Annie. 'You're quite right, of course. You couldn't possibly sell a gift; it would be quite unthinkable. It's good to know that standards are not slipping quite as much as one feared.'

Annie opened up her other bag, she'd deliberately left this until last. She draped a sprigged muslin across a chair and then diffidently said; 'If tha doesn't mind ma'am,' and arranged a fold of grey satin across Mrs Burnby's shoulder and knee.

'Why, it's lovely, Aunt.' Jane leaned forward and handled the shiny material. 'It would be just the thing for the Pattison's party if you could get it made in time.'

She came and stood at Annie's side. 'Do take everything out, I'm sure there'll be something for me too.'

Annie smiled to herself as she trundled back down the drive. She'd sold two lengths of satin to Mrs Burnby, the grey and a dark red. A blue wool and a short length of cream lace for Jane, and even the imperious Clara had condescended to buy a spotted muslin.

I can't get back tonight, she thought. It's too far. I'll make for 'next hamlet and see if I can beg a bed for 'night and then get off back tomorrow. She shivered and pulled her cloak around her. The sky had darkened while she had been inside and a cold wind had risen. Maybe these folk know what they're talking about after all. She sniffed the air. It was sharp to her nostrils. Maybe it will snow after all.

As she drove into the next hamlet the donkey appeared to be tired and walked slowly, his head down. She got out of the cart and walked alongside. 'Come on old lad, we're nearly there.'

There was only a scattering of houses, some were empty and the others were in a poor state of repair. One had a pig in a pen in the garden and as the old man opened his door two hens flew out. But no-one in the hamlet wanted to buy or give her a bed for the night, and they were anxious to close their doors on the gathering wind which was rushing down the valley.

'I'll go to 'big house,' she muttered. 'I'm sure to get a bed there.'

The long drive up to the house was dark and overhung with trees, and beneath her feet grass and weeds were growing. The shrubberies were overgrown and neglected and there was a general air of gloom.

Maybe the house is empty, she thought. There's no light showing. The heavy double front doors between columns which were shining white in the dusk, were firmly shut and the long windows on either side of the stone façade were shuttered. She cast her eyes to the upstairs rooms. Those windows too were shuttered, save one, where a dim light flickered.

She felt nervous. There was a sense of decay about the place, as if no-one cared if the house, which once must have been very grand, fell to pieces about them.

She grasped the donkey's rein, urging him on and led him around the back of the house.

There was a light in the kitchen and through the window she saw a young girl about to serve a man and woman with ale. She knocked and saw them look up. The woman came to the door and opened it.

'I know it's late,' she began. 'But I didn't want to pass thy door without offering to show thee my goods. I won't be by this way again 'till Spring.'

The woman invited her in. 'I can't promise to buy, but I'll have a look.'

'I've a few nice muslins left if thy mistress would be interested.'

'There's no mistress here,' she answered, tight-lipped. 'More's the pity.'

'No daughter of 'house, or son's wife?'

She laughed grimly. 'None. Nor likely to be.'

Annie waited to hear more but the woman didn't continue, but pointed Annie to a stool to sit down, which she did and opened up her two remaining packs.

'Does tha ever carry owt else?' The woman whispered as she ran her fingers through a length of wool. She looked towards the other couple seated at the table and lowered her voice even further. 'Tea or owt?'

Annie hesitated. How did she know if she could trust this woman? She decided she wouldn't take the risk and shook her head. 'No,' she whispered back. 'I onny carry legal goods. But if ever I hear of anybody who does, I'll send them to thee.'

A flash of alarm crossed the woman's face. 'Nay, don't. I onny wondered. I wouldn't want mayster to know.'

She bought only scissors and cotton and as Annie repacked her bag she asked her if she could have a bed for the night.

'Mayster won't have any strangers in the house.' Her face was stony. 'It's his rule, not mine. I'd lose my place if I let anybody stay.'

Dismay ran through her. There had been a soft flurry

of snow as she'd waited on the doorstep, and the next village was miles away. 'I'd sleep on 'floor – anywhere.'

The woman turned to the man who sat with his elbows on the table staring glumly into space. He was a dour individual with heavy-lidded eyes and a turned down mouth. 'Jed! See this young woman across. Make sure she's all right.'

'There's no need.' Annie answered huffily. 'I can manage on me own.'

Jed got up from the table. 'Nay. I'll see thee off. It's dark wi'out a lantern.'

Annie felt uneasy. She didn't like the look of this man, she'd rather risk the darkness of the drive on her own. 'I've got a dog,' she said. 'He'll look after me.'

But Jed followed her out of the warm kitchen and picking up a lamp he stepped outside behind her.

'Yon donkey's sick,' he said, as Annie put her pack into the cart. 'He'll not last long.'

'He's tired that's all, like me. We've come a long way.' She took hold of the snaffle. 'I'll be off then.'

'This way, missus.' He indicated with a turn of his head in the opposite direction. 'Come wi' me.'

'That's not 'way I came in.' She swallowed hard and looked for Charlie who appeared to have gone off on business of his own. She called him. 'Charlie! Charlie!'

'Ssh. Don't mek a row. Mayster'll hear thee and want to know who's been visiting.' He took her by the arm. 'It's all right missus, don't be frighted. I'll not harm thee. We've just got to be careful, that's all. Now, come wi' me.'

One hand held the donkey and the other arm Jed had firmly in his clasp so that she had no option other than to follow him. They rounded the back of the house – no light was showing except for the circle of light from the lamp which Jed held – through a heavy barred gate into a foldyard and towards a barn door.

The door was slightly ajar and Jed pulled it wider. She could smell the warm odour of hay and heard the rustle of mice as the halo of lamplight disturbed them.

'We allus keep this door open for travelling folk,' he said. 'Though mayster doesn't know it and would order it shut if he did. Mrs Rogerson back there wouldn't see thee without shelter. But young lass in kitchen is new and we don't want her telling tales to him upstairs.'

Annie could have wept with relief and she thanked the man profusely. He unfastened the donkey's harness for her and brought him a bucket of oats. The donkey didn't eat but shuffled off to a trough of water and drank thirstily.

'Here's thy dog,' Charlie came bounding up as Jed was about to leave, his tail wagging furiously.

She scolded him. 'Tha's supposed to be looking after me.' She shook a finger at him and he sat down meekly and put up a paw to her.

'That's not thy dog? I've seen him afore.'

'No, he's been loaned to me. His owner couldn't come on this trip, but he said I could have him. He guards me with his life,' she added, 'he'd attack anybody who tried owt.'

'Aye, that he would. If he hadn't gone off chasing rats or rabbits.'

Charlie put his head on his forepaws and gazed up at Annie as if he knew he was being chastized and Jed looked down at him, tapping his fingers against his mouth and a puzzled frown on his forehead.

Then his face cleared. 'Ah. I've got it,' he said. 'I've got it. Goodnight then missus.' He touched his forehead and moved away, leaving her in darkness.

She left the door open so that a sliver of light came through into the hay filled barn, and she arranged her packs around her to keep out the cold. But a wind began to rise and the door was blown wider and she got up to close it. She peeped outside. The snow was coming down fast and through the whiteness she saw a figure coming towards the barn. It was Mrs Rogerson and she was carrying a jug of milk and a piece of pie.

'Be off before light,' she said. 'And if mayster should see thee, don't tell him we let thee stay.'

Annie thanked her and closed the door firmly. She climbed back into her bed of hay and ate the vittals she had been given, and then lay down and tried to sleep. She heard the wind howling and called to Charlie to come beside her. She was so cold, her feet were like ice. She felt her boots, they were damp so she took them off and huddled her feet beneath her cloak.

When she woke there was a strong white light coming from beneath the door and filtering down though some broken tiles in the roof, and Annie hurriedly put on her boots thinking that she had overslept. She opened the door a crack and gasped. A thick white covering of snow cloaked the ground and the sky was heavy with the promise of more to come.

'Come on, Charlie. We'd better get moving afore we're spotted. I don't want them good folks to get into trouble 'cos of me.'

She looked round for the donkey. 'Come on Ned. I know tha'll not want to go out, but we're off home now.'

He wasn't there. He'd been standing by the water trough last night as she'd tucked herself in amongst the hay, she'd seen his dark silhouette just before she'd fallen asleep.

He can't have got out, I've only just opened 'door. She peered around the gloomy interior. Charlie left her side and went into a corner. He put his head down enquiringly and then barked. Slowly she went across to him and bent down. There was Ned, as stiff as a board and quite dead.

14

Her first thought was how would she tell the Trotts that their donkey was dead? The second was how would she get back without it, 'and then,' she said aloud to Charlie, 'How do I get rid of a dead donkey?'

She looked at the animal with some distaste. She wasn't too fond of animals, though she was getting to like Charlie, and Ned had been all right when he had been cooperative, which wasn't often. But dead, she decided, he was going to be a nuisance.

I can't bury him, I can't shift him for a start. And the ground will be hard. She stared at him. And I can't leave him here, it wouldn't be fair, he'll soon stink 'place out.

She sat down on a bale of hay and opened up her packs. There wasn't a great deal left and she managed to push all the lengths of cloth into one pack and strap it on her back and in the other pack she put the remaining small amount of tea and tobacco and fastened it around her waist. Then she opened the barn door and looked out. The snow lay pristine white, not a footstep on it, merely clawed imprints of pheasant or fowl.

She closed the door behind her and set off for the kitchen hoping that Jed or Mrs Rogerson would be about and she could tell them about the donkey, and ask if she could leave the cart with them until spring.

'Hey! You! This is private land. Clear off!'

It was Jed shouting at her. He had a shotgun under his arm and was accompanied by an older man. A man in warm though dirty breeches and a heavy greatcoat who was undoubtedly the master of the house.

'I'm sorry, sir.' She addressed herself to Jed's master. 'I don't mean to trespass. I arrived late last night and couldn't make anybody hear, so I took 'liberty of sleeping in 'barn. I had to force 'door, though I didn't break it. I knew a Christian gentleman like tha self wouldn't turn anybody away on such a bad night.'

She smiled as sweetly as possible and gazed up at him. But her persuasiveness didn't melt him for he gazed back at her with steely blue eyes.

'I don't allow strangers here, so move on. And if I find you've caused any damage then I'll have you arrested and charged.'

She gasped. 'Just for sleeping in thy barn? Why it wasn't fit to turn a dog out last night, surely tha wouldn't begrudge a bed of hay?'

'Confound you woman, don't answer me back,' he barked and she jumped at the ferocity in his voice. 'Don't you know that hardship is a necessity of life; that it's good for the soul? Now be off with you.'

'I'm going.' She hitched her pack higher onto her back. 'I can tell tha's well endowed wi' milk o' human kindness, sir, and tha'll sleep well at night I'm sure. I just hope as tha never has to stretch out a hand for charity and find none.'

She quickly moved away as the man's face grew red, and headed off down the drive. She turned and looked back and saw Jed nodding his head in answer to his master's raised arm which was pointing towards her, and Jed set off at a run after her. She too started to run, her boots sloshing in the snow, until she'd turned the bend in the drive and she slowed down and waited for Jed to catch her up.

'I've got to see thee off his land. Where's thy donkey-and-cart?'

'Donkey's dead in 'barn and cart's in there as well. Can tha get rid of him for me and I'll come back for 'cart in 'spring?'

He nodded. 'Aye, I'll see to it. But go now, don't linger

or he'll have my hide. Take 'road straight down 'valley, then when tha gets to three oaks at 'bottom, turn left, after that 'road winds quite a bit so watch out tha doesn't tummel into any deep drifts. Then there's a crossroad, if it's visible under 'snow. Go straight on again until tha comes to Hawksworth farm. They'll give thee a bed for 'night and directions to get back home.'

It wasn't until she was halfway down the valley that she wondered how he knew where she was going, or where home was, for she hadn't told him or Mrs Rogerson where she had come from.

'And where is home, Charlie?' She gazed down at the vast expanse of whiteness, not a hedge or fence visible to break up the landscape. 'Home should be with my childre'. Why am I wandering in a foreign country with a pack on my back? I'm a townie, used to cobbles and paving slabs; I'm a River Rat with my feet on damp staiths. Not a wanderer or gipsy in a place where there isn't a house to be seen, onny trees and hills and sky.'

By midday the sun came out briefly and its light intensified the brightness of the snow. She squinted ahead. Her eyes hurt and her feet were wet, and her legs ached like never in her life before as she staggered up and down the hills. I can't see no farmhouse. I hope I haven't taken 'wrong road.

She couldn't recall having passed a crossroad, but then the chalk road was so difficult to identify beneath the snow, and she was relying on Charlie, who was running ahead, to search out a track that she might follow.

The sky suddenly darkened, the sun could no longer be seen behind a curtain of grey, and within minutes she was drenched beneath a squally blizzard of snowflakes which eddied and swirled around her so fast that she had to catch her breath and bend double so that the force of it didn't knock her over.

'Charlie!' she screamed. 'Charlie!' She was so afraid of losing the dog. She was sure that she would step into a gully if he wasn't there to guide her.

She peered through the whirling flurry and shouted again. What if he had fallen down into a gully? The hillsides were steep and the snow banked high, it would be so easy to take a step too far.

There was no answering bark and she listened intently but all she could hear was the wind howling across the hillside. 'Now I'm done for,' she sobbed. 'I'll die out here. Me body'll be found in 'spring, and nobody will know who I am or where I come from. There'll be no name above me grave, I'll be unknown.'

A thought suddenly struck her and she took a deep shuddering breath. Toby'll think I've run off with his money, and 'Trotts'll think I've pinched their donkey, and Robin'll be that upset about his dog. She berated herself for her stupidity at coming out alone instead of listening to the warnings given by Toby and Robin, and she sniffed and snuffled in self-deprecation and wiped her streaming eyes with cold fingers.

She put her head down and walked on. There was no sense, she thought, in dying on the spot, she'd keep walking until she dropped. That way, it'll maybe be quicker and perhaps I won't suffer. Something snatched at the hem of her cloak and she pulled against it. Again it caught and she turned around to unloosen it from its hold, some bramble or twig protruding from the snow and holding her fast.

Charlie! Charlie, with his jaws firmly on the skirt of her cloak, and pulling her in the opposite direction from the one in which she was travelling.

She followed him. He seemed to know where he was going and she certainly didn't, for with the whiteness of the snow and the unfamiliarity of the landscape, she had completely lost direction. Though she seemed to think he was leading her across the hills at a different angle away from the road, to where the snow was deeper, past her knees, and where he leaped and bounded and almost disappeared beneath the snow.

He gave a loud bark and stopped and she looked up

from the thick white carpet where she had firmly kept her eyes, and saw before her a wooden shack, not a house or cottage, but merely a shelter, without windows but with a stout door and a roof.

'Oh, Charlie. What a clever fellow. Is it open?' She tried the sneck, it wasn't locked and lifted beneath her fingers, but snow was lodged beneath the door and she had to scrape with her fingers to free it. She pushed and it gave, and she almost fell through the doorway into the small dark interior.

'What does tha think it is, Charlie? A shepherd's shelter, maybe?'

The dog just lay down on the mud floor and closed his eyes. 'Poor old Charlie.' She patted his head. 'Tha's worn out, same as me, but tha did well and I'll tell Robin about thee when we get back.' Gone were her morbid thoughts of death. Now she had shelter, she also had hope. Charlie opened one eye at the mention of Robin's name and then closed it again and rolled onto his side and went to sleep.

There was no furniture in the room, just a wooden bed made from planks and set against the wall, and leaning in a corner were several long sturdy sticks, some with a crook like a shepherd's staff. Someone had made a fire at sometime, for there was dead ash in the centre of the floor, and a small pile of dry kindling, but she couldn't light it for she had no flint or stone. But never mind about that, she thought, I'm just glad to be inside. We'll stop here 'till blizzard blows itself out.

It wasn't until the next morning that the snow stopped falling and when she looked outside, it was as if the whole world was white. This must be what 'Arctic looks like, she thought. A field of ice, Alan said it was, when I asked him. Only it would be much colder than this. She looked up at the sky. It was blue with the sun just rising and not a sign of further snow.

Charlie whined behind her and put up a paw. 'There's

no breakfast if that's what tha's after. Not a bit o' bread, nothing.'

He whined again to go out and she opened the door and told him not to be long, and she lay down again on the bed and wrapped her cloak about her and wondered what to do. Should she risk walking on again or stay here without food and wait for the thaw? She closed her eyes. She had slept only fitfully through the night, being conscious of the wind howling, and wondering if the snow would blow deep against the door so that she couldn't open it and so trapping her inside. She breathed deeply and tried to relax. She was safe for the moment.

She was woken by the sound of Charlie scratching on the door. When she opened it he was standing triumphantly, his eyes bright and his tail wagging, and a rabbit between his jaws.

'I can't cook it without fire,' she said as he lay it at her feet and waited for praise. 'And if I had fire, I don't like skinning rabbits, 'thought of it makes me sick.' She had always turned away when the butcher in the Butchery in Hull had lifted his cleaver to chop the feet off a rabbit, or taken his knife and slit the belly, drawing the skin over its head like undressing a baby.

'But we'll take it with us. We'll not waste it.' She fastened it to the outside of her pack and picked up one of the sticks from the corner. She'd made a decision, they would move on.

They made slow progress, the snow was even deeper than before and though Charlie seemed to have a homing instinct for direction, she sometimes overruled him and headed off towards higher ground so that she could look down and try to find some familiar landmark.

By dusk they hadn't passed or seen any kind of habitation or sign of life, and again she started to worry. Once it became dark she could be walking round in circles getting nowhere and she knew if she became too tired to walk, then she was finished. She would fall asleep with exhaustion and die.

Charlie sat down on his haunches and pricked his ears. She stopped behind him and listened. What had he heard? His nose twitched. Stupid dog, she thought. He's got wind of another rabbit. He whined and then stood up and barked. Coming towards them was a figure on horseback.

Could it be Toby? He's come looking for me, she thought excitedly and waved her arm and shouted. 'Here, over here. Help.'

The man waved back and came towards her and her excitement faded as she realized that it wasn't Toby after all. But still, I'm glad to see anybody, anybody who can guide me back. She narrowed her eyes as he trotted closer. He was wearing a heavy dark cloak and a black hat. It was Roxton, the revenue officer.

She didn't think that he recognized her, he had only seen her once, on the night with Toby, when they had pretended to be young lovers, and it had been dark then beneath the trees; and now she deliberately kept her voice low and plaintive and not rough and raucous as previously when she had challenged him.

'Can tha help me, sir? I've lost my way. I need to get back to Welton. Am I on 'right road?' She didn't want to mention Hessle and once she was in Welton she knew she could find her way back to the river.

'You're miles away,' he said, 'but on the right road. Keep going for another two miles and there's an old farmstead. You'll perhaps get shelter for the night.'

She thanked him and prepared to move off, when he stopped her. 'What are you carrying in your packs?'

'Oh, nothing to interest a gentleman such as yourself, sir. Only cloth and knitting pins, buttons and such like.'

'It's a bad time of year to be out selling such things.' He leaned down and stared hard at her. 'Aren't you afraid of footpads and robbers?'

She shook her head. 'I have no jewels or fancy baubles such as they'd want, and when there's hungry mouths to feed and no man to bring in money, there isn't a good time, sir. My bairns will be waiting for me and worrying that I'm so late home.'

'Then I'll not detain you. I wish you a safe journey.' He touched his hat and rode off and she heaved a sigh of relief. If he'd asked to look at the contents of her bag he might wonder why such a poor woman had the remains of tea and tobacco and a bag of coins in her pack.

I'm lost again, she thought. She looked down into the next valley but couldn't see any farmhouse. Everywhere gleamed white as darkness fell and the trees were bowed down under the weight of snow, their branches bending low to the ground. She listened. She thought she heard a whistle. Charlie heard it too and stood, his ears pricked and body quivering. There it was again, a long sharp whistle and Charlie was off, flying down the valley into the darkness and leaving her alone.

She shouted. Her voice muffled against the blanket of snow. There it was again. Surely someone must have heard her, if she could hear them. She waited a few minutes and then set off downhill, trying to follow Charlie's paw marks set deep in the snow and testing every step with the long staff.

When an old man appeared out of the darkness she jumped in fright. Then Charlie rushed up to greet her, barking and running in circles around her. The old man peered at her. 'It's a good thing tha has a dog,' he shouted, his voice clipped and sharp. 'Tha'd never have got out of 'valley. 'Road's completely blocked.' He waved his thumb at her. 'Tha'd better come wi' me.'

'Where does tha live? I don't see a house.' She stumbled alongside him.

He didn't answer but kept on walking.

'I heard tha whistling. Did 'dog find thee?' Still he didn't answer and she bent her head questioningly to him.

He turned towards her. 'It's no use talking to me,' he shouted. 'I'm as deaf as stone.'

He led her out of the valley and up the hillside and into his one-roomed, low-beamed cottage where there was a fire burning and a pan of soup hanging over it. He ladled some into a bowl and passed it to Annie. He picked some of the meat from the pan with his fingers and gave it to Charlie. Annie silently handed him the rabbit and he nodded his thanks and took it and hung it up high on the wall outside.

Annie supped the soup, her eyes kept closing and her fingers and toes tingled from the warmth of the fire. She took off her boots and looked at her reddened toes and rubbed them with her hands. Then sleep finally claimed her and she lay down on the floor, wrapped her cloak around her and fell fast asleep.

She lost track of time as she slept on and on. She was vaguely aware of the old man giving her soup and as she gazed blearily around, found she was lying on a straw mattress. Then she was lost again in slumber. She dreamt she heard him opening the door for Charlie to be let out and seeing a flurry of snow blow in through the door. She got up once herself when she heard frantic scratching at the door and on opening it found the dog there with another rabbit in his mouth. She climbed back onto the mattress and closed her eyes and let the old man deal with it.

Finally she woke and felt refreshed, she stretched and wondered how she had got into this bed. She glanced warily towards the old man. Where had he slept? The mattress was narrow, no room for two and surely she would have known? Then she saw the blanket by the fire and realized that he had given her his own bed and he had slept on the floor.

'How did I get here?' she shouted, indicating the mattress. He gave a toothless grin and came towards her. She shrank back as he reached for her hand. But he was only placing it on his forearm and inviting her to test his biceps, which were as firm as a young man's and as hard as iron.

'Tha's light as a feather,' he chortled. 'No trouble at all.'

He went to the door and opened it wide. A soft drizzle was falling. 'Thaw's started. Tomorrow tha can travel. Tha'd best go whilst tha can, for we'll have another frost after, and then more snow.' He nodded his head. 'Believe me, I know. Next lot will be worse than this.'

Charlie came bounding triumphantly over the snow with yet another rabbit in his mouth. 'He's a good dog that one,' the old man said. 'Wilt tha leave him? My dog's gone missing.'

She shouted at him that she couldn't, that Charlie wasn't hers, and he nodded and sat down and gazed pensively into the fire. It was later that Charlie stood by the door with his ears cocked as if listening, and then whined and frantically scratched to be let out.

He didn't come back and night fell and she called and called, fearful that he had gone home without her. She insisted this time that the old man had his bed back and she lay on the floor on a canvas sack by the fire and worried about Charlie.

The next morning the old man woke her early. 'I'll take thee to 'head of 'next valley,' he said, pulling on his boots. ''Snow's thick but I know 'best way out.' He stood up and pointed up the hills. 'I reckon thy dog's gone, 'same as mine. He'll be in a gully or a trap, we'll find 'em both come spring.'

She shuddered and wondered if it was worth going back when she had to confess to losing both a dog and a donkey. Poor Charlie. He'd been so faithful. Poor Robin, what would he say?

She turned to pick up her packs and the old man dampened down the fire, when she suddenly remembered what she had in her other pack. 'Wait!' She called him back from the door. She handed him first some tea and watched his face crease with pleasure and then reached for his hand and opened it, and made him close his eyes. She delved into the waxed bag and pulled out a handful of tobacco and placed it on his open hand and waited for his reaction.

His grin spread from ear to ear and as he opened his mouth to speak, Annie heard a bark. She turned to the open door. There was Charlie, wet through and panting, and accompanied by another dirty, dishevelled and limping dog.

15

She stood on the ridge and looked back. The old man was halfway down the valley, heading back for the copse of trees which he had led her through, and which afforded them some shelter from the deep snow which was now turning to slush, filling her boots and soaking her cloak and skirt. He turned and waved just before he entered and she waved back. I didn't even ask his name, nor he mine. Yet he saved my life. I wouldn't have survived another night without him, that's for sure.

And Charlie saved his dog. Poor old man, he nearly cried when he saw him, and he wrapped the old dog in his blanket like a sick bairn and told him he wouldn't be long, that he'd just see us safe.

She gave a deep sigh and turned away towards the direction she was heading. There's some good folk about, just as many as bad, though I'd never have believed it once. Her gaze took in the dale below her and the narrow track running through it which was only just discernible as the snow melted on its chalk surface; a cluster of farm buildings nestled in its hollow, and as she raised her eyes she saw in the distance, the gleam of the Humber.

Instantly her spirits rose. She was nearly home. She felt animated and vigorous, filled with a resilient energy of spirit. What's happened to me? I'm not 'same person who left Hull all those weeks ago. I'm not frightened of life the way I was, and though I'm scared of what'll happen if 'law finds me, I think I can meet what's to come.

The stone spire of All Saints church guided her down the hillside towards the lanes of Hessle and she strode out singing, Charlie yapping at her heel or running ahead once he caught the familiar scents of home.

But as she approached the town square she slowed down and called Charlie to heel. The church bell was tolling a death knell, and a small crowd of people were gathered about near the cottages where Robin lived. She didn't want to intrude on anyone's grief by her sudden appearance. She was dishevelled and dirty, she knew, her hair tangled and her cloak muddy and wet around the hem and her boots fit only for the fire.

'Annie?' Robin, his face thin and white and his eyes red-rimmed, stood in front of her. 'We've been that worried about thee. Master Toby's had search parties out looking for thee.'

She glanced towards the cottage where Robin lived. 'I got stranded.' The door was open and a group of people, including Josh, were standing in the doorway. A horse and cart stood outside, the sides of the cart draped in black. 'What's happened, Robin? Who's died?'

His eyes were full of grief. 'My sister's bairn. He was sick in bed wi' me, does tha remember? He got took worse, poor little lad. We did what we could, but it were no use.'

She put her hands to her mouth to stifle a sob and felt hot tears welling behind her eyelids. Aye, she did remember. He'd reminded her of her own Ted, and she again wondered how her children were surviving without her. She must decide what to do about them. Now that she was fit and strong she should perhaps be brave and go back. Now, Annie, she told herself – boasting, tha was, about how tha can face life. Well now's thy chance to put it to 'test.

'Robin,' she said, her voice thick with emotion. 'Could I come with thee to church? To see 'little lad off? Would tha sister mind?'

'She'd be right glad, Annie.' A tear trickled down his cheek. 'This is 'time when we need all 'support of friends we can get. Come stand by me and we'll follow him to God's acre.'

*　　*　　*

After Toby had chastized and scolded her for going away on her own and then hugged her to death in delight that she was safe, he said that he would settle with the Trotts about their old donkey and get them another one.

'You're just in time, Annie, the *Breeze* is due in next week, so you can take over the distribution list and check with Josh over the lookout men, while I ride out and collect some money that's due.'

When the ship drew up river, Annie rowed with Toby in the coggy boat towards it and climbed on board. Matt was civil enough at first, though they didn't pass more than a few words as they exchanged papers. Then he complimented her on her foray into the Wolds under such terrible conditions. 'There's many a brave man wouldn't have attempted it,' he said with an ironical smile. 'Let alone a – lady.'

'Well, sir.' She flushed as she retaliated. 'That wasn't a problem I had to deal with, for as we all know, I'm neither a brave man nor a lady.'

'He makes me that angry.' She took an oar from Toby as they rowed back and pulled hard towards the bank. 'Why is he so disagreeable? He seems to take a delight in insulting me and reminding me of what I am. I know I'm only from 'gutter, but there's no need for him to act so high and mighty. He's certainly no gentleman, even if he was born one.'

'I don't know, Annie. I've never known him act this way before.' Toby helped her out and they stowed the boat beneath the rushes and hid several ankers of brandy beneath some bushes. 'He can be kind and benevolent.'

164

'How can two brothers be so different? Why does he hate me?'

They climbed onto Sorrel's back and cantered back to Toby's cottage. 'I don't think he hates you, Annie.' Toby spoke in only a whisper, keeping his voice down so that it wouldn't carry, though there had been no sign of soldiers or customs men. 'He's never met anyone like you before, I don't think he understands you.'

She put her head against his shoulder and her arms about his waist and squeezed. 'Not like you do, eh, Toby? Not like my friend, Toby.'

'I want to ask thee a favour, Toby,' she said the next day. 'I've been thinking about it since I was up on 'Wolds.'

He built up the fire with logs: there had been a sharp frost and icy patches covered the lanes and tracks, making it difficult to walk or ride.

'Don't ask me to go out, that's all. If we want bread, then we'll make it. It's freezing out.'

'No, it's not that. In fact if tha'll do what I ask, then we'll have to stay in.'

He stretched and yawned and then came over to her and put his arms around her. 'Annie!' His brown eyes were soft, yet humorous. 'What *are* you going to ask?'

She pushed him away. 'Stop fooling, Toby. I'm serious!'

He held her gently by her shoulders. 'So would I be, Annie, if you'd let me.'

'Please don't, Toby. Tha knows I care for thee. Don't let's spoil things.'

He turned away from her, but she saw a look of hurt cross his face. He's different from any man I've known, she thought, so tender and gentle. He deserves better than me.

'Go on, then.' He stretched out on his bed. 'What is it you want that is so important?'

She hesitated for a moment and then went and sat at the foot of the bed. 'I want thee to learn me to talk proper.'

He grinned. 'Teach you to speak correctly?'

'Aye. That's what I said. And to learn me – teach me, I mean, to read and write, and to do numbers. I can add up in my head, but I can't write 'numbers down. Will tha, Toby? Please.'

'Ask me again properly, and then I'll think about it.'

She took a deep breath and gathered her thoughts together. 'I want you to teach me to speak proper.'

He sat up. 'Almost right. But why, Annie? Your accent is part of you. You don't have to change. Is it my brother? Is it Matt who has made you think this way?'

She considered for a moment. 'Partly. I don't think of what I am when I'm with thee, but with him – well, I know that he thinks I'm nowt – nothing, and it makes my blood boil, 'cos I know I can be better.'

He looked wistfully at her. 'I see,' he said quietly.

'But it's not just Matt.' She got up and paced the floor. 'No. It was them two bitches up on 'Wolds. Them two she-cats. It was them that made me think.'

He laughed at her. 'Bitches are dogs, Annie. Cats are cats. What *are* you talking about?'

'Where I come from, bitches are spiteful women, and that's what them two so-called ladies were.'

'*Those* two, Annie. Not them two.'

'Tha'll teach me then, Toby?' She grasped him excitedly. 'Have we started already?'

'Tell me about the two ladies who have so disturbed you.' He looked enquiringly at her. 'And where have you been to meet such ladies?'

'Well, I didn't take 'usual route, not the one that Robin showed me.'

Toby raised his eyes to the ceiling in exasperation. 'No wonder you lost your way, silly woman.'

She ignored him and continued. 'I saw a big house, and I thought that I would take a chance and knock, and ask 'housekeeper if she wanted owt – anything. And as luck would have it, the housekeeper took me up to see her mistress, Mrs Burnby, who was entertaining two ladies, her nieces, I think they were, and they bought several lengths of stuff. Jane, that was one of them, said to Mrs Burnby, that she ought to buy the length of grey satin for a party they were going to.'

Toby sat forward and watched her, his teeth biting his bottom lip.

'But it was the other one, Clara, that was so – so – !' She shook her fists. She couldn't find the word that would fit the disdainful, haughty young woman who had laughed at her.

'Patronizing? That would fit, I think,' he said quietly.

'Aye. That's it. And that's when I started to think I could learn to talk better. I know my place, don't think I don't. I know I can't change what I am, but I can at least try, even for my own sake to pull myself out of 'sewer and not let folk despise me as soon as I open my mouth.'

'It wasn't just you, Annie.' Toby sighed and Annie looked at him curiously. How pale he seemed and melancholy. 'That's just how she is. It's her nature to be contemptuous and derisive. I know. I've felt the sharpness of her tongue. Even when she was very young she was the same.'

'That's not 'young woman you loved?' How could it be? She wasn't worthy of him. 'But you said she loved you too!'

'Huh. She said she did. But I was very eligible. I realize now that it was father's estate and name that she was after. If Matt had been around she would have set her cap at him instead. However, she seems destined to be an old maid for no-one has carried her off yet. Rumour has it that she'll have no-one that her father has chosen for her.' He shrugged. 'And so she gets more and more bitter and vindictive.'

'She is a bitch, then?'

'Absolutely.' He suddenly laughed. 'And a she-cat. What a lucky escape I've had, Annie.'

They spent every day for a month working on Annie's letters as she called them; and outside the wind howled and then it snowed, and after that it rained and rained, and the river rose and burst its banks and flooded the path and deposited its turbulent muddy water into the cottages which sat by its side beneath the low chalk cliff.

The lessons were not easy for her and Toby got bored, but she persisted, and soon she grasped the rudiments of reading. Numbers she had no trouble with at all, for, she said, she thought of the figures as shapes and she seemed to have a natural talent with a pencil to depict the figures in her head.

'You're amazing, Annie. You're so quick at adding up. Much quicker than I am.'

'It's because I had to be sharp, living on the wharves. We did so much bartering that we had to know 'worth of everything and convert it into money. And when I was married to Alan, I never had any money, he always spent it on grog or dogfights and I had to manage with what was left. Everybody thought I was a poor housekeeper, but it's hard managing on nothing.'

She put down her paper and pencil and gazed reflectively into space. I could manage now. I'd know how. I've got money of my own that I've worked for. I could feed my children. She turned towards Toby and found that he was watching her, his face soft and sympathetic.

'You're a very brave lady, Annie. You deserve to be happy.' He took her hand and kissed it gently, then he turned it over and kissed the palm.

She had never been kissed like that before. Never really been kissed so that she would like it. She had had her lips probed open by searching tongues and rough hands on her body. But never tenderness such as this. This was no brotherly kiss.

She gently stroked his face. He was such a boy. Untouched, somehow, by life, in spite of his daring adventuring spirit. She smiled at him and leant forward and kissed his mouth. 'I am happy, Toby. You have made me happy. You've taught me so much, and I don't mean letters and numbers. You've taught me that there are some kind folk in this world, and you are the kindest, bestest man in it.'

He smiled back at her, a crease showing around his eyes. '*Best*, Annie, if that is what I am, not bestest.'

The spell was broken as they laughed and they hugged each other.

'I've thought of something that will make you really happy, Annie.'

'What?' She packed up her books and pencil. 'I told thee – you, I *am* happy, just being here. I did think I'd go to York, but I don't think now that I want to.' And, she thought, I can't go anywhere until I've paid back that proud brother of thine. I'll make him eat his words. I know what it is with him. He thinks that I'm using Toby. Probably thinks I'm getting money out of him. He won't know that there's such a thing as a loving friendship.

'Your children,' he said. 'Why don't we fetch them here?'

She turned pale. 'How? I can't go to Hull. I've told thee before, folks' is after me.' In her anxiety she slipped back into her old dialect. 'And where would we all live?'

'That wouldn't be difficult. We can build another room, there's plenty of timber. And Mrs Trott would help to look after them, they could even go to school.'

She stared open-mouthed. He must be going mad. Mrs Trott look after Jimmy? And go to school? Her lads? Ted would like that, he was a bright little lad, and Lizzie was a good girl, she could go into service. But no, no, it was impossible.

'I've told thee. I daren't go back.' She started to cry. Her fears multiplied as she thought of Francis Morton lying in the mud, and the gallows creaking as a body swung, its eyes pecked out by crows. She sobbed and sobbed. 'I can't go back. Don't make me. Please don't make me. I'll swing. I'll swing!'

16

'I won't make you, Annie. How could I? It has to be your decision. But why won't you tell me why you are so frightened? You can trust me; you surely know that?'

She took a square of linen from her pocket and blew her nose. She gave a sobbing laugh. 'Look at me, Toby. Wiping my nose on a hanky and not on my shawl!' Should I tell, she thought wretchedly. Is it better to share my misery or keep it to myself. Some compassion in his face made her weep again. He told me his story; about his terrible father and his mistress, and that dreadful Miss Clara. He shared his sorrow with me.

'I killed a man.'

His face paled at her words and he grasped her hand. 'How? I mean – an accident?'

She took a deep shuddering breath. It was out. 'No. Not an accident. I did it intentionally. I took a knife and stabbed him.' She drew up her head and stared at him defiantly. 'And I'm not sorry. I'd do it again. He deserved it.'

Toby put his hand over his eyes and shook his head. 'No man deserves that, Annie. You can't mean it.'

'Aye. I mean it,' she admitted, her conscience unburdened. 'When a man behaves the way he did, then death is too good for him.'

'Tell me then, Annie. Don't spare me. I want to know what drove you to deprive a man of his life.'

'His name was Francis Morton. I'd known of him for a long time, he was well known in all the streets and alleys of Hull. He was a thief who was never caught – he had the law in his pocket. He was a seducer, a whoremonger with bastards all over town; and when he came into my life after

Alan died, I thought he was the most handsome, generous, charming man I'd ever met, and that all the stories I'd ever heard about him were just malicious rumours spread by vindictive people who were jealous of his good looks and the money he always had in his pocket.'

She wiped away a tear and got up and walked about the room. 'It wasn't until I'd accepted money and gifts from him, given, he'd said without pledge or promise of favours returned, that I realized that I was trapped. He *did* expect favours, and he tempted me with his soft talk and yearnings – and I was flattered, I have to admit it, and I thought I loved him—.' She stopped her walking and gazed into the fire. 'I was that desperate, Toby, to have someone care for me; but I soon came to realize that he was nowt but a cruel bully, who expected more from me than I'd willingly give.

'I put up with that, after all, I was used to being ill-treated, it was nothing new to me, and besides, he was giving me money, so I was able to feed my bairns.' She looked at Toby sitting so silently, pale and drawn, and now, she thought, I've lost him. He won't want to know the likes of me, the scum on dirty water. 'I don't think I can go on, Toby. I can't tell thee the rest.'

He drew her towards him and gently rested her head on his shoulder. 'Yes you can, take your time, it's best that you tell it all, then it's done with.'

Hot tears sped down her face, spilling onto his shirt. 'He'd hit my lads, they told me that he had, and I said that happen they'd deserved it, their Da was always chastizing them – our Jimmy was a young varmint, though Ted wasn't.'

She took another deep breath. 'Then one day I came home early from work. I found him in 'house with Lizzie.' She turned a tear-stained face towards him. 'She was eight years old, Toby – onny a bairn – and he'd taken off her apron and was unbuttoning her dress.' She shuddered. 'God knows what'd have happened if I hadn't come in when I did. I didn't say owt, just stood and stared – and then he laughed and made some excuse and left.'

She drew away from Toby and continued her pacing about the room. 'It was then that I decided. I knew that a man with an appetite like his would be back, and I couldn't be watching Lizzie day in, day out. And poor bairn, she was so frightened. So I locked her in the house and told her not to open 'door to anybody, and took my lads to Seaman's Hospital – I knew they'd be well looked after there. Then I took Lizzie round to some good friends of mine and asked them if they'd look after her for me while I attended to some business.'

A log on the fire spat crackling sparks onto the floor and she jumped and watched as Toby rubbed his boot on the scorching rug.

'I went back home and took Alan's flensing knife from where I'd hidden it and went looking for him.'

She sank down onto the floor. She felt sick and faint as she remembered the staining on Francis's shirt and the obscenities he raged at her in his death throes. She touched her cheek at the small scar left by the buckle of his belt as he'd lashed out at her, before she had kicked him down into the mud below the wharves.

'Annie?' She heard Toby's voice from a long way off.

'Leave me,' she whispered. 'Don't talk to me. Go away. Please!'

For two days she lay in her bed, too exhausted by the trauma of her confession to even talk or eat, she merely drank the water which Toby brought her and the warm milk in which he had stirred some honey.

On the third day she got out of bed ravenously hungry and with her mind made up. She would do as Toby suggested and fetch her children here. She had to defy the demons which haunted her and return to Hull.

'We'll have to wait until after the next run, Annie,' Toby reminded her. 'The *Breeze* is due in on Friday. We'll get the goods distributed and then go. I'll go with you, don't worry.'

But she did worry, she couldn't help it. She also worried when Josh appeared on Friday morning and said that soldiers had arrived in Hessle and that Bernard Roxton had booked in at the Admiral Hawke Inn.

'They've got wind of '*Breeze* arriving,' he said, his round face scowling. 'Revenue ship's moored at 'river mouth, but I reckon they'll try to nab her up river and us with her.'

'They won't catch us.' Toby was cheerful and optimistic. 'Their ships are not fast enough, and their cobbles were not built for the Humber, we can outrun them any time, and besides the mariners on board them couldn't care less, they never get their prize money even when they make a capture.'

'Aye, and some of soldiers'll take a bribe,' Josh conceded, 'only not Sergeant Collins, so I hear. He's straight as a die.'

It was as Toby and Annie were stepping out from the warmth of the cottage into the cold darkness to go to the river that he took her arm. 'Annie. Everything will be all right, I'm convinced of it––, but, if anything should go wrong, then you must get away as fast as you can. Go to the Trotts first, they'll look after you until you decide what your future is.'

'Toby! What are you saying?' She was horrified by the seriousness of his tone,

His mood changed and he laughed. 'I'm saying that we shall have great sport tonight. Roxton is out to catch me or my brother. He knows nothing of you or Josh or any of the others, and he must be as mad as can be. But,' he took her by the chin and looked into her eyes. 'If, by any chance things should go wrong, you must take over from me. Run the team as I do. Josh will help you. Take what you need from this house. You'll find money, clothes, cloth, everything you need to start afresh. Fetch your children and make another life.'

'Tha's frightening me, Toby.'

'What?' He smiled at her.

'You're frightening me,' she repeated.

He nodded. 'We need to be frightened, then we'll take more care. Come on, tonight we're seeking our fortune.'

There was a sudden exhilaration in his words, a feverishness in his manner and as she gazed closer at him in the darkness, there was, she thought, a spark of madness in his eyes.

'There'll be brandy and geneva, coffee and tea, maybe a roll of silk or two if Matt was able to make the contact, but that's for us, not for the others, they wouldn't know where to distribute it.'

She caught his enthusiasm and smiled. Silk. She'd love to have the feel of that between her fingers. 'Right then,' she laughed. 'Let's be off.'

*   *   *

While the men loaded the boats, Annie and Toby went with Matt to his cabin. Matt handed her a list of goods written in large bold handwriting.

'I understand you're going to help Toby with the distribution! Well, you'd better make a start. You'll find the number of ankers of geneva and brandy, and the amount of tobacco brought, the amount I've paid for it and the price it's expected to bring. Josh will be counting and his list should tally with this one.'

His voice was curt. He's still not happy about me being here, she thought. He gave them each a glass well filled with brandy and invited them to sit down.

'It's going to be a long night,' he said, and rubbed his hand over his eyes. 'And there's going to be trouble, I can feel it. There was another cutter, not as old as those the customs normally use, just off Spurn Head.' He scratched his beard thoughtfully. 'She made no attempt to confront us. That can only mean that there is some kind of plan afoot. They're probably hoping to trap us in the river. Have you heard of any customs ship being moored up at Brough?'

Toby shook his head. 'No. And the men have been very active up and down the river, we would have heard if a ship had been seen,'

'Then they're coming down from the Trent. God help them, the waters are treacherous enough in the day, even when you know them, but for them to attempt the mudflats in the dark is madness.'

'But you do it, Captain.' Annie had been dismayed by his news.

'But I know the waters, Mrs Hope. And though the mud and sand have a habit of shifting when least expected, I have a feeling for these home waters. Not like the mariners employed by the revenue who are often strangers to these parts.'

'Well we, too, have a scheme if needs be.' Toby drained his glass and stood up. 'We'd better be going on deck, the men will be almost finished.'

'Your plan?' said Matt.

'We have six boats which will carry only a small amount of goods. If there should be trouble, they'll draw away from the rest of us and hinder the customs from reaching us. Then when we are safely away they'll draw to shore, they'll be able to move swiftly, being lighter, and hopefully the customs will follow. Once they're on shore they'll abandon the boats and run. The Customs are sure to stop and search the packages, and it'll be worth the loss of a pound or two of tobacco if the rest of the goods are safe.'

Toby put out his hand to Matt. 'God go with you brother. I wish you a fair wind and a full sail.'

Annie thought she caught a fleeting look of apprehension on Matt's face, but then it was gone and he grinned. 'Who knows, God might well be on the side of Roxton and his comrades tonight. We shall see. But whatever happens we'll give them something to tell their grandchildren. 'Tis a pity we can't do the same.'

He glanced at Annie, staring into her face and then down at her bare feet, and then back to her face again.

'And you, Mrs Hope? Perhaps you will have a story to tell your children and grandchildren!'

'Aye,' she replied quietly. 'Perhaps I will. God willing.'

He grasped her hands. 'Don't leave it all to God. Life is in our own hands too.'

For a moment it seemed as if they were alone in the small cabin, as if Toby had gone, though he still stood by the door watching them. The muffled sound of barrels being moved above them, stilled. Then he suddenly released her hands and gave a small bow. 'Take care.'

Annie counted up to fifty small boats clustered around the *Breeze*, bumping against the hull and waiting for the signal to pull away. She climbed down the ladder behind Toby and clambered into the waiting coggy. Josh was in a boat next to them, his was one which was only half laden.

A light flashed from on shore. 'There we go,' whispered Josh. 'There's 'signal.'

'Bear away,' Toby called softly. 'Safe home lads.'

The boats pulled towards the shore and Annie turned her head back to the *Breeze* and saw Matt standing on deck. He raised his arm in farewell and she did the same, and then turning her back pulled hard on the oar in unison with Toby.

They were halfway to the bank when they heard a warning cry from the *Breeze*. They both looked back up river and saw a fleet of small boats heading towards them, and behind them, outlined against the night sky, the three-masted white sails of a frigate, the cannons on her gun decks clearly visible, was moving fast towards the *Breeze*.

'Damnation,' Toby cursed. 'What happened to the lookout? He was supposed to be watching up river.'

'I reckon he didn't see them,' Annie panted. 'Look where they've come from, they've rowed from Brough, there's a bend in the river, and 'tide is high so lookout's watching from the bank, not the shingle.'

When she had been on watch, she had stepped up to her

knees in water so that she could look up and down river, but if the tide was very high it would be impossible to do that for fear of being swept away.

The crack of a firearm made them duck low. 'It's all right,' Toby assured her. 'They're aiming above us. They'll not shoot to kill.'

Annie didn't believe him. She had heard the whine of the shot far too close to be reassured that the revenue men didn't mean them any harm.

'Change course.' Toby gasped. 'We'll make for the mill. There are people waiting there.' He steered away from the bank and pulled strongly down river towards the Hessle shore.

Several of the other boats were doing the same, the men on board pulling furiously to avoid capture, while behind, as Annie looked back, the revenue boats were chasing Josh and the other half-laden boats towards the shore, at the same time there came a sharp exchange of gunfire from the *Breeze* and the frigate.

'I think your plan's worked, Toby. They're chasing Josh and the others. Oh, what if they catch them?'

'They won't,' he breathed heavily. 'That area's low lying and marshy for one thing, and full of small creeks and reed-beds. They won't even attempt to follow. And for another, didn't you see that they're using Flamborough cobbles? They've a pointed stern, they have to moor them afloat and that means getting their feet wet if they want to give chase. No, they'll simply confiscate the goods and try again next time.'

'But what about the *Breeze*,' she said desperately. 'I can still hear gunfire. Why doesn't Matt heave to? There are no goods on board.'

'Yes, she's empty, but Matt won't trust the revenue men not to plant goods on board. He'll not let them set foot on her decks. He'll fight first.'

As they scrambled onto the pebbled shore, lanterns flashed in the darkness and men and women appeared from behind the old horse mill and within minutes the contraband was unloaded from the small boats. Tea and coffee, geneva, brandy, snuff and pepper, were loaded into donkey carts and panniers, wheelbarrows and back-packs, and were spirited away into the night.

Again came a crackle of fire and the sky was bright as if lit by lightning.

'Come on. We'll go back along the shore,' Toby said as they finished unloading their cargo and gave it into the charge of a man and woman. Annie peered at them. The man was unknown to her, but the woman, yes, it was, it was Mrs Trott. So she hadn't given up after all. She was still involved.

She picked up a lantern and as they turned to run along the shore they both stopped in their tracks. Coming up river from the direction of Hull was a revenue cutter, the *Mayfly*. It moved only slowly for the tide was turning against it, but its sails were full as the wind freshened.

''*Breeze* will be trapped! Toby! She won't be able to get away.'

Toby didn't answer but turned to run swiftly along the shingle. Annie followed him, stumbling in her haste. They ran as far as they could until the shingle ran out and they had to climb up onto the bank, pushing their way through scrub and scurvy grass to reach the path.

'There she is,' Annie panted. 'She's had some damage.'

The hull of the *Breeze* was blackened by gunfire and several holes were torn into her, but the revenue frigate had come off worse in the fight, one mast splintered in two and her sail flapping towards her decks.

They heard a shout from the frigate's captain. 'Captain Linton! You can't get away. Heave to or it'll be the worse for you.'

An answering reply came in the form of thunderous gunshot aimed not at the frigate but at the dark foaming water beneath her keel.

'Give me the lantern. I'll try to warn him.'

Toby snatched the light from her and gave two swift signals. 'They're not watching the shore or the river.

They're too busy watching the frigate. She'll be caught.'
Again he signalled, but there was no answering response.

'Keep trying,' Annie said urgently. 'Don't stop.'

Again and again he signalled until finally there came an answering light. 'She's seen us, but what good will it do. Here comes the cutter.'

But the *Breeze* had also seen the cutter and they heard the rattle of the anchor chain and the shout of command as she prepared to sail.

'He's left it too late.' Toby shook his head. 'That's not like Matt.'

The sails unfurled and filled as a sudden gusty wind blew and the *Breeze* moved towards the frigate.

'She'll crash into her,' Toby shouted. 'What's he playing at?'

They heard the shout of the frigate captain as he saw the *Breeze* bearing down on them and they watched as the tattered sails were raised on the remaining masts and it swung out of reach of the prow of the *Breeze*.

'Where's he taking her? Is he heading for the Trent?'

Toby shook his head. 'I don't know what he's up to. But I have a feeling that he was expecting this. I don't believe that he was surprised by the cutter at all. He's a crafty one, that brother of mine.'

The *Breeze* kept close to the Lincolnshire shore as she turned, followed by the frigate with the cutter not far behind to her windward side, each sending out bursts of gunfire towards the *Breeze*.

'They're gaining on her,' Toby muttered. 'Why doesn't he increase sail. She could easily lose them.'

It was as if the *Breeze* was in no hurry at all as she led the ships up river, even though the shot scorched her decks and a gaping hole appeared in the hull and she retaliated with occasional gunfire.

'I've got it,' Toby shouted, and Annie looked round anxiously, wondering if anyone was around to hear. The land above the bank was open, the ground chalky and dry and easily accessible for horsemen coming down from the hill above the meadows. A stone barn stood there, apparently deserted, but she worried that it could hide a legion of customs men or soldiers.

'He's drawing them onto Redcliffe Sands.' His voice dropped. 'If they get caught on there they won't be able to get off until the next tide!'

'But he might get caught too!' Annie bit at her fingers as she watched the ships moving steadily away from them.

'No. He won't. Not Matt.'

The *Breeze* suddenly started to pull away from the other ships and drew towards the middle of the river. The cutter, which had been lagging behind the frigate, seemed to become aware that the *Breeze* might get away and moved swiftly until it was in front of the frigate and heading towards the *Breeze*.

'Heave to. Heave to, or we fire.' The warning shout came from the *Mayfly*, but the *Breeze* with all her sails drawing moved steadily away and the shot fell into the water beyond its stern. Again came the rattle of gunfire and as the cutter chased towards her, the *Breeze* suddenly changed tack and beat to windward, sailing swiftly towards the windward shore.

The *Mayfly*, its impetus carrying it forward with no time to trim its sails to change tack, sailed on and came to a grinding halt as it hit the hidden sandbank and the frigate, following straight after, was unable to hove to and with a splintering of timbers crashed headlong into its stern.

Above the noise and confusion of men shouting and the crack of gunfire, Annie became aware of some other sound. She and Toby had lain flat out on the bank to watch the fray, and she thought she felt a tremor on the ground beneath her.

'Toby? I keep thinking that I can hear hoofbeats.'

'No. I don't think so. The soldiers won't come so far up here.' Toby was still engrossed in watching the floundering of the two revenue ships as they battled to free themselves from the sandbanks in the middle of the river, while the *Breeze* sailed impudently away beyond their range of gunfire.

Annie turned her head to look over her shoulder. She was nervous. Was that a shadow by the barn, or were her eyes playing tricks? No, there it was again.

The sky was brightening in the east. A pale streak heralding the dawn, while from the dark copse of trees across the meadow came the first faint twittering of birdsong.

'There's somebody, Toby, I'm convinced of it,' she whispered.

Toby turned towards her and smiled and reached for her hand. 'You're just jittery, that's all. And no wonder, it's been quite a night.' He got to his knees. 'Come on, let's get off home. I'm ready for my bed. Matt can look after himself.'

The musket shot that rang out echoed in her ears, resounding in its intensity and she flung herself to the ground, and Toby with a grunt did the same.

'I told thee, Toby, that somebody was there.' She heard the sound of hoofbeats again and lifted her head. The dark shapes of two horsemen were galloping from the shelter of the copse towards them. 'Toby! What shall we do?'

He didn't answer and she turned towards him. He was lying on his front, his back curiously hunched, and she put her hand on his shoulder. 'Toby? Tha's not hurt? Oh, say tha's not hurt.'

She looked up across the meadow, the horsemen were still coming but their pace had slowed, someone was shouting an order and they were looking back across their shoulders towards the barn.

'Toby, rouse tha self, we've time to get away.' She shook his shoulder. It was wet and sticky and in horror she looked at her hand. It was covered in blood.

She turned him over. The fear and trauma which she thought she had at last left behind, returned, chilling her to the marrow as she gazed at the bloody brown patch seeping through his coat in an ever widening stain, while his brown eyes, such deep brown, gazed sightlessly back at her.

17

She stared and stared, then as shock set in she felt a scream rising from her gut, bursting through her chest and compounding in the back of her throat. Her temples throbbed so violently that she thought her head would explode.

Then through a throb of beating heart and pulses she heard again the sound of a single horsebeat. She didn't look up but gathered Toby into her arms, wrapping her cloak around him. 'They'll not take us, Toby. They'll have to kill me first.'

With her arms clutching him tightly she rolled to the edge of the bank and looked down. The chalk bank was covered in scrub and sea lavender and was merely a ten or twelve foot drop, down to the shingle shore which now lay exposed as the tide retreated.

She curled herself into a ball pulling him on top of her, and with a huge heave launched them both over the edge. They bounced and rolled, crashing into the prickly scrub which broke their fall and which almost parted Toby's body from her. Frantically she pulled him back and rolled again and they landed with a thud, scratched and torn, on to the shingle.

'Don't cry, Annie,' she muttered. 'Don't weep and wail like you always did.' But she couldn't stop the tears which gushed unchecked down her cheeks.

She glanced westwards along the narrow strip. The two revenue cutters were marooned on the sandbank and there they would stay until the tide turned, and she wondered if they would attempt to put off a small boat to reach the shore; the *Breeze* was already lost to view in the obscure half-light of a grey dawn.

The bank curved, jutting out onto the shingle with a thick covering of shrubby undergrowth. She took a deep breath and got to her feet. She daren't look at Toby for she knew her nerve would fail if she saw once more the cold dead face and staring eyes.

She closed her eyes and bent towards him, intending to lift him under his arms and drag him towards the shelter of the overhanging bank.

A hand closed over her mouth, while another arm clad in red, grasped her round the waist and pulled her upright. She struggled, trying to bite the hand that was so firmly clenched about her mouth.

'Ssh. Don't struggle. And don't scream. I'll not harm ye.'

A thick Scottish accent whispered in her ear and her eyes flickered from side to side as she tried to see her captor. He released the arm around her waist but kept his hand on her mouth.

Her eyes opened wide as she turned to see the leathery face of Sergeant Collins. She lashed out at him. He grabbed her again.

'Don't make a sound. I'm here to help you.' He released his hand slowly. 'I'm sorry about your friend.'

'Sorry? Sorry?' she hissed. 'You've just killed a man. A man who did you no harm.'

'Not me.' He shook his head. 'One of my troopers. He's young and nervous. He had no orders to shoot and he'll get the lash because of it. But if we don't hurry and hide your friend, then they'll come looking for me, thinking I'm in trouble. I told them to give me ten minutes while I looked for the smugglers. We've had a merry dance tonight— '

His words were cut short as a pistol was placed below his right ear. 'Don't move. I'll fire if tha as much as breathes.'

Josh, with a scarf covering half of his face had crept up behind them and was brandishing not only a pistol but a heavy club.

'Wait. Wait.' Annie said urgently. 'Don't fire. I know him, he said he'll help us.'

'And tha believes him? I wouldn't trust any sodgers. They're in 'King's pay; it'll be a trick.'

'No trick.' Sergeant Collins spoke rapidly. 'You must believe me and hurry, my troopers will be starting to look for me. Let me go back and I'll tell them you've escaped, that there's no-one here.'

'Does tha believe him?' Josh kept his pistol firmly in place.

'Aye. He owes me a favour. Remember?' she queried the sergeant.

'I'll not forget it. We'll be even with this.' His eyes scanned hers. 'But I can't guarantee another time. You'll be as well to lie low; Mr Roxton is determined to stamp out this illegal trade.'

Josh lowered his pistol. 'Go on then. Get moving. And draw thy men away, keep them away from 'river.'

Sergeant Collins with a backward look at Annie, scrambled back up the bank. They listened intently for a few minutes and then heard the diminishing pound of hoof-beats as he cantered away.

Josh bent over Toby and touched his face. When he stood up he pulled the scarf from his face: he was deathly white. 'He's dead, Mrs Hope! I thought – I thought – when I saw thee fall down 'bank that he was onny injured. If I'd known – I wouldn't have stayed my hand with yon sodger.'

Annie pressed her hand to her mouth to control the trembling. She couldn't see for tears. 'He didn't feel anything, Josh. He was smiling when he died.'

She gave a sob. 'What do we do? It'll soon be light. We have to get him away from here.' She drew in a sharp breath. 'What about his brother?'

Josh stared at her as if not seeing, his eyes vacant. Then he shook his head as if shaking away a bothersome fly. 'We'll get him over yonder first, under cover – just in case that sergeant breaks his word and comes back with his men, or Mr Roxton.' As he uttered the custom's man's name he spat. 'We're worth a packet of money now, thee and me.'

He gave Annie the pistol and hoisted Toby's body across his broad shoulders and they crossed the shingle to the overhanging bank. He pushed into the scrub and carefully placed him down on the ground. Then tenderly he placed his thumbs over Toby's eyes and closed them. 'God bless thee, sir. Sleep peacefully.'

They sat silently for a few minutes, locked in their own thoughts, their eyes on the two ships trapped in the middle of the river. Then Josh screwed up his eyes and looked into the distance. He pointed up river. The *Breeze* was slipping silently back towards the marooned ships, keeping close to the northern shore.

Josh got up. 'Keep watch, I'll be back.' He slithered down the bank and ran westwards along the shingle and out of her view.

She felt the coldness of the pistol in her hand. I wouldn't know how to use it even if anyone came. I could only use it to threaten. She looked at Toby lying next to her. His face looked peaceful, as if he was merely sleeping. It was only the bloodstained coat which told her he wasn't.

Josh is a long time. She worried that he might get caught by the patrolling soldiers. What would I do if he didn't come back? She started to shiver. What was it Toby had said before we left? If anything should go wrong, make a new life for yourself. She started to weep and in her distress, some primitive urge caused her to rock, back and forth, her arms hugging her knees. I can't, Toby. I've come to rely on you. I never told you how much I cared, how much you meant to me, and now its too late, you'll never know.

Yet creeping into her consciousness came the knowledge that she had bared her soul to him, breaking open the seal of silence which she had avowed to keep. 'It's safe with thee, Toby,' she muttered. 'I know tha'll never tell.' And perhaps by telling, she thought, as she sat numbed by her misery, you realized that I did care for you, for I would never have told another soul.

She raised her head above the scrub. Daylight was

breaking ever faster, streaks of light stretching long yellow fingers across the sky, reflecting in the dark water like golden strands. The *Breeze* was sailing closer to the silent revenue ships, yet there was no movement on their decks and she wondered if the crew and revenue men had cast off in the darkness in their small boats, leaving only a single watch on board, to return on the next tide.

Hessle and Ferriby will be throbbing with rev' men if they have, she thought. But they'll not find anything. It'll all be safely hidden by now. She thought of Mrs Trott's henhouse and Mr Sutcliff's pit, and the countless other hiding places packed to the brim with contraband.

A boat was coming, she could hear the splash of oars as they dipped into the water. Josh. She saw his sturdy frame as he pulled towards the overhang and he beached the coggy on the shingle.

'Come on, we haven't much time. '*Breeze*'ll be on top of us before we know it.'

He lifted Toby across his shoulder and with Annie following led down the scrubby bank towards the boat.

'What are we going to do? Where are we taking him?' She kept her voice low as they lay Toby in the bottom of the boat.

'We're taking him to his brother. We can't take him back with us, there'll be too many questions asked. Cap'n Linton'll know what to do.'

The *Breeze* had passed the two ships, a single figure came on deck of the *Mayfly*, the frigate appeared to be deserted, and the *Breeze* now veered away from the shore towards the middle of the river.

'Right. Pull hard.' Josh heaved the boat into the water and jumped in. 'I don't want to hail her. I just hope that 'look out is on his toes and sees us, otherwise we'll be run down.'

He took an oar from her and they both pulled, drawing the coggy towards the middle of the river and into the path of the *Breeze*.

'They've seen us.' Annie waved an arm towards the

schooner. 'There's Captain Linton. Drop back. Drop back.'

The coggy boat dipped and rolled on the wash from the *Breeze* as she was brought up, and someone on board slung a ladder over the side.

'Go on up,' Josh said tersely. 'Tha'd best break 'news first.'

Annie felt the ladder sway as she put her foot on the first rung and thought of the first time when Toby had made her climb. She felt sick with fear and apprehension at breaking the news of his death to his brother.

But it was as if Matt Linton guessed as he took her hand and helped her onto the deck. He turned his hand over and looked at the blood transferred to his own hand from hers. Her face and cloak were spattered with Toby's blood as she'd wrapped him in a last tender embrace before falling over the bank, and her eyes as she lifted them to his face, couldn't hide the anguished grief which overwhelmed her.

He put his arm around her shoulder and called to a seaman to come and bear a hand to assist her. She leaned against him and watched vacantly as Matt climbed down the ladder towards the boat and as she looked over the bulwark she saw him gently touch his brother's face and then turn to Josh to say something.

With Toby over his shoulder he climbed the ladder and on reaching the quarterdeck laid him gently down. He knelt beside him for a few minutes, his head bowed and Annie wondered if he was praying. But when he looked up his blue eyes were ice cold.

'Who did this?' His voice was harsh and demanding as he stared at her. 'Roxton? He'll answer for this. Damn his eyes.'

She shook her head. No matter that the revenue man was hated, she couldn't let him take the blame for this. 'No. A soldier. He was young seemingly, and nervous. He didn't have orders to shoot.'

His eyes narrowed. 'How do you know this?'

'Sergeant Collins. I know him. He came. He helped us get away.'

'You have a soldier as a friend? They're in the pay of the Crown!'

'Not a friend.' She was beginning to feel faint, the events of the night sweeping over her. 'I once did him a favour. He was returning it.'

She thought she saw a sneering of his upper lip, a twitching which betrayed some emotion, but the sky seemed to be growing darker and her heart was hammering and his voice was drifting away, getting fainter and fainter and as she fell, he caught her in his arms.

When she came round she was lying in a bunk in the captain's cabin. Her cloak had been removed and she was covered with a blanket. She turned her head. Matt had his back to her, searching for something in a locker. He had taken off his jersey and was clad in a white shirt and black breeches and she saw that as she had imagined, his shoulders were as broad as Toby's had been. Her gaze followed down from the fair hair which curled below his neck, to the leather belt he wore around his waist, down past his black breeches to the tops of his boots.

He turned as she stifled a gasping sob and picking up a glass he came towards her. 'Are you feeling a little better?'

She nodded. She felt so empty, as if her mind had been displaced and she could no longer find the words to express her grief or anger.

'Will you take a little brandy and water?' A ghost of a smile touched his lips. 'The water is clean.'

She took the glass with trembling fingers and sipped but her teeth chattered and she couldn't swallow. She handed it back to him and put her head in her hands. 'I'm sorry,' she muttered. 'I know how bad you must be feeling and it's not that I haven't seen some dreadful things in my life. I'm not a feeble creature who faints with the vapours, but Toby – Toby meant so much to me.'

His face was sombre as he sat down beside her. 'Try to drink this. Believe me, I've had a tot or two already, though I must keep a steady hand and eye.' He held the glass to her lips while she drank, his hand over hers.

'Thank you.' She swung her legs to the floor. Her feet and legs were scratched where she had fallen over the bank.

'I'll get you something to put on those scratches,' he said quietly.

'No. It's all right.' She stood up. She felt unsteady, the floor beneath her feet was dipping and rolling. 'I'll have to be getting back. But what will you do about—. Oh,' she caught her breath. 'Josh! He'll still be waiting for me.'

He shook his head. 'No. He's gone. I sent him ashore. There's nothing he can do here. He'll break the news to Mr and Mrs Trott and tell the others.'

'I would have done that. They'll be heartbroken, she treats him – treated him like her own.'

'I know, she always did.' A veil of sadness settled on his face and she wanted to comfort him.

A sudden pitching sent her staggering almost into his arms. 'What's happening? Why are we rolling so?'

She bent her head and looked out of the square window in the bulkhead. The shores of Hessle had gone and there were other more familiar landmarks, windmills and spires and the tower of Holy Trinity Church.

'We're sailing!' she gasped. 'You have to let me off.'

'I can't,' he said tersely. 'It's too late. I had no alternative. The revenue men would have been back, they'd have boarded us and if they'd found Toby—, well it doesn't bear thinking about.'

'But what about me? Where are you taking me? Are you putting me ashore in Hull?'

He sat down at his chart table and busied himself. 'No.' He didn't look at her. 'You'll have to come with us.'

'Come with thee?' She stormed across to him, but her dignity was lost as the ship rolled and she grabbed the rim of the table to steady herself. 'Come with thee where?'

'Ah!' He looked up at her. 'I thought you'd lost your native lyrical tongue, but I'm pleased to hear that you haven't.'

'Don't you sneer at me, Captain Linton.' She leaned across the table and glared into his face. 'I thought that sorrow might have softened thy proud arrogant manner, but I see that it hasn't. Grief doesn't touch thee or melt thy marrow.'

His chair crashed to the floor as he rose angrily from the table and grabbed her by the wrist. 'Don't tell me about sorrow, you stupid woman. I know as much about it as the next man – or woman. I don't need you to tell me, not about grief – or death. I've seen plenty.'

He let her hand fall and turned away and there was something vulnerable in the bend of his head as he picked up his chair and sat down again.

'I couldn't put you ashore with Josh.' His voice was weary and he ran his hands across his eyes. 'Correction. I *didn't* put you ashore with Josh because you were ill,—and, mistaken as I may have been, I thought that perhaps you would want to come with us. I shall give Toby a burial at sea. I just thought that you would want to be there.'

He sat unmoved by her weeping, simply staring into space. Then he rose to his feet and went to the door. 'The pilot will be along shortly to guide us out of the Humber. I'll be obliged if you'll keep below and out of sight. The fewer people who know you are here the better. Also, the crew are not happy about having a woman on board, though under the circumstances they're not raising any objections. I'll have food sent down to you as soon as we reach open water.'

Her grief turned to anger once more as she gazed through the window in the cabin and saw the house roofs and spires and towers of Hull receding on the skyline. The wind thundered through canvas and rigging and she felt the pitch and roll as they rounded the point of Spurn and made headway into the heavy swell of the German Ocean.

18

For two days and nights she tossed, sick and wretched in the captain's bunk. Brandy and water and a dry biscuit were the only sustenance which passed her lips for she refused all other food which the cabin boy brought to her. Of Matt Linton she saw nothing, but she cursed him each time she retched or staggered to look out of the small square window and saw the surging water and the far horizon and not a sight of land.

Then the following morning the boy knocked and calling for him to enter, he came in carrying a jug of hot water and clean towels and then returned a few minutes later with a bowl of hot soup.

'Beggin' your pardon, ma'am. Captain Linton's compliments and he says will you prepare yourself.'

'Prepare myself?' She stared at him dully.

'Aye, ma'am. Today's the day for Master Toby's burial. Sails are already scandalized.'

'Scandalized?'

'Aye, ma'am. It's tradition. Sails are hanging loose in the buntlines. It's the way we honour the dead. If you take a look yonder, you'll see that ships nearby are flying flags at half-mast out of respect.'

'But they don't know Master Toby,' she whispered as she looked out and saw several ships, schooners and brigantines, with their ensigns at half-mast.

'No ma'am, but they know Captain Linton and he's well respected.'

'Is he?' she said curtly. 'Thank you. Tell Captain Linton I'll be up shortly.'

When she came up on deck the air was sharp and cold

and she took several deep breaths. The cabin had been hot and stuffy and she realized that she might well have felt better if she had dared to come up earlier.

The crew were all assembled. Matt looked pale and haggard she thought, and she wondered where he had slept as she had taken his bunk. She took her place at his side and he nodded to her. 'I trust you are feeling better.'

That cabin boy, she fumed. He must have told him how sick I was.

'It takes a little time to earn your sea legs.' His voice was low as if it was an effort to talk to her. 'Another day and you'd even enjoy a sea voyage.'

She shook her head. 'It's been very rough. I thought several times that we were about to capsize.'

He permitted himself a slight smile. 'Smooth as a millpond, a cat's paw only.' His smile vanished. 'A perfect day for a burial.'

She lifted her eyes and it was then that she saw the platform attached to the bulwarks and strapped to it was a white shroud, wrapped in heavy sailcloth. She started to shake and Matt took her by the arm.

'Nearly all over,' he murmured. 'Bear up if you can.' He called to a seaman. 'Bosun. Is all ready?'

'Aye, aye, sir.'

'Parson White. Be so good as to start the service.'

A more unlikely parson Annie had never seen. He was a rough looking fellow with a pock-marked face and a patch over one eye, and wearing a ragged, striped shirt beneath a fancy embroidered waistcoat. On his head he wore a soft woolly cap which he pulled off as he stood forward; but when he opened his mouth he had a deep stentorian voice, well suited for a pulpit.

'Dear Lord. Bless this thine servant, Tobias Linton. He was a fine man as we well know, and though he was but a landlubber, he was a good one.' He raised his voice, getting into full swing. 'And now his great storm has passed and he is coming in to shelter in thine harbour.'

Matt raised his head and stared at him in his good eye. Parson White coughed and cleared his throat and started to sing a hymn, his voice deep and rich, the crew joining in lustily.

When they'd finished, Matt let go of her arm and stepped forward, his head bowed. He waited for a moment as if composing himself, then lifting his head spoke clearly with only a trace of huskiness to betray him. 'We brought nothing into this world and it is certain we can carry nothing out of it. The Lord gave and the Lord hath taken away. Blessed be the Name of the Lord.'

'Amen.'

'Commit the body to the deep.'

The inboard end of the platform was raised and Annie closed her eyes. The white shroud sliding into the water was nothing to do with Toby. Toby was back at the cottage, laughing, joking, his dark eyes merry and waiting for her.

*   *   *

'May I join you for supper?' She had left the door open to let in some air and Matt stood in the doorway.

'It's your cabin, Captain. Your ship.'

He cleared the table of charts and instruments which had been left littered there since she had first joined the ship, and called the boy to bring supper. A white cloth was laid with silver cutlery, two engraved glasses with the initial L carved on them and a matching decanter filled with red wine.

The boy brought in a tureen of soup, followed by a large platter which held a boiled fowl surrounded by dumplings.

She ate a little soup, but then looked warily at the cutlery. 'I'm not very hungry,' she said to hide her confusion. There seemed to be an uncommon amount of knives and forks.

He carved the bird and with a quick glance at her

picked up a chicken leg with his fingers and started to eat. 'You must excuse me, Mrs Hope, with my common seaman's manners, but I don't stand on ceremony whilst I am at sea.'

She too picked up a leg. 'Then why bother with all of this.' She waved the leg at the table.

'I like to at least observe standards even if I don't necessarily follow them, and besides its good for the lad. He might one day better himself and he would at least know which knife and fork went where.'

He's laughing at me again. She tore into the meat with her teeth. It was good. She hadn't realized just how hungry she was.

'I have a proposition to put to you, Mrs Hope. I know that we have had our differences, but those I think stem from our similarities.'

'Similarities!' She took a long draught of wine from the glass. 'I think that we have none!'

'We both have a quick temper and can be rude. There. I can admit it, why can't you?' There was a sparkle in his eyes, a challenge.

'I don't admit that I'm rude – but *if* I ever am, I'm only ever rude to you. Never anyone else. You're the only one that has ever deserved it.' I'm lying, she thought. I was never rude to Alan or Francis. I never dared. I was too scared. Scared of getting a beating. So why do I behave this way with him? Why does he rile me so much?

He raised his eyebrows and shrugged. 'Very well. Do you want to hear what I have to say or not?'

She gulped some more wine. 'Why not? There's nothing to lose by it.'

Nothing to lose. That's what she and Toby had said. Tears came into her eyes and she blinked them away. And now Toby was gone. They had both lost.

'Are you all right?' His voice had become more gentle. 'I'm sure all of this has been a strain for you.'

She swallowed and brushed away the tears. 'Aye. It

has. And now I must think again about my life, which way it'll turn. Sometimes – sometimes— ,'

'Yes?'

'Nothing. It's nothing.' I was so happy, she thought, and now I'm so full of misery again, just like before. Sometimes I wonder what life is about.

'I need someone else to organise the running on shore now that Toby – now that Toby has gone. Will you do it?' He was matter-of-fact, emotionless, and kept his eyes on her glass as he poured her more wine.

She stared at him. 'Me? But I don't know how. I don't know the team or where they go.'

'Josh can tell you all of that.'

'Then why can't Josh do the running. Why do you need me. I might have other arrangements to make.'

'Josh can't keep accounts or read, and though names are not written down, numbers are, each team member has a number and he or she is allocated a certain amount of goods. It needs someone with a sharp mind to keep a tally.'

'I suppose I should be flattered.' He doesn't know that I've only just learnt to read and write, she thought smugly.

'Flattery is the last thing I would think of Mrs Hope, especially where you are concerned.' He got up from the table and she did also. 'You have a few days to think about it. We're homeward bound. You can give me your answer when we reach port.'

He gave her a small bow. Well you can tell he was born a gentleman, she thought scathingly, his manners can't be faulted, but I know that it's an act, he doesn't mean any of it.

'By the way.' He turned towards her. The cabin was small and he was very close, almost brushing her skirt. 'What were your intentions now that Toby isn't around to – er, take care of you.'

Her eyes flashed. What was he implying. 'You thought I stayed around for what I could get out of Toby. You thought I was his mistress! His doxy! Someone like you just wouldn't understand what there was between us.'

He grabbed her by the wrist and pulled her towards him, his face flushed and close to hers. 'Make no mistake, Mrs Hope. I understand perfectly about my brother. But I don't for one moment expect ever to understand you.'

They glared at each other, their eyes wide, and she caught her breath as she saw his lips so close to hers. She felt the powerful strength as his arms came around her and enfolded her in a crushing embrace. His mouth was demanding and passionate as he sought hers, his hand on her head clasping her hair. She closed her eyes and responded, for a moment only. Then reason took over, some judgement of mind which she had never before experienced – before she had only a devious instinct for survival. She pushed him away, hitting him on the chest with her fists.

'Don't treat me like some street woman that you've picked up,' she snarled.

'How should I treat you?' His smile was scornful as he pulled away from her and headed for the cabin door. 'Like a lady that you're trying to be and not the alley cat that you are?'

In anger at his words she picked up a knife from the table and held it aloft as if to strike, and he lifted his arm to parry, but as the blade glittered, another memory came to mind and with a small sob she lowered it.

'I meant you no harm, Captain,' she whispered. 'I'm sorry.'

He looked at her and opened his mouth as if about to speak, then with his hand on the door latch stopped for a moment. 'Forgive me, Mrs Hope. I can't think what came over me. It's been a wretched day, emotions are running high. Shall we forget this little scene ever happened?'

She lifted her head. 'It's forgotten, Captain. It was nothing.'

*   *   *

But she couldn't forget it. Not the look in his eyes nor the touch of his mouth on hers nor the salty smell of the sea in his beard. She could taste it as she licked her lips and as she lay in the bunk at night she felt again his arms around her.

As she thought of him, other images came into her mind. The sight of Toby sitting with her, reading with her, his long brown hair falling over his eyes, and his mouth moving, telling her something.

'What is it? What must I do?' She paced the floor of the cabin as the ship cleaved its way through the seas back to port.

She left the cabin, wanting to clear her head, and climbed the companion-way to the upper deck and felt the wind on her face and heard the rush of it as it swept and filled the sails. The sky was dark with a million stars and as she stood, her head lifted up gazing into space, Matt Linton appeared beside her.

'I couldn't sleep.' She explained her presence. 'I came up for air.'

'You should have called for someone. It isn't safe for you on deck alone. The winds could freshen, you could so easily be swept overboard.'

'And then I'd join Toby,' she whispered.

'No. We're near enough to land, your body would be swept to shore, Toby's won't. He's weighted down and I did soundings for the deepest water, that's why we've been so long at sea. This is a shallow sea, but Toby won't come to shore.' His eyes looked sad. 'I made sure of that. Not ever.'

'I'm so afraid,' she said. 'He's in the dark.'

He looked up at the stars, then he turned to her. 'No,' he said quietly. 'He's in the light.'

They stood silently, their animosity forgotten as their sorrow united them. Then softly he spoke. 'I shall tell my father he died of a fever whilst he was taking a trip with me. He need never know what really happened.' He swallowed hard. 'I'll tell him that we couldn't bring his body back. He'll understand – or think he does, the reason why.'

'Your father? You'll go to him?' She didn't know why she had picked up the idea that Matt and his father never met.

'Yes. He's a hard, unreasonable man and there's no love lost between us, but he still deserves to be told of his son's death. Also there's a housekeeper and man who'll want to know, they became fond of him. They came later, after Mrs Trott. We shall dock the day after tomorrow. I'll hire a horse and go straight away. I can take you as far as Hessle,' he added.

'No,' she said quickly. 'I won't go back just yet.' She had finally made up her mind and she'd remembered what it was that Toby had said to her. 'I have some business to attend to in Hull,' she said. 'When I've dealt with that, then I'll come and I'll tell you what I've decided. I'll tell you if I'm in with you or if I'm moving on.'

He looked annoyed as if his plans had been dashed, as if someone else had had the bad manners to make a decision without consulting him.

'As you wish,' he said coldly. 'I'll meet you at Toby's cottage in four days time.'

They said goodnight and she returned to the cabin and lay down on the bunk. She wouldn't sleep again, not now that she had to think of the day after tomorrow. The day after tomorrow was the day she would brave the streets of Hull and risk the danger of being recognized. The day she would go and search for her children.

19

'Can you lower a boat to take me off? I don't want to sail into the dock.'

She felt Matt eye her curiously but she didn't explain why she didn't want to sail with the *Breeze* into the New Dock. That she might see someone she knew was her greatest fear, and though the morning was still dark as the ship was manoeuvered from the Humber into the river Hull, or the Old Harbour, as it was known in the town, she knew that there would be women waiting there as soon as they heard that a ship was coming in.

She guessed that there would be no wives or sweethearts waiting for the crew of the *Breeze*, for these were not local men, but from Liverpool and Bristol and some, whose sharp accents she could hardly understand were from as far away as Kent on the south coast. The women who would be waiting for these men were no friends of hers, nor would she acknowledge them, but it was possible that someone from amongst them might recognize her as once being a friend of Francis Morton, in the days when she accompanied him to the inns and taverns around the waterfront.

A sea boat was lowered from the davits into the river and she descended the ladder, her toes curling around the rungs, following Parson White and another seaman who were to row her across the narrow waterway to the quayside.

She raised her arm to Matt who was standing on deck watching her as the boat pulled away. The schooner continued down the river, past the warehouses and riverside homes of ship owners and master mariners.

He didn't return her wave but folded his arms and turned his back.

'You'll take care now, miss? There's some scoundrels about. You can't trust anybody these days, they'll have the coat off your back if you as much as turn it for a minute.' Parson White helped her out of the boat and she climbed the iron steps to the quay.

She almost laughed as this villainous looking scoundrel gave her advice, but she promised that she would heed his warning as she ran in the darkness towards the narrow familiar alleys which until only five months ago she had always called home.

I'll go first for Lizzie, she panted as she ran through the alleys and courts, taking short cuts across the town. Will and Maria will be up, Maria will be off to work afore long. She slowed down to catch her breath. Or maybe not. She'll have had her bairn. She might have got 'sack – and poor Will, I wonder if he got work, hard enough to get work with two legs, but with onny one—!

She slipped through a narrow slit in a brick wall which led into Wyke Entry, the small court where her friends the Fosters lived, and where, in the room above them, had lived the late, but not lamented, Francis Morton.

There was a candle burning in the lower window and she bent to look through. She frowned and rubbed the dirt from the glass with her finger. Maria had always been clean and houseproud, but now the room looked dirty and there were people, men and women, sleeping in heaps all over the floor. Three dogs were tied to a chair leg and one looked up, its lips starting to curl as it saw her.

She pulled back from the window. They must have shifted. Where will they have gone?

Upstairs in the Morton house, she heard a sudden cry and pressed herself against the wall. The window was flung open and a bowl of slops thrown out, splashing onto the floor just beyond her feet. A loud cursing told her that Mrs Morton was alive and well, and in fright Annie dived back through the slit, the smugglers slit, they used to call it, and ran as fast as her feet would carry her away from the court.

I'll go home and see what's doing, she thought, at least to what *was* home. Though how I ever lived in that dirty alley, I don't know. Realization was dawning on her that for the past few months she had lived a life of comparative luxury in Toby's wooden cottage.

But the room which had been hers was now occupied by several Irish families, she could hear the lilt of their voices as they called on each idle beggar to shift themselves and get off to work.

What'll I do? She hugged her cloak around her. The morning was cold and a light drizzle was falling. Everywhere looked grey and dingy. She looked up at the upstairs windows of the buildings. There was no light showing, but then, there wouldn't be, few people in this alley could afford candles or oil for light. They did what they had to do by the dim natural daylight which filtered down through the narrow walls and rooftops, and when that was gone, if they had no fire they sat in the dark or went to bed.

A window above her was raised, and a bucket was emptied down into the alley. The stench of urine and excrement was strong and she put her hand to her mouth and retched. 'Old woman's still there then, she never would wait for muck cart. Poor old lass. What a life, stuck in one room. Annie, get going, there's nowt for you here.

The iron gate to the Seamen's Hospital in the long street of White Friar's Gate, where orphans of seamen lost at sea were given a home, was chained and padlocked. She looked up for the bell and pulled on a rope, she heard it jangling across the yard and inside the building.

A man opened a door to the building and looked out. 'Tha's too early. Come back at six.'

'I – I want to find out about some bairns who were left here. Two lads.'

'Whose lads?' He didn't move from the doorway or

come out into the yard but simply poked his head round the side of the door.

'Er – my sister's lads, Swinburn's the name. She left them here while she went to find work.'

He came out buttoning up his jacket. 'I don't remember that name.'

'Are you sure? She – she asked me to come for them.' She grasped the iron bars of the gate. 'Is there anybody tha can go and ask, Matron or Master?'

She had seen the matron when she had brought them. A formidable woman, she had asked her to sign a form, and Annie hadn't listened to her when she had read it out; she had been in such a turmoil of despair over Francis and his treatment of Lizzie, and she'd blotched the paper as she struggled to sign her name.

'Can't ask Matron, she's busy supervising breakfast, and Master isn't here.' He put his hands in his pockets and jingled some coins. ''Course I could go and look on 'list.'

'Oh, please. Would you?' She gripped the railings and looked through at him. 'They're here, nobody else would have fetched them out.'

He stood and stared at her, then let his gaze drift skywards.

Oh, God. He wants money and I haven't any. She patted her thigh where her money bag would normally be. But she hadn't brought it out with her. She hadn't expected – we thought, Toby and me – we thought that we wouldn't be long down at 'riverside. I didn't need money. And I left my moneybag hidden at the cottage.

'I haven't any money, but I can bring thee some later. Please, go and look at the list. I'm desperate to see my lads.'

He drew himself up. 'Did I ask for money? Did such a question pass my lips? It's more than my job's worth to ask for money!' He started to turn away. 'Tha'll have to come back later after breakfast is finished and cleared away, about half-past-six or seven, Matron might see thee then.'

She fingered the silk scarf around her neck. She'd vowed that she would never sell it, it was given to her in friendship, but she needed to know if the boys were still there. They might not have stayed she worried, young Jimmy might well have decided to run away and Ted would have followed him.

She slipped it from her neck. It had been stained with Toby's blood and she'd washed it in the cabin. The blood was still there, a dark stain on the pale blue; it was creased, but it was soft, soft as the down on Mrs Trott's ducks.

'Here. I'll give thee this if tha'll go and look at 'list. It's real silk. I need to know if they're still here and not run away. I have to get back to my sister, she's sick and wants to know if they're all right. I told her that I'd take care of them.'

He took the neckchief from her and ran it through his fingers. Then he grunted and with a twisted smile handed it back. 'I don't know how tha came by this, and I wouldn't be so bold as to ask, but if I took that home to my missus, she wouldn't believe I hadn't been up to some sort of mischief. Folks like us can't afford goods like that.'

His glance took in her gold-lined cloak and her bare feet. Then he pursed his lips and considered. 'Aye, I reckon it's worse for them as has had plenty, to lose it, than it is for them who's never had owt. Wait here. I'll get 'list.'

She leaned her forehead against the railings and closed her eyes as she waited for him to come back. Please, please let them be here. I'll take them back with me to Hessle, just like Toby said. We'll not have much, but more than we used to have, and I'll be a better mother than I was, now that I'm not so frightened. I'll go hawking and I'll work with the team. I'll do anything.

She looked up, there was a clatter of hooves on the cobbles. A platoon of soldiers were riding down the street and a man in dark clothing riding alongside them. One of the town constables. She drew in a breath and pulled her hood over her face as they drew abreast of her. They must have been chasing a misdoer. And they'd caught him. Running behind the platoon was a young man, no shirt on his back or boots on his feet, and both hands tied to a rope which the last soldier had fastened to his saddle.

He stumbled as he passed Annie and fell his length onto the floor, his arms stretched in front of him, his wrists red and raw from the rope and his chest scratched and bleeding. The soldier reined in. 'Get up,' he ordered. 'No use trying to dawdle.'

The man spat towards him as he clambered to his feet. 'Curse thee militia men, tha's worse than 'press-gang.'

The soldier laughed and jerked the rope, he was no older than the prisoner and was obviously enjoying his power.

'There's nobody of that name listed here, miss. Maybe they're in one of 'other hospitals.' The porter had come silently to the gate and had a paper in his hand. 'I can't make out a name of *Swineburn*. Here, have a look for tha self.'

'Swinburn.' She was trembling as she turned away from the scene behind her.

'Here, – Charlie! Charlie Thompson! I knew they'd catch thee in the end!' The porter shouted and craned his neck to see the prisoner as he was dragged away. He shook his head. 'I knew he'd come to this. Allus looking for trouble he was, never knew when to keep his mouth shut. Well, he'll keep it shut now. It doesn't do to make trouble, it comes fast enough on its own.'

He thrust the paper through the bars. 'Can tha make out if they're there?'

She took it from him and held it in shaking fingers and stared after the platoon as they trotted down the street towards the gaol, the man slipping and sliding in his attempt to keep up. She glanced down at the paper. There were no names beginning with S.

'What has he done?' She pushed the paper back through the bars.

'Who?' The porter frowned. 'What's who done?'

'Him.' She jerked her thumb down the street. 'Charlie Thompson.'

'Stole a horse and then sold it,' he said carelessly. 'His bairns'll be begging in 'streets now. He'll not get off this time. He'll be swinging, will young Charlie.'

She clasped her hands together to stop them trembling. Horse stealing was a capital offence, but it didn't seem right.

'It's not that he ever hurt anybody though, didn't Charlie, he looked after his ma – fed his bairns. Still— .' He shrugged and turned away. 'He'll have to take what's coming. Miss! Shall I tell Matron tha's coming back?'

'I've made a mistake.' She shouted back as she ran. 'I've remembered. They're not here. They're somewhere else.'

'That's right, miss.' His voice grew fainter as she ran, her toes catching on the cobbles. 'They are, I've remembered. They're somewhere else. At least, one of 'em is. I can't speak for the other one.'

She ran, choking and sobbing, unable any longer to keep from her mind the spectre of the young man swinging from the gallows; even the iron bars of the Seaman's hospital seemed to be a threat as she'd clung to them. She turned into an alley and sank to the floor, she wanted to be away from any curious stares of passers-by, or shopkeepers who were now unbolting their doors and taking down wooden shutters.

Her cloak she wrapped around her and she crouched with her arms around her knees into a black ball, trying to ease her trembling. The cloak smelt warm and comforting, an aroma of grass and horse, of wood smoke and the salty smell of the sea, and if she kept her head well down she wouldn't see or smell this stinking alley where she had sought a temporary refuge.

A sharp kick on her leg brought her out of her reverie and she raised her head. Standing in the entrance to the alley was a man, so big and hairy that he blocked out the light and her first fleeting sensation was that it was an escaped bear from a travelling fair.

He kicked her again. 'Who are you? Where's Lottie?'

'I – I'm just going. I was onny resting.'

'Where's Lottie?' he repeated. 'This is her spot.'

'Sorry. I didn't know. I – I haven't seen her – anybody.'

He moved towards her and put down his pack. He had a great bushy beard and a huge nose. 'Well it doesn't matter. Tha'll do just as well, I'm not particular.'

'No. No, you don't understand.' She scrambled to her feet. 'I'm not a street girl.'

He grinned. Most of his teeth were missing and those that were left were black and misshapen. 'I said, I don't mind. Come on, I haven't got all day. I've got a job to go to.' He grabbed her cloak. 'Get that off and thy skirts up.'

Her way out was blocked by his bulk. She couldn't possibly slip past him and neither could she fight him off.

She edged her way round so that she was sideways to him and he moved too so that his back was to the wall.

'How do I know what tha's got to offer?' she asked softly, 'money, or— ,' she gave a cynical smile, 'equipment?'

He raised his hand and she flinched. 'I've had no complaints,' he growled. 'They get what they deserve.'

She took a deep breath and dared. 'Let's see then. Get thy breeches down.'

For a moment she thought he was going to strike her. Then he suddenly opened his gaping toothless mouth and roared with laughter. 'By, lass. Tha's a right one. I'll show thee all right.'

He unbuttoned his breeches and let them fall to his knees. His enormous buttocks were white and fleshy and his monstrous member, distended and syphilis scarred, quivered obscenely towards her. 'What about that, eh?'

She smiled and lifted the hem of her cloak and skirt.

''Best I've ever seen,' she purred and lifted her foot; her bare foot, hard and firm, met its mark and the giant of a man bent double and fell, retching and groaning as he grasped his shrinking penis.

'I'll kill thee,' she heard him gasp as she gathered up her skirts and ran. 'Whore! Bitch! I'll get thee.'

Her decision was made. There was nothing else she could do. She would run to the riverbank, taking the pathway again to Hessle. She'd live in Toby's cottage and become Annie Hope once more. Here she was frightened Annie Swinburn. A woman terrified of every knock on the door. Here there was only poverty, danger and sorrow in front of her. Surely, surely there had to be more to life than that? We've only one life, Annie; wasn't that what Toby had said? Well at least he'd died smiling, which was more than she could hope for if she stayed here.

20

Matt Linton left a small crew on board the *Breeze* in the New Dock and strode across the town towards the Cross Keys Inn in the Market Place. He hadn't docked in Hull for over twelve months and mused that the dock, which had been opened less than thirteen years before, in 1778, was more congested than it had been the previous year, and that it was more difficult to pilot a ship in or out of the entrance than it was to sail across the German Sea to Holland.

Ships from all over the world, from Russia, Sweden and Gothenburg docked in Hull, as well as the barges and small boats which came up the Humber and Trent and other canals and waterways, bringing iron and brass, pottery from Stoke and lead from Derbyshire for onward distribution and shipment. Here too came the whaling fleet, the principal industry of the town from whose by-products issued the stinking aroma floating in the air.

It's a prosperous town, he mused. A man could do well here if he was in the way of commerce or shipping, there have been several fortunes made. But he also knew that many of the men who had made their fortunes here in this thriving town, took their wives and families out of the confines of the town boundaries, which were now stretching further and further into the outlying country and built their homes, their mansions and desirable residences, where they didn't have to have the embarrassment of seeing the other unfortunate populace of the town. Here were the people who had no hope, no fortune, no proper roof over their heads, except perhaps one which they shared with many others, and who behaved so annoyingly in complaining and rioting about injustice.

He glanced up at the portico of Trinity House and felt a thrust of envy. Boys could now be sent to school here to learn the science of navigation as well as being given a good grounding in general education. I wish – still, it's no good wishing, what's done is done, but if only I had been able to attend a school like this, instead of learning the hard way by running away to sea. He had been at the mercy of disreputable seamen who worked him all hours of the day and night, and then gave him the lash for disobedience.

He strode across the Market Place. The vendors were setting out their stalls in front of The Holy Trinity church, and sweeping up the debris of the night before. Rotting vegetables, mouldy fruit and bedding-straw left from the pens of pigs, hens and ducks were swept away into the middle of the street, there to be dispersed by the hooves of horses and donkeys and the tramp of feet from the hordes of townspeople who would shortly descend on them.

'Good to see thee again, Captain. It's been a long time.' The landlord of the inn drew him a tankard of ale. 'Breakfast?'

Matt nodded. 'Please. Eggs, ham, beef, everything you've got. I shan't be eating again today. And I'll also need to hire a horse from you for a few days, maybe a week.'

'That's soon done, sir. I've got a grand fella, just suit thee fine.'

Matt eased off his boots and stretched his toes. 'I'm trying to find out about a seaman who I believe is from this town, and I wondered if you know of him. Name of Hope? I don't know his first name, and in fact I did hear that he'd died, but it may well have been a rumour.'

The landlord pursed his lips. 'I know most of 'seamen from this town, but I can't say I know that name.'

Matt took a long draught from the tankard and wiped

his mouth with the back of his hand. 'He has a wife I believe, er – Annie, I think she's called.'

'Bless thee, sir. They don't bring their wives in here, not if I can help it, and not that they want to. No, I'm sorry but I can't help thee there. Now if tha'll excuse me, I'll just go and see to breakfast.'

A hearty slap on Matt's back made him splutter into his ale. He stood up and put out his hand when he saw Gregory Sheppard, captain of the ship *Maiden*, standing in front of him, a smoking pipe in his mouth which even a wide smile couldn't dislodge.

'Good to see you, Greg. Have some breakfast.'

'Aye, I will. I'm famished. I've had nothing but dry tack for the last three days. The *Maiden*'s been beset with problems since we left home port and I must have a quick turn around.' He bent his head to whisper. 'I've got a good shipment promised for next week. You could do well to get back to Holland.' He raised his head and spoke normally. 'I didn't see you this trip, where were you?'

Matt rubbed his eyes, he was suddenly very weary and depressed. The loss of Toby was just beginning to hit him. 'I didn't manage to get there. I too had problems.'

Greg Sheppard nodded and took his pipe out of his mouth. 'And who's this dead seaman that you're looking for?'

Matt started. He'd just been thinking about Toby, seeing again the body wrapped in sailcloth shooting down below the waves, but not identifying it with his own brother.

'I heard you,' Greg persisted, 'as I came through the door.' He too took off his boots and stretched his feet onto the table. He gave a sly grin. 'Or is it his widow that you're looking for?'

Matt frowned, he hadn't realized he'd been overheard. Greg would think it great sport to be chasing a comely widow, as he too might have done under different circumstances. They had both done considerable carousing and chasing of agreeable willing females. But Annie Hope is not a comely young widow, he told himself, she is not comely by any means, she is skinny and underfed, anyone can see that by those high cheekbones and enormous eyes, and as for being a widow. 'Pah.' He gave an exclamation, she's probably lying.

'What? Come on, tell. Who is she?'

'She's nobody. Mrs Hope, she calls herself. She's just someone my brother knows – knew. Knows. Someone my brother knows.'

Greg put his pipe back in his mouth and sucked thoughtfully. 'And how is your little brother? Getting into trouble with other men's wives is he?'

Matt hesitated. Greg had been a good friend for a lot of years but he didn't want to tell him of Toby. Not yet. Not until he'd broken the news to his father. Nor did he want the news to get to the revenue men, and it could if Greg or his men should get caught, which they would sooner or later, for Greg was a hard man who took far more risks than he did himself, his fast rakish schooner was badly scarred from the frequent gun battles with the revenue men.

'He's away – gone out of the area for a bit.'

Greg's grin widened. 'And left the little filly alone? So while the coast is clear,—?'

The landlord brought in a tray of food before Matt could reply. A dish of eggs and fatty bacon was set in front of them, and slices of roast beef, chicken legs and boiled onions and a crusty pigeon pie were placed on a table near at hand.

They ate hungrily, dipping thick chunks of bread into the egg yolks and mopping up the fat from their platters. The landlord brought more ale in a jug but Matt shook his head. 'I'll never get on the horse, let alone stay in the saddle if I have more. You draw a grand brew, landlord.'

He pushed his chair back from the table when he'd finished and reached for his boots. 'That'll last me the day. I'll have to be on my way. I'm visiting my father.'

Greg whistled. 'I thought you never saw him?'

'Sometimes I do. Not often. But I have to deliver a message to him.'

'And the little widow? When are you going to see her?'

Matt shrugged and leaned on the table. Greg was still trenching, his teeth around a chicken leg, grease running down his chin. 'You're on the wrong tack. It's not what you think. I have no interest in the woman, apart from finding out if she is who she says she is. I only know that she told Toby that she was a widow, that her husband had died at sea. She's not the type of woman I'd go for. You know me.' He surveyed his friend seriously. 'I like them sweet-faced and agreeable. This one's from the gutter and acts like she's a princess. She's impudent and opinionated. She gives herself airs and has an accent you could cut with a knife. She annoys me to *Hell*. She's got under my skin and I just want to prove that she's the liar I know she is.'

Greg picked a piece of chicken from his teeth. 'Who do you want to prove it to? Your brother? Or yourself?'

Matt turned to go, heading for the side door which led out to the yard.

'And when you've proved it,' Greg shouted after him. 'What then?'

He didn't answer. He thought of when he'd impulsively kissed her. What a fool he'd been. What on earth had possessed him? He felt anger burning inside him. And she'd spurned him. Pushed him away as if he was some callow youth trying out his manhood. He felt a pain in his chest as the greasy food fought its way down into his stomach. He shouldn't have eaten so much or so quickly.

He turned at the door. 'Why then I can see the look on her face when I tell her that she's found out – that she's not who she says she is. She's probably got some poor cuckold of a husband with half a dozen children waiting for her at home.'

His face tightened as he thought of the possibility of his flippant remark being true and Greg smiled and reached over for more pie.

'I'm sorry for you, old fellow.' Greg belched. 'Really sorry. This woman's got you well and truly scuppered.'

'Hogwash. You don't know what you're talking about.' Matt eyed him angrily. 'And ease up on the ale, captain. You're half seas over already. You'll never get your ship out of harbour.'

Greg put his head back and guffawed. 'Farewell old shipmate. You're off course and drifting. It happens to the best of men, but I never thought it would happen to you.' He gazed down into his tankard and hiccupped. Then he waved it towards Matt standing frozen faced in the doorway. 'Let's drink to the little widow – to Mrs Hope; *wherever* she may be, and *whoever* she may be.'

*　　*　　*

It was twelve months since he had been on horseback and two years since he had seen his father. He paid the landlord for the food and the hire and rode out of the yard. He hesitated for a moment before deciding on a route; some of the roads were in a perilous state especially in bad weather, though there were more turnpikes being opened every year which made it easier for a long journey. But today only a light grey drizzle was falling and he knew that by the time he reached the Wolds the weather would have changed.

He decided to ride via the Spring Dyke, a pleasant track where the clear water alongside was now being channelled into Hull, and then onto the village of Anlaby before starting the gentle climb up into the lower reaches of the Wolds. He was loath to take the route by the river towards Hessle in case, by chance, Mrs Hope should cut short her visit to Hull and decide to go back to Toby's cottage and so meet him on the road. Blasted woman, he thought. I'd be obliged to offer her a ride, and the thought of her being up on the saddle behind him made him very uneasy.

Besides, I might well meet up with Bernard Roxton if he's still sniffing around the riverbank, and it would take a lot of effort for me not to throttle him with my bare hands. He still blamed the revenue man for Toby's death and not the unknown soldier.

A two hour ride brought him up to the hamlet of Riplingham where he followed an old watercourse to reach the summit of the dale. He dismounted and let his horse graze while he stretched his legs and surveyed the view. Below him, almost lost in the distance lay the towns of Beverley and Hull and the gleam of the Humber, and in the land between, a rolling multi-shaded landscape of pale spring green and dark woods, lit now by a midday sun.

He swallowed hard. How he loved this countryside. He had been contrary, he knew, in defying his father who wanted him to stay at home and help him run the estate. But as a young man nothing could have been more unacceptable than the thought of staying with a man he considered no more than a petty tyrant, who had no regard for his servants or even his wife's and children's desires.

Just a vast sheep walk, he thought as he stood looking down, that's what it was, nothing more. And I wanted to see the world. If only he had agreed to my going, just for a short time – I would have come back – I surely would have come back. This is my heritage after all, so why didn't he listen? And then, he wouldn't have lost Toby either. He should have known that Toby wouldn't stay without me.

But now as he looked down he saw that changes were taking place. Land was being enclosed, hedges were planted, pasture was being ploughed and cereal crops being sown in its place and the face of the Wolds was changing. Plantations of new trees were growing and copses of young larch were showing the first tips of green needles and high above him he heard the song of skylarks.

He dropped down into the next valley and rode for another half hour, taking tracks framed by hawthorn trees, still green and without their mantle of white May flowers whose perfume used to fill him with delight. Banks of young nettles and cow parsley were pushing their way through an undergrowth of ground ivy, and as he cantered, crushing them beneath heavy hooves and leaping a fast running stream, he came into the dale where his father lived, and which once had been his home.

Well, at least Mrs Rogerson is pleased to see me. He paced the drawing-room where the housekeeper had ushered him. She seemed to be at a loss to know where to put him, there was no fire in here or the library and though the room was clean and elegant with vestiges of his mother's hand still lingering in the choice of furniture, carpets and hangings, the house had a desolate unlived-in air, no books or flowers or cards on the mantelpiece, no music on the pianoforte, therefore presumably no visitors for his father to entertain.

'So, you come at last, sir.' His father made no concession of welcome. A big man, dark as Toby had been, and still handsome despite the glower on his face and the deep red veins around his nose; he simply came into the room and sat in a chair and stared at Matt. No handshake, or pat on the back to welcome home his eldest son.

Perhaps I deserve it. Matt gave a small stiff bow. It has been a long time.

'How are you, father?' He doesn't look well, he thought. He's not yet fifty, yet looks ten years older.

'I'm as well as can be with all the work I have to do. It's not easy at my age, running this place on my own.'

'What happened to the steward you had last time I came? He seemed a good man.'

'Pah. He was full of hot air and new-found nonsense. Wanting to do this, that and the other. I had to get rid of him. I've only got Jed Harris and he's not much good,

215

though better than nobody I suppose. At least he does what I tell him and doesn't argue.'

'Farmers are enclosing their land, father, it's more economical. Perhaps you should consider doing the same.'

'Pah. That's what the other fellow said. He went over to Sledmere. He'd the cheek to tell me that they're more enlightened over there. Imagine. Telling *me*! And this family has been here for generations!'

'Perhaps it's time for change. Cereal crops are needed, the population is expanding, commerce is—'

'What would you know about it?' His father bellowed at him from the depths of his chair. 'What would you know when you spend your time between one harbour tavern and another? You know nothing. You're not even a proper seaman. You've not got a bit of gold braid to your name.'

Matt clenched his teeth. This is what had happened last time. He'd come in good faith and they'd finished up having a terrific argument and he'd stormed out of the house vowing he'd never come back again. He took a deep breath. 'I'm master of my own ship. I have a good crew who obey me. I care nothing for a piece of fancy ribbon.'

He glanced around the room. On a small table by the window was a half full decanter and a small silver tray set with brandy glasses.

'May I pour us a brandy, sir?'

'It's a bit early in the day, isn't it?' his father grunted.

Matt hid a wry smile and looked at the ornate French clock on the mantelpiece. He'd never known his father keep to a strict timetable when a glass of brandy was offered. 'I think you're going to need it, sir, and I certainly do. I have some bad news for you.'

His father motioned impatiently towards the table and Matt took off the stopper from the decanter and sniffed the aroma of the golden liquid, then poured a generous measure into two glasses. He gave one to his father and then sat down opposite him.

He took a sip and then with a deep sigh looked across at him. He was startled to see his father gazing steadily at him, his eyes unveiled and beseeching. It was for a second only, then the blue eyes took on their usual cold hardness.

'Well! What is it? What news? Have you sunk your ship and want some money for another?'

'Drink your brandy, father. It's about Toby.'

There was a measure of uncertainty as his father lifted his glass, but he took a sip and growled. 'What about him? What's he been up to? Getting into mischief? I always told your mother she ruined that boy.'

'He's dead, father.'

Matt wished that there could have been some other means of breaking the news. Three simple words seemed somehow stark and cruel to tell of the ending of a life, especially when that life was still unfledged. He watched his father's face from over the rim of his glass as he took a deep draught to steady his own nerves and finished off his brandy.

His father's face seemed to crumple and suddenly grow old and his hand shook as he put his unfinished drink on the table beside his chair. 'How?' His voice cracked and he cleared his throat. 'How did he die?'

Matt took a deep breath and prepared to lie. 'He decided to come with me on a voyage. He said he needed some sea air. But he caught a fever, and – you know how quickly these things catch hold, – we did what we could for him, but it was no use.'

'And you've brought him back? He can lie with his mother?'

'No, sir. You know how virulent these fevers are. I daren't risk it. The men—,' he stumbled over his words and he fought back tears. 'You know the procedure, sir, I don't have to explain?'

His father shook his head. 'No, no, of course not.'

Matt blew his nose. 'We gave him a decent sea burial. It seemed fitting. I have a former parson on board, he said a few words, and I as captain, did the same. He's resting peacefully.'

There was a knock on the door and the housekeeper entered. 'Begging your pardon sir,' she addressed Mr Linton. 'I've taken the liberty of lighting a fire in the dining-room and prepared a light supper.' She turned enquiringly to Matt but addressed her question to her employer. 'And I wondered if Master Matthias will be staying the night? I'll need to air the bed.'

'Yes. Yes. He'll be staying. Won't you?' He looked up suddenly and Matt saw again the appeal in his eyes.

He nodded. 'I can stay a couple of days, then I must get back to my ship.' He followed Mrs Rogerson out of the room, ostensibly to wash before supper.

'I'll light the fire in your old room, sir,' she said, 'and put a brick in the bed whilst you're at supper.'

He stopped her. 'Mrs Rogerson. I'm the bringer of bad news, I'm afraid.' Her face crumpled as he told her. Toby had been everyone's favourite. His mother's, Agnes Trott; all the other servants and they had had many in his mother's day, they all fussed and spoiled the merry, laughing boy.

But no-one was allowed to spoil me, he thought bitterly as he climbed the stairs to his room, leaving Mrs Rogerson weeping her way back to the kitchen. I was but a child and not even my mother was allowed to hug me. It will make him weak, his father had said, and he must grow up to be hard and strong, my eldest son, not a namby-pamby weakling. One day he'll take over from me and have to make hard decisions, he'll have tenants and staff to deal with.

He gazed at his reflection in the oak-framed mirror that stood on the table in his old room. A tall, fair-haired, weather-tanned man gazed back at him, where once had been a boy. 'But I paid you back, didn't I father?' he muttered. 'I paid you back for depriving me of love and affection from everyone but Toby, he was the only one who cared, or dared to care. Everyone else, including my mother was too frightened to defy you.'

He laughed softly at his reflection, and with a start, saw for a second, his brother's smile on his own lips, that slight gap between his front teeth, which everyone said meant happiness.

'But I defied you. I scotched your plans. I upped and ran, and in running took away your selfish dreams.'

21

Annie kept her emotions firmly locked away until she reached Hessle. She first of all went to see the Trotts and found Mrs Trott tight-lipped and silent and Henry Trott bereft with grief. 'What a waste,' he kept repeating. 'What a waste.'

Then Annie, too, gave way to her grief as she reached Toby's cottage door. She lay down on his bed and stayed there most of the next day, weeping and sobbing, not just for Toby, but for her lost children and for herself.

Finally she got up and opened the door and looked out. The river was glinting and she could hear the chattering of finches and the trill of song thrushes. She traced her fingers over her swollen face and through her tangled hair and ran down the meadow and along the track down to the river. The shingle was sharp beneath her toes as she neared the water's edge and the water cold as she waded in.

When it reached her waist and the buoyancy lifted her feet from the bottom, she took a deep breath and ducked. She gasped as she emerged, the water streaming from her hair, and ducked again. Then re-emerging she took a huge breath of air and turned back towards the bank. A ducking was always a good way of bringing anyone to their senses, that's why the ducking stool at the riverside in Hull had always been so popular, though why, she wondered as she sploshed her way back to the cottage, it was only used for women, she couldn't imagine, there were plenty of men she would gladly tie on and duck.

'Mrs Hope! Tha's had an accident.' Josh stood on the path, his grimy face creased with anxiety and his hands white with dust from the quarry.

'No. No accident.' She didn't feel inclined to explain, especially not now when the wetness of her clothes was beginning to make her shiver.

'I was coming to see thee. I heard tha was back. We wondered if tha was staying? Robin was asking and the team are bothered that their supply'll dry up, now that – you know.'

'Come with me, Josh. I've things to talk to you about, but I'd like to get into something dry first.'

He followed her up the path and through the undergrowth to reach the meadow and she knew from the fact that he didn't question her that he knew the way. There wasn't any path or track in this area that Josh didn't know of. He waited outside, lounging on the grass in the deepening dusk, while she changed into a dry skirt and shirt, and then she joined him, sitting on the grass beside him. It smelled good here. She could smell the river in her hair, but she could also smell the grass which they crushed beneath them and the sweetness of the yellow flowers which nestled beneath the hedge bottom. There were no foul smells here, even the chalk on Josh's clothes had a clean, soft, earthy aroma.

'Captain Linton has asked me if I'll take over the running. I suggested that you might want to as you've more experience,' she added, not wanting to offend him. 'But he seemed to think you'd be better as a sort of team leader.'

'Oh,' he interrupted her. 'I've no head for figures, Mrs Hope, and I couldn't bargain with 'toffs and landlords and such like, besides I'd be better as a go-between, 'men trust me tha sees.'

He chewed on his lip. 'But, I'm not sure as they'd like to be run by a woman, they wouldn't expect that she could do it, and what's more they'd be a bit aggrieved if they thought that somebody like—,' he flushed, 'beggin' tha pardon, Mrs Hope, but they wouldn't expect that somebody like thee'd be able to read and write better than them.'

'I know, Josh. Don't apologize. I know I'm no lady, and even some real ladies can't read.' She drew herself up and smiled. 'But I can. And I can write. I'm not very good yet, but I will be,' she said with a determined set of her chin. 'I wonder if—?' An idea started to form. 'Do you think—?'

'What?' He peered into her face.

'Well the men haven't seen me yet. Not properly.'

'They've seen thy bare feet,' he grinned. 'And thy ankles as tha climbed jack ladder.'

'But they've not seen my face.' She smiled. These men of Hessle should go to Hull if they want to see bare feet, there are plenty of women there who can't afford boots. 'I've kept my face covered with my hood.'

'I don't know what tha's driving at, Mrs Hope. They still won't want a woman as master, if tha sees what I mean – no matter how she looks. They'll say it's not right.'

'All right.' She got up from the grass. 'We'll give them a master. Somebody with breeches and boots. They'll only see him at night, and as nobody has a name but only a number, they'll be none the wiser.'

Josh gaped up at her nonplussed, then as comprehension filtered through, he scrambled to his feet. 'Tha's not suggesting—?'

'Aye. I am. And if we can fool the team, we can also fool Mr Revenue Roxton. He'll be looking for Toby and won't be able to find him.' Her face saddened. 'Not ever. And the other man,' she waved her arms in the air, 'will simply disappear.'

Josh started to grin, his smile getting wider and wider. 'What a ruse,' he laughed. 'I wasn't too sure at first, it didn't seem right, but, oh.' He kicked a tuft of grass. 'What the heck. Let's do it.'

After he'd gone she went inside and lighting the lamp took a fresh look around. Toby's other boots were lined up against the wall and she knew he had more breeches in the chests. Tomorrow I'll sort through and find something to fit, and also look to see if there's anything to sell, any linens or cottons and such, 'cos if there isn't, well, I don't know where Toby got them from. That's one thing he didn't tell me.

Take what you need, he'd said, if anything should happen to me, and make a new life. It's almost as if he knew. But I can't take it without asking Matt first. This is his by rights. But if there's nothing to sell, then me and Robin are going to be on our beam ends again come summer. Poor Robin. He doesn't even have a stake in the run goods. Something will have to be done.

*　　*　　*

When Matt knocked on the door the next morning and immediately opened it, she was startled, she hadn't expected him back until the next day. She was sitting on the floor next to a half-empty trunk, its contents scattered around her. She flushed and hoped that he didn't think that she was taking what didn't belong to her.

'There are lengths of linen and muslin here which I think Toby intended for selling,' she explained, 'and over here,' she reached over to a separate pile. 'This is silk, I'm sure of it.' She picked up a length of deep blue and handed it to him and flinched as his hand brushed hers.

He ran it through his fingers. 'Yes. It was a special consignment. There should have been more on the last trip but there was a scare on in Holland and we weren't able to ship it.'

'What do you want me to do with it?'

He stared down at her. 'What?'

She gazed back. His eyes were so blue. They were as blue as the sky on a summer's day and she felt as if her spine was melting, as if the heat from that same sky was beating down on her.

'What do I do with it?' she repeated huskily. 'Shall Robin and me sell it for you?'

He shook his head as if waking from a sleep. 'Erm.

It's nothing to do with me. I've been paid already. It was Toby's.'

'Toby said – he said, if anything should happen to him, then I had to take what I needed and use it to start a new life.'

'Then take it,' he said coldly. 'If that's what you want. But it won't last you long. What will you do when the money you get from it is spent?'

'No, you don't understand. I meant for Robin and me to take it up into the Wolds, like we did before, only we'll sell it for you instead of Toby.'

'I don't need to be in this kind of business. I'm a seaman. Not a draper.'

She started to get angry. 'But I need to earn money in the summer, when your ship isn't coming in with goods.' Toby had told her that there were very few runs during the summer months when the evenings were light and the possibility of being seen and caught by the customs men was inevitable. 'Where did Toby buy this stuff?'

'I've no idea. Absolutely none. Some merchant from Leeds or such place I imagine.' His tone was sharp and abrupt. 'You'll have to find out for yourself, I can't help you.'

'I'm not asking thee to help me,' she snapped. 'I asked a simple question.'

'And I'm asking you one,' he retorted. 'I haven't got all day to stand around arguing, I've a ship waiting for me. Do you want to run this operation or not? Or are you going to play at shopkeepers?'

She got to her feet and faced him. His eyes were flashing angrily and his mouth was tense.

'Then if you're in such a hurry what's keeping you?' Her own blue eyes locked antagonistically into his, her voice low and scathing. 'Yes. I'll do the running and I'll do the selling up on 'Wolds, one way or another I'll find out where Toby bought this stuff – without thy help, Captain Linton.'

He nodded abruptly and turned to go. 'I'll see you

in about ten days then. Post a lookout as usual. You'll find that Toby keeps a book somewhere, it has numbers in it, but no names. Josh knows which man has which number.'

She put her hand to her head. 'Wait. Wait.'

He looked up, his expression was glacial, though his mouth turned down petulantly.

'We have to do this properly,' she pleaded. 'If we're to be partners we have to be organized. We have to talk to each other, or else it won't work and somebody will get caught. I'm sorry I haven't thought it all through yet, but I wasn't expecting you until tomorrow.'

He sat down as if weary. 'I'm back earlier than I thought. I – I wanted to get back to the *Breeze*. I'm listening,' he gazed into her face. 'Please, continue.'

It was harder than she expected it to be, explaining what she had in mind and how she would organize the men, harder because he kept his eyes on her the whole time. He didn't look away, not into the fire or up at the ceiling and even when she got up to cut them some bread and cheese and pour a cup of milk, she felt his eyes following her.

He's going to say summat scornful when I've finished, she thought. He's going to tell me that none of it will work, that I'm just a stupid woman who's getting above herself. Well, I'll show him, just give me 'chance.

The only shadow of a smile which came to his face was when she told him that she was going to dress in Toby's breeches and boots because Josh had said the team wouldn't accept the leadership of a woman.

When finally she finished talking he got up to go. 'That's fine,' he said briskly. 'I'm sure you've covered everything. And that's a clever touch to dress like a man. Or, a youth at least,' he added whimsically. 'You haven't the shape for a man.'

He immediately realized his error. 'I beg your pardon. I didn't mean to be impertinent.'

She smiled icily. 'Nor to flatter, if I remember correctly.

Don't be embarrassed Captain, I've been insulted many times and a slip of the tongue doesn't bother me one bit.'

'I didn't mean to insult you.' He walked across to the door and paused. 'It seems we're doomed to misunderstand each other. It's just as well we shan't meet too often.' He gave her a civil curt bow and was gone.

*   *   *

It was barely a week later that she had the opportunity to try out part of her plan. She had the door open catching the last of the daylight when she heard a man's cough.

'It's onny me, Mrs Hope.' Josh called to her. 'I hope tha doesn't mind me coming up uninvited, but I wasn't sure what to do.'

She stood in the doorway and greeted him warmly. She hadn't seen a soul since Matt had left and had spent her time morosely sorting out the linens and cottons which she hoped she and Robin would be able to sell. The silks she had repacked, knowing full well that they wouldn't be wanted by the wives of the Wolds. Now she had just one more box to empty.

'It's just that there's a fellow, name of Moses, asking for Master Toby over at 'Admiral Hawke. Landlord forestalled him and sent for me. What shall we tell him?'

'What does he want?'

'I don't rightly know. But landlord says he's got a couple of boxes with him and Robin seems to think that Master Toby dealt with somebody called Moses. He says he once heard him mention his name.'

'Oh.' She clapped her hands to her mouth. 'Maybe he's the one who sells the cloth. Wait for me. I'll get ready now and go and meet him.'

She dashed indoors to brush her hair and get her cloak, then slowly turned back to the door. Josh must have had the same thought for he stood in the doorway staring at her.

226

'He won't talk to me, will he Josh? He won't deal with a woman?'

Josh shook his head. 'And it's no use asking Robin. He's a great talker, but he's nobbut a bairn when it comes to business.'

'So am I, Josh, but we both have to start sometime, so we'll collect him on the way. How have you come? Have you walked?'

He looked abashed. 'I came on Sorrel. I was going to ask thee what we should do with him? Maybe Captain Linton would like him for when he's here.'

'Never mind that now.' She spoke quickly. 'Wait here for me. I'll be as quick as I can.'

She pulled on the breeches and tucked her shirt inside, then on second thoughts pulled it out and left it loose. Though her breasts were not large they were firm and rounded and any man would be sure to notice. Toby's grey coat was still hanging over a chair, he'd worn his black one the last time, she thought sadly, so that he wouldn't be seen. She slipped it on and fastened it and searched for a piece of black ribbon for her hair which she tied back and tucked inside the coat collar. Then she padded the toes of his boots and pulled them on.

'Sorry to keep you, Josh.' She tried to keep her voice low and to stop the laughter from bubbling out as she watched his awestruck expression.

'By! Well I never! I'd never have thought! Tha looks grand, Mrs Hope. I mean – what am I to call thee?'

'I'll have to keep to Hope. It'll get confusing otherwise. But I'll introduce myself as Toby's partner and try not to mention a name.' She giggled and her laughter started to flow so fast that her nose wrinkled and she opened her mouth wide and hooted. 'You can call me sir, if you like!'

Josh bent double as he laughed and laughed. 'Very good, sir. If that's what tha wants, sir.' He wiped his eyes. 'We'd better get going or we'll find yon chap's got tired of waiting and has cleared off.'

They ran down the meadow and collected Sorrel, then Josh put out his hands for her to step into and mount. Then he took a step back and with an agile spring launched himself behind her.

'I'll drop you to collect Robin and then come as fast as you can, won't you?' she said as they cantered towards Hessle. She was beginning to enjoy herself, tasting a freedom that came with the clothes she was wearing. I don't feel like a pitiful weak-minded woman. Nor yet do I feel like a man. I just feel like – like me!

'Take 'horse into 'yard at 'back of 'Admiral' Josh said as he slipped down from Sorrel's back. 'Groom there knows him, he'll see to him.'

Her heart pounded as she trotted into the yard and dismounted. Remember you're a man, she kept reminding herself. Keep your voice low.

The groom took the reins from her and gave her no more than a cursory glance as he touched his forehead and led Sorrel away. Then she stopped in her tracks as she heard him call.

'Other door, sir. That one leads to 'kitchen.'

She heaved a sigh of relief and nodded her thanks and went in search of Mr Moses.

'Sorry to keep you, Moses.' The landlord had pointed him out and she strode to where he was seated alone at a table. The room was dim, not all the lamps yet lit. She extended her hand and shook his firmly. Her hands were small and she kept her grip as tight as she could. But Mr Moses was a small man too with a flaccid handshake and as she released his hand he rubbed his together. 'My man had difficulty finding me,' she continued. 'I'm pretty busy just now as I'm dealing with Mr Linton's business.'

'But where is Mr Linton? Nobody seems to know, or if they do, they're not telling.' He leaned towards her, his dark eyes gleaming. 'He's not in trouble with the law is he? For if he is, then I can't deal with him. My company has to be very careful.'

'Good heavens! Mr Linton? You obviously don't know him well or you wouldn't ask.' She bristled indignantly.

'Oh, but I do sir,' he spluttered. 'We've been dealing amicably for nearly two years now, and he's always a gentleman I must say.' He leant forward confidentially. 'Not the sort that I usually deal with, I can tell you. But you can tell quality, I always say.'

She backed away. She didn't really want him staring too closely into her face. The landlord brought her ale as she'd requested, she lifted the large pewter tankard with two hands and took a long draught. Things were going quite well so far but she wished that Josh and Robin would hurry up, she could do with some support.

Other men came into the room and sat at the table next to them and lit their pipes but did no more than glance in their direction. They were probably used to salesmen and travellers coming in to the inn, she thought. Hessle was on a direct route to and from Lincoln via the ferry and travellers from York and London would be regular visitors.

She called the landlord over. 'Do you have a room we can use, just for a half hour or so? Mr Moses here has some cloth for me to look at and we need some space.'

Moses looked startled for a moment but then followed her as she marched after the landlord.

'But – erm, I never said that I'd—,' he began as he sat down in the small dark room where they had been ushered. 'Do I understand that you're acting for Mr Linton, Mr er—?'

'Hope,' she said briskly. 'I'm Linton's cousin. I've recently joined him. He's told me all about you. From Leeds aren't you?'

She held her breath for a moment, then exhaled softly as he nodded. 'Aye, Cartwright of Leeds. Foremost cloth merchants in the West Riding. We can get you the best deal you want.'

The landlord brought in another lamp and placed it on the table. 'Well, Moses, it's like this,' she said, moving it nearer to him so that her own face was in shadow. 'Mr Linton isn't available at the moment and I don't have the authority to spend as much as I would want, but I do want cloth. I have several customers up on the Wolds who are crying out for good hard-wearing stuff at a reasonable price, as well as some of your better cloth. So let's see what you've got.'

Moses hesitated for a moment only, then excusing himself went up to his room to bring down his samples.

She leaned back in her chair and gasped. He hadn't noticed a thing, no doubt at all, he had just accepted that she was who she appeared to be.

The door opened and Robin put his head round. 'Oh. Beg tha pardon, sir,' he muttered. 'I was looking for somebody.' He touched his forehead and backed away.

'Robin!' she hissed. 'It's me!'

He looked round the door again, his eyebrows drawn together, a frown puckering his forehead. 'Beg pardon. Did tha speak, sir.'

'It's me, you idiot,' she whispered hoarsely. 'Come in quick and shut the door.'

Robin stood open-mouthed staring at her, then he gasped. 'Josh said as how I might not know thee, Annie. But I never thought—!'

'Ssh. Moses will be back in a minute. Say as little as possible and call me sir. Whatever you do don't call me Annie!'

He grinned. 'No, sir. I'll try not to. What a lark, eh, sir? What a lark.'

She introduced Robin as a junior partner, and explained that they were trying to build up a separate business from Mr Linton's. With his approval, she added. They could only buy a small quantity of goods, she said, and that Mr Moses would have to let them have it on trust.

'But I don't do business that way,' he objected. 'It's got to be cash until we know you, then we can negotiate credit.'

She shook her head. 'But you know Mr Linton, he

won't let you down. A gentleman, I believe you said. Let me have what you've shown me tonight. I'll take it off your hands and have the money for you by the time you come again. Then,' she said persuasively. 'I'll order some of your better cloth – only with this year's designs.'

She saw him hesitate. She was fairly sure that he was showing her last year's patterns and samples, some of it she recognized as being similar to that she had sold to Mrs Corner and the other wives on her last visit to the Wolds.

'You drive a hard bargain, sir,' he said sitting back and folding his arms. 'Harder than Mr Linton did. He always paid for his goods before he got them. But I'm prepared to take a chance, you're young but enthusiastic and I approve of that, so if you'll take all the samples I've got here,' he pointed to the box on the floor. 'I'll give you a good deal.'

'Done.' Annie stood up and put out her hand. 'Let's shake on it as gentlemen.'

22

She insisted that Robin went straight away to the Wolds. 'Sell what you can,' she told him. 'Stay until everything's gone. Visit Mrs Corner and find out the name of her relatives and where they live and visit them. And go to the Sutcliff's, she'd added with a smile. They'll be glad to see you, and tell them I'll be along when I can.'

The *Breeze* was due at any time, so she couldn't go herself. But there would be plenty of opportunities soon for spring was well under way and summer only just around the corner, and then the *Breeze* wouldn't be coming with any goods for them. Captain Linton will be busy with his coastal trade, she mused. I won't have to put up with his surly, argumentative manner. But although she told herself that she would be glad to see the back of him, she knew that their quarrelsome banter exhilarated and excited her, making her feel mettlesome and full of vigour.

Josh came to tell her that the ship had been sighted on the river and would be at the designated place by midnight. She changed into Toby's breeches and boots and rolled her cloak into a bundle and tied it to Sorrel's saddle. She'd decided to keep the horse in the meadow during the summer and would use him for her journeys into Hessle to meet Moses, and also to reconnoitre the dropping places on the river bank.

'Just you and me in this boat, Josh. I can row almost as well as any man, and I'd rather the men didn't see me too closely.'

They saw the signal from the *Breeze* and set off and Annie climbed the ladder, musing that it was easier in breeches than in a skirt, though she preferred her bare feet to boots.

Matt stiffened and moved forward as if to help as she climbed over the bulwark, but he stepped back again and none of the crew moved to help her as they'd done previously, when their hands had been eager to assist her.

She followed him below decks to his cabin where they would discuss the cargo and the dates for the next run. She handed him a wad of money in payment of the last ill-fated consignment. 'Well, Captain. You recognized me. You weren't fooled, I could tell. Why was that? Your men didn't know me.'

He stared at her and she felt herself grow hot under his scrutiny. She took off her jacket and hung it over a chair. The sooner they got the discussion of the run over with, the better, then she could go back to shore.

'You warned me, if you remember,' he said stiffly. 'You said that you were going to dress in Toby's clothes.'

There was an agitation about him that she couldn't quite fathom, a look of intensity in his eyes as if he was trying to hide something, some passion. She gave an exclamation. 'Oh. I'm sorry.' Impulsively she reached out and touched his arm and he started and drew back. 'I'm sorry. I didn't think. It was cruel of me.'

'What are you talking about.' His voice was a hoarse whisper. 'What game are you playing now?'

Sudden tears came to her eyes. His words were like a slap in the face. How insulting he was, when she was trying to make amends. She blinked. 'No game. I thought you were upset because I was wearing Toby's clothes. I thought I reminded you of him.'

He gave a sudden laugh. 'How just like a woman. Just the sort of thing a woman would think of. No, Mrs Hope, you don't remind me of Toby one bit. Nothing like him. As if dressing in a few old clothes could make you look like him.' He laughed again, amusement lighting up his face and she longed to hit him, to wipe the smile off his face.

'Never,' he crowed. 'Never, never, never!'

*   *   *

Three more runs and they decided to finish for the summer. It was now too risky on the river-bank and though the soldiers were not seen, Roxton was: he and two other men were constantly in Hessle, asking questions but not getting answers. One night Annie had had a fright when he stepped in front of Sorrel as she was cantering home, the horse had reared, almost unseating her and she was relieved that she wasn't carrying any goods, that Josh had taken a donkey-and-cart and loaded it and gone along another road. She had gathered her long cloak about her for she was wearing breeches, and on impulse had loosened her hair and removed her boots and strapped them to the saddle in a bundle in front of her, her feet were bare in the stirrups.

'Ah. The barefoot lady,' Roxton had sneered, holding on to the horse's snaffle. 'No use asking if you've seen anyone acting suspiciously? No? Of course not.'

'Let me pass,' she'd said curtly. 'You've no cause to detain me.'

'No, I haven't.' He released his hand and stared up at her from within the shadow of the trees; she could barely see his face for the rim of his hat and she hoped he couldn't see hers. 'But one day I will have. Both you and your lover.'

She'd laughed aloud at him and slapping Sorrel on the flank she'd cantered away, almost knocking him over.

The evenings were light and the days hot and long, and Annie and Robin packed their bags with Mr Moses' new cloth that he was now happy to supply – for Robin had sold all the other samples – and went off to the sweet chalk pastureland of the Wolds, where the air was filled with birdsong; yellowhammers called and willow warblers and whitethroats sang their tiny hearts out, and beneath the huge summer moon the air was heavy with the perfume of honeysuckle and bluebells and the fragrance of meadow grass and wild thyme, and thousands of cowslips lay like a carpet of gold.

And while Annie breathed in a beauty that she had never before imagined, Matt sailed between Holland and England with his authorized merchandise on which duty was paid; and met with the fishermen off the coast of Scarborough and Whitby, who were happy to relieve him of a considerable amount of brandy and geneva on which it was not, and Bernard Roxton went back empty-handed to the port of Hull.

*   *   *

When autumn came and Matt sailed again up the Humber, the *Breeze* laden with a cargo of duty free brandy, tea and tobacco, he could scarcely contain the turmoil inside him. He had passed the foreshore of Hessle several times as he'd sailed towards the Trent and Ouse taking legitimate goods towards their onward destination of the Midlands, and had looked in the direction of his brother's cottage, searching for woodsmoke or some other sign that she was there, but there was none and he guessed that she had gone off to the Wolds.

Blasted woman. Why she's just a hawker, nothing more. That's all she's fit for, selling a few ribbons. Yet he knew that it was just a fit of pique that made him think so, for he had to admire the way she had organized the run. She had ridden or rowed to all the hidden, lonely creeks and watched the tides and shifting mudbanks, so that she could be sure of a safe dropping place. She had shown him the lists that she had drawn up and the plans she had made, bending her head close to his as they sat at the table in his small cabin, so that he'd felt suffocated and had to make an excuse to go on deck.

And he'd laughed at her; he could kick himself. He'd seen for a moment that she dropped her fierce, hostile manner and shown him a tender side when she'd thought he was hurt over her wearing Toby's clothes. He laughed again, softly, as he thought of her slim body within the breeches and her rounded breasts within the shirt as she'd unbuttoned the neck, her face flushed from the heat of the cabin. As if she could ever look like a man. The crew and the men from on shore must have been mad or blind not to have seen who and what she was.

He'd still searched for the elusive seaman Hope in the taverns and inns of Hull, and Greg Sheppard had turned laughing, cynical eyes on him and remarked: 'It's no use old fellow. You're going to have to bed her, it's the only way to get her out of your system. Take her and have done with it. She probably won't mind.'

But he'd turned away with a sharp word. If he'd wanted a woman then there were plenty available, more shapely and handsome than Mrs Hope, and he'd never yet taken a woman who wasn't more than willing. Besides, she was Toby's friend. He'd got there first and he certainly wasn't going to have any cast-off.

No, Toby had always had first choice, even though he was the younger brother. First with his mother's affections and spoiling by the servants. Even his father—.

Even my father. He stopped and thought of the night he'd told his father of Toby's death. He thought he'd taken it well, asking the relevant questions and then remaining silent until bedtime. It wasn't until during the night when he himself couldn't sleep, and had come downstairs to walk around, that he found his father hunched weeping over a dying fire.

They'd never been demonstrative, and he'd put his hand diffidently on his father's shoulder and said a few halting words. But his father had turned red eyes towards him and brushed him away.

No, he thought. Much as I loved him, I don't want Toby's leftovers. I don't want any comparisons made. Though—, it's strange, he mused. Toby always said that he was finished with women after that episode with the dose of clap and Clara. He sighed. Silly young fool, if only he'd come to me.

She's put on weight, he thought, when he saw Annie again. And her hair has bleached with the sun. And she probably doesn't even know that the sun has turned her skin golden. She looks like a country maid not a woman from the town.

'We've had a good summer.' She smiled and looked triumphant. 'We've made money from the cloth and I've enough now to buy some brandy and stuff of my own.'

'I don't understand.' He faced her once more in his cabin. 'Do you mean that you haven't been buying any of the goods I brought last winter?'

She shook her head and a strand of fair hair fell from out of the ribbon which held it. 'I hadn't much money of my own, and what I had I wanted to save, in case – in case I had to move on.'

A shiver ran through him. Where was she thinking of going?

'So you did all of that, organizing the runs and distributing the goods, for nothing?'

She nodded and eyed him narrowly. 'I've lived by my wits all of my life captain, but I'm fairly honest – except when I'm desperate – and I'd never be so shameless as to take from people who trusted me.'

He thought her mouth trembled but she turned away from him and when she turned again to face him she had a defiant glare in her eyes.

'I knew that you weren't sure about me, even though you'd asked me to be the runner. I've not taken a penny so far, but I've earned money of my own up on the Wolds. I've paid Mr Moses for what I've had from him, and now I can have equal shares in the running.' She tossed her head in the direction of the upper deck. 'Same as the men up there.'

He fell silent. He really didn't know what to say. She was quite extraordinary.

He watched her from the deck as she pulled away towards the shore and disappeared into the darkness.

'Captain? Shall I give the call?' His bosun stood beside him, a frown on his face.

'What?'

'Man the capstan, sir?'

He gave himself a shake. Drat the woman, she's going to scupper me if I'm not careful. 'Aye. Man the capstan. Hoist the mainsail.'

'Aye, aye, sir.'

There was a scurrying of feet. The men had been mustered and waiting for his command. He'd a good crew, the best he'd known. He mustn't let them down, mustn't let some ragamuffin female so disorganize his mind that he was in danger of sheering off course and scuttling his own ship.

As they headed up the estuary, Parson White stopped by the helm. He pointed over his shoulder towards Hessle. 'That's a grand young fellow back there, sir. Got the team well organized and some good dropping places so they say.' He winked and lowered his voice. 'But beggin' your pardon sir, if you'd take my advice, you'll tell him to wear some thicker tunics. It gets cold on the river this time of year. Slip of a lad like that'll soon take a chill.'

Matt hid a grin. He might have known an old salt like Parson White wouldn't miss a trick. Then he remembered that he had been the one who'd rowed her to shore in Hull. He would have had a good look at her. He had an eye for the women had Parson White, that's why he was sailing the seas instead of preaching in a pulpit.

'I'll tell him,' he said. 'Next time I see him.' As a matter of fact there's something else, he thought, and made a sudden decision.

'Bosun! Ahoy, Bosun,' he called. 'Bear a hand.'

* * *

238

Matt slipped the *Breeze* into Brough Haven and dropped anchor and had a boat lowered. The sky was still dark and there was no sound from shore, no early birdsong, only the gentle lap of water against the keels of the ships anchored there. 'Put on a harbour watch, Bosun, and make sure the crew don't imbibe too heavily at the Ferry Inn,' he called as he shoved off. 'And be polite if the Customs or Excise should happen to call,' he grinned. 'We've nothing on board that they'll be interested in.' He pulled hard on the oars and turned downstream towards Hessle. 'I'll be back as soon as I can.'

A lambent flame defined the horizon as he pulled into the haven at Hessle, a soft tongue of light licking the skirts of a new day. A mist hovered, shivering tremulously as it spread its ghostly dissolving strands above the surge of the river. This was the time he loved best of all. The break of a new day, the assurance of another beginning, when broken promises of yesterday could be absolved and a whole new life could begin.

This was the time, when as a youth, full of hope and enthusiasm, he had ridden out at dawn, galloping through the lush, dew-wet grass, breathing in the heavy perfume of bluebells and cow parsley and the musky dampness of wet sheep, and had sat in the saddle of his mount and looked down over the lands belonging to his father, lands which he had known would one day be his. Until came the day when he decided that the promise of that land – his heritage – was not worth the misery and wretchedness of the present, that he was living in a fool's paradise, full of false hopes, and so had left it all behind.

The door to the cottage was closed as he clambered through the undergrowth and entered the meadow. He walked slowly, taking his time, his boots imprinting in the wet grass. Toby's horse was standing by the far hedge and whinnied softly and for a moment he was startled, forgetting, only for an instant, and then sadly remembering that Toby wasn't there to mount and ride his beloved Sorrel.

He stopped. The door was opening. Was she an early riser – for she couldn't have had more than a few hours sleep – or had she heard the horse's warning? She stepped out of the threshold and looked towards the river; she hadn't seen him and he didn't move. He didn't want to startle her, but he did want to watch her.

She stretched, arching her back and raising her arms to the sky as if in greeting; she spread her fingers wide, her head and neck dropping back and her long hair swinging free.

Her neck was long and white and her waist and hips slim, but through her thin cotton shift he could see that her breasts were full and firm. He felt his heart pounding and his loins grew hot with an eager craving as he thrilled to the uninvited sight of her almost unclothed nakedness. The thin shift, he breathed, as aroused he licked his dry lips, was more erotic and sensual than if she had been standing stark naked in front of him.

She appeared fragile, like a piece of delicate porcelain, yet he knew that she had a strength running through her. Had she acquired this tensile thread or had she been born with it? Had she suffered or been hurt? She had known fear, he was sure of it, for when he had first met her he had seen in those enormous eyes set in a pale white face, a moment of fear, to be replaced a second later by defiance.

But what had caused that fear? He needed to know. Instinctively he started forward and she saw him. His sudden movement startled her and he saw again the fear in her eyes, a flutter of her body like a bird about to take flight.

'I'm sorry. I didn't mean to frighten you.' His words came out abruptly. He was overwhelmed by the nearness of her. She clasped her hands together and the pressure brought the blood rushing to her long fingers, and she curled her bare brown toes in the grass.

'What does tha want?' she whispered. 'Why is tha here?'

He heard the words she spoke in her natural tongue and thought how right they seemed for her. No artifice or polish, but pure and unpretentious. Why then had she tried to change? He watched her lips as they moved.

'Why, Captain Linton?'

Why indeed. Why had he come? His conversation with Greg Sheppard came to mind: 'You'll have to bed her, old fellow. It's the only way to get her out of your system.' Is that why he'd come? To take her whether or not she was willing? To rape and violate her slender body? And what then? Then, he knew she would flee and he'd be lost once more, and she would have one more hurt added to her score.

'I don't know.' He was honest. 'I don't know why I've come. I only knew that I had to.'

She hesitated for a moment then said, 'Excuse me. I'll just get my shawl,' and disappeared inside leaving him feeling like a fool.

She reappeared in the doorway with her shawl around her shoulders. 'Will you have some bread and cheese? I'll make tea when the fire is hot.'

He nodded and followed her inside and watched her as she pushed twigs into the hot ash in the hearth. He saw that her hands were trembling and he bent down beside her. 'Let me do that.' He took the kindling from her and felt the touch of her shoulder on his. She drew back and he saw again a look of apprehension in her face.

Damn it, he thought, with a sudden burst of anger. I'm not going to touch her. What does she think I am? Some good-for-nothing reprobate? He made a pyramid of twigs and watched them catch alight, then placed the trivet and kettle of water on top.

'So why did you come, Captain?' She sawed up a loaf of bread and reached for the cheese in a cupboard. The knife, he noticed, she left at her side of the table.

He pointed towards it. 'Do you always protect yourself so?' he asked, thinking of the time in the cabin when in a moment of anger she had raised a supper knife to him.

241

'You're not answering my question.'

He saw the nervous swallow in her throat as she spoke and he shook his head. 'I told you. I don't know why I've come. Only that I wanted to see you.'

'Do you mean me harm?' The question was direct and he saw the imperceptible movement of her fingers across the table.

'Harm? Why should I mean you harm?' The question hit a nerve and angered him and his voice was harsh.

'Some men do.' She stared at him as if trying to analyse what his intentions were. 'Not all. I've met only a few kind men in my life and I could count them on one hand.' She held up one finger. 'Mr Trott, who asked me in when I was hungry, he made Mrs Trott feed me and let me take his bed.' She raised another finger, 'and Toby.' She raised two more fingers, and added with a small smile, 'oh yes, and Robin and Josh. They've been kind too.'

He gave a harsh laugh. 'And how was Toby kind? Did he let you take his bed too? Or did he share it with you?'

The words were out, the question which had been simmering for so long, asked, and too late he remembered the truckle bed hidden beneath Toby's bed, which he had many times pulled out himself, and slept on when he'd taken time off from being a seaman and become a landsman again.

'Get out.' Her eyes were like fire, her lips wet as she spat out the command.

He gave a gasp. He hadn't intended—! Why did he insult her so? He wouldn't have done it to any other woman, so why her? The reason came sharp and clear. He was jealous. Jealous that Toby might have held her in his arms, might have kissed her lips and throat, when that was precisely what he wanted to do.

He took a step towards her. 'I'm sorry. I shouldn't have said that.'

'No. You shouldn't. And even if I did share his bed,

then it's nowt – nothing to do with you – or anybody else for that matter. Now go.'

So she did. They had. That was it then. His anger dissipated and he just felt drained and sick and disappointed. He shrugged and turned away.

'I'm sorry,' he muttered as he reached the door. 'Please believe me.' He stepped out into the morning. The sky was streaked with gold and purple and in the middle of the river was a tide-rip, the surface of the water breaking and rippling as opposing currents met. He squared his shoulders and strode out down the meadow towards it.

23

Annie leaned heavily on the table and bent her head. She wouldn't cry. She screwed up her eyes to keep back the tears. She wouldn't cry, for hadn't she just won a victory? She had seen him, her adversary, crumple in front of her. His strong manly features falling apart at her words, so that he looked like a shamefaced boy.

I'm even with him, she thought. I'm even for all the hurtful things he's said to me. But why, she wondered? Why do we fight? He's the only man that I've ever dared to antagonize. God knows I never dared with anyone else, I was always too afeard of getting a beating, that's why I always kept my lips firmly shut.

But he wouldn't have hurt me, I should have known that. Why did he come? What was it he wanted? She went to the door and opened it wider. He was halfway down the meadow and had stopped close to Sorrel. She saw him stroke the horse's nose, and then, she drew in a breath, he laid his head against the horse's neck and put his arms around it.

I've hurt him I think. I didn't mean to. He makes me feel so strange. I have feelings about him that I'm not familiar with, that I don't quite understand. But I didn't want to hurt him, and I have.

She saw him stand back from Sorrel and then he gave him a last pat on his flank and started to move away. If I let him go now, I'll never see him again. We won't want to face each other after this. If only he hadn't said what he did about Toby. I didn't want him to think that about us. Perhaps if I'd explained myself better. Should I call him back and tell him?

I don't want him to go; not like this. I don't want him to go.

A deep agitation stirred within her, she put her finger to her mouth and gently nibbled, pressing her teeth to the flesh. She didn't want him to go. She wanted him to come back, yet reason told her that if he did, then she had a very clear idea of what might happen. He wants to bed me. That can be the only reason why he came.

As if her eyes were suddenly opened, she saw the daylight; the sky was streaked with colour, the river was shimmering, the wave crests sparkling and dancing.

I have a choice, she realized. It's up to me. Do I want him?

The answer unfolded like a manifestation. Of course she wanted him. She wanted to feel his arms around her, his lips once more on hers as they'd been that night in his cabin. She must have been brainsick not to have realized before. The provocation and tension within her each time she saw him, wasn't caused by aversion – but by desire. A longing for—. What?

When she'd opened the door earlier and greeted the morning, she had been filled with a bright expectation. She had slept but little after returning from the *Breeze*, feeling restless after the evening's events and her meeting again with Matt on the ship, and when she'd seen him there in the meadow, staring at her, not knowing how long he had been watching her as she made her obeisance to the day, she'd felt that fate was taking a hand, that here was her predestination. She could reach out towards it or turn her back.

She watched him striding further and further out of her reach. She was afraid. She knew men only too well. They coaxed and tempted you with sweet words, and then they changed and became bullying, abusive tyrants. The fear was real and she trembled. She took a hesitant step onto the grass. 'Wait,' she whispered. 'Wait.'

You're a fool, Annie, she considered. You'll be hurt

245

again. But I have to learn to trust, she pleaded with herself, or it'll be too late!

She stepped forward again. 'Wait,' she shouted, her voice breaking huskily. 'Wait! Matt. Please wait.'

He stopped and turned, hesitated, and then turned back and walked on. She started to run. 'No, wait. I must tell you something.' She'd explain; about her and Toby, then he'd understand. Maybe he was jealous of her being with Toby, they were fond of each other, she knew. She ran faster, the meadow sloped steeply. Maybe he was jealous of her and Toby – of Toby and her – of Toby!

Why hadn't she thought of that before. If it was true! The possibility of such reasoning sent a warm glow through her. 'Wait.' Her breath was going, she felt a stitch coming in her side. Why didn't he turn around?

She fell headlong in the grass and she gave a loud gasp, but still he didn't turn. She picked herself up and ran again, leaving behind her shawl. 'Please stop. I want to tell you.'

He started to turn as she almost reached him, and she felt herself falling again, her momentum pitching her forward into his arms which he opened to catch her.

'I want to tell you,' she said breathlessly. 'About me and Toby. There was nothing.' She shook her head, too breathless to go on. 'We didn't—'

He put his fingers on her lips to silence her. 'It doesn't matter,' he said quietly.

'But it does.' She took his hand away from her mouth and held it. 'We were like brother and sister. That's how we both wanted it.'

He gave a short laugh and gently stroked her bare arm. 'Toby!'

'You don't believe me?' She stared wide-eyed at him, wanting to convince him.

His eyes were tender, why had she always thought they were hard? She felt as if she was melting beneath his gaze; her legs were giving way.

'I was wrong to ask. As you so rightly said, it's nothing

to do with anyone else, but yes, I do believe you. It would be typical of Toby, playing at brothers and sisters.'

He gazed down at her and hesitatingly he caressed her face, tracing her cheekbones, touching her lips. He shook his head. 'He must have been touched in the head, wanting you for a sister!'

'But I wouldn't have wanted to be anything else,' she whispered. No need to tell him, not now that Toby was no more, that he had been changing towards her, that his brotherly kiss was becoming more tender and that she hadn't wanted it.

'You know that I want you?' He moved a strand of hair and bent and kissed her forehead and then each cheek.

She didn't answer, but only nodded and felt happiness filling her mind, her whole being.

'I want you so badly that I can't sleep for thinking about you. I've been so consumed by needless jealousy that I was rude and unkind towards you.'

'So that was the reason,' she whispered and smiled, her face lighting up. 'I thought it was because I was just a nobody, – a nobody off the scrap heap.'

He flinched. 'Did I really say that? I don't know how you can bear even to talk to me.' He took hold of both her hands and drew her closer, she saw the wisps of curl in his beard and could smell the sea in his hair. 'Can you ever forgive me? I didn't mean to hurt you, it was unpardonable. But what now? Will you send me on my way now that we have made our peace? Shall I come on another day so that we can start again on a different understanding?'

She was puzzled and a frown wrinkled her brows. Did he mean that he wasn't going to stay? That he wasn't going to take her into the feather bed and whisper sweet nothings to her, before he forced his body into hers? Did he mean that she should decide?

He gave a gentle laugh. 'But don't make me wait too long, Mrs Hope. I'm a man after all and my desire is strong.'

'There's no need to wait.' She felt suddenly shy; she bent her head against his chest and felt the pounding of his heart. 'You can stay.'

He lifted her chin with his finger and kissed her lips, his mouth was firm yet tender. 'Only if you're sure,' he whispered.

She lifted her arms around his neck and held him in a swift embrace. 'I'm sure.'

They walked hand in hand back to the cottage, not speaking, but merely gently squeezing fingers. She was surprised by his actions, for he made her sit down while he made a dish of tea from the hissing steaming kettle, and he finished cutting the bread which she had left on the table, and then bade her come and eat and drink. She didn't speak but watched his every movement. What manner of man was this who didn't want to take her straight to the mattress?

When they had finished eating, and she didn't eat much, finding it hard to swallow, he rose from the table and put more kindling on the fire and then stood in the doorway looking out.

He turned round and smiled and held out his hand. 'Come and look, the geese are flying in on their way to the feeding grounds.'

She stood next to him, the morning smelt sweet and pungent, the smoke from their wood fire and others from the cottages on the cliff was drifting down to the river, aromatic scents of brushwood and apple and pine cones filling the air, while above the water flew vast flocks of greylag geese and, close behind, came the long necked brent, barnacle and Canada geese.

He put his arm around her and led her back inside and closed the door. She trembled a little but he appeared not to notice, yet he led her, not to the bed but to the chair, where he sat down and drew her onto his lap. He lifted her hair from her shoulders and gently kissed her neck and throat.

'Why are you afraid?'

She looked plaintively at him. So he had noticed. 'I was allus afraid,' she whispered. 'Every time.'

'You won't be afraid with me.'

And she wasn't, for every touch and caress was gentle, yet persuasive, his kisses light on her body, tempting her with their seductiveness, yet still she sat in his lap, her body soft and yielding, feeling the hardness of him beneath her. Her body was pulsating, her breathing coming faster, this was such bliss, this wasn't something she had known before. Why didn't he take her? She stood up from his knees and with her eyes drawn to his she lifted the hem of her shift, drawing it up above her head so that she stood naked before him.

He closed his eyes for a second and then opening them, he followed the line of her body with his hands, touching her breasts, arousing her nipples and running his fingers down the pale dappled stretch marks on her belly, round the curve of her hips and through the fine bush of pubic hair. 'You are so lovely. I thought – I thought I could imagine how you would be, but – you are so much more beautiful.'

He rose from the chair and with a swift movement lifted her into his arms and carried her to the bed. She reached up to help him unfasten his shirt buttons and as he turned to drop it onto the chair, she gazed at his shoulders and back, tanned from the sun and sea air. But she flinched as he started to unfasten the buckle on his belt, as another memory returned, and she touched the scar on her face.

He saw the movement and bent over her, taking her fingers from her face and studying her. 'Has someone hurt you?' he asked quietly.

'Yes,' she whispered. 'But I deserved it.'

He lay down beside her and held her in his arms. 'No woman deserves to be hurt, though I know I hurt you with unkind words, and I shall always regret them. You're meant to be cherished. To be loved.'

'I know nothing of love with a man, onny with my

childre'.' She looked up at him, her eyes wet with emotion. 'Can tha teach me?'

'I know nothing of love either,' he answered, kissing each moist eyelid in turn. 'We must learn together.'

24

The long cold winter became her summer. Annie felt like the chrysalis which Robin had shown her while they were on the Wolds. It had hung on a fine silken girdle from a plant stem, and he assured her that soon it would be gone and in its place a butterfly would emerge. 'Lady of the Woods,' he'd said, 'the prettiest of them all.' She hadn't believed him, not until they returned to the place and found the shrivelled pupa cast on the ground and above them a free and fluttering orange tip butterfly.

She felt that she too had cast off her old life. She had shed her past, forgotten her beginnings, let slip even the memory of her children, as love and passion absorbed her. The desire of wanting Matt replaced all else and her days were spent watching for his ship; riding through the night to greet him and rowing with breathless anticipation towards the *Breeze*; mounting the ladder with practised ease and wanting him so desperately that there was no waiting for him to join her in the cottage before dawn, just falling into each other's arms with an urgency born of need, the moment they reached his cabin.

Exhilaration gripped her; she was invincible. She took tremendous risks, drawing Roxton away from the river as the men unloaded the goods and leading him on a chase through the saltmarsh and scrub land and into the darkness of Hesslewood where she lost him. She had bought a donkey-and-cart with her own money and carried her goods in baskets in the back of the cart through the streets of Hessle and under the very nose of Roxton. She stopped him and asked if he would buy some ribbons for his lady and he brusquely turned away and didn't hinder her; she cracked her whip and laughingly drove off to visit the big houses where she asked for the master and unloaded the ankers of brandy and geneva which they so gratefully received.

'I must visit my father.' Matt lay on the bed next to her, stroking her thigh. 'I haven't seen him for months. I'll go tomorrow.'

'Don't be long away, will you? I'll miss you. I'm greedy for you. I can't bear it when you're away.'

He rolled over and pulled her towards him. 'I'll miss you too.' He placed his lips around her nipples and she breathed in a sigh of delight. Her fears had gone that first day, when he'd soothed and enticed her, seeking to please her, finding hidden secret places of ecstacy, so secret that she had never known before that they were there. Her body throbbed. Never had she felt so desirable. Never had she thought she could give or receive such pleasure. Never had she felt so much love.

*　　*　　*

When he returned he was brimming over with glee. 'Father has been invited out yet again. A neighbour, Mrs Burnby, was visiting when I arrived and has invited him to a supper party. He declined of course, and then she asked me. I too declined saying that I had to get back to my ship. "Oh" she said, "But it's not for another three weeks, Captain, you have time to come back again." Again I declined, but then she went on to say that it was to be a masked party – and what do you think?' He picked Annie up and whirled her round. 'I said I would only go if I could bring a partner.'

Annie stared at him. What was he talking about?

'She was a bit put-out I think. I'm sure she was angling for me to partner that whingeing niece of hers who was once set on Toby. Anyhow, she could hardly withdraw the invitation, and then father said that if I was going, then he might as well go also.'

'So who is this partner that you're taking?' Annie said resentfully. This was a part of his life which she couldn't share, and could never be a part of.

'Why you, of course. Who else is there? Who else is there that I should choose to partner me?'

Hungrily he began to undress her, fumbling with the buttons of her blouse in his eagerness to hold her.

'Stop.' Her lips mumbled beneath his. 'How can *I* partner you? How can you take *me*, a waif and stray?'

Sometimes she teased him, reminding him of the time when he had said such things. He became penitent, or sometimes angry with her for reminding him. He was angry now.

'Don't tell me what I can or can't do.' He pinned her down on the bed. 'I will if I want to.' Then his eyes became soft as he gazed down at her. 'I want you to come with me, I hate it when I'm away from you. I wanted you with me on the Wolds when I visited my father, I want you with me on the *Breeze*, only I know that it is too dangerous.' Then he laughed. 'Do come. Josh can take care of the running this once. We won't be needed. Think what a jest it would be!'

What a jest indeed. To go from a life on the dank and muddy wharves of the river to a fine party in a great house. It was a great house as she well knew. But Matt didn't know that she had been, he didn't know that she had met Mrs Burnby, that she had sold her satins for her gowns, maybe even for one that she would wear for the party.

She smiled. She had gone into the great house by the back door. If she attended the party with Matt she would enter by the front. What a jest. But it was time now for some truths to be told.

'Matt?' She reached up and touched his lips. 'I've something to tell you.'

He sighed and held her close. 'Can't it wait?'

When she told him that she had met Mrs Burnby and her two nieces and that she thought that it was probably his father who had turned her off his land, he was more determined than ever that she should go.

'But my voice will give me away, even if I wear a mask. You knew that I was a nobody – no, be honest, you did,' she added as he started to protest. 'And besides I haven't a dress. How can I go in what I have?'

He grinned. 'Now you're making a typical woman's excuse. There's a trunk full of silk which will make a dozen dresses. And as for your voice – well. I know – we'll say that you're Dutch and that you don't speak much English! You could be, quite easily, with your fair hair, and if anyone asks you an awkward question then just shake your head and say that you don't understand. I'll say that you're a widow, which is true, and that your name is, erm – Annaliese Hope.'

She started to laugh. What a lark it would be, and if they were found out, what did it matter. Matt wouldn't care and neither would she.

They opened up a chest and brought out silks and satins, and then Annie remembered the other chest, the one she hadn't yet looked in, which was covered in rugs and cushions which Toby had said he'd stolen from his father's house. They took off the coverings and beneath they found a sandalwood chest, sweet smelling and carved with scrolls.

'I remember this,' said Matt quietly. 'I didn't know that Toby had it. It was our mother's. She kept it in her room.'

'Toby said he brought things away bit by bit, so that no one would notice,' Annie stroked the carved lid. 'Though how anyone could fail to miss this I can't understand.'

'The servants would know. They would just be pandering to Toby's games.' He shook his head sadly. 'He could get away with anything, could Toby.'

She took his hand and held it. 'And you couldn't?'

'Not then.' He lifted his head and laughed. 'But now I can. Let's show them all, Annie. We can do whatever we want.'

The chest contained silks which Matt had brought from abroad, clocks and trinkets which Toby had brought from his father's house; and wrapped in a muslin cloth was a string of pearls. Matt placed them around Annie's neck. 'Pearls for a princess,' he said and kissed her.

'But I can't wear these,' she protested, fingering them lovingly. 'It doesn't seem right.'

'It doesn't seem right that they're locked away in a chest. Perhaps they were my mother's, or maybe Toby bought them intending to give them to Clara.' He shrugged. 'Who knows? But now they're yours. And pearls should be worn,' he added. 'They need the contact with a woman's skin to give them their sheen, their translucency. Keep them on,' he said and gently touched her throat, 'and by the time we go to the party they will be beautiful. Their colour will be matched only by the colour of your skin.'

At the bottom of the chest was a sheet covering a large yet soft bundle. They opened it out and shook it and out spread a gown of silk, the most beautiful thing that Annie had ever seen. It was the colour of a newly opened damask rose, a flush, a blush of a virgin's cheek, with silver silken threads running though it. The neckline was low and heartshaped, the skirt full and trailing.

'There!' Matt said triumphantly. 'There is your gown.'

Annie wept. 'I can't. I don't deserve it. It's meant for a lady.'

'You will be a lady,' he laughed. 'Even if it's only for one night. Mrs Trott will dress your hair – yes she will. We'll give her something.'

Annie smiled through her tears and picked out a piece of shiny satin from the heap on the floor. 'Yes, she will. We'll give her this to add to all the others in her chest.'

Matt took Annie and the dress down to Mrs Trott and told her what he wanted her to do. She took the dress from him and handled it softly, drawing its silkiness through her fingers.

'I remember it,' she nodded. 'It was your mother's. Only she never wore it. She got took ill and it was put away in a chest and never brought out. I often wondered what happened to it.'

'Tidy it up, will you, Mrs Trott? It's badly creased and I have it in mind to give it as a present for someone. Oh, yes—. Mrs Hope and I have a wager on. She said that she could never look like a lady, and I said that if you dressed her hair, the way you used to my mother's, then she could – that there was no-one more expert than you. What about it? Can you help me win the pledge?'

'I reckon she needs to win 'pledge more than thee, Captain Linton, tha doesn't need money, of that I'm sure.' A gleam came into her eye. 'It's been a long time, a long, long time since I dressed my lady's hair, but aye, I reckon I can still do it.' She glanced at Annie who still felt there was a trace of animosity lingering towards her. 'It'll be a challenge mind, but aye, I'll try.'

By the time the three weeks had passed and Matt was due to return, Mrs Trott had once more become an expert. Annie's hair had been washed and brushed and washed and brushed until her scalp was sore, but her hair was shining like a mirror, and as soft and luxuriant as silk, and Mrs Trott had piled and pinned the long straight tresses into various styles. Finally she decided. 'Tha hasn't got 'type of hair for owt elaborate. It's too fine and silky. I'll have to coil it. I'll coil it over each ear and I'll twist the back, and if tha was really going to a party or a ball, then I'd dress it through with flowers or pearls.'

Annie smiled secretly. 'Tomorrow Captain Linton will be back. I'll come in the morning and then we'll be ready for him. Does tha think he'll win his wager?' she asked mischievously.

'Aye,' she admitted. 'I've not been beaten.'

He came that night. He'd dropped anchor in Hessle Haven and rowed to shore bringing with him a circlet of pearls to match the necklace. 'You can wear it in your hair tomorrow,' he said. 'That's what the *proper* ladies do.'

'I know,' she laughed. 'I've just been told.'

*   *   *

Matt carried a leather valise; Annie's dress, which was wrapped in a cotton sheet, he draped over his arm as they walked into Hessle where he had ordered a carriage for their journey to his father's house.

Annie carefully covered her hair with her hood. She was wearing just a simple skirt and shirt beneath her cloak and would change at the inn at Welton where Matt had reserved two rooms.

'Two rooms?' she'd asked with a smile.

'Of course,' he answered. 'Don't forget that you are a respectable young widow, and that rumours can soon spread. It's a very well-known inn and it's possible that other guests of Mrs Burnby will be calling there.'

She was beginning to be nervous. Suppose someone guessed what she was? Suppose someone spoke in the foreign language of Dutch and engaged her in conversation? The only Dutch person that she had known was her late husband's former captain on his whaling ship. She remembered his fair good looks and broken English accent. She fell silent and began mentally practising stilted conversation.

The carriage was already waiting for them at the Marquis of Granby Inn and Matt helped her in. She breathed in the smell of leather and commented. 'It smells like a slaughter house.'

'Ssh,' he said. 'You're a lady. You're not supposed to know about such things. You only know about music and theatres and fashion.'

'But I don't,' she implored. 'Matt – I don't know. Only 'flutes and drums and shops that I've seen in 'Market Place in Hull.'

'Then tell about those.' He laughed at her. 'Make up a story, I know full well that you can, and everyone will think that that's the way it is in Holland. The ladies that you'll meet tonight know nothing. They'll believe everything you say.'

They swung into the coachyard of the inn in the small village of Welton at the foot of the Wolds and he whispered into her ear. 'Now don't forget, you're foreign. You don't understand. Just nod and smile if I should speak to you.'

The innkeeper's wife took charge of her when Matt explained that she spoke little English, and would require the services of a maid to help her dress. She stared wide-eyed at him but dare not speak. What was he thinking of? She was perfectly capable of dressing herself.

He handed the dress to the landlady and then unclasped his valise and took out another bag which he handed to Annie and spoke in a language which she didn't understand. He gave her a small bow and then turned and went upstairs.

Annie watched him go and then turned to the landlady with a question in her raised eyebrows.

'Molly will look after you, ma'am,' the woman shouted at her. 'She's here now.'

A young girl in cap and apron appeared and she too shouted instructions at Annie to please follow her.

Do they think I'm deaf? she wondered as she followed the girl to her room. Or stupid, not being able to dress myself?

The room was warm and comforting with a four-poster bed draped with thick hangings and beside the fire was a table with a bowl and jug of hot water and warm white towels upon it.

'I'll just fetch thee refreshment ma'am, like 'gentleman said,' the girl shouted. 'Tha'll be tired after thy long journey. Then I'll help thee dress.'

'Excuse, please.' Annie pointed to her ear and shook her head. 'I not deaf.'

The girl nodded. 'Aye, that's right, I expect, ma'am,' and giving Annie a bright smile she bobbed her knee and went out of the room.

Annie chortled with laughter and taking off her cloak, bounced on the bed testing it for comfort. She stretched herself luxuriantly, how wonderful to sleep in such a bed. She closed her eyes for a moment, then remembering that soon Matt would be coming for her, she climbed off and unbuttoned her skirt and shirt and pouring water into the bowl began to wash. She remembered the bag which Matt had given her and wondered what was in it. She picked it up from the chair where she had left it and opened it. Inside was a silk underslip and petticoat, white stockings and a pair of white kid shoes, and long, elbow-length gloves. She delved to the bottom of the bag, something else was there. She held the garment up. Pantaloons!

She laughed and took off her shift and put them on and paraded in front of the oval swing mirror. She had never worn such things. How strange it felt to have her legs encased in such a fashion. She picked up the underslip and petticoat with a happy exclamation and pressed their softness to her cheeks. How thoughtful of him to think of such things. Then she reflected wryly on how he would have known what to buy. But she dismissed the thought. He'd had a life before her, what of it? Now was the time that mattered.

She stuffed the old shift in the bag and continued her bathing. The maid, Molly, came in bearing a tray with a bottle of wine and two glasses and a plate of thin slices of beef. She stared at Annie standing almost naked before the fire and hurriedly closed the door.

'Dear me,' she muttered. 'I knew foreigners did strange things, but teckin' all their clothes off, well I never!'

Later, she poured Annie a glass of wine which she slowly sipped, and then helped her into her stockings, underslip and petticoat. She took the gown from its wrap and shook it and invited Annie, by way of nodding and pointing, to step into it.

It was like looking at someone else in the mirror. It certainly didn't seem like her. She didn't know that she had such fine cheekbones, shown to such an advantage with her hair drawn away from her face, dressed with pearls and coiled and twisted about her ears. And the gown, how it showed off her slenderness as it nipped her waist and pushed up her breasts to swell the heartshaped neckline.

She fingered the pearls about her throat. Matt had been right, they glistened much more since she had worn them, now they had a lustrous sheen as they nestled so comfortably on her pale throat.

There was a knock on the door and Molly hurried to answer it.

'Is Mrs Hope almost ready?'

Annie turned from the mirror to see Matt standing there in naval uniform with white breeches and stockings and carrying a tricorne hat. He looked so handsome she wanted to run and put her arms around him.

'She's almost ready sir.' Even Molly seemed overawed as she stared at him, then remembering herself, she bobbed her knee.

'Please. Come in, Captain.' Annie extended her hand. 'I am ready.'

Matt brushed past the maid and took Annie's hand and bending low, kissed it. 'You are beautiful,' he murmured.

The maid watched the handsome couple, her eyes shining and her mouth open. 'Oh, sir,' she said. 'Isn't madam lovely? Beggin' her pardon, and I know it's not my place to comment, and it doesn't seem right talking of her when she doesn't understand – but she looks so handsome.'

Matt smiled, 'I'm quite sure that she wouldn't mind in the least. I'll convey your comments once we are on our journey.'

Molly dipped her knee again and went out, closing the door after her. Matt strode after her and opened it again and heard her cry out to the landlady. 'Oh, mum. What a handsome pair. And so in love, tha can tell.'

'How handsome you look.' Annie put out her hands to hold his.

'My father says that I am not a proper seaman, because I don't wear a uniform or gold braid.' There was a note of bitterness in his voice and he fingered the gilt buttons on his frock coat. 'So I'm going to show him how I would look if I wanted to.'

He tipped up his hat. 'Here. Here is our disguise.' Tucked inside the hat were two masks, one in white silk for her and one in black for him. 'We'll put them on now to go down to the carriage.' He gave her a sudden smile. 'The fun is about to begin, Annie. You are a beautiful but penniless Dutch widow, and I a respectable naval captain. And not one of my father's honourable and dignified acquaintances could begin to guess otherwise.'

25

The party was due to start at ten o'clock and it was twenty-minutes-past-the-hour as they rattled up the sweeping, winding drive to the house. Annie peeped out of the carriage window. It was just as she remembered it. An imposing residence built of stone with pillars gracing the massive front door.

'I'm that frightened, Matt. 'Last time I was here, I went to 'back door. I had to wash my hands and tidy my hair afore I could go and see 'mistress.' In her nervousness she slipped back into her own comfortable dialect.

He took her hand. 'Don't be frightened. They won't eat you, and Mrs Burnby won't possibly remember, nor will Clara or Jane if they're here.'

She gasped. She hadn't thought about those two young women being at the party. She fingered her mask. They wouldn't recognize her of course. Not dressed like this and with her hair up. Besides, she'd noticed that they hadn't really looked at her previously, not even when they were speaking to her. It was as if she was nothing, as if she wasn't there.

The wide hall with its stone-flagged floor and a long table groaning with food and drink, was already crowded with guests in party dress. Roman emperors and Greeks roamed the room – men in togas with thonged sandals strapped on their feet and laurel circlets on their heads. A shepherd was there with his smock and crook, and ladies as duchesses and dairy maids simpered and giggled and admired as they fluttered their eyelashes behind their masks.

'Captain Linton? It is you?' Mrs Burnby, resplendent

in red wig and powdered face as Queen Elizabeth, bore down on them. Her extravagant dress of velvet, trimmed with satin and lace floated above a farthingale, and a gauze ruff rose like wings above and behind her head. 'I could tell, your smile gives you away. And this lovely lady? Please present her.'

Matt bowed. 'I thought, ma'am, that we were to remain an enigma until the end of the evening?'

'Oh, but not to me, dear boy. I must know who my guests are, particularly such a lovely one as this. How perfectly charming.'

'May I present Mrs Annaliese Hope. I regret that she is unable to engage in conversation, her English is limited I fear. She is Dutch, erm – a widow. I knew her husband, a sea captain like myself.'

Annie threw him a dazzling smile as she inclined her head to her hostess. Why he could tell a better tale than she could. And Mrs Burnby, was it really her? The quietly spoken mistress of the house who had bought her cloth, bore no resemblance to the elaborately dressed apparition greeting her now. Perhaps this evening would be fun after all. She took a glass of wine proffered from a passing footman and drank, the bubbles effervesced and made her hiccup. She finished it off, it wasn't strong, not like gin or brandy and she took another, and with her other hand on Matt's arm they circled the floor, nodding and smiling until they reached the wide staircase and ascended it to the ballroom.

'You see the tall man without the mask? Over by the window. He's the one who turned me off his land.' She whispered from behind her gloved hand. 'And the one talking to him – the rolypoly with the powdered wig – he's one of my contacts. He takes brandy and geneva and tobacco.'

'Does he indeed?' Matt gave a sardonic chuckle. 'Beddows! He's a pillar of society. He's a magistrate; he's raised a company of militia men to keep our shores safe from the enemy and to prevent smuggling – and you tell me he barters with the self-same smugglers! Well, I can tell you, he doesn't do it because of want or necessity as most of the suffering classes do, he's well able to pay duty, so he does it because of greed. And,' he added ironically, 'the man with him is my father!'

'Yes.' She nodded. 'I know.' She too gave a chuckle. 'Why don't you introduce me? Let's see if they remember me. Mr Beddows first met me when I was dressed in coat and breeches. I told him I was Toby's partner and collected money from him. I also said that I would be sending a woman with the goods and that he must be sure to take them from her in person. He did, and pinched my bottom into the bargain.'

Squire Linton looked closely at Annie as Matt made the introductions, and then gave a bow. 'Coming to your senses at last are you?' he barked at Matt. 'About time you settled down. You say she doesn't speak English? Well, give me a woman who doesn't have much to say, anytime.' He guffawed. 'There's plenty of other things they can do, what?'

'I said she doesn't speak *much* English, Father,' Matt said stiffly. 'I'm quite sure she can understand your meaning.'

'Oh, don't be so stuffy, Matthias. I don't mean harm.' He invited Annie to sit. 'She's handsome, I'll say that for her.'

Matt spoke again to her in a language she didn't understand, and then to her horror he moved away, 'Take care of her for a moment, Father. There's someone I must speak to.'

Mr Beddows bowed to her and he too moved away and left her alone with Matt's father. 'So you're a widow are you?' he boomed. 'And looking for another husband, no doubt?'

Annie gave a genial smile and nodded her head, and then shrugged and pursed her lips.

'You'll have some money, I expect. Did your husband leave you much?' His voice carried and several people

264

turned round with raised eyebrows and a smile on their faces.

'Excuse me please?'

'Money,' he said, rubbing his fingers together, 'You know,' he patted his coat and brought out a money bag. 'Do you have any?'

'Ah.' Annie brought an expression of comprehension to her face, then sadly turned down her lips and shook her head. 'Nay, no money.'

'Oh well, I suppose it doesn't matter. Matt will have plenty one day; if he stops fooling around that is, and comes back home.' He folded his arms and viewed her. 'Pity you can't understand. I'd like to have had a chat. Don't get the chance to talk to pretty young women these days. Used to though, by jove I did. You wouldn't think so now, but I was quite handsome. Aye, the ladies used to follow me around.' His voice dropped to a whisper. 'That was my problem – I couldn't resist.'

He fell silent and Annie glanced at him from behind her mask. He was still handsome, more so than she remembered, for on the day he'd ordered her off his land he was dressed in a shooting jacket and dirty breeches, and now he was wearing a silver-grey tailcoat, unbuttoned to show a silver embroidered waistcoat that was a perfect foil for his thick, silver-streaked dark hair. He was a tall, thin man and wore black sateen breeches and white silk stockings on his long legs. Yes, she thought, he could still turn a woman's head.

He pointed across the room to where Matt was engaged in conversation with two ladies, both with nodding plumes in their piled high hair and wearing black masks. 'You see the one in blue?'

She followed the direction of his finger, it was Clara with Jane, she was sure of it.

'Well that young filly was set on my youngest boy at one time – Tobias. He was much too young then to think of marrying, and she was a prissy little madam, not good enough for one of my sons.' He sighed and glanced at Annie. 'He died you know,' he said softly. 'Well of course, you wouldn't know. Yes, he died of a fever. Such a waste. Such a waste.'

He took out a linen handkerchief and blew his nose, then he gave a croaky laugh. 'He was always a rascal. After he left home, he used to steal things. Whenever he visited there would be something missing. I suppose he thought I wouldn't notice, but I did. Just trinkets and stuff, you know. His mother always spoilt him when he was a child,' he went on, talking as if to himself. 'I warned her, but she wouldn't listen. My own fault I suppose, for I wouldn't let her spoil Matthias. I told her – this boy will have responsibilities.' He gazed into the distance as if remembering. 'He was a fine young fellow – perhaps I was too hard on him – I don't know. And now he can barely bring himself to talk to me.' He sighed. 'It's not easy bringing up sons.'

She could almost have felt sorry for him, until she remembered his treatment of her, when he was prepared to deny her shelter on a cold winter's night.

'Hm,' he muttered as Matt came across the room with Clara and Jane, one on each arm. 'I shouldn't sleep easy if I thought she was going to be mistress of my house. Miss prim and proper. She's got no warmth, none at all.'

Annie and Squire Linton stood up as Matt and the ladies approached. Annie was taller than both of them and they raised their heads to greet her. Clara frowned slightly. 'Have we met? You seem familiar.'

Annie turned enquiringly to Matt who spoke to her in Dutch, then she said laughingly. 'No. I *sink* not.'

Matt turned away and coughed to hide a grin, then turning towards Annie he took her by the arm. 'If you will excuse us ladies – sir – it is time I introduced Mrs Hope to the delights of the minuet.'

'Oh, Matt,' she whispered as he led her away. 'I'm having such a time. This is another world. Any minute now I shall wake up and find I've been dreaming.'

He smiled down at her. 'And I was about to ask if you

would like to leave? Can you bear to go? I've had enough of these pompous people, and besides——.' His eyes kindled behind his mask. 'I don't want to share you. I want you to myself. I need you.'

She heard the music begin to play. She didn't know how to dance and, right now, she did not want to learn. She was having a wonderful time, here was a life she had never even dreamt of, of richness and opulence, but she had no craving for it – more than anything she wanted to be held in Matt's arms. She lifted her head towards him and he bent to kiss her lips. Behind her she heard someone gasp. It was Clara. 'Ssh,' she heard Jane whisper. 'They do things differently abroad.'

'How disgusting,' Clara replied.

Annie turned her head. Behind the two girls, who were watching with outraged fascination, was Matt's father, who was also watching them, a half smile on his face and an approving gleam in his eye. He nodded his head to her and raising his fingers to his lips he blew her a kiss.

Mrs Burnby didn't want them to leave. She had plenty of guest rooms available, she said. No need to make such a long journey at this hour. But no, Matt insisted that they must go. Mrs Hope had lodgings booked and he must get back to his ship.

'You and your ship,' their hostess said playfully. 'You'd be fonder of it than a wife, I declare,' and looked pointedly at Annie.

When he refused to be drawn, she announced that if they insisted on leaving, then first of all everyone must now remove their masks.

Annie drew in her breath. This was it. Was she to be exposed? Mrs Burnby, Matt's father, Clara and Jane, Mr Beddows, all had seen her before. She could hardly refuse, people were already taking off their disguises and laughingly acknowledging that they had known all the time who their partners had been.

Matt removed his mask and stood behind her as he

unfastened hers. 'Don't worry,' he breathed. 'No-one will know you.'

She lowered the mask and defiantly stared out at the crowd who had gathered to see Captain Linton's partner.

There was a hum of voices, of approval, faces smiled at her. 'What a beauty.' 'Her husband was in shipping, so I hear.' 'Linton will do well to catch her, what?'

She put her head back and laughed. Clara and Jane were standing at the front of the crowd. Jane had an admiring look on her face but Clara still looked puzzled. Mrs Burnby was watching them quizically and Mr Beddows came across and bowed. 'So glad to make your acquaintance, I trust we'll meet again.'

I'm sure we will, she thought as she bowed her head to him, and turned to Matt's father who was coming towards them. He bowed and took her hand and kissed it.

'I'm delighted to have met you. I hope that son of mine doesn't let you slip through his fingers.'

He raised his eyes approvingly to her face and caught sight of the pearls. He touched them sensitively. 'Exquisite,' he murmured. 'My wife—,' he closed his eyes for a second, when he opened them she thought she saw a look of regret. 'My wife had such a necklace. I bought them for her – she had skin and features like yours, fine and delicate. Pearls are right for you.' He bowed once more and turned away.

'Am I really going back to lodgings and you to your ship?' She leaned her head against him as the carriage pulled away from the house.

'We're going back to the inn. I asked them to keep our rooms.' He kissed her softly on the mouth and ran his fingers across her bare shoulders. 'I thought that we could have the comfort of a proper bed for once rather than Toby's old feather mattress.'

But he also wanted her away from the atmosphere of the cottage, which he still thought of as Toby's home and which still held vestiges of him there. Much as he'd cared for his brother, he couldn't get rid of a feeling of jealousy that Toby had shared a part of Annie's life before he had known her.

They were perfectly proper. Annie was shown once more to her room where the fire was still glowing and a fresh jug of wine was set on the table. Molly helped her out of her dress and looked about for Annie's night attire.

'Sank you,' Annie said in a clipped tone. 'You may go.'

The girl raised her eyebrows and nodded. She lit another candle from the one which was guttering and placed it on the table beside the bed. 'Goodnight then, ma'am. Sleep well.'

'Goodnight, *ma'am*. Goodnight, *ma'am!*' Annie chuckled and squeezed her arms about herself. 'What a lark. I've been a real lady!' She fingered the softness of the dress which lay across a chair and gave a deep sigh. 'I'll never forget this night, never in my whole life.'

A gentle tap came on the door. She opened it to admit Matt. She felt weak as she saw him standing there. Her body pounded, her mouth was dry.

'I thought we could share a drop of wine before we sleep,' he said huskily.

'Sleep?' She drew him into the room and closed the door. 'I don't want to sleep, not unless you're beside me.'

He remained silent but held her face in both of his hands.

'Tonight,' she whispered as she put her arms around his neck, 'I saw how real ladies behave. They seemed to me to be trapped behind their masks and beautiful clothes. It's as if they can't be themselves, they can't say how they feel. Well, I'm glad that I'm not a real lady, that I'm just a nobody, for I want to say to thee, Matt, that you're the only man I've felt about in this way. I was always afraid of being with a man for they never treated me right. But with thee—.' She shook her head, she

269

could feel the tears welling behind her eyelids, her lips trembling. 'It's something special, something beautiful. I love thee, Matt.'

Gently he kissed her and then picking her up he carried her across to the bed. Love. He had never heard the word spoken before. His father and mother he assumed had loved their sons and perhaps each other, though they would never have dreamt of saying so. The women he had bedded didn't know about love – or tenderness, for that matter. How strange then, that he should learn about it from someone who had never known it either, but was not afraid to proclaim or show it.

26

Josh was waiting for them as they arrived back at the Marquis of Granby Inn, he had an anxious look on his face.

'I'm sorry, Captain. I've got bad news for thee.'

'What? Is it the *Breeze*? What's happened, man?'

'*Breeze* got away, sir, they saw what was happening and hauled up 'anchor.'

Annie touched Matt's arm to quell his anxiety. 'Is anybody hurt, Josh?'

'No, thank God, though they could have been. Revenue men appeared just as we were shipping stuff on shore. They must have been watching for 'ship, they seemed to come from nowhere. I'm sorry, Captain, Mrs Hope – and just when I was left in charge an' all. I feel that bad about it.'

'Did they get all the stuff? Nobody was caught?' Annie pressed him for details.

'They got most of 'brandy and geneva, and all 'bales of tobacco and they caught one man. He stayed to fight instead of running like 'rest of us. Master Toby allus said that if 'Rev men turned up we was never to argue or stand up to 'em, but to tail it as fast as we could. But he was allus a bit hotheaded was—!' He was about to say the man's name, then checked himself. 'He's on 'list as number eighteen, Mrs Hope. Tha'd better cross him off, he won't be around for a bit.'

'Have they taken him to Hull?' She had a vision of the crumbling dank old gaol.

'Aye. Onny I don't know where they'll house him,

they're pulling 'old gaol down. But they'll find somewhere secure no doubt.'

'Will he talk?' Matt frowned. 'Does he know names?'

Josh shook his head. 'He'll not talk, and onny name he knows is mine, but he'll not give it.' He gave an ironic snort. 'He's a sort of relation, my wife's sister's husband—, he'll not talk cos he knows I'm onny one left to look after his wife and bairns while he's in gaol.'

'That's a damned shame.' Matt cursed softly as they walked back towards the cottage. 'We'll have to ease off for a while. I'll take the *Breeze* along the coast for a week or two, Roxton will get fed up of hanging around the river-bank. It's me he's after of course, not the men on land, though he'll get a bonus for capturing the goods. That's if the commissioners pay up, they're notoriously slow.' He laughed. 'You can hardly blame Roxton and his colleagues for being frustrated.'

'He's after me too,' Annie added. 'Only he doesn't know it's me! The last time I met him he said he was after my lover – he meant that stranger in breeches and boots who gallops around the countryside on horseback!'

Matt put his arm around her. 'You must take care. They'll put you in gaol as readily as any man.'

He kissed her goodbye when they reached the cottage. 'I won't come in,' he smiled as she tried to persuade him. 'If I do, I won't want to leave, and the crew will be waiting for me.'

'You'll take care won't you? Don't antagonize the Customs men.' She suddenly felt afraid, she couldn't bear it if he should be captured, or killed as Toby had been; her life would be finished.

He laughed. 'Would I do such a thing as that? Not I! The next time I come up river I shall have only legitimate goods, duty paid. So warn everyone there'll be no activity for a few weeks.'

*   *   *

It amused her to visit Mr Beddows again, dressed in her breeches and boots and with Toby's hat pulled over her face. She met him at night in his orchard on a pre-arranged meeting and they spoke only in whispers as he handed over the money he owed. She told him that there wouldn't be any goods for him for a while as the customs were getting too close to take the risk.

'Mm,' he pondered. 'That's a pity, and Roxton can't be bribed, it's been tried. He's as straight as an arrow that fellow. Well, never mind, young man, we'll just have to be patient.'

Snow was falling as she rode into Hessle and she knocked on Robin's door to ask him to tell Josh to collect Sorrel and have him stabled as the weather was obviously going to get much worse. Robin answered the door and she thought how pale and thin he looked, he hadn't got over his last bout of fever, and his left hand was bandaged.

He held it up at her query. 'I've been working at 'quarry,' he said. 'But I nearly sliced me finger off wi' one of pick axes. I can't go in now until its healed, so there's no wages coming in.' He shook his head. 'I'm not cut out for this sort of life, Annie. I was meant to be a gentleman, I'm sure of it. It's just unfortunate that I was born at 'wrong time and in wrong place.'

She laughed with him. He could always make a joke, could Robin, but she couldn't help thinking that his slight frame wasn't meant to be wielding a pick or crowbar in an effort to extract chalk from the quarry; or even to be breathing in the fumes as the chalk was burnt to make lime mortar for builders, for the work was hard and arduous and needed strength and muscle such as his brother Josh had.

The time hung heavily as the weather worsened and she brought in extra kindling and logs for the fire and fetched in another bucket of water from the spring. Then she opened her door one morning to find that snow had been falling heavily and had drifted halfway up the door frame. She'd brought in a spade just a few days before and with some effort managed to make a way through. The snow lay pristine and sparkling, a white carpet down to the river which in contrast to the snow, looked grey.

The following two days she couldn't get out at all for the wind had blown the snow almost to the top of the door and window, so she built up the fire and crept back into bed to try to keep warm and hoped the thaw would soon come. On the third day she busied herself sorting out the lists of numbers for the contacts on land, the farmers and men of property who were eager to buy from those who ran the risk of smuggling the goods from across the sea, the labouring men and women who supplemented their meagre income by waiting on wet wintry nights by the river for the ship to appear and offload into their coggy boats.

She put her head onto the table. She felt tired and lethargic and slightly nauseous. I haven't had much to eat, she thought. I'll make some gruel, that'll settle me and give me some energy. She poured water and oats into a pan and placed it on the fire to boil. It started to bubble and thicken and when it was cooked she poured some of it into a bowl. It was thick and glutinous and stuck to the spoon.

'I never was much of a cook,' she muttered to herself, 'but I suppose it's better than nothing.'

She ate no more than half of it when she started to feel sick again and so lay down on the bed. But a minute later sat up retching.

'Oh,' she groaned, her eyes streaming and the back of her throat strained. 'I haven't felt as sick as this since – since – our Jimmy!'

Realization hit her like a blow and she closed her eyes and put her hand to her head. 'Oh,' she whispered. 'I never thought! I didn't think I could!'

She never imagined that she would become pregnant again after the dreadful labour she had had with Jimmy. The midwife had shaken her head and said she needn't worry any more. Her flux had never been regular and when she thought back she couldn't even remember when her last one had been.

For a few minutes she was elated. This is coming 'cos of love, she thought, a bonding between Matt and me. I wanted him just as much as he wanted me. She went to fetch the hand mirror and held it up above her, looking to see if there was any change in her body, any thickening of her waistline, but there wasn't, she looked just the same. She ran her hands across her belly and her hips, there was no sign, and yet she knew.

She thought of the first time she became pregnant, with Lizzie. She hadn't known then. I was that ignorant, she thought. She hadn't realized that she was pregnant or why she kept being sick, but Alan did, and when he came home one day and saw her retching, he'd hit her, knocking her onto the floor in his fury at her being caught with a child.

He hated me when I was big. Big and ugly he said I was, even though I wasn't very big, not like some women. But he couldn't stand the sight of me. She gave a sob. Each time, each time – as if it was all my fault. But at least he kept away from me, he didn't want me then. Not 'till it was all over.

So how will Matt feel about it? Do all men feel the same? I expect they do. And will I be an embarrassment to him? 'Yes, of course I will,' she whispered despairingly. 'He'll not want a bastard child. It doesn't matter to folks like me, there's no shame in it – but he's gentry, no matter that he tries to deny it.'

She went across to the window and peered through a small gap where the snow hadn't reached. The sun was up and the snow crystals were sparkling and scintillating like shards of glass. I'm trapped, she thought, and I thought I was free. As she stood pondering, she saw two figures, dark against the white background, break through the hedge into the meadow and stand up to their knees in the snow, their hands shielding their eyes and staring at the cottage. They turned to each other and as if making a decision started to make their way laboriously towards it.

'Mrs Hope! Mrs Hope. Is tha all right?' Josh and Robin stood by her door, both with a spade over their shoulders.

She knocked on the window and called back. 'Aye. I'm all right, but can you dig me out?'

'Aye, that's why we've come. We guessed tha'd be snowed in when we hadn't seen thee.'

She could hear their grunts as they tried to clear a path to her door and then the scraping of the spades on the door as they reached it. She tested the kettle, just in time, this was the last of her water, the bucket was empty. She put it on the fire to make them a drink and then tried the door to see if it would give.

Her eyes watered with the brightness as daylight flooded in and with it the sharp cold air.

'By, tha doesn't look well, Mrs Hope. Has tha had nowt to eat?' Josh was concerned as he peered at her face. 'Tha looks that pale.'

'Well I've been cooped up for a few days, and even if I could have opened the door I couldn't have gone anywhere.'

They scraped their boots free of snow and came in at her invitation, she made them tea but didn't drink any herself, the thought of the strong brown liquid turned her stomach and she poured some hot water into a cup and sipped it.

She felt Josh observing her with some consideration and presently he said to Robin, 'Now tha's finished tha tay, why dossn't thee finish clearing 'path? I'll come and help thee in a minute.'

Robin did as he was bid and Josh leaned towards her. 'Tha's got caught, hasn't tha?' he whispered. 'In family way!'

'How can you tell?' she stammered. No point in denying it, not to Josh.

'My wife allus drinks hot water to take away sickness, she can't keep owt else down.'

'What am I going to do, Josh? I'll have to leave won't I?'

He drew in his breath. 'He'd look after thee and 'bairn; he wouldn't see thee go short, but tha might be a hindrance to him; he's gentry after all. And wives are for breeding and doxys' for summat different, if tha'll beg my pardon, Mrs Hope. I've seen how tha's cared for each other, but he's bound to take a wife of his own kind one day.'

A doxy! A mistress! She stared at the kindly man opposite. No word of reproach; he was only telling her that that is how it would seem. No-one would understand what love there had been. And of course he was right. He would need a wife one day to run that fine house on the Wolds. She imagined the scorn Matt's father would pour on him if he found out about her, even though he probably had bastards of his own, if what Toby had said was true.

'So do you think I should go? Should I leave?' She willed him to tell her no, that everything would be all right, that Matt wouldn't mind.

'I'd be sorry to see thee go, but it's how tha feels about him. Passion's a strange thing, but love's summat different, and if tha cares for him then tha'll not tie him down.'

How strange, she thought, that this short, plain, homely-looking man, should give out wisdom on the aspects of passion and love. You don't need to possess a handsome face or winsome grace to know of it. She smiled sadly. How lucky he was. Just as she was; for even though she knew the decision she must make, nothing could take away what she had shared with Matt.

*   *   *

A message had been passed on that the *Breeze* was on the coast somewhere near Whitby and would be in Hull in a week, she would then make her way up river towards Hessle.

Annie was desperate. I need to see him one more time.

How can I go without holding him in my arms and kissing him goodbye? But it was impossible. He would know that something was wrong, she wouldn't be able to hide it. He would be kind, she knew, and say that he would look after her. But she didn't want that. She didn't want to hold him because she was dependant on him, and she was so afraid that he would feel tricked or caught and would cease to love her.

And now doubts started to creep in and she started to wonder if he did indeed love her. He had said so many wonderful things, but maybe men of his class did that. How could she tell, never having known it before?

Tha's tired Annie, she told herself, and depressed. Once more she slipped into her own tongue as doubts and self-deprecation flooded over her. But she gave herself a mental shake and cried out loud. 'Don't doubt him. What tha had was wonderful.'

She packed her bags with cloth and muslins and carried them down to the bottom of the meadow where the cart was hidden. The donkey had been stabled for the winter but Josh had brought it back for her and it was cropping on the hard ground. Then she took out all the silk from the chest and carefully folded it and packed that also. She took out the silk dress and lovingly stroked it and thought of that special night, then shook it to free it of creases and hung it on a peg on the wall.

It will be the first thing he sees as he comes in. He'll remember that night when we never slept, and maybe he'll always think of me lovingly. She sat and stared at it, at its shimmering softness, and remembered its luxurious sensuousness as it clung to her body, and of the enchanting evening when she had known such happiness.

'I shan't ever forget. How can I when I'll have a constant reminder?' She ran her hand across her breasts and down her waist to the special place where a new life was beginning.

She said goodbye to the Trotts. 'I have to be moving on for a bit. I allus said I would, didn't I?'

'We'll miss thee, Mrs Hope,' Henry Trott said, nodding his head. 'Where's tha off to?'

She answered vaguely and waved her hand in the direction of the river. 'I might take the ferry, I haven't decided yet.'

Mrs Trott whispered in her ear out of Mr Trott's hearing. 'What about 'running? Who's going to do that if tha's not here. Tha's letting a lot of folks down.'

No word of sorrow at her departure, only concern that the goods wouldn't be coming in.

'Josh,' she whispered back. 'He'll tell you what's happening.'

She'd persuaded Josh that he could organize the running on his own and had suggested that he asked Robin to become the agent and collect the money from the farmers and landowners who were supplied with goods.

'He's a presentable lad,' she'd said, 'and can add up in his head, and I'll give him a letter to say he's taking over. He can give up work at the quarry then for he's not suited for it.'

'I'll not disagree with that,' Josh had pondered, 'but I was going to ask if tha'd take him with thee. Tha'll need somebody on 'road to look after thee, there's some villains about, robbers and that.'

'I can't, Josh. I can only be responsible for myself and the bairn I'm carrying. But, maybe I'll send for him one day – if I get settled. I'm fond of him, you know that don't you?' And she'd asked him to say goodbye for her when she'd gone for she couldn't bear to see the disappointment on the boy's face.

'Aye, he's fond of thee, he'd do owt for thee would Robin.'

Sorrow gripped her as she left the Trotts' cottage. She'd miss them all. She'd found real friendship here. Toby, Robin, Josh, Henry Trott, she'd even miss Mrs Trott, with her funny grasping ways, and at least her dislike was predictable.

As she walked back up the meadow towards her cottage

she fingered the pearls beneath her shirt, the ones she and Matt had found in the chest and the ones he had brought for her hair. I'll never part with these, she thought, never, even if I'm on my last crust, nor the scarf that Toby gave me. They were given in love.

Josh had asked her when she was leaving and where she was going, and again she'd waved vaguely towards the river. 'Tha's never going to try for London, Mrs Hope? They do say there's fortunes to be made there, but it's a long way off.'

She hadn't denied it and told him that she would leave first thing the next morning, and she knew that he would be there to see her off. But that was the last thing she wanted. Lingering goodbyes would bring tears and she must harden herself for this parting.

She sat on the doorstep watching dusk fall. The river was turbulent, the crests of the waves were creamy brown as they tossed and tumbled. The air was cold and the ground hard with the frost that was still lingering. It's not a time to be travelling, she told herself; once before I set off on a journey when winter was approaching, and now here I am again, continuing my travels in the middle of it. Well at least this time I have warm clothes and boots, and money – and goods to sell and a donkey-cart to ride in. What riches! If the folks in Hull could see me, wouldn't they wonder at it!

But my poor bairns. It seems that I'm destined to be always parted from them. I wonder if you're being a good lass, Lizzie? Maria and Will 'll take care of you, I'm sure of that, God bless them. And my lads—! She bent her head and silently wept. It's a punishment. I'm being paid back for what I did.

As darkness came she went inside and lit a lantern and packed bread and cheese into a cloth. She put on warm stockings and her boots and took the cloak from behind the door. She picked up the lantern and turned towards the door. I'll not look back, she thought. Only forward.

But she couldn't help herself. She turned and lifted

the light. It lit on Toby's boots, the ones she had worn, which were leaning lopsidedly against the wall. 'Goodbye Toby,' she whispered. 'God bless thee. Sleep in peace.' It shone on the dress, catching the silken scintillant threads in shimmering, radiant splendour. 'Goodbye Matt, my only love. Don't ever forget me.'

She closed the door behind her and hid the key where she knew Matt would find it, and holding the lantern high she strode out down the meadow.

27

Matt ran up the meadow. There's no fire, he thought. No smoke from the chimney. What a woman, he smiled, she's no housewife, no cook. But she's—. He grinned with elation. She's something special.

He'd met his old friend Greg in Hull, who on greeting him had said, 'So, you found your little widow? I knew there was a reason for the smile on your face.'

'She's *wonderful*, Greg. The most wonderful woman I've ever met.'

Greg had slapped him on the back. 'But I seem to remember, *you* said, she was impudent and opinionated and came from the gutter, and wasn't your type of woman at all!'

'I was wrong,' he'd grinned. 'She is from the gutter, but she's my type of woman; she has fire and guts and isn't afraid to say what she means.'

Greg had looked at him curiously. 'And what do you intend to do with this wonderful woman? Are we going to get a chance to look at her? Will you introduce her to your father?' he added cynically.

'I shan't let *you* clap eyes on her, you old sea dog. I wouldn't trust you. And as for my father, he's met her already.' He'd stroked his beard and mused. 'She was play-acting, pretending to be a foreign lady.' He told Greg about the party. 'But I think he liked her, he seemed to find her unique – which she is.'

He smiled now as he reached the cottage door, Greg had had such a look of incredulity on his face and had shaken his head in mock despair at his friend's apparent derangement.

He banged on the door. 'Come on, Annie. Where are you hiding?' He peered through the small window. There wasn't a fire, nor had there been for some days by the look of the dead ash in the hearth. He put his hand up to shield the reflection of the glass. Her dress was hanging up on the wall. Had she put it there to remind her of that wonderful night? The night when he had known that there would never be anyone else in his life but her.

He looked round for the key and on finding it opened the door. The cottage was cold and empty; the blankets were folded neatly at the bottom of the bed and the table was cleared, no milk jug or crockery, only a bread knife lying on a wooden board. He knelt and felt the ashes, they were cold and burnt through to a fine dust and hadn't been warmed for a long time.

She must be ill. He came out in a cold fear. Mrs Trott will know, or Josh, yes Josh, he'll know what's happened. He dashed out of the door and ran back down the meadow.

Josh was waiting for him in the lane beyond the hedge. 'I was waiting on thee, Captain. I knew tha'd be here about now.'

Matt grabbed his arm, 'Mrs Hope, where is she? She's not at the cottage. Is she ill?'

'No sir, she's not ill, not so far as I know, anyhow. But she's gone, sir.'

'Gone! What are you talking about, man? Gone where?'

'I don't know, Captain. She said as how she was having to be moving on, and when I came to give her a hand to load her things, she'd already flitted.'

Matt ran his fingers through his hair and clasped his head. 'I don't understand what you're saying, Josh. Why should she go, especially without telling me? You say you knew she was going? Why didn't you get a message to me?'

Josh drew himself up in a dignified manner, yet touched his forehead. 'Beggin' tha pardon, Captain, but it wasn't my place.'

Matt gave an exclamation. 'Oh. No. Sorry. Of course not.'

He put his hand to his mouth. 'There has to be a reason,' he muttered. 'Something has happened.' There came a vague recollection of something Toby had once said. Something about her being in trouble with the law. But she had never discussed it with him. They had never spoken about their pasts, either of them. They had always been so wrapped up in the present. He cursed himself for not asking before. She might well have had fears and anxieties that I didn't know of, that I could have shared, helped her with, he thought.

'There'll be a note,' he said abruptly. 'Bound to be. I'll go back and look.'

'Yes sir.' Josh had a frown on his forehead as Matt turned and raced back towards the cottage. 'I hope as I haven't made a big mistake,' he muttered. 'I allus thought gentry was different from 'rest of us, but I could be wrong.'

There wasn't a note, no sign to indicate where or why she had gone. Matt went down to the Trotts' house to enquire, and then to the river for they seemed to think that she was catching one of the boats across into Lincolnshire.

'Did she mention the ferry to you, Josh?' he asked after returning from fruitless enquiries of the ferry men. 'Try to remember if you can. What exactly did she say?'

He watched Josh's face. There was something he wasn't telling him, he wasn't looking him in the eye.

'She didn't exactly say she was going across 'river,' Josh said slowly, 'Though I got 'impression that that's what she meant. And – and I think we mentioned London, though I'm not altogether sure of it.'

'London! Good God, man. She'll never get to London. Do you know how far it is?'

Josh shook his head miserably. 'It's a long way, I believe, sir.'

'A long way! The woman must be mad! How has she gone? Is she walking? She's taken Sorrel?'

'No sir, she's taken 'donkey-and-cart. They were hers. She gave me 'money for 'em some time back and I bought 'em for her.'

It had been planned then! A sudden anger brought a flush to his face. She'd never intended staying! Matt stared at Josh as he comprehended what had happened. She'd gathered some money together from selling her cloth and bought the donkey-and-cart and now she'd gone. She was probably off on another adventure. Well, men do it, he sneered sceptically. They have a good time with a woman and then clear off to pastures new. But why would she when they'd been so happy together? They had been happy hadn't they? It wasn't just him?

He was suddenly aware that Josh had been speaking to him. 'What? The goods? No, nothing this time. I told Annie – Mrs Hope – that we wouldn't risk it this time. In about three weeks. Then we'll have something for you. We'll carry on as usual. If we can.'

He turned and strode back to the cottage. He'd have one more look and then he'd have to leave; his crew would be getting anxious.

The room seemed so bare and deserted. He sat down on the bed and stared into space. Nothing. She had taken all that was hers, but she had left Toby's clothes and his boots, she had taken nothing that didn't belong to her. Not even the gown which she could have had, for no-one else will wear it if not her, he thought, as he stared at it hanging there. No-one else will wear it. He stood up. No one. No-one. He picked up the knife which lay on the table and holding the blade high, lashed out at the flimsy fabric, ripping it with sharp sweeping violent slashes until it hung in shredded tatters.

*   *   *

'All hands on deck!'

'Aye, aye, sir.'

He couldn't wait to sail away. To leave behind the solid earth, the meadowland and the cottage which had been Toby's, but where at last he had laid Toby's memory to rest. And now it held nothing for him, not now that she had gone.

'Helm's alee!' He uttered the warning cry as he put the helm down to swing the ship up to the wind.

He'd told Josh that he would be back in three weeks but he doubted if he would return. I can't face that river if she's not going to be there to greet me.

He barely spoke to his men, giving them orders only and not indulging in his usual conversation with them – although they respected him as their captain they were not afraid to speak or joke with him – most of them had crewed with him for a long time.

They were two days and nights out into the German Ocean and the coastline of Holland had been sighted, when Parson White came to speak to him after supper. 'Beggin' tha pardon, cap'n, but some of the men, me included had been wondering if all's well?'

Matt looked up from his table and ran his hand over his eyes. He'd drunk too much brandy, he decided, his head was swimmy and he couldn't concentrate on writing up his log.

'All's well? What do you mean? Hasn't the bell been struck?'

'Sorry, sir. I wasn't referring to the nightwatch; no, the crew are concerned that you are a bit under the weather – not quite yourself, sir.'

'Kind of them to be so considerate,' he said sharply. 'Give the men my compliments. I'm perfectly well.'

'The landlubbers are going to be disgruntled that there's nothing for them this trip.' Parson White rumbled on. 'I reckon most of them rely on us to add money to their pockets.'

'Well, there might be some changes,' Matt replied abruptly. 'There's going to be another agent, and if it doesn't work out we might have to find another port of call.'

Parson White squinted through his one good eye. 'Why

would that be sir? Mrs—, erm, – the young gentleman that is, seemed to be doing well.'

'Oh, give up, Master Parson! I know that you know, that Mrs Hope and the *young gentleman* as you call her, are one and the same. But she's gone. She's moved on elsewhere.'

'Ah.' Parson White had a keen sense of perception and turned down his lips. 'And do we know why or where she's gone sir? It just seems a pity,' he added as Matt turned a sour look at him. 'She seemed to fit in just right – with the running and such, I meant.'

Matt rested his elbows on the table and put his chin in his hands. 'No. I don't know why or where, but only that she's gone and probably not coming back.'

'Women are strange creatures,' Parson White said chattily. 'They get strange fancies, but usually they're happy to stay where they're comfortable. Mrs Hope was comfortable enough, I fancy?'

Matt nodded but made no reply.

Parson White eyed the captain. 'She'd want for nothing, I wager. Probably had more now than she'd ever had in her life: yet she should choose to leave!'

'What are you getting at? Come on, man, spit it out.' Matt heaved a sigh and sat back in his chair and looked at the former cleric. He forgot sometimes that the man had taken holy orders. He was an intelligent man and but for his misbehaviour with the ladies of his living, could have been ensconced comfortably in a nice house with servants, a carriage to drive and a goodly supply of food and drink.

'May I sit down, sir?' He placed himself into a chair before Matt could reply and nodded his head as Matt moved the brandy decanter towards him.

He lifted his glass and reflectively studied the amber liquid. He spun it around the glass and then held it between his hands to warm it. Matt lit a candle and placed it in the middle of the table and the parson leaned forward and rotated the glass above it, warming the drink. He sniffed it appreciatively and then took a sip.

'This is good,' he nodded. 'We must try for more of this,' and it seemed to Matt that they could have been cronies in a gentleman's club and not man and master on board a sailing ship.

'As I was saying, sir. There has to be a reason for a woman leaving, or a man for that matter, and in my own experience, it's usually the man who cuts and runs. It would have to be something very serious for a woman to leave the place where she's most comfortable: they have no rights, as we know, the poor unfortunate creatures. Where would she go for one thing?' He took another sip of brandy. 'If she's a lady, she might go to her family, though it's doubtful that they would want her back. And if she's not a lady—.' He glanced at Matt: 'then there's only one way to go, I should say, and that's downhill, for though she might get work – as a servant or a maid in an inn or such thing, it's a very precarious existence for a woman, fraught with every kind of danger.'

Matt stared, horror-struck. He'd been so overcome by his own loss that he hadn't thought that Annie might be in peril.

'So, what we have to establish is why Mrs Hope went.' The parson reached over and helped himself to another tot. 'She has either done something dreadful and is running away to escape the law and its consequences – and I know only too well about that subject – or she has a conscience about something and can't face you.'

'You see.' He stretched out his legs and crossed them. 'I ran away several times, but only when I got found out or when the women were starting to bother me, as women do from time to time. It was a pity,' he said, 'for I was often very comfortable, but they *would* make demands on me, or start getting possessive, or pregnant, and then they would want me to marry them, and I couldn't – for I was already married – several times.'

Matt smiled in spite of himself, the man would be in gaol if ever the law could catch him.

'Yes,' Parson White continued. 'I remember one of my wives; the third one I think it was.' He sighed. 'She was a pretty little thing, but she started to get all kinds of strange notions when she became pregnant. They change you know,' he added, 'they become quite different, not rational. Anyway, she got these fancies that I wouldn't love her when she became fat, and that I would go off with someone else if I was given half the chance. Which, of course, is exactly what I did do.'

*   *   *

Matt stood in the prow of the ship, his feet apart and his arms folded across his chest. The wind blew through his hair and he watched without seeing as the *Breeze* cut through the foaming waves. Above him the night canopy glittered with a million stars.

She's expecting a child! Our child! Why didn't she tell me? Did she think I would abandon her or not want her any more? Surely she knew me better than that? Out of his despondent melancholy came the recognition that she didn't know him, that she only had a general opinion of men of her own class, and by her own admission had been hurt by them.

Why should she think that I'm any different? I could be worse. Men like me do take advantage of women like her, women without money or hope; they use their bodies for their own satisfaction and then abandon them, just as Parson White said. How cruel I must have seemed when I first met her – so harsh. And if indeed she loves me as she says she does, then she wouldn't want me to be compromised and she wouldn't want to be just taken care of – not with money – like some doxy.

He leaned against the bulwark and stared into the distance. How intolerable for her. He thought of his friend Greg and his question, 'What will you do with this wonderful woman?' Annie wouldn't know of my intentions, even I don't know what they are, I haven't thought about it. I've just been so besotted by her. But I would never abandon her, or my child. My child! He felt a warming of his spirit. A child of his loins.

He turned towards his cabin below decks. He'd try to sleep. Tomorrow they would reach Holland. They would load as quickly as possible for an immediate turn around. With luck and a following wind they would reach home shores in just a few days and he would set in motion all posible means at his disposal of finding her and bringing her back.

But he lay sleepless and restless in his bunk. She had already disappeared once, from her life in Hull. Was she being searched for by someone from that town? She had hidden from the world in Toby's cottage and he had protected her.

He sat up and put his head in his hands. She could so easily disappear again, only this time she might not be so lucky to find someone like Toby. The possibilities of the hazards facing her loomed large and menacing and he was gripped by a grim cold fear.

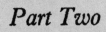

Part Two

28

Annie looked down from the window into the street and saw the regiment of soldiers trotting by, the flash of their scarlet tunics brightening the dull day.

'Henry!' She called to the child playing on the floor with his wooden bricks. 'Come here and see the soldiers.'

The little boy came to her and lifted his arms for her to pick him up that he might see out. She stood him on the wide oak windowsill and he pressed his nose against the small-paned glass. 'Where they go, Mamma?'

'Back to their barracks for their breakfast,' she smiled at him and planted a kiss on his fair head. They've been practising their killing games, she thought. What violent times we are living in. A reign of terror raging in France, Louis XVI and his queen dead, and England at war with France.

'Mrs Hope! Mrs Hope!'

Henry lifted his head and chortled. 'Mrs Hope, Mamma!'

She opened the door of the room and looked down the stairs. 'Yes, Mr Sampson? Do you need me?'

'If you could just come down.' The elderly man, clad in a silk embroidered waistcoat and an old-fashioned frock-coat and curled wig was standing at the bottom of the stairs, looking anxious. 'Mrs Downham has come in and insists on seeing you.' He looked rueful and whispered, 'It seems that the proprietor of this establishment is no longer good enough for the lady.'

Annie laughed. 'I'll be down directly.'

She put her son into his cot and gave him his bricks

to play with. 'Stay and play, there's a good boy. Mamma won't be long.'

Henry pulled a lip. 'Where's Polly?'

'Polly will be here soon. Now be good, I'm only in the shop, not far away.'

She took off her apron and hung it behind the door, and looked into the mirrored glass on the wall. A composed dispassionate face stared back at her as she smoothed her hair, which she wore in a coil at the back of her neck, and adjusted the lace edging on her bodice. Turning away with a small sigh she lifted the hem of her grey dress and hurried downstairs to greet her customer.

Mrs Downham had taken a fancy to Annie when she had come into the shop and met her for the first time. She had watched as Annie draped satins and velvets across the oak counter, swathing them into drapes and simulating skirts and trains, and listening as Annie made suggestions for trimmings and accessories.

Since then she had been a regular customer and Mr Sampson was only too pleased, for not only had Annie released him from the pressure of suggesting styles for ladies of ample build like Mrs Downham, but word had spread of the new assistant at the draper's shop who knew about cloth and who had even brought samples with her that couldn't be bought elsewhere.

As she courteously greeted Mrs Downham, Annie recollected the first time she had attended her. It had been her first day as an assistant and she was so nervous, wondering what she would say to the fine ladies who came into Aaron Sampson's drapery shop.

'You'll be all right,' he'd said to her. 'You know more about brocades, damasks and flowered satins than they do, they'll trust in your judgement.'

But I don't know much, she'd thought at the time, for though she hadn't lied to him about her past, she had embellished a little about the length of time she had handled and sold cloth. But Mrs Downham had been impressed and she had bought some of the muslins which Annie had brought with her and sold to Mr Sampson.

Today Mrs Downham only wanted new gloves to match a garment she had ordered previously. Annie wrapped them for her and opened the door and wished her good-day, and then turned with a broad smile to Mr Sampson.

'I could have done that,' he said, grumbling in a jocular manner, 'But no, it has to be Mrs Hope! Still,' he said approvingly. 'You were right, I'm glad you suggested that we stock gloves and fans and such, it's been a nice little sideline.'

Annie nodded and listened. She heard Henry call for her. 'Where's Polly?' she asked. 'She's late.'

'I sent her on an errand, she'll be back presently.'

'Good, she can take Henry for a walk and then perhaps we can change the window display. I thought we could have something patriotic, red and white, like the soldiers uniforms, with a swathe of black satin like their boots.'

He shook his head. 'You're amazing, Annie. Why didn't I think of that.'

'Why don't you go up to my room and make a dish of tea and talk to Henry while I empty the window?' she suggested. 'We shan't be too busy just yet, the morning is too grey and unsettled for the ladies to venture out shopping.'

She knew he would need no further persuading. He loved to play with the little boy, he'd had no children of his own, and said he hadn't missed them, but he would dearly have liked grandchildren to spoil.

He had been so kind to her, especially that first day when she had arrived in York, unsure of herself and her surroundings. 'You were like a lost soul that day,' he'd said later when he knew her better.

And indeed she had been lost, her spirit was lost, her strength was lost after the long, long journey from Hessle to the Wolds, across to Market Weighton and down towards the bowl-shaped valley that was the Vale of York.

She had set off in darkness, taking the paths she knew

and skirting the town of Hessle to avoid being seen. She regretted not seeing Robin, but she was sure that he would have tried to persuade her to stay or else insist on coming with her. She'd found a sheltered spot within a copse and spent the long night huddled beneath a blanket and it was then that misery had descended, she thought of all she had lost and wept in despair.

When the morning broke and the first streaks of dawn stroked the receding night sky, she'd moved on; she'd shivered with cold and so walked at the side of the donkey to try to get her blood warm. She ate at midday and then was sick and nauseous and vowed she would only drink water for the rest of the day.

But as chance would have it, she had seen Mr Sutcliff and Rose driving towards their village and they had both insisted that she should go home with them and spend the night there. In the bedroom that night she had confided in Lily and told her that she was heading for York.

'Don't tell of me, Lily, will you?' she'd asked. 'I don't want Matt to be charitable towards me. I want his love, not his pity.'

Lily had listened wide-eyed at her story and said how lucky she was to be carrying her lover's child. 'It'll be hard for thee, but tha'll always have some reminder, Annie, not just a ribbon.' She'd touched the ribbon in her hair, 'but something tha can love instead.'

As she had driven away the next morning Rose had come to her and asked about Robin. She'd smiled at the girl and touched her cheek. 'Be patient, Rose, I'm sure he'll come for you one day.'

But she wasn't sure, she wasn't even sure that Robin would agree to becoming an agent for the contraband goods. He was such an honest lad, she mused as she'd cracked her whip and headed off down the rutted frozen track – he would probably rather work in the quarry doing honest hard labour than sully his hands with illegal goods.

She emptied the window of the display and fetched

a cloth to dust away the cobwebs and grime that had accumulated since she had last cleaned it – and watched through the new, squared, plate glass window, which had replaced the bow-shaped bubble glass, as Polly sauntered down the street, with a basket in her hand. The girl saw her watching and immediately quickened her step.

'Sorry, Mrs Hope. I got delayed.'

Polly had been employed, at Mr Sampson's insistence, to help look after Henry and run errands, so that Annie would be free to help him in the shop. But she was lazy, and Annie had caught her on two occasions fast asleep in a chair with Henry wide awake and wet and hungry in his cot.

Still, she's just a child, she thought, as she draped a length of red satin over a stand, twelve years old; I shouldn't expect so much. She'll be about my Lizzie's age, I should think. She sighed, where has the time gone to? She thought back once more of her journey towards York after leaving the warmth of the Sutcliff household.

What a simpleton I was, thinking that I should be able to travel alone, just me and my donkey. She remembered the bitterly cold frosty nights, when she'd slept in the cart, and the muddy impassable roads once the thaw had started. And she shivered when she thought of the footpad who had held her up, who had kept his hand on the donkey's snaffle and demanded money from her.

She'd held out a money bag towards him. It had three coins in it, the rest of her money was tucked securely beneath her skirts, where, she had vowed it would stay. I'll be raped or murdered before anyone gets their hands on that.

He'd taken the bag from her and emptied it into his hand. 'Is this all tha's got?'

'Aye. If tha relieves me of that I'll have nowt to buy bread with.'

'There's no place up here where tha can buy bread,' he'd grinned and put the money in his pocket. 'So tha'll not be needing it.'

He'd demanded she open her packs in the cart, and she'd deliberately opened one which had contained rich velvets and heavy satins, knowing that he wouldn't be able to sell them as they would look so obviously like stolen goods.

'Would tha rob thine own kind?' she'd been emboldened to ask.

'Think thaself lucky tha can keep yon donkey,' he'd growled. 'Tha must have had money for that.'

She'd shaken her head and lied. 'It's not mine, it's my master's. If tha takes that he'll have 'constables after thee.'

He'd let go of the snaffle then and slapped the donkey's rump. 'Go on then,' he snarled. 'Get going before I change me mind.' He stepped away, but the donkey who was normally mild, took exception to the blow and lashed out with her back legs and caught him on the shin. Annie cracked her whip and left, leaving the thief hopping on one leg and cursing.

As she arranged her display she nodded to several people who were passing by, a butcher from the Shambles, his apron splashed with blood, a floury-faced girl going home from the bakery where she had spent the night kneading dough, and a young maid who called often on her mistress's errands. Then her eye caught sight of someone crossing the street and she groaned inwardly. Mrs Mortimer, Mr Sampson's sister, and she was coming straight towards the shop.

Annie gave her a polite smile as she entered the door, the bell jangling loudly.

'It's time that clapper was fixed.' Mrs Mortimer gave no other greeting. She leaned heavily on a striped parasol which was made of the same material as her walking dress which showed beneath a short grey cape. 'It's far too loud. Is Mr Sampson at liberty?'

'Good morning Mrs Mortimer. Yes, he's upstairs. I'll tell him you're here.' Annie knew that Mrs Mortimer didn't like her, had never liked her, but the feeling was mutual. Annie considered that she was mean and grasping;

she ordered her brother around as if he was still a callow youth, and seemed to consider Annie a threat.

Mr Sampson moaned when Annie whispered to him that his sister was here. 'She gives me heartburn,' he complained. 'She'll ruin the day with her grousing.'

Annie continued with her window display while Mr Sampson took his sister to the small room at the back of the shop where a fire burned and where the draper took his midday meal of ale and bread and cheese.

'I'm just a simple man,' he'd told her when he first offered her the position of assistant and the use of the room upstairs. 'I can manage here for what I want,' and in the evening he went home to the small lodging house in Jubbergate.

She draped a swathe of black satin along the base of the window and remembered standing at the top of a hill and gazing down into the valley, wondering if the donkey-and-cart would get down safely or if the steep descent would tip them all over. She'd had to take a rest from the long pull up the hill and had marvelled at the landscape unrolling in front of her. It had been almost midday and the mist was still lying like a mantle in the valley bottom, but as she watched, it had lifted like the raising of a diaphanous skirt until the whole valley lay open before her.

A troop of soldiers had ridden up and she'd called to them, asking where she was. 'That's the Vale of York,' the trooper captain had said. He'd looked at her mode of transport. 'Two days and you can be in the city itself. We'll help you down the hill if you like.'

She'd accepted gratefully, for she had been exhausted. One of the soldiers ran a lead to the donkey's snaffle and another had tied a rope to the cart to hold it back, and together they had descended into the valley bottom.

But it had taken her longer than he'd said because she had been so weary that she had tethered the donkey to a tree, and climbed back into the cart and slept for a whole day. It had started to rain, clearing away the remaining drifts of snow, but dripping in through the tarpaulin which covered her and her precious parcels of cloth.

She'd moved on when she'd felt better and on crossing a stone bridge over the flowing river Derwent, she'd stopped again. Willows were bending their slender naked branches towards the water and she too bent to wash her hands and face, and brushed her hair with the silver brush which had belonged to Toby and Matt's mother, and which she had decided she could reasonably claim as her own. Take what you need, Toby had said, and she needed this reminder of what had been, for she felt very lonely.

The day had only just begun as she'd entered the old city walls through the Walmgate Bar. The walls were still standing with their gates and posterns intact, and though decayed in parts because of their antiquity, they were not destroyed and broken like the walls of Hull which were being demolished to enlarge the town. She'd felt lost, unsure of which way to turn.

She'd seen the draper's shop as she'd led the donkey through Fossgate and thought that the next day, after she had found lodgings and had had a good night's sleep, she would call with one of the packs and see if she could sell some of her cloth. It was good quality, she was sure of it, for she had felt the difference in the samples that Mr Moses had shown her and had seen the approval in his eyes when she had chosen a particular weight and quality.

The lodgings were simple but clean and she had stabled the donkey in the yard and carried the packs up to her room. She had paid extra to have a room to herself, for she dare not risk losing any of her merchandise to any dubious fellow traveller.

Mr Sampson had raised a wary eyebrow as she entered his shop with a pack on her shoulder, but she spoke moderately and politely, not just for the sake of politeness but because she was also nervous, never having stepped within the threshold of such an imposing establishment as this, with its silken hangings, waxed oak counters and polished wood floors. Mr Sampson himself made her quake – for he looked every inch a gentleman with a fine waistcoat beneath his grey frock-coat, and knee breeches on his portly figure, and flat buckled shoes – though reason told her that he couldn't possibly be.

She'd laid out some of her muslins for him to see when a lady had entered the door. Annie had stood back and tried to make herself invisible while Mr Sampson made his obsequious rites to the imperious client. She had spotted Annie's samples on the counter and fingered them and asked if they were available in another pattern, and Annie had given a nod to Mr Sampson's imperceptible silent query.

Annie shook her head reproachfully as she completed her display. She could hear Mrs Mortimer's wittering voice carrying through from the back room and Mr Sampson's weary inaudible reply. She folded away the unused material and placed it neatly on one of the shelves. It never ceased to amaze her that she had become so neat and tidy, but it gave her such pleasure to see the rows of shiny satins arranged in descending shades of colour, the pretty sprigged muslins, the warm shades of wool set to compliment each other.

She knocked on the open door of the rear room where Mrs Mortimer was finishing a cup of tea. 'I do beg your pardon, Mrs Mortimer, but I just wanted to tell Mr Sampson that I've finished the display. I know you wanted to have a look at it before you went out, sir, – to put the finishing touches to it, and there's just time before your appointment.'

Mr Sampson jumped up. 'Bless my soul, I'd almost forgotten. Charlotte, my dear, do feel free to stay, Mrs Hope will look after you, but I really must dash.'

Mrs Mortimer rose pompously to her feet. 'Why you should think that I have time to linger, I really can't imagine, brother. I have a million things to do.' She swept towards the door and nodded briefly to Annie. 'Goodday, Aaron. Think about what I have suggested. Ralph is only too eager to join you.'

Mr Sampson mopped his brow as he closed the door

behind his sister. 'Phew. Thank you, Annie. You couldn't have chosen a better time. I couldn't think how I was going to get rid of her.' His brow wrinkled. 'Did I have an appointment? I can't remember.'

Annie put her hand to her mouth in mock shame. 'I made a mistake,' she said grinning. 'It must be another day.'

He sat down wearily on a chair in front of the counter, and gave a sigh. 'I don't know what excuse to make to her. I've tried them all but she won't take no for an answer, and as for that odious son of hers!'

'Ralph?' Annie had met him infrequently, they had first passed in the shop doorway and he had given her a fawning bow, thinking that she was a client and not an assistant in his uncle's shop. She had taken an instant dislike to his foppish, dandified appearance, and had since avoided him whenever possible. 'What has he been up to?'

'It's what he wants to get up to that's the trouble. His mother and he have hatched a plot; he wants, or at least his mother wants him to come into the business with me.'

'But what is your objection, Mr Sampson? He'll surely inherit it one day.' Annie felt secure enough in her friendship with the draper to make so bold a statement. 'Better to train him in the art of selling cloth now than risk him making a hash of it later.'

Aaron's face grew scarlet. 'I'd sooner give my shop to charity than let him get his hands on it. When I think how my poor dear wife gave all her time and money to this venture – why she'd turn in her grave if she thought that young dog was squandering it away, which is just what he would do if he could.'

Polly came downstairs carrying Henry dressed in his outdoor clothes and ready for his walk.

'Now, Polly. Don't under any circumstances let go of Henry's hand,' Aaron shook a finger at Polly. 'Indeed I think that perhaps you should take him in his carriage.'

Polly raised her eyebrows in dismay and Annie interceded. 'He's far too big for his carriage now, Mr Sampson. Polly will take care of him, won't you Polly?'

The girl nodded and smiled gratefully at Annie. Henry was growing into a strapping boy and had already lost his baby roundness. Annie had recently breeched him, taking him out of his wrapping-gown and putting him into trousers and buttoned-down jacket, and he was far too heavy to be pushed in the hand-carriage.

'If you'd had children you would have spoilt them to death, Mr Sampson. Men don't usually have an interest in children. My husband didn't, they were just a nuisance and another mouth to feed.'

'Not all men are the same, Annie, and Henry's father might well have been happy to have a son.'

She nodded and sighed. She'd felt compelled to tell Mr Sampson of her circumstances when he'd been so generous to offer her a position with him, and had explained that though she was a widow, her husband wasn't the father of the child she was carrying.

'I suppose I've become fond of the boy because he was born here,' he said. 'I've never seen a newborn baby before. Such a miracle,' he said, his eyes shining. 'Such a miracle.'

He had been most anxious for her as her pregnancy progressed and instead of dismissing her as she expected him to, he'd insisted that she should rest whenever possible. But she had felt strong and healthy, and because she didn't know when the birth was due, on the Saturday afternoon when she felt tired, she merely thought that she had been overdoing things. However, as Mr Sampson was preparing to leave that night, she had asked him casually if he would give a boy a copper to send a message to the midwife.

But the midwife was late, as the message given wasn't considered urgent and by the time she arrived, the baby had been born. Squalling lustily he'd proclaimed his arrival as soon as he was free of her. She'd wiped his face with the bed sheet and moistened her fingers with her tongue and cleared his mucous-covered eyes and nose, then bit through the cord which bound them.

The door bell jangled and they both turned, a greeting ready for a client, but both their smiles faded when they saw Ralph Mortimer standing there, his white-gloved hand clasping a silver-topped cane and sporting a fashionable top hat.

'Good Morning, Uncle – Mrs Hope. I understood that my mother was calling this morning—'

'You've only just missed her,' Aaron interrupted. 'If you hurry you'll catch her, she went—'

'No, no. No matter. I'll stay a while and chat to you. Are you well, Uncle? You're looking a little strained. Not overdoing things are you?'

He turned to Annie and smirked confidentially. 'We shall have to watch him, won't we, Mrs Hope? Don't want him to become ill. It's a lot of responsibility running an establishment like this.'

What would you know? Annie thought. You've never had responsibility in your life, you exist on your late father's legacy and your mother's indulgence.

'I've run this business for twenty years,' Aaron bristled. 'I don't think I have need of advice from you, young man.'

'Oh, no – I didn't mean – I was only concerned.' He fingered his sideburns as he sought to placate his uncle. 'Mother and I are both concerned, we think that you ought to be taking things easier now. You're no longer young you know,' he added waggishly.

'I know perfectly well how old I am,' Aaron said impatiently, 'and I do take things easier. I have excellent help in Mrs Hope, 'couldn't wish for better, so please don't worry on my behalf.'

'If you'll excuse me, Mr Sampson,' Annie made her excuses. 'I have to make up orders which are wanted for this afternoon. The maids will be coming for them and I promised they would be ready.'

'Ah. Of course.' Mr Sampson bustled round the other side of the counter and started sorting out fabrics. 'I shall come and help you in one moment.' He stared at his nephew. 'Was there anything else, Ralph? You'll understand of course, being familiar with the intricacies of business, that we don't have time to chat, except of course to our clients.'

Ralph was lost for words for a moment as he was given his dismissal, but he smiled politely at his uncle and tipped his hat and said as he opened the door, 'Perhaps you would allow me to give you some extra assistance as you are so busy, – my time is my own. I have a good head for figures, I could perhaps relieve you of the boredom of adding up your accounts. Do think of it, Uncle, I should be only too pleased.'

As he left the shop door he almost fell over Polly and Henry who were returning from their walk, rain had started to drizzle down and their faces were wet.

He looked down at Henry and then glanced back at Annie inside the shop and touched his hat with his cane. She felt, she knew not why, as if she had just been assaulted.

Aaron rubbed his chest with quick anxious movements and then adjusted his toupee forward onto his brow. 'I'm going to have to do something soon, Annie. I don't know how long I can fight them.'

Mrs Cook the drapery assistant came in to help in the shop
on three days a week. She worked from ten o'clock until
four, whereas Annie was on call all the day, as was Mr
Sampson, from Monday to Saturday, nine o'clock in
the morning until eight in the evening, and they took
refreshment or rest whenever they could.

Polly also looked after Henry all day, feeding him and
playing with him, which Annie preferred, rather than
sending him out to a childminder. There were many
respectable women who took on the task of looking after
other people's children, but Annie had a picture in her
mind of some of the women she had met in Hull who
had that same occupation and who dosed the children in
their care with laudanum to keep them quiet, just as soon
as their mothers had disappeared over the doorstep.

Annie had tried to teach Polly her numbers so that she
could in turn teach Henry to count his bricks and beads,
but the girl had no aptitude for it, so today while Mrs Cook
was dusting shelves and there were no clients in the shop,
Annie brought Henry down and sat him on the counter
with his bricks and counted them out for him. She built
a pyramid of red bricks and another of blue to teach him
the colours and the child looked up at the shelves of cloth
and pointed.

'Well I never,' Mr Sampson looked up from his tall desk
in the corner. 'What a bright child. He's matching up the
colours.'

'He knows his colours already,' Annie smiled indulgently, 'and he can count up to ten.' Her face saddened.
Lizzie and Ted and Jimmy had never learnt to read or

write, there had been no one to teach them, she thought. Alan could read a little but he never taught the bairns. This child will be different, she decided defiantly. He'll have a better chance than they did.

'He should go to school – when he's old enough, I mean. There are excellent schools in York. We should put his name down.'

Annie laughed at the old man's earnestness. 'I don't think I'll ever have enough money for him to go to school,' she said. 'Though I don't mean to grumble, sir,' she added. 'The wages you give me are fair.' More than fair she thought, for where else would I get a room and coals included. She bought food for herself and Henry, and clothes were made by a dressmaker from the remnant ends of material which she bought cheap from the shop. And Mr Sampson paid for Polly's pittance, giving the excuse that she was available for errands if he needed her.

She never had any money left over, but she didn't mind; she felt secure in her occupation and comfortable in her room over the shop premises, and when the fire was lit and the shutters closed, a warm fragrance exuded from the old oak panels, and she felt almost happy; except at night when she was alone with her young son sleeping in his cot, and the darkness pressing heavily on her, and then she would think of Matt and imagine that this small room was his ship's cabin and he was lying next to her with his arms around her, his warm breath on her face, the beating of his heart in unison with hers.

So real was her illusion that sometimes she would awake and reach out for him, and on finding him gone would be filled with desolation once more.

Mr Sampson was speaking to her. 'I said, he'll make a draper one day!'

'Such dreams,' she answered jokingly. 'Perhaps we'll make him an apprentice! We'll dress him up in frock-coat and waistcoat.' She picked up a piece of embroidered satin and held it against Henry's chest. 'And of course he must have silk stockings, just like those that Mr Ralph wears!'

Aaron Sampson put his chin in his hand and nodded thoughtfully. 'He is already three, isn't he?'

Annie nodded and lifted Henry down from the counter. 'Yes, childhood almost gone, six more years and I must think of what he must do for a living.'

'Too young.' Mr Sampson declared. 'Too young by far.'

Mrs Cook joined in the conversation. 'My nephew went to work for a baker when he was nine, but the hours were too long for such a young child, he was always falling asleep and burning himself on the ovens. Now he works in the market running errands, but the wage is paltry; his poor mother is desperate for money and can't wait for the time when the next one is old enough to go to work.'

The doorbell jangled and they became busy and Polly took Henry upstairs out of the way. Annie got out a pair of tall steps to reach to the top shelf for a length of red satin, the customer in the shop had seen the same material in the window and wanted to handle it, and Annie made a mental note to keep the stock from the window in a more accessible place.

Mr Sampson insisted on climbing up the steps and reached awkwardly to pull the material from the shelf. He grimaced as he reached and Annie watched anxiously in case he should drop it.

'Are you all right, Mr Sampson?' she whispered. 'Did you jar yourself?'

'No, no. I'm perfectly well. Just a bit of a stitch, that's all.'

During a lull in the day he went into his back room and there Annie found him stretched out in a chair with his eyes closed. 'Mr Sampson, are you not well? Can I get you something?'

'I'm a little tired, Annie, and I get a pain down my arm when I stretch for the shelves, but it's nothing much.'

'I'll get you a drop of brandy,' she said and hurried upstairs. She'd brought a half anker of brandy with her three years ago and had used it only sparingly, now there was very little left, but without hesitation she poured a generous measure into a glass for Mr Sampson, and ran back downstairs with it.

Mrs Cook was putting on her shawl to leave and Annie asked her to wait for just another five minutes in case anyone came in, and hurried through to her employer. It often crossed her mind that if ever anything happened to Aaron Sampson, or if he should decide to retire, she would have to look for other employment, for she wouldn't want to work for Mr Mortimer or his mother. But, she mused, I have experience, I'm known in the city. I could get other employment if I had references.

She thought of this now as Aaron sipped the brandy. She really ought to ask him, though not just yet. It would perhaps seem rather unfeeling, particularly as he was now unwell. But don't be soft, Annie, tha has to think of tha self.

She didn't often lecture herself these days, life had fallen into a steady pattern, but occasionally if a small worry bothered her, then her thoughts would lapse into her native cant.

Aaron sat up and took a deep breath. 'Tell Mrs Cook she can go, it's past her time. I'm feeling fine now, Annie, don't worry.'

Annie did as she was bid and when Mrs Cook had left she busied herself writing out the amounts the clients had spent, and entering them into the large ledger so that the accounts could be sent out at the end of the month. She noticed that some of the accounts had been outstanding for six months or more, some of them belonging to ladies of esteem and she wondered what was done to encourage the client to clear the account.

Mr Sampson came through into the shop, his round face a little pale. 'Thank you, Annie, I was just going to finish those.'

'Some of these clients owe you a lot of money,' Annie said. 'And yet they still come in buying more goods.'

'I know.' He shook his head. 'I keep sending the

accounts to their husbands, but they're very slow to pay.'

'And soon they'll be ordering material for their ballgowns for the autumn season, how can you possibly give them credit for so long?'

'If I don't give them credit I lose their custom, and if I insist on them settling their bill, I lose their custom also. They'd go elsewhere, there's no shortage of drapers in the city.'

Annie called Polly downstairs to mop the floor and she went up to her room to sit down and talk to Henry, but the little boy was engrossed in a game of soldiers and didn't need her attention and so she sat, quietly watching and reflecting. Presently she got up and satisfying herself that the child was still occupied she went downstairs again.

'Mr Sampson – Aaron,' She was in the habit, at his request, of using his first name when there were no clients around, 'I've been thinking.' Polly was still there, idly swishing the mop around the floor and gazing out of the window and she motioned her to go back upstairs to Henry. 'About these overdue accounts.'

Aaron sighed. 'It's not as if these people can't afford to pay,' he said. 'It's just that they don't want to.'

'That's just what I thought. Most of these ladies are married to rich merchants, the tradesmen's wives always pay on time because you trade with them and pay them promptly. But these wealthy customers have no incentive to pay – they know that you won't press them for fear of losing their custom.'

'That's true,' he nodded. 'But think of the stock I could buy if they settled.'

'Quite right,' Annie grew quite animated. 'So this is what I suggest. Offer them an incentive. Offer them a discount, quite a large one, say, ten per cent, if they will settle their existing account within a month; and on any future business, a smaller discount, maybe two-and-a-half per cent if they pay on a monthly basis.'

'It sounds a good idea,' he said slowly, 'but won't they

then delay the paynent of future business so that they get the larger discount.'

'No,' she answered briskly. 'Say that this is a special once only arrangement, designed in order to release money for a new consignment of stock which you are expecting for the autumn.'

She felt exhilarated as she watched her employer's face become wreathed in smiles. She loved bargaining, it was part of her character, born of necessity so many years ago. Yet she was amazed at herself, at how quickly she had learned to add and subtract, better in her head than on paper, and, although she often spelled a word wrongly when she was writing, she could read as well as most.

'Annie, you're a wonder. How ever did I manage without you?'

'Perfectly well. I'm the one to be grateful,' she smiled back at him, feeling a tearful lump in her throat. 'But you're too nice a man to be in trade – people take advantage of your good nature. I've always had to fend for myself, to be one step ahead.'

'Yes, you're like my wife used to be. Nobody got past her. She was as sharp as a blade.' He took Annie's hand and patted it. 'I'm grateful, Annie. We'll work something out together in the morning, and then get the printer to set it up.'

He said then that he was tired and would go home if Annie could manage the last two hours alone. 'Shut up shop early if you want, we've had a good day.' He put on a caped greatcoat and picked up his cane, but before walking off to his lodgings he stood for a moment looking at the display in the window, and then lifted his head to look at Annie as she stood behind the counter. As she smiled a goodbye he touched his hat with his cane and gave her a small formal bow and walked briskly away.

*   *   *

She always took a walk in the evening after the shop was closed, no matter what the weather. The air was warm and sultry tonight as she took Henry's hand and made her way towards the river. Henry hadn't wanted to come, being busy still with his soldiers, but she insisted, it was the only time she felt that she had the child to herself without the company of others. She liked to show him the ships that were on the river, and tell him what they were carrying and where they had probably come from or were going.

York was a pleasant and beautiful city, she had decided that on first arriving. It had a magnificent cathedral, noble churches, elegant houses and pleasant gardens and many ancient crumbling monuments. Mr Sampson had told her that it was once a Roman colony and the seat of Roman emperors.

There were good families living here and much lavish entertainment for them, with theatres and grand balls, and music in the Assembly Rooms, while for the ordinary citizen there were travelling entertainers, tumblers and tightrope walkers, wild animals which had been taught to do tricks, and, of course, the inevitable cockfights, set on a raised circular stage which were held in various parts of the city and advertised on posters displayed on the city walls.

Annie always averted her eyes if by chance she should pass a building when a fight was in progress, for she never could abide the thought of the two creatures locked in battle, their silver spurs flashing as they fought to the death, neither did she like the shouts of the crowd as they watched the bloody spectacle.

She did like to stand and watch the specatacle of the gentry arriving at the Assembly Rooms for a concert. They came in their carriages and sedan chairs, in elegant gowns and flowing capes, and she watched eagerly to see if any of the fashionable ladies were wearing silks and satins from Mr Sampson's drapery. She gazed, her eyes misty as they entered the portals and saw through the window the flickering candles of the candelabras, and thought of the magical time when she too had worn a a ballgown and listened to the strains of music with the man she loved at her side.

Her reason for coming to York had been a simple one. It was the only town accessible enough from Hessle of which she had any knowledge. Once she had lied to Toby that it was her home town and he had questioned her familiarity of the strange sounding streets. Now she had traversed the lanes and alleys, the snickets and ginnels of which he had spoken: Hornpot Lane, Whip-Ma-Whop-Ma Gate, Jubbergate, Lady Row. She knew Micklegate which was the old road to London, with its mixture of merchants' houses and shops; she watched the builders working on its timber-framed buildings which were being rebuilt and refaced in the modern style and the earth floors being replaced with stone flags.

But, above all, her decision to take the long arduous track across the Wolds towards the city of York, was because she didn't want to cross the Humber. She was afraid of taking the ferry into Lincolnshire, the ancient line of communication towards the south of England. A great fear had shaken her to the core as she'd hesitated on the river bank when she had finally left the cottage, for she felt that once she had paid the ferryman and traversed the waters, then she could never return.

So she had turned her back, comforted by the fact that she was still on the Humber's northern shores. Now she was secure in the knowledge that in this city of white stone and hidden courtyards and gabled roofs, which, though welcoming her, she could never call her own, there ran two rivers, the Ouse and the Foss, which linked with the Humber in their run to the sea.

'Tell me again about my father,' Henry tugged at her hand. She lifted him up and sat him on a bollard by the Ouse.

'He sails in a ship, bigger than any of those.' She pointed

down at the yawls and ketches and single-masted cutters lying in the water.

'And is he still very brave, like you said?' The child looked up at her eagerly.

'Oh yes, very brave and strong and very handsome.'

'And when will he come to see us?'

It was a question Henry always asked, ever since she had told him about Matt, when he had asked was Mr Sampson his father.

'He'll come when he can. He may be fighting the enemy.'

She wondered about Matt all the time. Was he alive or dead? Was he captured and languishing in gaol or still trying the patience of the customs men?

'James has a father and a grandfayther, they all live together and he sees them all the time.'

James was the son of a baker, and Henry sometimes played with him when he was out walking with Polly.

'Then James is very lucky,' she said, lifting him down to continue with their walk before bedtime.

'Why haven't I got a grandfayther?' He started to whine. 'Is Uncle Sampson my grandfayther?'

'No,' she gently admonished. 'I told you, Uncle Sampson is a very dear friend, but not your grandfather.'

She started to laugh. 'But you do have a grandfather, Henry. He lives a long way from here. Your grandfather, my little peazan, is a Squire!'

30

The letters and leaflets to the draper's customers were printed and sent and money started to come in, slowly at first and then in a steady flow, even from those notorious for delay. Annie had suggested that they sent an enthusiastic account of the new cloths and materials due in from the manufacturing towns in the West Riding and the Brussels lace and silks expected from the Continent.

Already, ladies started to appear, anxious to be the first to buy and to put in their orders with the dressmakers. Annie visited some of these busy sewing women, and persuaded them that if they recommended Mr Sampson's establishment to their ladies, then there would be a considerable saving to themselves in their purchase of needle pins, sewing cottons and ribbons. 'We can help each other,' she explained. 'These are hard times.'

A tall, stooped gentleman, a beaver hat on his greying hair, came in to the shop one day and asked, 'Mrs Hope?'

'Yes sir.' She bobbed her knee. 'Can I assist you?'

'I wished to speak to Mr Sampson, but I have just this moment seen him hurrying across the street. Perhaps you would permit me to wait?'

She brought him a chair to sit on and then busied herself making up stock and straightening the rolls of cloth. He looked vaguely familiar and she thought that he had been in the shop at some other time. Perhaps he was the husband of a client, come to discuss his wife's spending.

'You keep busy, Mrs Hope, you obviously enjoy your work here?'

'Yes indeed. Mr Sampson is a good employer and the

work is interesting. I love handling cloth.' She looked at him quizzically. 'If you'll beg my pardon, sir; you know my name, but I regret I can't recall yours, perhaps your wife is a client of ours?'

'Not at all. I have no wife. I'm a bachelor; always have been, always will. I have no small talk for ladies, they find me very dull.'

He rose to his feet. 'Forgive me for not introducing myself, another reason for my not marrying, I forget the niceties when speaking to the fairer sex.' His brow furrowed. 'Where was I? I was going to say something.'

She gave him a broad smile. 'You were about to tell me your name, sir.'

'Ah yes, of course. Marcus Blythe, of Blythe and Green, solicitors of law, though there is no Green any more, no, just myself and then nobody. It's a pity, don't you think, when there's no line to carry on a profession or business that's been worked for?'

'But you choose surely, sir, to indulge in a business or a profession for your own satisfaction, not just for the pleasure of handing it on; and perhaps a son or other relative may not have the same gratification or sense of achievement that the originator had.'

'My word, I believe you're right. You're a thinking woman, I can tell. Not one to sit around gossiping about the theatre and the latest novels and such!'

Her smile faded, she felt exposed and vulnerable. Was he laughing at her? He could surely tell what kind of woman she was? Why else would she be working for a living? It was pure luck on her part that she was nicely dressed and employed in a shop and not working as a drudge in a big house, or washing clothes in the wash-house, or even, as she had once done, sorting fish in the fish-houses.

But she spoke politely in answer. 'I might well gossip about the theatre, given the opportunity, and I'd like to read, given the time, but my hours are taken with my work and my small son, so there's little chance and certainly no money to do either of those things.'

'Ah.' He appeared a little confused. 'Of course, I was forgetting. You have a son. Henry, isn't it? Yes, indeed. Mr Sampson has spoken of him, he's quite taken with him. Children never did appeal to me, I fear.' He walked up and down the shop, swinging his cane. 'Never felt the urge to beget them. The ones I know have generally been noisy and a veritable nuisance. But I expect yours isn't? Mothers are usually very indulgent.'

What a strange man, she thought; and why should Aaron discuss Henry with his lawyer?

When Aaron came back he ushered Mr Blythe into his sanctum at the back of the shop and closed the door. Annie shrugged and got on with serving two ladies who came in, but she could hear Mr Blythe's voice quite clearly. 'I quite agree,' he said. 'If that's what you wish, but it may well kill you off dear fellow; mark my words, if you're here to remember them, at your time of life it can't be good.'

At the end of the day, Aaron sent Polly off and locking the door behind her, he pulled down the blind. 'Another day over, Annie. I feel quite tired, I must say. The days seem to be getting longer.'

'You ought to take more rest, Aaron. It's too much for you standing on your feet all day.' She surveyed him thoughtfully. 'Could you afford more staff? An apprentice perhaps? It would be a good idea, you know. A young man could handle the heavy fabrics and lift down the bales and so save you the effort.'

Annie was strong and often lifted the bales of cloth herself rather than ask Mr Sampson, but if he was there, then he would insist on lifting them himself and she had noticed recently how taxing it was for him.

'Perhaps I might consider it,' he said. 'I have been slightly unwell lately, not quite myself.' He coughed, putting his hand to his mouth. 'That is why, Annie, Mr Blythe called. I have consulted him in his chambers, but being the man he is, he wanted to see the erm – that is, he wanted to visit the shop to see who, erm I mean, how, we conduct our business.'

'Surely he knew that already? I remember you saying that you had had the same family lawyer for years!'

'Ah, yes, but you see, things are different now.' He nodded enthusiastically. 'Improving, I might even say, especially under your organization. So – erm, I needed his advice about something rather important.'

Annie nodded. 'I see,' and turned away.

'No, don't go, Annie, I need to talk to you. This does concern you – and Henry.'

She turned back in some surprise, his face was flushed and he fingered the stiffened stock around his neck.

'As you know, my sister and her son have been hankering after joining me in this business, and I know my weaknesses only too well. They would soon be taking over, lock, stock and barrel.'

'I said, didn't I, that you were too soft-hearted,' Annie interrupted. 'Your wife wouldn't have let them get away with anything, I'll be bound.'

'Indeed she wouldn't, not her.' He took a deep breath, 'and neither would you Annie, would you, if you were in charge?'

She laughed. 'I wouldn't have them over the doorstep, Mr Sampson, even though they are your relatives.'

'Exactly. So Annie, what about it? Will you join me here and make a partnership – a proper one I mean – oh dear, I'm not doing this very well and I've been rehearsing what to say for weeks. I mean my dear, will you become the next Mrs Sampson?'

Annie drew in a breath, for once she was lost for words.

'I wouldn't expect – what I mean is – I'm an old man, you wouldn't be afraid that I'd force you to do anything that was disagreeable to you. Women, I know have much to put up with; although my wife never complained, but I'm older now and couldn't—.' He paused, his cheeks pink. 'But in any case even if you didn't want to – marry, I mean, I still intend to leave the business to you and Henry, when I'm gone.'

Annie sank down onto a chair quite bewildered. That Aaron Sampson was fond of her and Henry had always been apparent. He had been so kind, especially during those first few weeks when she had felt lost and lonely in a strange city, endeavouring to put on a brave face and manner as she faced the customers in the shop, yet feeling that her life no longer had any meaning.

Not until she had felt the child stir within her had she realized that she *did* have some reminder of Matt, someone she could love and who would love her in return. Aaron had seemed to sense the turmoil she was going through and had been patient and understanding. He would make a good husband and father to Henry if she should consider it. She'd want for nothing, and the business would be hers, hers and Henry's to do with as they wished.

'Aaron,' she began. 'I'm proud to have your regard and affection, and you know, don't you, that you have mine in return?'

He nodded, his face lighting up eagerly.

'But, you also know that I love Henry's father. How can you ask me to marry you knowing that?'

'My dear girl, you are still so innocent, in spite of the life you have led.' He took her hand in a fatherly fashion. 'Don't you know that in most marriages there is no love? Even in my own, which lasted many years, we married because we made a suitable arrangement satisfactory to both parties – we came to care for each other but only over time, we became comfortable together.'

'I've been married once,' she said dully as she remembered her life with Alan. 'But that was like some other life. There was no love there or comfort.'

'I'm not asking for an answer now,' he said patiently. 'But will you think about it?'

She squeezed his hand. 'You're a dear man. Yes, I'll think about it.'

Yet the more she thought about it, the more she realized that she couldn't marry him. She considered him more as a father-figure – the father she might have wished for –

rather than a husband. But if I don't marry him, then he might change his mind about leaving the business to Henry and me, she thought. And then when he's gone, God willing it won't be for a long time, then Henry and I must move on again.

In her own room she bent her head and wept a few tears. She could survive alone, she didn't care how, but for Henry she wanted a good life, she didn't want to risk losing him in poverty and hardship the way she had lost Lizzie and Ted and Jimmy.

*   *   *

'I've had an idea, Aaron.' She ran down the stairs from her room one morning about two weeks later. 'I've been thinking about it all night.'

'Have you made a decision then,' he asked quietly. He hadn't pressed her for an answer to his proposal but had bided his time.

'Not yet, but I promise I will soon, very soon. But hear what I have to say. We discussed didn't we, that it would be an idea to get an apprentice to help in the shop?'

'Yes, yes, but I haven't liked any of them that came for an interview. Either too rough with scratchy hands or too foppish to attend the customers, let alone lift the bales.'

'Well,' she said excitedly. 'It came to me during the night, I couldn't sleep and I got thinking, you know the way you do during the dark hours.' When the night seems never ending and all you can do is weep for what you have lost, she thought.

'But I started to think about someone I knew, someone who knows about cloth and who knows how to talk to women, and to ladies too if he'd known any. His hands may be rough now,' she added as she thought that Robin might have gone back to the quarry, 'but we can soon do something about that with creams and lotions.'

'Then you'd better send for him,' Aaron said. 'I trust

your judgement. We'll need someone soon, now that we have all this fabric coming in.'

Day by day shipments of fabric were arriving, down through the Aire and Calder waterways, and along the Ouse to arrive in York. Cargoes of soap and perfume, casks of porter and Jamaica rum, brandies and geneva were snatched up on arrival by the shopkeepers as the war with France made these commodities rare.

'I can't send for him,' she explained. 'He can't read. We'd have to teach him when he got here.'

'How do you know he'd be willing to come? He might be doing some other work that he can't leave. Could you persuade him?'

'Yes,' she said thoughtfully. 'I think I could. But how to find him and get him here, that's the problem.'

'Why, you must go, of course. Go to where you last saw him and talk to him.'

She stared at him. Go! To Hessle! Risk seeing Matt's ship in the Humber and know that he was there, breathing the same air as she was. She became breathless as she thought of it, and yet, the thought excited her, to know that he was still living and breathing, to catch one glimpse of him perhaps for the last time. And if he wasn't there, well then she could enquire of Robin or Josh and ask news of him, and swear them on their honour to secrecy.

'I haven't got my donkey, how will I go?' She searched for excuses.

'Bless my soul, we can afford the coach. We can charge it to business. Let me see now,' Aaron ruminated as Annie continued to stare bemused. She'd been in a coach only once, when she had gone with Matt to the fancy dress ball, that wonderful night when Henry had been conceived, she'd worked it back from his birth, it had to have been then.

'You'll have to get the coach to Hull, and then I'm not sure what you'll do. Will there be transport to this place Hessle?'

She smiled. 'My own two legs or I'll hire a mare.'

She nodded at the look of surprise on his face. 'I can do either.'

They arranged that she should go the following week, before they began to get busy with the autumn custom, Mrs Cook agreed to come in each day while Annie was away and Aaron booked her a twelve-shilling seat for the seven hour journey, on the inside of the Hull light coach. At the last minute she decided to take Henry with her rather than leave him to the precarious protection of the well-meaning Polly.

I'll show him the Humber, she thought, and the town of Hull where I was born. He's so young and he'll no doubt forget by the time he's a grown man, but at least *I'll* know that I showed him my beginnings. She had great aspirations for Henry, now that she had almost made a decision about marrying Mr Sampson.

As the horses pulled away and they waved a final goodbye to Aaron Sampson, she sat back against the seat and breathed in the smell of leather and remembered. How many memories I have, she thought. What a life I have led; from poverty to a lost love, and now riding in a coach back to Hull and my past.

31

'Heave to or we fire!'

'Then fire and be damned!' Matt shouted back at the cutter captain who was chasing the *Breeze*.

'In the name of the King, heave to!'

Matt ignored the command, he'd not have revenue men boarding his ship. He gave orders to increase sail and drew away from the range of shot from the revenue cutter. He stood with his arms folded and laughed at the incompetence of the captain of the *Royal Swan* who, acting in the name of the Customs, couldn't keep pace with the swiftness of the *Breeze*. His crew too stood at the ship side shaking their fists and jeering at the desperate attempts of the cutter to score a hit.

They had dropped the last of the contraband, brandy and geneva, at Scarborough, after a hazardous journey across the sea from Holland where they had encountered French privateers who had attempted to board her. They had fought them off and continued to Whitby and then Scarborough to discharge the goods to the waiting fishermen.

Then they had been chased along the coast towards Bridlington by the King's frigate which had discharged shot at them, penetrating the hull and damaging rigging before they had finally lost it, only to be approached later in the day by the revenue cutter, the *Royal Swan*, who had ordered them to heave to and who was now well out of the chase as they drew further away from her.

'Will we sail to Hessle, captain, or stay in port?'

'Stay in port, Bosun. We'll need to get repairs done to the rigging, and I have some business to attend to, besides we've nothing for them, everything went at Whitby and Scarborough. They cleaned us dry.'

'Customs'll still come looking though, sir.'

'Well let them, we're clean as a whistle.'

They rounded the sand flats off the tip of Spurn Head and followed the pilot boat up the Humber towards Hull and into the crowded Old Harbour to a berth in the equally crowded dock.

Matt went as usual for his breakfast at the Cross Keys Inn and then ordered a mount. I've been going through this charade for three years now, he thought, as he mounted the stallion and rode off in the direction of Hessle, and what good has it done? Absolutely none. Not a sign or sighting of her; not across in Lincolnshire, not in Beverley, nowhere. Nobody has heard or seen anything, or so they say.

Robin or Josh would tell if they'd heard. Mrs Trott wouldn't, she didn't like her. Old Henry would protect her I'm sure of that – he'd only tell if he thought I was going to do the honourable thing by her. But Robin, well he's in my pay. I pay him well to look for her, he surely wouldn't do a double cross?

He'd brought Robin out of the quarries to look for Annie, asking him to search on the Wolds if necessary, and Robin had told him that while making his enquiries, he had come across Mr Moses. That gentleman having lost a lucrative outlet now that the young *Mr* Hope had disappeared, had asked Robin if he was willing to take some of his samples.

'You seem a likely sort of young fellow,' he'd said to Robin. 'Do you think you could sell cloth like Mr Hope did?'

'I could try,' Robin had bantered. 'But tha'd have to give me credit for stock, same as before, cos I've no money of me own.'

Moses had agreed, and so as Robin searched the towns and villages of the area for Annie, while in the employ of Captain Linton – even travelling across the Humber into Lincolnshire and scouring Barton and

Goxhill – he also sold cloth on behalf of himself and Mr Moses.

Being an honest kind of lad, he had informed Matt of his intentions. 'I'll do my duty by thee, captain,' he'd said. 'I'm as anxious about Annie – Mrs Hope, as anybody. And while tha's paying me I'll keep looking for her, but I want to mek summat of meself and I can onny do that if I have money, and I can mek it wi' selling cloth and stuff.'

Matt had studied him. He was a pleasant-looking fellow, he'd thought, with an open, honest face, and he'd refused the job of agent for the distribution of contraband, saying that though he wouldn't say it was wrong to defy the King and his officers, it wasn't something that he would want to do, preferring to keep his hands clean. He'd laughed then and looked down at his hands which though clean were still pitted and cracked from the quarrying.

'You'll need more than money, Robin, if you're to make something of yourself. You need to be able to read and write and to speak properly. You'll always be considered a street urchin if you speak like one.'

'I remember Annie saying summat similar,' he'd said eagerly. 'Robin, she said, you and me'll have to learn to talk proper if we're to better ourselves.' He'd given a great sigh. 'Well, she did; Master Toby learned her. But now she's gone and I wonder if it did her any good. We all miss her, captain, more than we can say; Josh, and me – even Sorrel.'

Matt arranged an interview with the schoolmaster in Hessle, who on meeting Robin told him he would give him lessons in reading, writing and speech, and if he proved adaptable he would then teach him arithmetic. He couldn't take him during school hours as Robin at fourteen was too old, but he agreed to take him on three evenings a week at a private fee which Matt would pay. Robin's gratitude knew no bounds.

So when Matt dismounted at the cottage door where Robin still lived with his sister, it was a quite different young man from the gawky lad he had once been, who opened the door to him. At almost eighteen Robin had grown several inches and though not tall, he had broadened considerably, his face had lost the plump roundness of boyhood and though still ready to smile, had a mature confidence about it.

'Come in, captain. It's good to see you.' He motioned Matt to sit down in the small room, which for once was devoid of the usual brood of his sister's children. 'Will you have a glass of ale?'

Matt refused. 'No. I won't stay long. I came as usual to enquire if you had any news.'

'None, sir, I'm sorry to say.' Robin faced Matt. 'I was hoping you'd call for I wanted to talk to you. I'm sorry to say, Captain Linton, but I think we're on a fool's errand. We're not going to find her and I can't keep taking money from you pretending that we are. I'll look and enquire wherever I happen to be, but I don't want any more payment from you. It isn't fair.'

'Come Robin, are you now so rich that you can afford to throw money away?' Matt hadn't intended that his voice would be cold and harsh, he was disappointed and couldn't help that it showed, even though he knew that the youth was right.

'That I'm not, sir.' The old Robin showed through. 'And never will be, though I'm better off than I ever was. 'Summer months are always good to me, though when the bad weather comes I spend all I've earned when I can't get up on 'Wolds.'

'Yes it's a fair weather job you've got, no doubt about that. That country can be a killer if you get caught in the winter.'

He felt a gnawing sense of guilt about his father as he spoke. He'd visit him the next time around. He didn't go as often as he should, but he hated the questioning by his father of the whereabouts of Mrs Annaliese Hope and his derisive comments on what a fool he'd been to let her slip away.

'All right,' he said, rising to his feet from the small

wooden chair. 'We'll call it off, but if you should hear—'

'I'll hot foot down to Hull and be waiting at 'harbour side, captain. Have no fear of that.'

Matt nodded and left. A sense of loss and desolation filled him. While someone had been actively looking for Annie, even after all this time, he had felt there was some hope, but now there was nothing; no anticipation that Robin might speak to someone who had come across a woman alone; or turn a corner and find her there.

But she might not be alone now, he pondered. She might have a child if she was safely delivered, or she might have a husband and even more children. Or, he breathed in softly as he mounted his horse and turned down the river path towards Hull, she might even be dead.

By the time he reached the town boundaries, his sense of sadness had fermented from despair, into frustration and finally anger that she should go, leaving him without a word or message. 'Damn and blast the woman,' he muttered as he trotted through the Market Place putting to flight scratching hens and scattering small boys from their games as they played on the dusty road.

'Hey, Mister, better watch out,' one of them called after him, but he cracked his whip in the air and rode on towards the Cross Keys.

'Bring me a tankard of ale,' he barked at the landlord as he entered the door. 'No, make it a jug, and a brandy, large.'

'Drowning tha sorrows, captain?' The landlord raised an eybrow. 'Is tha not sailing today?'

'No,' his answer was short. He didn't want to talk, only to get drunk. If only Greg was here they could get drunk together, just like the old times. Yes, that's what he would do from now on, he'd meet up with his old cronies, go carousing again. Not sit mooning around over a woman who might or might not be the mother of his child.

The smoky room started to fill up as dockyard workers finished their shift and other seamen, discharged from their ships came to relax and drink away their wages before they went on board again. He listened to the hum of conversation around him.

Two whaling ships had come in, both with a good catch. It was good news for the town which relied on the whales as their chief industry. Soon the inn would be packed with the whaling men come to celebrate their good fortune, while outside, women would wait, some with children by their sides waiting for their share of money that they might buy food and pay their debts, and others with painted faces who waited in anticipation of a good time.

He narrowed his eyes, his vision seemed to be blurred as he looked across the room. There was Parson White and Bosun, they gave him a nod but he didn't respond. He didn't want to talk. He looked down at the table. Two jugs. He picked them up one at a time. Both empty! Someone had been drinking his ale!

He let out a roar. 'Another jug, landlord, and be quick about it.'

The landlord came across. 'It's not for me to refuse custom, captain, but doesn't tha think tha's had enough? Tha'll be sailing tomorrow, no doubt?'

'I might, or I might not. It's my ship and I'll sail whenever I damned well choose.' He glared balefully at the double image of the man and hiccoughed. Why didn't the rogue keep still?

He got unsteadily to his feet. 'But if you won't serve me, landlord, then I'll find some other hostelry that will.'

'Sir? Take care, there's trouble—!'

Matt waved a dismissive arm and staggered towards the door. The room was stifling, he needed some air. As he reached the door it swung open, almost knocking him over. It was Greg Sheppard.

'Now then, my old shipmate.' Greg slapped him on the back, making him wince. 'You're well in front of me by the look of you. I'm going to have some catching up to do.'

'Landlord here won't serve me,' Matt mumbled and

grabbed Greg's arm. 'I'm going on. The George – they draw good ale. That's where we'll go.'

Greg laughed, throwing back his head. 'You'll have a devil of a hangover in the morning, you're three sheets to the wind already! But yes, my friend, let's make a night of it, it's been a long time since we did. You've been a miserable drinking partner for far too long.' He tapped Matt's chest and whispered with a grin. 'We'll find a couple of ladies and have a good time. Just give me five minutes whilst I have a word with somebody over there and I'll be right with you.'

Matt staggered towards the George just off the High Street, Greg would know where to find him; another few drinks and then oblivion, he'd be able to forget her even if it was for only a short time.

He pushed his way through the crowd; there was a large crush of people. Something must be happening, the local militia were out, their disparity of uniform contrasting with the scarlet tunics and flashing cutlasses of the cavalry, who with their muskets slung over their backs rode towards the Market Place where the biggest press of people was gathering.

Greg caught him up as he crossed the George's yard. 'There's trouble afoot,' he said. 'The mob are out. There's been a rise in the price of flour and the townsfolk are being egged on to blame the millers; the press-men are in town and the whole place is about to blow!'

Matt didn't answer as he reached for a chair in the inn. His mind was befuddled; he couldn't cope with other people's problems, he had his own. He couldn't remember what they were, but he knew he had some.

Greg beckoned to the serving maid and pinched her bottom as she poured him a tankard of ale from a large jug. She winked at him and he slyly slid his hand under her skirt.

Matt drained his tankard and watched their antics through bleary eyes. He wanted no part of this. He wanted no loose woman to share his night. He wanted to get back to his ship and lie down alone in his bunk and wallow in misery. He suddenly felt sick. His head ached and he needed to get outside for some air. He pushed back his chair sending it clattering on to the floor and muttering something incomprehensible into Greg's grinning face, he hurried towards the door.

Once outside he rushed towards the corner of the building and retched and retched, then gasping, he leaned against the wall. What a mess, he thought. What a fool I am, getting into such a state. He drew away from the pool of vomit and took a deep breath. Phew. I feel terrible. He turned towards the door of the George and then on second thoughts turned away. He couldn't face the smell of ale again. Greg would have to find his own entertainment for the night.

He stood, his hand clutching his brow as he tried to remember where he was going. The *Breeze*. That was it. That's where he was going.

'Now then, my old matey. What's your trouble?' A friendly voice greeted him. 'Lost your way home, have you?'

'No, no.' He looked warily at the group of men gathered about him. Perhaps he should have gone back inside to find Greg. Two men had more of a chance against a mob than one.

'Do you need some help? There's a lot of trouble tonight.'

They seemed friendly enough, decently dressed in dark clothes, probably just pals out for a drink after work.

'I'm going back to my ship. I can manage.' But could he? His legs didn't seem to belong to him; as he took a step his knees buckled and he stumbled.

One of the men took him by the arm, his grip was firm. 'We're going that way ourselves, sailor. We'll walk along with you.'

Another man came to the other side of him and took his other arm and they marched him out of the George yard.

He became alarmed and resisted. 'Let go!' he demanded. 'I'll find my own way.'

'We're taking you, in the King's name, sailor, so don't struggle. There's a pistol in my hand and I'll use it.'

The press-men had him! He groaned. Through his own stupidity, he had let slip his caution. Caution which a seaman should never abandon, for they were wanted by the navy more than any other able-bodied man with their knowledge of the sea and ships.

They hustled him around the corner and in the darkness of an alley clapped an iron on his wrists and led him away towards the docks and the naval ships.

'Stop in the King's name!'

The cry rang out as Matt and other pressed men were being hustled towards the docks. He had spent the night in a locked room along with a motley assortment of other men, most of them the worse for drink, waiting the turn of the tide. Matt had spent most of the time battering on the door demanding to speak to the authorities, until the other men had turned nasty and made him stop.

'Stop! In the King's name, I arrest this man.' Roxton, the customs official put out his arm to halt the naval lieutenant who was escorting Matt.

'In the King's name he's mine.' The officer pushed Roxton away. 'I have his papers. Look, he's volunteered to serve in the navy.'

'I did not!' Matt made to grab the paper but the lieutenant snatched it away.

'It has your name on it, Captain Linton, and your signature, therefore you've volunteered.'

'I have a warrant for his arrest. A seizure of contraband was made on his ship.' Roxton turned to Matt. 'I arrest you on a charge of smuggling goods on which duty was not paid.' He raised an arm to summon a cavalry sergeant who dismounted and stood at his side.

'The devil you will, Roxton.' Matt raised his voice in

anger. 'My ship was clean. There was nothing on board that wasn't paid for.'

Roxton sneered. 'I knew I'd get you sooner or later, Linton. You or your brother, it didn't matter which.' He drew out a list from his pocket. 'Two half ankers of brandy, one of geneva and one cask of tobacco. We've seized your ship and the men on board her.'

Matt made to attack him, but was restrained by the soldier. 'You've planted that,' he snarled. 'I wouldn't keep such a miserable amount on board. You took it on board with you!'

'Are you accusing me of connivance, Linton? That's a serious charge against an officer of customs!'

Matt rubbed his beard. Roxton had been known as a man who wouldn't take a bribe or get up to dirty tricks. Strange that he should fall now.

Roxton stared hard at Matt as he made no answer. 'Bring him along sergeant.'

'Whoa! One minute if *you* please.' The naval lieutenant stopped the sergeant. 'I said this man is mine. I got to him first therefore I have first claim on him.'

'Then I shall send for the magistrate and he can convince you.' Roxton glared at the officer. 'I'll not leave without him. He's going to gaol – and not before time.'

'He's going to sea, where he belongs.' The officer stood his ground.

'Well, gentlemen, until you've decided my fate, you won't mind if I sit down?' Matt dropped to the ground by the harbourside and crossed his legs as if to make himself comfortable, and the men behind him grinned and did the same.

'We're going to have some sport, captain, by the look of it.'

Matt turned on his haunches at the familiar voice behind him. 'Master Parson! So they caught you too?'

'Aye, sir. Just coming out of the inn and there they were waiting, like rats in a pack they were. Bosun got away though, they couldn't catch him.'

'They'll let you off, Parson White.' Matt dropped his voice. 'Tell them your sight is poor, I'll vouch for it – walk into something!'

'Aye, sir. I would, but what'll I do without a ship to sail in? The *Breeze* has been captured and the crew that were left on board.' He eased nearer towards Matt, elbowing the other men out of the way. 'If you go with the navy, I'd just as soon go with you.'

Matt was touched by the man's loyalty and patted him on the shoulder. 'If we don't go with the navy, it seems we go to gaol, and of the two I'd rather do the former. That'll spike Roxton's guns. But what I don't understand,' he mused, fingering the ring in his ear, 'is, if he didn't put the goods on board, then who the devil did?'

Parson White blinked his eye and cleared his throat, 'Erm, begging your pardon, captain—'

Matt stared as the man's face took on a hangdog expression. 'Master Parson! You didn't? Did you?'

32

Dusk was falling as the coach carrying Annie and Henry, along with three other passengers, clattered through the periphery of Hull. Though it was only a few short years since she had lived there, she was amazed at the change. Where once had been green meadows outside the town, there were long streets of elegant houses, and in the town itself as the coach drew towards the Market Place, changes had been made. Gone was the old gaol and guardhouse; finished and consecrated was the new St John's church. Old buildings had been demolished, and flagstones laid in the new streets instead of cobbles.

Yet still there were signs of poverty; children were still begging in the streets and the haggard faces of the poor showed their desperate situation as they milled around the Market Place. She felt, as she descended from the coach that there was an undercurrent of discontent waiting to flare.

She hid a wry smile as she entered the Cross Keys Inn where a room had been booked. How often she had been in here, but not dressed as she was now in her travelling habit of grey beneath her much loved black woollen cloak, a white lawn shirt and leather laced boots. Nor did she then wear a tall beaver hat as she did today. Then, she had worn whatever cast-offs she could beg and dressed them up with feathers and bits of lace, for she had always hankered for finery.

The landlord greeted the passengers who were staying overnight and she wondered if he would recognize her, for she had once been a regular customer along with Francis Morton.

But he didn't. He wiped his fingers on his apron and greeted her courteously and called for the maid to show her to her room.

'If tha's taking a walk to stretch tha legs, ma'am, take care.' He called to her as she mounted the stairs. 'There's an ugly mood in 'town.'

'What's happening?'

'Oh, usual complaint, ma'am,' he said cynically. 'Folks complaining that they're starving – no money to buy food – but nowt for thee to worry about. Just keep away from 'crowds if tha goes out and keep hold of bairn's hand; press-men are in town and there might be trouble. Nobody likes them.'

They took a short walk down to the Market Place, Annie wanted to show Henry the gold statue of King William III, or King Billy as the townspeople called him, as he sat on his horse in the middle of the road, but there were pockets of people standing around who were shouting abuse at a company of soldiers who were riding past and they couldn't get near. Two men were fighting round a street corner and while some others kept watch for the law, another group shouted encouragement at the participants.

Annie smiled a wide smile and Henry looked up and asked. 'Why you laugh, Mamma?'

She squeezeed his hand. 'I'm laughing to think that some things never change, Henry. Come, we'll go back for supper and an early night, then tomorrow I'll take you to see the big ships in the dock before we ride to Hessle.'

The landlord sent supper up to their room. 'Too noisy downstairs, ma'am. Two whaling ships came in today and 'men are celebrating. Things might get out of hand. Best stay in tha room.'

She was tempted to question him on the names of the ships and the company who owned them, but on second thoughts decided against it. No sense in arousing his suspicions, she thought, and later as she lay in her bed with a sleeping Henry at her side, wondered if any jolt of memory might remind the landlord of who she was, or

335

remember her bullying husband who'd died in the Arctic, or even worse, recall the death of Francis Morton.

For they must have found him, she thought, even though the mud was deep. They'd find him with the knife embedded in his chest. She sat up in the bed, her hand over her mouth. She'd never felt remorse for what she had done and yet, now she was back in the town where it had happened, in the very streets where she had roamed barefoot to save her boots, searching for cheap food to feed her children, she felt something like penitence.

'I'm sorry, Francis, if tha's listening anywhere.' She whispered in the darkness and watched wide-eyed as the candle flame flickered in a draught and sent quivering shadows across the ceiling. Outside the inn she could hear shouting and the sound of breaking glass. 'I know that what I did was wicked, but you were more wicked than me. Tha was going to hurt my bairn, my poor Lizzie.'

She looked down at Henry and moved a strand of fair hair from across his chubby pink cheek and knew in her heart that if anyone should attempt to hurt this child then she would do the same again.

Sleep deserted her and she slipped out of bed and looked out of the window. Outside the inn an affray had broken out between gangs of men. They were shouting and cursing and in the scuffle she saw the flash of a drawn cutlass and the raising of cudgels. She closed the shutters to muffle the noise and climbed back into bed and stared with sleepless eyes into the darkness.

In the hour before dawn she got up once more and looked down at the now quiet street. The only movement was from the muffled and bent figures of the night-soil-men with their odorous baskets, which as she watched they shouldered into the carts on their way to the muckgarths outside the town.

The next morning she woke heavy-eyed and could have slept on but Henry was awake and anxious to be off to see the ships.

'There was trouble last night all right.' The landlord

served them first with gruel, then brought a platter of ham and boiled fowl and sausages, and a seperate plate of eggs made into an omelette. 'Will tha have ale to drink, ma'am, or milk?'

'I prefer to take tea – or chocolate.' She smiled, revelling in being able to use the phrase which Toby had taught her. 'And milk for the child.'

'Aye, a heap of trouble,' he gossiped. 'It's a wonder 'noise didn't keep thee awake. Press-men were outside waiting to catch 'seamen. There were a few fights I can tell thee and plenty of clearing up to do this morning.'

As they went outside she saw the results of the disorderly and violent night. Market stalls had been overturned and produce trampled on. A wooden cart had been set on fire and was black and smouldering, whilst nearby a lone donkey munched from a basket of carrots. Glass and bricks littered the street and amongst the rubbish, women with torn and tattered clothing and children by their sides, poked about looking for something to eat or sell. Lying in the road in a sticky brown pool, the overflow from a brimming muck cart, was the still form of a man, either drunk or dead, and by his side a dead cat.

'Aye,' Annie stood in the inn doorway holding Henry's hand, and surveyed the scene. 'Nothing changes.'

She wanted to get away, to sit astride the horse she had hired, with Henry in front of her and ride away from this town and its memories. But she had promised him that he could see the ships in the dock, and from first rising he had constantly asked when would they go.

There were a great number of soldiers about, both the regular troopers, cavalry and infantry, and the militia, and they were all heading in the same direction, towards the dock. The New Dock, built to replace the Old Harbour and which was always crowded with shipping from every corner of the world.

Lines of men were being marched towards the dock, some holding their heads as if they were in pain, others openly weeping and she guessed that these were the pressed men, on their way to join the naval ships. Women were running by their sides, some crying, others clinging to the naval officers' coats, imploring them to let their men free.

'Excuse me. Can we come through.' She elbowed her way through the crowd. 'We want to see the ships.'

'I shouldn't go over there, miss – ma'am. There's too great a crush. Are you looking for somebody.' A young naval lieutenant spoke to her.

'I promised my son he could see the ships, but we can't get near.'

'Like ships do you, young man?' The officer bent down to Henry and ruffled his hair. 'Perhaps you'll join the King's navy when you're big enough?'

'Not if I can help it,' Annie's rejoinder came swiftly though she smiled amiably enough. 'I'll not have my son sailing to a watery grave.' Then she shivered as the words were out, as if in premonition.

'If you come with me, I'll find you a space.' He made a way through the crowd, still talking to Henry. 'You'll be able to see from over here, there are whalers and schooners, cutters and sloops, every kind of ship from all over the world.'

He found them a space near a group of men who were sitting on the ground near the edge of the dock. 'Don't go too near the edge.' He smiled at Henry. 'He's a fine boy, ma'am. I have two of my own. I haven't seen them for two years. I can hardly remember what they look like.'

'I'm sorry,' Annie began, but he saluted her and turned away.

There was a gusty wind blowing and Annie took off her hat for fear of losing it in the water. She pointed towards the dock. 'Look, there's a whaling ship, Henry. See how well the hull is built? That's because it has to break through the ice. And those small boats hanging at the side are what the men use to row out from the ship to capture the whale.'

'These men here?' Henry turned to look at the men

sitting near them. 'Are they going to row out and catch the whale?'

There was general laughter and one man answered. 'No, son. We're going to row out and capture the enemy, whoever that might be.'

Annie turned away from the sight of the ships and smiled sympathetically. She felt sorry for these men. They may well have had regular work and a home and family, but now they were in the hands of the navy, whether they liked it or not.

From the corner of her eye she saw a fair-haired man rise slowly to his feet and stare in her direction. 'Here you!' A soldier called to him. 'Sit down.'

She turned to face the man as ignoring the command he strode over the men sitting on the ground, and came towards her.

It was as if the world stood still. As if time had taken a deep breath and was suspended. They both gazed, one at the other and didn't speak. Then a veil of uncertainty showed in his eyes, to be replaced immediately by a flash of tempestuous fire.

'So, Mrs Hope. We meet once more.' His voice was cold though it trembled.

Oh, Matt! He's hurt, she thought and felt hot tears gathering behind her eyelids. And he's angry with me, just like he used to be. He doesn't want to show that he once cared.

'Indeed we do, Captain Linton,' she answered softly.

Matt gave a harsh laugh. 'Not Captain Linton any more, I fear. Just a common sailor in the navy.'

'You've been pressed!' Distress made her raise her voice. 'Oh, no.'

'Thank you for your sympathy, but it's of no matter. One ship is very like any other.' He continued to gaze at her and she wanted to put out her arms and hold him close to her.

'That isn't true. I know how you feel about the *Breeze*. It's what you most care about.'

'Is that what you think?' he asked in a bitter tone. 'You think I care only for tree trunks and sailcloth?' He gave a wry laugh which twisted his mouth but didn't reach his eyes. 'How little you know of me.'

She fell silent and hung her head. Perhaps then she had made a mistake, one that she would pay for forever. And now it was too late.

Henry had crouched down on his haunches and was playing at throwing pebbles with one of the men in the crowd, and she put out her hand to draw him towards her.

Matt drew in a sudden intake of breath as she stood the boy beside her.

'This is my son, Matt.' She saw his eyes glisten and the tears held back in her own eyes, spilled over.

He bent down and smiled at the boy and shook him by the hand. Then he ran his hand over his Henry's head and stood up, keeping his hand on his shoulder.

'And mine too, I think.'

She took a step towards him and he put out his arms and wrapped her within them. She felt the strength of them around her and started to sob. She had never thought to hold him again, to feel the softness of his fair beard against her face, to smell the sea in his hair.

He kissed her. A tender loving kiss which told her all she wanted to know, and from somewhere in the background, she could hear the cheers of men around them and felt Henry pulling on her skirt.

'Come on now. Break it up. Break it up!' A soldier on guard came towards them.

'This is my guard,' Matt said and kissed her wet cheeks. 'He's afraid I'll run away before Roxton gets back.'

'Roxton?' she breathed. 'What has he to do with this?'

Matt laughed. All signs of strain had gone from his face and he looked quite merry. He kept his arm around her.

'The Customs and the navy are fighting over who should have me, we're waiting for the magistrate to get out of bed and decide for them. And in the meantime, this poor fellow has charge of me, me and this blackguard of a parson who insists on staying with me.'

She glanced down at the man sitting almost at her feet and recognized the seaman with the eyepatch who had conducted Toby's burial and warned her of the dangers in the town when he had rowed her to shore from the *Breeze*.

Parson White shook his head despondently. 'Aye. I'm no good for anything. I'm a poor parson and an even poorer smuggler.'

Annie wiped away a tear and glanced at the soldier who was staring impassively at her. Sergeant Collins! Guarding Matt! For a moment, wild improbabilities raced through her mind. She would get him to turn his back while she spirited Matt away.

Then she remembered the kind of man that Sergeant Collins was. If he could give up Lily, whom she was sure he loved, because of his honourable regard for the wife he never saw, then he wouldn't risk his life or career for a pressed man.

She looked around her. Besides, there were too many other soldiers and navy men around. They wouldn't hesitate to fire their muskets or pistols if they saw a man escaping.

'I know this soldier,' she said simply. 'He helped me once when Toby was killed.'

Matt's eyes flashed as he remembered. 'One of your men was it, who killed him?'

Sergeant Collins nodded. 'Aye. A lad of sixteen drafted into the army from gaol where he'd been sent for stealing bread. He hardly knew one end of a musket from the other. He fired because he was frightened.' His voice was matter-of-fact. 'Perhaps you don't know about fear, captain. But young soldiers do. They know what it's like when their bowels turn to water and their legs tremble beneath them. But he was punished for disobeying orders and letting the smugglers get away. He'd hardly any skin left on his back by the time they'd finished.'

'But why was he so afraid? We wouldn't have hurt him. Not Toby or me.' Annie was aghast that the young soldier should have suffered.

'It's a game you've been playing, Mrs Hope.' Sergeant Collins drew closer and addressed them quietly. 'Both of ye, and your dead brother, sir. It's just been sport to ye, avoiding the law, never getting caught. But for some it's more than that. I've seen my men shot at and beaten to a pulp by these law breakers. We've sat all night on a cliff top in the pouring rain because no-one, not a house nor hostelry would give us a bed for the night in case they got their windows smashed by their own kind the next morning. Just think about it next time you're drinking run brandy or sipping duty-free tea; somebody might be paying for it with his life.'

He moved away from them to the edge of the crowd and they remained silent. Then Matt said quietly. 'It's true, all he says. I know that some of the men I meet are nothing more than ruffians; but then there are others who are trying to keep body and soul together by selling these run goods.'

He gathered her towards him again. 'But let's not talk of such things. Where I'm going there'll be no brandy, no tobacco, no silk. Not in gaol or on the high seas.' He squeezed her tight. 'How can I bear to lose you, Annie, when I've only just found you again. I've searched and searched for you these last years. I've had people looking for you and no-one knew where you'd gone.'

He put his head against hers. 'There were times when I thought you were dead.'

'I'm sorry,' she whispered. 'I'm sorry. I thought you wouldn't want me, not when I had a babby. I thought I'd be an embarrassment to you. I went to York. I work for a linen draper. We have a room above the shop, Henry and me.'

'Henry?' he asked, his brow creasing.

She nodded. 'I gave him the name of the first man who was ever kind to me – Henry Trott – and your name: Matthias – his father's name.'

'Annie! You know don't you, that I'll have to stay with the navy? They need men with my background.' He spoke softly and calmly. 'The magistrate won't let me rot in gaol when I can be usefully employed at sea. The sergeant was right when he said it was a game we were playing. Well the game is over. God knows I've no grudge against the French, at heart I'm a farmer, a landsman, but I'm in up to my neck now, and I'll have to go.'

Her face crumpled with dismay. She might never see him again. Henry might lose the father he had never known.

'Will you marry me, Annie? Will you give our son my name?'

She put her head against his chest and wept. 'How can I marry you? I'm nobody. Just a woman from the gutter who has pulled herself out. That's why I ran away. How can I marry a man like thee?'

He held her at arm's length and contemplated her. 'A woman from the gutter, a smuggler, a hawker, a Dutch widow, a draper, a mother. You have been all of these things, Annie; why can you not be a wife?'

He grinned. 'A wife of a common seaman who's just been pressed into the King's navy!'

'I have to tell you something first. You might not want to marry me then.' She took a deep breath. 'I ran away from Hull because I'd killed a man.'

He was silent for a moment and she felt a dreadful despair. He would reject her now. He was bound to.

'He must have deserved it, Annie,' he said softly and stroked her cheek. 'You must have had a compelling reason. I want you for my wife, no matter what you have done.'

She searched for a piece of linen to wipe her nose and streaming eyes, but couldn't find one and so put her arm up to her face and wiped it with her frilled sleeve.

Matt put his head back and laughed though his voice broke with emotion. 'Oh, Annie. How wonderful you are. Don't ever change.'

'Begging your pardon, captain.' Parson White stood by

343

their side. 'With my one bloodshot eye, I spy Roxton at the far end of the dock. If you were planning anything then it had better be soon.'

'Planning anything? What do you mean, man? Have you got a pistol hidden beneath your hat and intend that I shoot the varmint?'

'No sir, you know as well as anybody what a law-abiding fellow I am. No, what I was meaning sir, for I couldn't help overhearing, was if you and the good lady were thinking of getting wed, then we'd better be sharp about it.'

'How can we wed,' Annie asked, her face pink and blotchy from crying. 'We've had no banns read, no licence, and Roxton wouldn't let us go to church, even though St Mary's is just a step away.'

'A step too far,' Matt mused. 'He wouldn't allow it, nor would the navy.'

Parson White gave a huge sigh and tutted. Matt stared at him. 'What are you suggesting—? You're not suggesting—? You *are* suggesting that you should marry us?'

'I was ordained to conduct marriages as well as burials,' he boomed in a pontifical manner. 'And though the church might have thrown me out, God knows where my heart is; and if you want me to bless the pair of you in His presence then I can do it here, as well as any other parson in a pulpit. With or without a magistrates licence,' he added.

'Will you be happy with that, Annie?' Matt gazed seriously at her. 'It might not be strictly legal, but it's the best I can offer you until I return.'

They both knew that the words he uttered were only of hope. There was every possibility that he wouldn't return.

She nodded, too overcome to speak, then she drew Henry, who had been contemplating both Matt and Parson White, towards them. 'Henry.' She swallowed and wiped her fingers across her eyes. 'Henry. This is your father.'

The little boy raised his eyes and solomnly contemplated Matt and then smiled, his cheeks dimpling. Matt bent down and kissed him on both cheeks and Henry put his arms about his neck and hugged him.

'I knew he was mine, the minute I saw him,' Matt spoke in a choked voice. 'Look at his smile, he's got the same gap as both Toby and me.'

Annie patted the boy's cheek and said huskily. 'His milk teeth, Matt, all children have it.'

'No matter, you'll see when he's grown—.' He couldn't finish the sentence and Annie held them both close, Matt and their son.

'Now then, cap'n, – ma'am. We'd better get started if you've decided.' Parson White's voice broke in. 'There's not much time.'

'I have nothing to give you, Annie! No token for you to remember me by.'

'I have your son,' she whispered.

He nodded, his eyes loving. 'Wait.' He put his hand to his ear, and took from it the gold ring which pierced it. 'I have this, take it and wear it.'

She took the small gold ring and slipped it on her little finger; her hands were unadorned, she had never before had a ring. The only jewellery she possessed were the pearls which Matt had given her and which she always wore.

They stood side by side with Henry between them as Parson White conducted the unorthodox ceremony. The parson took off his hat and putting his hands together and closing his one eye, raised his head to the heavens.

Some of the pressed men who had been listening and watching with some interest, got to their feet when they realized that they were to be witnesses to a ceremony. They dusted themselves down or straightened their neckchiefs and pulled down the sleeves of their coats, and took off their caps and hats.

'Dearly Beloved. We are gathered here today in the presence of the Almighty, who deems Himself to be in all places at all times wherever two or three are gathered in his name, to bear witness to the marriage of Captain Matthias Linton and Mrs Annie Hope.'

345

He opened his eye and raised an eyebrow at Annie.

She bit her lip. This was no place for lies and subterfuge. If God was listening, He would know. She leaned forward and whispered. 'Swinburn. Annie Swinburn.'

Matt shook his head in amused admonishment, but she gave no answering smile. What if any of the men here remembered the name?

Parson White continued, 'And the woman,' he lowered his voice so that only Matt and Annie heard, 'Annie Swinburn, better known as Hope.'

From the corner of her eye Annie could see Roxton approaching, Sergeant Collins had seen him too and stealthily moved away from the ceremony in the direction of the customs official.

Parson White had seen her glance away and he too looked over his shoulder, and proceeded in a faster tone.

'If there is anyone here who would dare to object or give cause to say why these two people should not be joined together in Holy Matrimony in sight of God, then let him speak now.'

He glared dissuasively around, but there was not a sound from the men. Sergeant Collins was still in conversation with Roxton and Annie saw him put a restraining hand on his arm.

'Then I now pronounce you man and wife.'

A cheer went up from the men and from the ranks of the army and navy who had joined the crowd, and hats flew into the air.

'Now for a hymn,' one of the men shouted. 'Let's have a bit of music to give them a good send off.'

33

As the men sang lustily and Matt held her close, Roxton threw off Sergeant Collins' hindering hand and strode towards them. The naval officer who had confronted him the previous evening, and had been watching the marriage ceremony also hurried forward.

'What news Mr Roxton?' he called cheerily before he could reach the wedding party. 'Are you to have him after all, or shall the King keep him?'

Roxton's face was livid. He shook an angry fist. 'I've waited for years to catch that felon! He deserves to go to gaol!'

'Oh, come now, Roxton.' The lieutenant admonished him. 'You know as well as I do, that life on board one of His Majesty's ships is as fitting a gaol as those on land, especially for a pressed man. There'll be no luxuries on board for him.'

'I wanted the satisfaction of taking him to the courthouse myself and hearing the door of the gaol clang behind him.' Roxton's voice was hostile and resentful.

The officer laughed. 'Well, you can wave goodbye from the quayside for we can be off now, and not a half hour too soon for we'll miss the tide if we delay any longer.' He turned to another officer. 'Muster the men, and stand by. Tell the army we are ready to sail.'

The quayside bustled with activity as naval men and soldiers obeyed the commands.

'I didn't realize that the soldiers were going too,' Annie said. 'I wondered why there were so many of them here.'

'Most of them won't come back,' Matt answered grimly. 'It's hard enough being a sailor, far worse to be a soldier.'

He looked down at her and wound a strand of fair hair which had escaped from the coil at the back of her neck, around his finger. 'You're a real lady, Annie. The only one I could have wished for to be the mother of my son. Go now, and don't look back. God willing I'll come back to you.'

She clung to him not wanting this moment to end; he kissed her and pushed her away. 'Go,' he said. 'Don't make it any harder for me to bear.'

She kissed him once more and brought Henry near that he also might kiss his father. Holding back her tears she shook hands with Parson White and some of the other men who were standing near, their faces wracked with emotion. Then she turned again to kiss Matt a final goodbye.

'Don't look back,' he whispered. 'Just go.'

She turned and holding tight to Henry's hand, walked away.

'Mrs Hope!'

Instantly at the sound of her name, she turned around. Matt was smiling at her, his eyes creased with pain.

'Mrs Linton!' she exclaimed through her tears. 'My name is Annie Linton.'

'I love you, Mrs Linton.'

Before she could reply, Henry tore out of her hand and ran back towards Matt. 'If you're my father now, do I have a grandfayther like James?'

Matt gave a small exclamation, something between a gasp and a sob, and crouched down to be on the same level as the child. 'Indeed you do, young Henry.' He kissed the boy and sent him back to his mother.

'Annie!' He called urgently. 'Take him to my father.' He made to step towards her but the impeding hand of a navy man stopped him.

'Your father!' How could she? How could she take Henry to the man who had rejected his own sons. How could she confess that the poor hawker and the Dutch widow and the wife of his eldest son, were one and the same?

'Take him,' he called as he was pushed into line ready

to embark the ship flying the royal ensign. 'He likes you. Take him and tell him, and wait for me there. Take him to his grandfather – Henry Linton!'

She walked slowly back towards the Cross Keys, holding Henry tightly by the hand. She felt the sun warm on her face and remembered once before when she had walked from the same quayside on such a day as this, when she had been told that her husband, Alan Swinburn, had been killed on board the whaler *The Polar Star*. Then, though she had cried and wailed, she had felt no emotion for the dead man, no sorrow, only terror that she would have to fend for her children and herself without a man to support them.

But now, she knew that she could support herself and Henry. She had become self-reliant, had grown in stature and had a better opinion of herself than she once had. But, she thought sadly, it means nothing. I want only Matt. I can't bear to think that I might never hold him in my arms again, never hear his laugh or kiss his lips. I've been without him these long years and now that I've found him again, the pain is harder to bear than ever.

Henry tugged her hand. 'Mamma?'

She smiled a weak smile. But I have his son. I'll watch him grow in his likeness. While I have him, I have Matt.

'Mamma.' Henry's voice was persistent and he wrinkled his small nose in distaste. 'What's that smell?'

She hadn't noticed. It was inherent in the town and so familiar that she hadn't realized its presence. The smell of boiling blubber which brought industry to the town.

'It's blubber,' she said, 'from the whale. It's what keeps this town alive and prosperous.'

They passed a group of women and children. They were neither prosperous nor hardly alive she thought, looking at their pinched faces and tattered clothing. She kept her head down so that her hat shielded her face, in fear that any one of them might recognize her, and in humility that

349

she had escaped from the poverty and servitude which held them down.

How grateful I should be, she thought. For even though Matt is bound to a ship which might take him away for ever, I have the knowledge of his love; I have his son, I have work and a roof over our heads. What more could I ask?

What more? Yet, still something more.

She called to the landlord as she waited for the hired mount to be saddled. 'Do you know of a family by the name of Foster?'

He would know. He knew everyone in this town and Will Foster was well known. Everyone knew Will and had been shocked at his injuries sustained on the same voyage that had killed Alan.

Caution veiled his face. 'Foster?' He pursed his lips. 'Can't think of any travellers of that name.'

'No, no, not visitors. They live in the town, or they did.'

He shook his head. 'Folks' is moving out of 'town; gentry and trade. Grand houses are being built out Hessle and Ferriby way.'

He was evading her questions. If I should speak as I used to and say, 'Come on Jack, tha can tell me. Where have 'Fosters and my bairns gone?' Then he would tell me, but not now; not in case this fine lady means them mischief.

They looked after their own, the people of Hull, and she realized now why there had been no pounding of the feet of the law chasing her when Francis Morton had died. If questions had been asked about her, a wall of impenetrable silence would have descended, impossible to scale.

But now she had crossed to the other side. The landlord would know that she wasn't gentry, he might even find it difficult to know where to place her, but all the more reason for the hedging of answers. Until he knew that she meant the Fosters' no harm, he would give her no satisfactory answer.

The groom, in a canvas smock covering his coat and

breeches, came to tell her that the mount was groomed and ready. She paid the landlord and thanked him for his hospitality. 'I shall come back, one day,' she said. 'Perhaps then you might be able to tell me of the Fosters. It's important to me.'

He narrowed his eyes and viewed her quizically and she knew that first he would make his own discreet enquiries.

'Take care on 'road, ma'am. I hear that a man's escaped from a navy ship. He'll be desperate. I'm not saying he'd harm thee, but he might want 'hoss. Dost tha carry a firearm?'

She stared dumbstruck. 'A man? A seaman, do you mean?' Wild delight ran through her and she felt her cheeks grow hot, then cold as she thought of the consequences. If he was caught, he'd be hanged.

'Is tha not well, ma'am?' The landlord pushed a stool towards her. 'Better sit down for a minute.'

She sank down and Henry came and held her hand and watched her anxiously.

'A seaman, did you say?' she whispered. 'One of the pressed men?'

'No. I didn't say that.' He gazed at her as if to remember her face. 'A soldier. Didn't fancy a sail on one of His Majesty's ships apparently, and I can't say I blame him. It wouldn't be anybody that you would know, ma'am, not an officer, just a common soldier.'

She closed her eyes and shook her head. 'No. For a moment I thought – but no, I know no soldiers.'

'Look at the ships, Mamma. Look at the ships.'

The Humber was thick with ships, schooners and brigantines, sloops and commercial boats, plying their way towards Hessle and the towns beyond the Trent.

The river was choppy, the tide full. The waves surged and swelled, and they watched from the high cliffs near Hessle as one of the ferry boats battled its way towards the Lincolnshire coast, tossing and plunging as the billowing body of water made sport of its shaking timbers.

We'll go to the Trotts first, she decided as she urged the horse forward. They can meet Henry. Then we'll go to see Robin and put forward the suggestion. I'll not go to Toby's cottage. She stifled a sob as she cantered past the track which led there. The door can stay locked on those memories. The memory of two loving brothers.

'Yes?' Mrs Trott answered the door and Annie felt as if she was reliving time. Except that Mrs Trott's grim expression changed to disbelief when she saw who it was.

'Who is it, Mrs Trott?'

Annie smiled as she heard Henry Trott call. 'Not a beggar,' she called back. 'Just somebody down on her luck.'

He came to the door and Mrs Trott stood back, her eyes fixed on the child.

'Bye. I'm glad to see thee, Mrs Hope. We've been that worried. Talked often of thee, haven't we, Mrs Trott? Captain Linton's searched high and low. Come in, come in. We'll have to get a message to him.'

Mrs Trott said not a word, but stared at Henry as he clung to Annie's cloak.

'And who's is bairn?' he asked as he noticed Henry hiding behind her.

'Can't tha see whose bairn it is?' Mrs Trott's voice broke in. 'Can't tha see?' She put her hands to her face and started to weep.

'Mrs Trott? What is it?' Annie put her hand on the old woman's arm.

'Daft beggar that he is, hasn't got eyes in his head.' Mrs Trott wiped her nose on her clean apron. 'Anybody can see who he belongs to.'

Henry Trott looked bewildered. 'I suppose he's thine, Mrs Hope? I'm not much good at seeing likeness in babbies.'

Mrs Trott gave a great sigh and leaned forward to draw Henry towards her. He resisted for a moment and looked up at Annie, but she nodded reassuringly and he went towards the old lady.

'He's a Linton all right, he's got his father's eyes and his grandmother's hair.' She stroked the boy's head. 'She had beautiful hair, your grandmother.' Her mouth trembled, 'and a face like an angel.'

Annie smiled to herself. No matter that she too had fair hair and blue eyes. She would let it pass. If it pleased Mrs Trott to attribute all Henry's beauty to the Lintons, she wasn't going to complain.

She told them of finding Matt and of him being pressed into the navy. She didn't mention Roxton for she thought that Mr Trott would still be unaware of the smuggling.

'We were married before he sailed,' she said. 'I'm Mrs Linton now.'

'Married!' Mrs Trott's mouth dropped open. 'He married thee!'

Annie took no offence. She felt she knew Mrs Trott well enough now. The old woman had never liked her, but it didn't matter any more.

'Yes,' she said. 'He wanted to give Henry his name before he went away.'

'Henry?' Mrs Trott repeated.

'That's what Mrs Hope – Mrs Linton said, you silly old woman.' Mr Trott displayed an impatience Annie hadn't seen before. 'Don't keep repeating everything she says!'

'Henry!' Mrs Trott ignored the old man. 'Called after the squire I expect?' She gave a short laugh. 'Well I doubt that old scoundrel will accept either of thee, in spite of it.'

'No,' Annie faced her. 'That wasn't why. I didn't know that Squire Linton's name was Henry. I named him after Mr Trott.' She looked fondly at Henry Trott. 'You taught me that there were some kind men in the world and I met several more after you. But you were the first, you took me into your home and fed me and gave me shelter, and so I gave my son your name.'

Henry Trott blew his nose and then thanked her. 'I'm honoured, Mrs Linton, and very proud. Proud to have your son and grandson of Squire Linton named after me. I'll live with that in my heart for 'rest of me days.'

She went then to see Robin, he was out, his sister said, but she was welcome to come in and wait, she was sure he would be back for supper. The house was neat and seemed to be more comfortable than it had been. She was offered tea.

'Is Robin in work?' she asked as she sipped the tea.

'Aye, he is. He sells cloth in 'summer and goes in 'quarries in winter if he's hard pressed for money. Then he's been in Captain Linton's pay, until recent. He's been good to him 'as Captain Linton. I thought as how Robin might get ideas above his station, but he never. He's allus been a good lad, our Robin.'

Annie didn't quite follow but asked no further questions. Robin would no doubt tell her all when he put in an appearance.

'And your other brother, Josh?'

'Still in quarry. Works all hours God sends. He looks after his wife's sister as best he can, as well as his own; her husband died in gaol; he had a nasty accident after he was imprisoned for being with them smugglers.' She pulled her shawl closer around her and though the room was warm and stuffy, Annie too shivered.

'Aye,' the woman said softly. 'It's folks like us that allus gets caught. Never 'nobs.'

'Sometimes they do,' Annie whispered. 'Sometimes.'

It was getting dark as Robin returned and after greeting her with enthusiasm and some amazement at being presented to Henry, he forgot himself enough to give her a smacking kiss on her cheek.

Then he suddenly said. 'I'll have to get a message to Captain Linton. I promised I would.'

'Robin?' Annie queried. 'There's something different about you.'

'Aye,' he said grinning all over his face. 'Bye heck there is.'

'Come with me to the Admiral Hawke,' she said

suddenly. 'I'll need to get a room for the night for Henry and me. It's too late to go back into Hull, and we've a lot of talking to do.'

They uncoupled the reins of the hired mount from the hitching rail and while Henry rode on its back, Robin and Annie walked by the side and talked and talked.

'So the Captain's been pressed? Well, he's better at sea than rotting in gaol. Roxton would have had him sooner or later, aye and Josh. That's all over and done with now, I hope.'

'Did you always know, Robin? About the smuggling?'

He nodded. 'Aye. I wasn't so dim that I didn't know what was going on. But I just didn't want to be involved; somebody has to make a stand about what they think is right.'

She gazed admiringly at the young man who had emerged from boyhood with his ideals still intact. She'd been right. He was just the person they needed at Sampson's Drapery.

She booked in at the inn and after giving Henry his supper, put him to bed and joined Robin downstairs in the small dark snug where she had once persuaded Mr Moses to let her have cloth to sell.

'I met up with Moses again,' Robin said as if reading her thoughts. 'I came across him when I was searching for thee. *You*, I mean! Sometimes I forget,' he laughed. 'Though I always use my own voice when I'm up on 'Wolds.'

'When I'm alone I often think in my own voice, though not always, as I once did.' She studied him questioningly. 'When you're on the Wolds, do you see Rose?' she asked.

He blushed. 'Sometimes. Sometimes I stay there when I'm travelling, but her sisters watch her all the time. They know, I think, how I feel about her.'

'How do you feel, Robin? Dare I ask?'

'I don't mind telling theè, Annie.' He fidgeted in his seat and looked down at his feet. He was wearing, she noticed, a finer pair of stockings than the knitted ones he used to wear and his short leather boots were new. And though he was wearing the same coat as he previously wore, which was now shiny and rather short in the sleeve, his flannel shirt was good and hard-wearing, as were his brown breeches.

'I'd like to wed her one day. But I've nowt to offer her yet. I can make money in 'summer when I can get out to sell cloth, but I know her fayther wouldn't let her go unless I was in regular work. He's not short of brass himself so he won't let her go to a pauper.'

Annie's smile went from ear to ear. Now she had an extra cherry to offer Robin.

'Well, Mr Deane,' she said solemnly. 'How would you like to become a draper in York, and take your wife, Rose, with you?'

34

'How shall we travel, Annie?' Robin could scarcely contain himself for joy. 'We still have Sorrel, Josh keeps him well shod. And I hire a cart when I'm travelling.' He added anxiously. 'Though perhaps it's more fitting for you to travel post-chaise now that you're married to the captain?'

'Being married to Captain Linton hasn't put more money in my pocket,' she said. 'I have money belonging to Mr Sampson which he gave me to bring you back, but we won't spend it unwisely. Besides, no chaise could get up those roads. No, if I'm to go and see Mr Sutcliff and persuade him that you're a suitable person for his youngest daughter to marry, I'll travel with Henry on Sorrel, and you can follow in the cart with your belongings, when you've made your arrangements with Moses and said goodbye to your family. Oh, and you'll bring Charlie?'

She knew it would be hard for Robin to take his leave of his sister and Josh who had cared for him, and guessed too that he might want to make arrangements with Moses to visit him when he was settled in York. He had an eye for business had Robin, now that he was older, she was convinced of it. And as for Charlie, the dog had greeted her deliriously, giving her great licks with his pink tongue and his long tail swishing.

'Aye, I'll not come without Charlie, he'd pine without me, besides, he can guard young Henry when we're busy in 'shop.'

Already he was assuming an essence of propriety, ever since Annie had told him of the draper's shop in Fossgate, York; of its large window and open floor and oak counters,

357

and the walls of shelves which were stacked with rolls of linen and muslins and silks and satins, and of the hangings which she draped for display.

As she urged Sorrel on towards the rolling hills and dales of the Wolds, she felt a surging emotion. It was almost a feeling of going home, yet she hadn't felt this before. When she had come the first time she had been overwhelmed by the openness, by the vast green pasture-land. Then she had been loath to leave behind the safety of the river, feeling unsure of herself as she left the long ribbon of water behind.

But now, as she trotted along the narrow tracks, scattering pheasants and rabbits and pointing out to Henry the disappearing tail of a fox as it slid beneath a hedge, and showed him the foxgloves and leafy ferns that were growing along the stone walls, she felt a sense of belonging. There was a sweet smell of wild thyme and the heavy scent of elderflower and a great joyful sound of birdsong as if she was being welcomed back.

'This is where your father lived when he was just your age, Henry. This was his home.'

'But where is his room?' Henry looked about him. 'Where is his shop?'

'Your father didn't have a room above a shop; he lived in a great house with a lot of rooms and large gardens, gardens as big as the park where Polly and I take you to play, and he had a horse of his own, and dogs.'

'I'm going to have a dog,' said Henry decisively, looking about him. 'I'm going to have Charlie. Robin said I could share him. Then I'll bring him out here to play in this park.'

Annie smiled down at him and then reined in to point down a valley. 'Over there, Henry. Hidden in that hollow, is the house where your grandfather lives.'

'Can we go and see him? I'll tell him about James's grandfayther; he might know him.'

She shook her head. 'Perhaps one day, but not now.' I don't know if we'll be welcome, she thought, in spite of what Matt said. 'We must get on if we're to see the Sutcliff's. There'll be a welcome there for us, I've no doubt about that.'

But, though the Sutcliff girls greeted her with open arms, and made a great fuss over Henry, she felt a slight restraint from Lily. She was welcoming enough, but seemed nervous and jumpy. Mr Sutcliff had hurt his back lifting a barrel of ale and was hardly able to get out of his chair and all of his daughters were scurrying around trying to do the jobs which he normally did.

'There's a lot of heavy work running an inn,' he complained. 'The lasses are strong enough but they can't shift ale barrels around.'

'They can if they do it properly,' Annie said. 'I know how, I'll show them.' She had shifted many barrels of fish in her time, she was sure she hadn't lost the knack.

'Find the pivot,' she told them. 'Then it's easy.' She rolled the barrel on its axis as easily as she ever did. 'I can't think why your father hasn't shown you before.'

'He allus took care of the ale,' Lily told her, wiping her pale face with her shawl. 'We allus looked after 'house. Annie,' she whispered anxiously. 'I have to talk to thee. I'm that worried.'

She took Annie up to her room, and left Henry in the charge of Rose. 'It's Sergeant Collins,' she blurted out. 'He's here, hiding in 'barn.'

Annie stared. The escaped soldier! Not Sergeant Collins?

'He said he'd had enough. Something happened to make him run off, but he wouldn't say what. I'm that scared of what me fayther will say if he finds out. It's onny by chance that he didn't find him, he can't get outside because of his back. Oh, Annie, I want him to stay. And if he can't stay, then I'll go with him.'

'His wife?' She put her hand to her mouth as the words came out. She'd forgotten that Lily didn't know that Sergeant Collins was married.

'He told me,' Lily nodded, 'but he says he has no wife, onny in name. He hasn't seen her for years. And now, well, he can't go back, not now; there'll be a warrant out on him.'

'No,' said Annie softly. 'He can't go back.' Only to the gallows or a flogging to the death.

'Take me to him,' she said urgently. 'We'll have to decide what to do before your father finds out.'

They slipped out of the kitchen door and across the yard and into a foldyard. Annie remembered the way, this was where Mr Sutcliff had brought her when she'd brought the run liquor and they'd stored it in the pit.

Sergeant Collins was lying in a corner of the barn with a blanket wrapped around him. He'd discarded his red tunic and wore a shabby coat which Annie suspected had once been Mr Sutcliff's. His once shiny boots had a film of dust and his breeches were muddy.

He sat up instantly as they opened the door and Annie saw him reach for a heavy stick which was lying by his side. He relaxed when he saw who it was and stood up. His face was pale and he looked younger than he did when he was in uniform.

'I've brought Mrs Hope to talk to you, she has a clear head.' Lily stood by his side. 'She might know what we can do.'

Sergeant Collins glanced at Annie. He'd been there when she'd changed her name to Linton, but she hadn't yet told the Sutcliffs.

'Why?' Annie asked. 'Why now? I thought you were a soldier through and through.'

'I was,' he muttered grimly. 'Even though the army wasn't what I would have chosen – if I'd had the choice. But who of us does have the choice? And they made it sound tempting. There was regular pay, though it was a pittance, and I did have some satisfaction out of an orderly life, even though it was hard.'

He put his hand to his head. 'But there are so many injustices. You can feel the dislike of the ordinary folks, the hatred of the mob. I got to be able to smell the fear of the young soldiers when they had to face them.' He nodded his head towards Annie. 'Like the soldier who fired at you and Master Linton.'

'But you'd put up with it for so long, and you had responsibility!'

He gave a grim smile. 'Aye, but not for much longer. Roxton was out to get somebody for losing Captain Linton, and he told me that day on the dockside, that I'd obstructed him. He was set to stop the marriage.'

Lily had a puzzled frown on her forehead but she didn't interrupt.

'But neither did I fancy a sea voyage. Half those men won't come back and though I'm no coward I'd already decided that there must be some other life, a better one than dying on foreign earth.'

'But,' he said in merely a whisper. 'It was when I saw ye and Captain Linton that I made my mind up. Ah. Ye might not have the chance of a life together, who knows what might happen out there on the ocean? But I watched you make a pledge in spite of that, and I knew then what I wanted. I wanted to be with Lily. It might not be for long if I'm caught. But even so, it's what I want more than anything else. I'm sick of battling with my Calvinistic conscience. I want a taste of happiness too.'

He sat down on the floor and put his head in his hands and the two women stayed silent. Then Lily gently stroked the top of his head. 'Don't worry, Stuart. We'll take our chance. I'll run with thee if need be.'

Annie made up her mind to speak to Mr Sutcliff immediately. She went into the room where she had tasted the sumptuous food which Lily had prepared on her first visit and found him with Henry on his knee. He'd miss Lily's cooking, she mused. Joan isn't nearly as good a cook and Meg is so scatty she'd burn everything. And dear Rose, I hope, is coming with me.

She'd managed to whisper to Rose that she had some good news coming to her and the girl's lovely face had lit up with a huge smile. She had been a pretty child but now she was beautiful, just grown into womanhood. There was no wonder, Annie thought, that Robin was so smitten, she would turn any man's head. But she worshipped Robin, there was a smile in her eyes at the very mention of his name.

'Run and find Rose,' she told Henry. 'I want to talk to Mr Sutcliff.'

Henry obediently slipped off his knee. 'Are you a grandfayther? I've got a father and a grandfayther just like my friend James.'

'Has he, Mrs Hope? Have you told him his fayther's name?' Mr Sutcliff looked up at her from his chair.

She nodded and sat down opposite him. She knew that he wouldn't know anything. Lily was the only one who had known about Matt and Annie knew she hadn't spoken of it. The others had expressed complete astonishment on meeting Henry.

'Yes,' she said. 'He knows his father, my husband – Captain Linton.'

Mr Sutcliff tried to rise from his chair. 'Well, I never. Please excuse me Mrs Linton – I had no idea. Does Lily know.'

His face was red with embarrassment and she hastened to reassure him. 'She does now.' Sergeant Collins was no doubt telling her of the marriage at the quayside in Hull. 'Captain Linton has been pressed into the navy.' She dropped her voice to a whisper. 'He was also caught by the Customs; there'll be no more goods I fear.'

'Dear, dear. Not a naval ship! That is hard luck. Can't he buy himself out?' he added. 'A man like him – his father would have influence!'

It was something she had pondered on too. Money and influence could have done much to persuade the authorities to release him. But she knew how proud Matt was. He wouldn't go to his father for help, not at any price.

'If he bought his way out of the navy then the Customs would be waiting for him; he couldn't easily avoid gaol. There's a price to be paid for what we do, Mr Sutcliff –

we're none of us innocent as we both know, and if Captain Linton stays in the navy then the Customs can't bring him to court.'

'That's true.' Mr Sutcliff ran his fingers thoughtfully through his short beard and she thought she saw a vestige of relief in his eyes. 'And though we know that the captain wouldn't give evidence, there's a few folk will sleep easier if they know there's no-one to give out their names. And I'm not talking about folks like thee and me, like me, I mean to say,' he added hastily and she hid a wry smile, 'I'm talking about some of 'nobs who don't mind handling run goods.'

She nodded and thought of Mr Beddows the magistrate who would be very embarrassed if it came out that he had a regular delivery of smuggled brandy and tobacco.

'I wanted to talk to you, Mr Sutcliff, about a young man I know, who so far in his life has managed to avoid temptation. He's had no brush with the law and has always managed to work honestly for his living.'

'If there is such a man, I'd like to meet him,' Mr Sutcliff snorted. 'It's not possible to keep tha hands clean these days. I don't know of anybody, except for my four lasses, and they're both honest and trustworthy, and that's why they're not wed. There's nobody fit for 'em round here. They'll stay spinsters even though I'll miss out on having a grandson like your young 'un.'

'This young man has,' Annie insisted. 'And what's more he's about to embark on a new career in trade. He's set to make his mark in drapery. But,' she sighed. 'His heart isn't in it. He's so smitten with a young lass that he can't bear to leave without her.'

'Then why doesn't he wed her and take her with him? It's the obvious thing to do. He can't be that bright if he can't see that!'

'Oh, he knows that. But he thinks that the girl's father won't let him near his daughter.'

'Then her fayther must be off his chump. By, I'd let one of mine go if I thought there was a chance like that!'

'Would you, Mr Sutcliff?' Annie leaned towards him. 'Would you let Rose go?'

'Rose?' His mouth opened wide in astonishment. 'Little Rose! Does somebody want that bairn?' He blew out a breath. 'Well I never.'

His eyes narrowed as he pondered. 'I might have trouble persuading her. I think she's smitten with young Robin Deane. You know, yon fellow who first brought thee here. I've seen 'em with moon eyes every time he comes, they think I don't notice. He's an upright young fellow, but no prospects. Tha'd have to help me talk to her, Mrs Linton.'

She sat back in the chair and waited for the notion to sink in. It took only a few minutes. He looked up. 'It's him, isn't it? Robin Deane? I think tha'd better tell me about it.'

She finished her explanation and an agreement was made. Robin would present himself formally to Mr Sutcliff on arrival. Rose would be informed and Robin would speak to her and then she would accompany Annie back to York.

'If onny my back wasn't bad I'd come wi' thee,' Mr Sutcliff said. 'First of my daughters to be wed, – she'll be onny one I expect, unless tha can come up wi' some others,' he added roguishly.

'You'll need one daughter at home to look after you?' she asked. 'You couldn't manage otherwise?'

'Oh aye, but our Lily'd stay. She'll not wed, she's past 'time of passion. She'd not leave her Da.'

'Mr Sutcliff! Now that we've got the business of Rose settled – I need to talk to you about Lily.'

It was as difficult as she expected it to be. He ranted and raved about deceit and trickery and she sat and waited until the fury over the alleged duplicity had blown out. Yet though he blustered that he'd have no soldier living under his roof, she felt that his real fear was in losing Lily.

'I have to warn you, Mr Sutcliff, that Lily will go with Sergeant Collins if you won't accept him here. She said she would go with him. They'd have a life of misery, for ever hiding and moving on, but still she would go. You wouldn't want that would you – not for Lily?'

He heaved himself painfully out of his chair and staggered across to the window. He stood for a few moments just staring out, not speaking. Then he turned towards her.

'It's not been easy bringing up four lasses. I did my best by 'em and tried to treat 'em all equal. But Lily, she was allus special to me, being 'first. I wanted a lad of course, what man doesn't. A lad that could take over here when I'm past it, which won't be long,' he groaned as he eased himself back into the chair. 'But Lily was like a mother to other 'bairns. It was hard for her when her Ma died, but she never complained. Never once as far as I remember.'

'Then isn't she due for some happiness, Mr Sutcliff?' Annie pleaded. 'They might not have long together. If the army finds him and takes him back, then she'd lose him for good. You can't deny her a chance.'

He shook his head. 'Military wouldn't find him up here. They never come now. They're too busy fighting 'French to come looking up here for a deserter for one thing; and for another, we get very few travellers in this part of 'Wolds for 'word to get out. And if local folk round here did find out about him, their lips 'd be sealed, they'd say nowt.' He folded his arms across his chest purposefully. 'Not if he was wi' me, they wouldn't.'

She was halfway to victory. She rose to her feet. 'I must relieve Rose of Henry. Perhaps you'll think about it?' She opened the door and a smell of onions and wild garlic drifted through from the kitchen.

'Something smells good,' she said lightheartedly. 'She's a good cook is Lily.'

'Aye, she is,' he said gloomily. 'She takes after her mother.'

As they were preparing to sit down to supper, Mr Sutcliff pulled out a chair at the table for Annie, and one next to her for Henry. 'Rose,' he said. 'Come and sit by me. If I'm to lose thee soon then I'll have thee next to me.'

Rose blushed and glanced shyly from beneath long dark lashes at Annie and then at Joan and Meg who were bringing in the supper dishes.

They both looked up and glanced at her and then their father, but asked no questions. Joan put a pie dish on the table, its contents hidden beneath a golden crust.

'Mm, that looks good Joan, thy hand's improving then?' her father remarked.

She giggled. 'Don't tease, fayther. Tha knows it's not mine. Nobody makes paste like our Lily.'

Her father sighed. 'Aye, tha's never spoken a truer word.'

Lily sat down and cut into the crust and a fragrant spiral of steam rose from the incision. Her face was drawn and she avoided looking at her father.

'Excuse me, Lily, but hasn't tha forgotten summat.' Mr Sutcliff's words broke the silence.

She dropped the spatula with a clatter, spilling gravy on to the table and looked up in fright, her face whiter than ever.

'Nay lass. Don't look so scared,' he said quietly. 'I'm not going to bite tha head off.'

'I'm sorry fayther. Wh- What have I forgotten? Everything's out I think – extra gravy and 'taties.'

'I was thinking that it'd be polite to wait on our other guest to join us before starting on our supper, and tha hasn't set an extra place at 'table!'

Lily stared at her father, her face set, her eyes enormous. She said nothing and the other girls moved only their eyes from one to another, as if aware that something momentous was about to happen, but dare not for the life of them ask what it was.

'Joan'll dish up,' he continued. 'Meg, fetch another plate from 'rack. Go on then, Lily,' he said gently. 'Bring tha friend in before 'supper gets cold.'

35

Annie, Rose and Robin waved goodbye to the Sutcliffs as
they gathered in the inn yard to see them off. Mr Sutcliff
leaning on a stout stick stood between Joan and Meg, both
of whom were weeping copious tears, while a little apart
from them stood Lily and Stuart Collins. As they made
a final wave before turning a corner they saw him put a
hand on her shoulder.

'You don't mind about not being married from home,
Rose?' Annie looked at her anxiously. 'You don't feel as
if you're being rushed?'

Rose shook her head. 'Local folk would have expected
a wedding breakfast, and under 'circumstances – with Mr
Collins here, it would have been awkward for our Lily.
I'm so glad for her, Annie. She's been so good to all of us,
she deserves to be happy.'

Rose and Robin had barely spoken to each other since
Mr Sutcliff had given them his blessing, they both seemed
so overcome with the swift events, the impromptu family
party that they'd had to celebrate, the hurried packing
of Rose's things, that it was as if they had run out of
things to say.

They hardly know each other, Annie thought. They're
going to have to learn, I'll keep Rose close by me until
she's ready.

Robin had hired a bigger cart than usual, and a swift
mare. He'd brought all of his cloth and trimmings, though
his own belongings were in one small bag, so they all rode
in the cart with Sorrel tied behind and Charlie running
alongside.

'We'll be there before nightfall,' Annie said. 'This is

faster than by donkey-cart. I thought I was travelling to the ends of the earth when I first came.'

'Tha left at a bad time, if I remember rightly,' Robin said. 'Wasn't it winter and snow on the ground?'

'It was,' Rose interrupted. 'I remember you came out looking for Annie, Robin, and we were all surprised at you coming at that time of year.'

She blushed as she spoke as if remembering it with pleasure.

'That's right I did.' He glanced at her from over his shoulder as he urged on the mare. 'And we took that walk across the valley and all the branches of the trees were covered with snow. It looked so beautiful.' It was his turn now to blush as he too remembered.

And the Sutcliffs didn't give me away, Annie thought. If they had – how different things would have been. Robin would have found me and told Matt. How hastily I acted; what wasted years.

As they drew up outside the shop in Fossgate the lights were burning though it was after eight o'clock, the normal closing time. Annie glanced in the window. Someone had changed her display. Instead of the red and white and black which she had arranged, there was a conglomeration of colour; purples and maroons, yellows and orange. The window was filled to capacity with rolls of velvets and satins set in a hotchpotch fashion.

She opened the door, the bell gave a tinkling chime and she looked up. The clapper had been taken out and a coin put in its place. She looked around. What had happened? Everything looked different. The rolls of cloth had been taken down from the shelves and placed in boxes on the floor. Ralph Mortimer stood behind the counter watching her.

'What's happened?' she asked breathlessly. 'Mr Sampson—? He's not ill?'

'Good evening, Mrs Hope. So you're back at last? We'd quite given you up.' He adjusted his fine neckcloth and perfunctorily brushed hair powder from his shoulder. He had on his head a full bottom wig after the fashion of the traditional London drapers, and a green watered silk waistcoat embroidered with lace, beneath his grey cutaway coat. He wore white stockings and tight grey breeches.

'Where is Mr Sampson?' she demanded. 'Why are you here and where is Mrs Cook?'

'I've sent Mrs Cook home, and alas my uncle is confined to bed. My mother, Mrs Mortimer, is with him now, taking care of him. Oh, and the girl, Polly, has gone also, we have no need of such a person here.'

'But is Mr Sampson ill? What's the matter with him?'

He surveyed her from down his long nose. 'I think it's no concern of yours, Mrs Hope, except of course,' he laughed scornfully, 'you will be worried about your position here!'

Mine and that of Robin and Rose, she thought, glancing through the window where she saw them sitting in the cart waiting for her to tell them they could come in. But poor Mr Sampson in the clutches of that pair!

'But there is no need to worry,' he assured her patronizingly. 'I'm sure we can usefully employ you in a similar capacity to the one you had previously. I shall need your room, however. I shall stay on the premises until, or if, such time as my uncle should return.'

'But my things—, have you been in my room?' She couldn't bear to think that his thin white hands had been straying over her possessions.

'Only to assess what I shall need.' His thin smile told her that he had indeed been prying.

The bell tinkled again and Mrs Mortimer filled the doorway, her bearing arrogant as she saw Annie. 'Ah,' she gushed. 'So you came back, Mrs Hope!'

'Of course I came back, Mrs Mortimer.' Annie's temper got the better of her. 'Surely Mr Sampson told you that I had been away on his behalf? We have a new manager, Mr Deane, who is at this moment patiently waiting to be let in!'

Robin had dismounted from the cart and was waiting

outside the window. 'He is most experienced,' she continued, 'and has been employed especially at Mr Sampson's request, so that he might now take things a little easier. I can't understand why he didn't inform you if you are as close as you maintain.'

Mrs Mortimer and her son exchanged glances and two bright pink spots appeared on Ralph's cheeks.

Annie smiled sweetly. 'Did Mr Sampson not also tell you that he had asked me to marry him?'

Their mouths dropped open and they both took a breath.

'Yes,' she continued. 'I said I would inform him of my decision on my return. I intend to go to his lodgings and tell him my answer just as soon as we have unpacked Mr Deane's belongings. So if you will excuse me—? Don't worry about locking up,' she said, opening the door. 'I'll do that after you've gone. I have my own key.'

Dumbstruck they both walked towards the door. Annie picked up a cane which was lying on a chair and handed it to Ralph Mortimer. She viewed him with her head on one side. 'Are they still making those wigs?' she asked. 'Or was it your father's? All the London dandys are wearing their own hair now, so I hear. Still,' she added sweetly, 'wear what suits, I always say. Good evening.'

After they had unpacked the cart, she sent Robin round to lodgings nearby where he would spend the night and stable the two horses. Henry had fallen asleep in a chair and Robin had gently lifted him up and taken him up to bed. Rose watched him as he covered the boy with a blanket and her face became soft and loving.

'Will you be all right here with Henry, Rose, if I leave you for half an hour? I must go and see Mr Sampson even though it's getting late. I want to put his mind at rest, God knows what state he'll be in if he thinks those two have been in charge of the shop. Go to bed if you're tired.'

There was a knock on the shop door as she went down the stairs and Robin peered through the glass. 'Can I leave Charlie here, Annie? The woman at the lodgings won't let me take him up to my room, 'says he has to sleep in the stable, but I'm afeard of him running back home if I'm not there with him.'

She opened the door and let him in and Charlie greeted her joyously as if he had been parted for days instead of only a half hour.

'Will you stay until I get back, Robin? I think Rose is a little nervous in a strange place.'

'Aye, she will be. She's not been in a town before, she'll wonder at all the strange noises. At the carriages rattling past, not to mention the drunks going home from the gin shops. I'll stay, you don't have to rush.'

'Robin?' she said as she turned to leave. 'Rose is not much more than a child. I leave her in your care. I trust you!'

He swallowed. He knew exactly what she meant. 'Aye,' he said. 'You can.'

Not much more than a child, she thought as she hurried towards Mr Sampson's lodgings. Yet older by far than I was when Alan took me. She shuddered at the memory. Then she smiled. It wouldn't be like that for Rose.

Mr Sampson's landlady took Annie upstairs to his room where she found him in bed, his face white beneath his nightcap and his lips blue. His blue-veined hands were outside the coverlet and she noticed for the first time the dark spots of age.

'Thank goodness you're back, Annie,' he wheezed. 'Don't let those two take over will you? They'll ruin us. How's Henry?' he asked. 'And did you find the young man?'

'I won't let them take over if you give me the authority, Mr Sampson. I did tell a little white lie,' she smiled. 'I told them that Robin Deane was to be employed as the manager so that you could take things easier, and I'm afraid they went off in a huff. And Henry is fine, and Robin is at the shop now; I'll bring them to see you tomorrow, shall I? Oh, yes, and Robin is to be married – to Rose – he's loved her since they were children. I've brought her with me and she'll stay with me until they're married; if that's all right with you?'

He nodded in agreement. 'Well, well. You have been busy.' He gave a weak smile and she thought that he was tiring. 'You look different, Annie. Has anything else happened? You seem more serene somehow, and yet, are you sad? Did it upset you going back to that place?'

'Just a little.' She patted his hand. She wouldn't tell him about Matt yet. That would keep until he was feeling better.

'Annie!' He tried to ease himself higher onto the pillow, but he winced and slid down again. 'If anything should happen to me, go straight away to Marcus Blythe, you remember him, don't you? He knows what to do.'

'Come now, nothing is going to happen to you, Aaron. You've just been overdoing things. You'll soon be out and about.'

'No, no. We must be realistic, my dear. It was quite a turn I had. I'd been lifting a roll of cloth down from the shelf and it brought on such a terrible pain. Mrs Cook sent for the doctor straight away and he brought me home in his own carriage, he was very good. But he said I must rest or it would be all up with me. Still,' he added with a sigh. 'I can rest easy now that you're back and you've got Mr Deane to help you.'

She didn't light a candle as she entered the shop but made her way in the darkness to the stairs. There was no sound from above but she could smell smoke, Robin or Rose must have lit the fire, the room had been cold when they had first arrived back.

She opened the door cautiously, and then gave a small cough, anxious that she shouldn't appear to be prying on them. Henry was fast asleep in his cot and her bed lay smooth and unruffled. The fire was flickering steadily and already the room was warm and comforting.

Rose sat in a chair by the fire, her body perfectly still, her head resting against her shoulder and her eyes closed. How beautiful she is, Annie thought. The firelight flickered sending golden reflections to her dark hair and lighting up her face. Robin was sitting on the floor close by her feet with his head in her lap and her hand resting on his hair.

Annie patted Robin's cheek gently and he woke with a start. 'Come on,' she whispered. 'Off you go to bed. We have a busy day tomorrow.'

'I must have just dropped off,' he croaked. 'We were talking, and,' he looked at Rose just slowly opening her eyes. 'Isn't she lovely, Annie?' he said huskily. 'I can't believe how lucky I am, that somebody like Rose would have a peazan like me.'

'She knows a good man when she sees one, Robin.' Annie swallowed a tear. 'She knows that one day you'll make her very proud.'

Robin kissed Annie goodbye before leaving for his lodgings. 'I'll be here at eight o'clock, on the stroke. Thank you Annie for all tha's done, I'll never forget it.'

He turned to Rose, her eyes glazed with sleep, and took her hand and kissed it, holding it ardently against his lips. Then he put his arms around her and held her close, pressing his cheek close to hers.

Annie let the tears run unchecked down her cheeks as she watched them in their innocence proclaim their love. Yes, Robin, you are lucky. She drew in a deep sobbing breath. You both are.

They spent the next day rearranging the shelves and putting back the rolls of cloth that the Mortimers had taken down. Annie put back the window display, this time with yellow and gold and green to reflect the summertime. She thought of the Wolds as she draped the fabric, of the vast greenness of the meadowland, the yellow gorse and the golden sun.

She watched as Rose handed up the rolls of muslins to Robin who was perched on a pair of steps. He'd taken off his jacket and was wearing only his shirt and breeches and she thought that one way or another they would have to get him some new clothes.

Mr Sampson obviously had the same thought, when on the same evening, Annie took them all to meet him. Rose stayed at the door and gave him a curtsey, but Robin went up to the old man's bed and shook him gently by the hand and told him how grateful he was.

'I've brought a supply of cloth with me, sir. Woollen stuff and muslins, all manufactured in the West Riding, and you can have it gladly to sell in the shop,' he said, eager to please. 'I can never get hold of cloth from other parts, not having the contacts, but I hear there's good fabric coming from Manchester and the western counties. We have no need to rely on foreign goods and pay the high duty, especially just now when it's so difficult to bring in.'

Aaron Sampson smiled at his enthusiasm. 'You'll do, Mr Deane. I can see we'll make a fortune with you to look after our interests.' He waved a finger towards Annie and Henry. 'Bring the boy here that I might speak with him, and then I must ask you to excuse me, I'm very tired.'

Robin bowed and left the room and Annie took Henry to the bedside. Mr Sampson spoke quietly to him, asking him if he had enjoyed the outing and the coach ride and Annie held her breath in case Henry should mention meeting his father. But the boy became shy and tongue-tied at seeing the old man in bed, looking unfamiliar out of his usual old-fashioned frock-coat and wig, and declined to talk.

'Annie.' Mr Sampson tried to take a deep breath, his words were slow and halting. 'Mr Deane is a fine young man.' He nodded and closed his eyes as if the effort of speaking was too much for him. 'But you must see that he gets a more suitable set of clothes.'

He opened his eyes and she saw that they were quite merry. 'We can't have our manager dressed like a country labourer, can we? Find some good cloth and send him off to the tailor, and don't let the customers see him until he's properly dressed. He'll need a suit of clothes for the shop and for one for outdoors; we can't have him looking shabby, not even when he's about his personal business, it just won't do.'

Robin chose a dark-green fine wool cloth for his coat, and buff coloured waistcoat and breeches for his work in the shop, with a linen shirt and neckcloth, white cotton stockings and black buckled shoes.

'I don't want silk coats, Annie, that's not my style. Nor embroidered frippery. Not yet – maybe one day.' He'd looked in the mirror when he was dressed and smiled at her standing behind him. He had long since abandoned his queue and his hair was long on his shoulders. 'Is it me?' he asked. 'Pinch me so I can know if I'm dreaming.'

Obligingly she did. 'Ow,' he complained. 'No. I'm not.'

For his other set of clothes he had chosen a plain black coat and grey breeches but had allowed himself the extravagance of a red wool waistcoat and this they decided was what he should be married in.

Rose had brought three other dresses with her, all Sunday clothes and perfectly good, but Annie decided that if Robin was going to be dressed in new clothes then Rose should be too and that she would pay for the fabric out of her own money as a present. After much deliberation Rose chose a dark blue muslin, shot with paler blue flowered stripes. A flounced white cotton petticoat edged with lace was to be worn beneath it and the bodice was to be pleated.

'I can make it myself,' she said. 'I have a neat hand. Lily was the cook in the house, but I was the seamstress.'

Rose asked Annie to be witness and Robin said he would like to ask Mr Sampson also if he was well enough. He was delighted to be asked and said he was sure he would be up and about in time, but just in case he wasn't they asked Mrs Cook as well. Mr Sampson also said they could shut the shop for the morning whilst they went to the ceremony at the nearby ancient church of St Denys in Walmgate.

The day before the ceremony a hired chaise drew up

outside the shop and Mr Sutcliff, hobbling painfully, and accompanied by Joan, climbed out.

'It might be 'onny marriage my daughters make,' he said, sitting down gratefully as Robin brought him a chair. 'And when we got your letter telling us the day, we decided to come.'

Rose was overjoyed to have her family with her and accompanied them to Robin's lodgings to ask if they had two more rooms.

'Stay the night with your sister, Rose, and hear all the news from home,' Annie said. 'Ask her about Lily, and take your gown and let her help you dress in the morning; she'd like to share your joy, I'm sure of it. I'll call for Mr Sampson and bring him along with me.'

And then I can sleep alone in my bed, but for Henry, she thought, and think of my wedding day and how different it was from how yours will be, which will be full of hope and expectation.

When she called for Mr Sampson at ten o'clock the next day, he was dressed and waiting but extremely unsteady. She decided that he couldn't walk all the way to Walmgate and so went out into the street to look for a boy to send for a sedan chair.

The wedding party was waiting for them outside Robin's lodgings and Mrs Cook came hurrying up a minute later.

'What do you think, Annie,' Robin said gleefully. 'Mr Sutcliff has booked us a breakfast at the Bay Horse. We can have a private room until one o'clock.'

'In that case,' Mr Sampson put his head out of the chair. 'Perhaps I can buy the ale? I would like to make a contribution.'

Robin took Rose's arm on one side and her father, leaning more than assisting her, took the other. Annie, and Henry, who was wearing a new pair of pantaloons and short jacket, Mrs Cook and Joan, brought up the rear while Mr Sampson was whisked away in front of them.

After the simple ceremony inside St Denys's church, they merrily made their way to the Bay Horse, this time Mr Sutcliff also calling for a chair. The landlord had prepared a splendid repast of cold meats, including pork and tongue and sweetbreads, a crusty raised pie and a selection of pickles and chutneys. There was plum cake and jelly and sweet apple tart.

Annie noticed that Mr Sampson only picked at his food and once or twice patted his chest. She asked the landlord to bring him a brandy which she gave to him and watched anxiously as he sipped it slowly.

'Shall I call for a chair, Mr Sampson? Would you like to go home?'

'I think that perhaps I would,' he said wearily. 'I don't want to break up the festivities, but I am very tired.'

She said that she would go with him but he became most distressed at the suggestion and insisted that she should stay. In order to pacify him she said that she would, but looked on worriedly as he tottered unsteadily towards the door.

She called the boy. 'Take him home as fast as you can and then go and ask the doctor to call on him.' She gave him the address and a coin and told him to come back when he had given the message and she would give him extra.

When the festivities broke up at one o'clock, Joan said she would take Henry for a walk to the park, Mr Sutcliff went back to the lodgings for a rest and the others walked back to the shop. It was fortunate that it was a quiet day with not too many customers for they were all feeling the effect of the food and drink.

'Why don't you and Rose go up to my room and put your feet up for half an hour?' Annie said to Robin. 'Mrs Cook and I can manage and if we get busy I'll call you.'

Robin nonchalantly agreed and escorted a blushing Rose upstairs.

'Ah,' said Mrs Cook watching them go. 'Bless 'em.' Then she sighed. 'Pity that bliss doesn't last, isn't it?'

Joan brought Henry back and at eight o'clock Annie locked up the shop and Robin and Rose prepared to go back to Robin's lodgings.

'Why don't the two of you stay the night here?' Annie suggested. 'Henry and I can share with Joan – you wouldn't mind, Joan? I dearly want to talk to you about Lily and Sergeant – er, Mr Collins.' She deemed that the newly-wedded pair might be more at ease in the privacy of the quiet room above the shop, rather than in the room sandwiched between those of Rose's father and sister in the lodging house.

'Oh, yes please, Annie,' Rose seemed overcome with relief. 'It's so cosy and warm in your room.'

'Aye,' Robin quickly agreed. 'And I'll make an early start in 'morning seeing as I've had time off today.'

Annie settled Henry into the bed which they would share with Joan and Joan had started to tell her how things were working out with Stuart Collins.

'Tha'd hardly know him, Annie, he's grown a beard and his hair is long, he looks quite different; and he's been such a help to fayther, lifting things and all that, that I think fayther's quite accepted him. But Mr Collins won't help inside, not when visitors come, he says he'll stay out at 'back where he can't be seen, just in case. And he says if 'soldiers come, then we have to warn him and he'll go off into 'woods for a few days. He doesn't want any of us to get into trouble.'

Annie pursed her lips and thought sadly of the life he had now chosen, to be forever watchful or else face the terrible consequences.

'Mrs Hope! Mrs Hope!' An urgent knocking disturbed them. The mistress of the house was at the door. 'Mr Deane is downstairs, he's got a message for thee.'

'It can only be from Mr Sampson,' Annie said, reaching for her shawl. 'Will you watch Henry for me, Joan? I'll try not to be long.'

Robin was waiting outside with Charlie. 'A boy came from Mr Sampson's lodgings. He said for you to go straight away. I'll come with you,' he said, taking her arm, 'it's getting dark.'

'There's no need,' she claimed. 'I'm used to making my own way. Go on back to Rose.'

'I'll walk part of 'way with you then,' still he persisted. 'I was just about to take Charlie for a walk when 'message came. Rose is just busy with a few things.'

She said nothing and he walked by her side until they came to Mr Sampson's lodging house. The doctor's chaise was outside. 'Thank you, Robin. Now go,' she said, 'back to Rose; she'll be waiting.' She didn't want him to wait in case there was bad news. No sense in spoiling their wedding day.

He looked down at the ground and then scraped the side of his shoe in the dust. 'Fact is, she's a bit shy is Rose, that's why I was coming out to walk Charlie, so's she could prepare herself. And,' he swallowed. 'I've not been with a woman afore, Annie, so I'm just a bit afeard missen.'

She smiled gently and patted his cheek. 'Just hold her close in your arms, Robin, and everything will be all right. You have my word on it.'

'He's sinking fast,' the doctor said when she came to the small stuffy room. The curtains were drawn tight and there was just one oil lamp burning, and a low fire. 'I told him he must stay in bed or risk another attack, but he didn't listen. I can do no more for him I fear. He'll go by midnight.'

'I'll stay and keep watch.' Annie spoke from between clenched teeth. She felt fear at the passing of someone she was fond of and didn't at all care for the death-watch vigil; yet she felt that the old man deserved a friend by his side as he drew near to his eventide.

'Should we send for his sister?' the landlady whispered after the doctor had gone, 'though poor old fellow never wanted her up here.'

Annie shook her head. 'No, it's too late to disturb her, she'll be in her bed and it might well be too late by the time she gets here. We'll tell her in the morning. That'll be soon enough.'

The woman nodded meaningfully. 'Aye, and no sense in disturbing his spirit. It's peace he's after now, not strife.'

She brought Annie a cup of warm chocolate and built up the fire so that she might be comfortable, and she sat quietly reflecting and wondering what the morning would bring. A niggling worry scurried about her mind as she felt the responsibility weighing upon her of Robin and Rose, who she had brought to this city with the promise of work and a future together, promises which now might come to naught at Aaron Sampson's demise.

A sound of a sigh, the exhalation of a last breath woke her and a swift glance at the slight form in the bed told her that he was gone from this world into the next. His eyes were closed and his hands folded together as if in a last prayer. There was no pain in his face, no sign of suffering and she felt no sadness for him for he looked peaceful – only sorrow for herself that she had lost a kind and compassionate friend.

36

She sent a runner with a letter for Mrs Mortimer at eight
o'clock, and as the clock struck nine that lady arrived on
the doorstep in a complete set of mourning clothes. Rose
and Annie had quickly stitched black lace bands onto their
gowns and wore black ribbons in their hair, and Robin
hurried to the tailors for a black ready-made waistcoat.

Mrs Mortimer, however, was in full mourning dress of
black bombasine with a black silk crepe hat and gloves.
She lifted her veil and wiped her eye on seeing Annie.

'My poor brother, and to go alone. Not a soul to stand
by him in his final dark hours.'

Annie was quick to placate. 'Oh, no, Mrs Mortimer.
Don't distress yourself on that account. I stayed by his
side. He was very peaceful.'

'*You* stayed by his side?' Mrs Mortimer's powdered face
beneath her veil creased with anger. '*You* who are of no kin
to him – though I know that you had aspirations of being
so. Well your plans are scotched now and no mistake. *I*
should have been sent for – I or my son. Arrangements
have to be made. A funeral service. And plans for the shop.
You must close today out of respect.'

Annie remained silent but pointed towards the door and
window. The blinds had been drawn and a notice written
by Robin to say that they were closed, was pinned to
the door.

Mrs Mortimer sniffed and looked around her. 'I see
you've put the cloth back on the shelves. That won't
do, it's far too difficult to reach up there.' She pointed
to Robin. 'Take them down and stack them on the
floor.'

He glanced uncertainly at Annie. 'Should I do that, Mrs Hope?'

Mrs Mortimer gasped. 'You will do as I say, young man or there will be no position here for you in this drapery.'

Annie spoke up. 'I'm sorry to go against your wishes Mrs Mortimer, but nothing must be touched until Mr Blythe gets here. I've already sent for him and he will issue instructions according to Mr Sampson's wishes.'

'You think you have been very smart don't you?' Mrs Mortimer spat out. 'My brother didn't get around to marrying you did he? No, nor do I think he ever intended to. Never mentioned it to me, his only sister in the world. His only confidant.' She gave a snort. 'Marry! At his age? As if he would!'

'Please be seated Mrs Mortimer,' Annie said quietly. 'Or perhaps you would prefer to sit in Mr Sampson's room while we wait for Mr Blythe? There's a comfortable chair in there and a warm fire.'

Mrs Mortimer glared at her but turned her back and stalked into the back room and Annie rushed upstairs to her own room before anyone could see her tears.

She had forgotten, in the rush of organizing messages and notifying those who needed to be told of Mr Sampson's death, that Robin and Rose had spent the night in her room, and though the bed was neatly made, there were vestiges of their presence still lingering.

Rose's bedgown and robe were draped across the foot of the bed and Robin's striped nightshirt still with its pristine creases was folded beside it. Annie sat on the bed and started to sob. She hadn't cried for such a long time, but now the uncertainty of her future alone but for Henry, plunged her into a deep well of depression.

Squire Linton's image flashed into her mind but she brushed it aside. She'd not ask him for help. If she ever went to him it would be on a visit as his son's wife, not begging for shelter as she'd once done.

Wearily she got up from the bed and wiping away her tears, opened her chest of drawers and taking out her belongings laid them on the bed. If she had to leave this place then she would be prepared. Mrs Mortimer might keep Robin, she thought. She'll realize that someone who knows about cloth is needed. And she thinks he's the manager, she won't realize that as yet he hasn't had any shop experience. Mrs Cook will help him; they'll keep her on. It'll only be me that they'll want rid of.

When she'd emptied all the drawers she sat down in the chair by the low fire. She was very tired, she had had little sleep that night. It had been late when she had arrived back at the lodging house and there was little space in the narrow bed which she shared with Joan and Henry, and her sleep had been scanty, beset as she was by worries.

Rose knocked softly and opened the door. 'Annie. My fayther and Joan are here, they're leaving now, they said they wouldn't linger on account of how things are. Joan has brought Henry back but I'll watch him if you're busy.'

There was a brightness about Rose, a warm sparkle in her eyes; no sadness for the old man who had died for she didn't know him, but a sympathetic respect at a bereavement. Annie blinked away her tears, she was glad at least that someone was happy.

She went downstairs to say goodbye. Mr Sutcliff took her hand and gave a bow. 'I wanted to talk to thee, Mrs Linton,' he said in a low voice, 'but it'll have to wait now, this isn't 'right time. I'll settle summat for Rose now they're wed, they'll not go short, I'll see to that.'

Annie was relieved. If Mr Sutcliff would help Robin and Rose financially, then it would be something less for her to worry about.

As the chaise drew away and they waved goodbye from the doorway, another drew up and Marcus Blythe got out. He touched his hat solemnly. 'Good morning Mrs Hope. This is sad news, sad news indeed. But death comes to us all, there's no avoiding it.'

They all turned as an open curricle drawn by two sleek horses drew up beside them and Ralph Mortimer in a shiny black topper and black frock-coat jumped down.

'That's a fine carriage, Mr Mortimer.' Mr Blythe moved closer to inspect it. 'Almost as good as new I would say. It must have cost you!'

Ralph Mortimer looked slightly embarrassed, Annie thought, and neither could she remember seeing him drive his own carriage before.

'A snip at sixty guineas, Mr Blythe. Too good to miss don't you think?'

'That depends on whether you have sixty guineas, Mr Mortimer,' Mr Blythe commented wryly. 'But you young men seem to have money to throw away nowadays.' He turned to Annie. 'Shall we go inside, Mrs Hope, and proceed with the formalities?'

Annie led the way into the shop and then suggested that they remove to Mr Sampson's old room where Mrs Mortimer was already waiting. There wasn't a great deal of room for the four of them, but Mr Blythe placed himself behind a small table and opening a leather bag took out a roll of parchment.

'I do not intend reading the deceased's will here today, but ask that you all, Mrs Hope, Mrs Mortimer, Mr Mortimer, will kindly attend my premises on Wednesday of next week at ten o'clock when I will acquaint you of Mr Sampson's wishes.'

He scanned them all gravely from beneath frowning brows. 'In the meantime however, according to my instructions, it is requested that Mrs Annie Hope proceeds with a complete assessment of stock in hand in the drapery establishment herewith; details of which shall be given to me. Mr Sampson also instructs, Mrs Hope, that you alone shall supervise this stock-taking with one other person of your choice, with the purpose of it being completed for next Wednesday. Salary of course will be paid for the time taken as usual.'

Annie heaved a sigh of relief. At least Mrs Mortimer and her son would be kept out of the way for a few days. She'd ask Robin to help her and Rose could look after Henry. There had been no sign of Polly since the Mortimers had told her to go.

'And what about the funeral, Mr Blythe?' Mrs Mortimer put her handkerchief beneath her veil to wipe away a tear. 'I suppose Ralph and I must attend to that being his only relatives?'

'Not at all, Mrs Mortimer,' Mr Blythe gave her a small smile. 'All taken care of, there is no reason for you to trouble yourself; Mr Sampson was meticulous in his arrangements. Tomorrow at three-fifteen at St Denys'.'

First a wedding and now a funeral, thought Annie, then a—? Her mind drifted to Robin and Rose, but then Mr Blythe was speaking to her.

'Will you be able to manage in time, Mrs Hope? Before Wednesday?'

'Yes. I'll ask Mr Deane to help me, he has the experience of checking stock, but perhaps we could close until then? It would be a sign of respect too.'

Mr Blythe agreed and snapped closed his bag. 'Until Wednesday then. After you, Mrs Mortimer. Can I perhaps drop you anywhere?'

Gratefully Annie showed them to the door as Mr Blythe ushered Mrs Mortimer in front of him. Ralph lingered for a moment, glancing around proprietorially, and catching sight of sweet-faced Rose standing by the window, gave a bow, his hand to his chest.

Robin wagged a finger as they drove away. 'Don't think we're staying here if he takes over, Annie. I'd rather go back to my donkey-and-cart. I've seen that sort of dandy afore, they don't think twice about dallying wi' other men's wives; but he'll not dally wi' mine!'

Annie put her head back and laughed out loud as Robin, the man of the world, thought to protect his new wife.

They started checking the stock immediately and finished five minutes after the stroke of midnight on Wednesday morning. The small church of St Denys had been packed to the doors for Aaron Sampson's funeral, which they had thought would be attended by only family and staff; but the old draper was well thought of by members of his trade, and drapers and haberdashers came from all over the city to pay their last respects. Even some of his customers came, not just the wives of the confectioners and bakers and innkeepers who bought from him, but those whose husbands were bankers and businessmen, sent their companions and maids to represent them.

Annie was pleased that the man who had been so kind to her should be remembered by so many others, and Mrs Mortimer had fairly preened as she took her place at the front of the church.

As she walked across the Ouse bridge to Micklegate towards Mr Blythe's house, Annie was once more beset by the fears she had put aside while following the instructions left by Aaron Sampson.

I wouldn't have had this worry had I married Aaron, she debated and paused to look at the shipping in the water below. Supposing I had married him, or even promised, before I went to Hull? How would I have felt then, meeting Matt? How strange fate is. But I wouldn't have had it otherwise. Henry has his father's name, nobody can take that away from him. And I have a husband, even though – she gave a silent sob – even though he might never—, no, don't think that way, Annie. She gave herself a mental slap. Don't think that way.

But I'm so lonely without you, Matt, she thought sadly. Meeting with him again had rendered the loss much worse than before. She thought she had hidden away the pain, storing it at the back of her mind, yet now, when she had in her presence the loving Robin and his wife, it was brought to the fore once again. She, too, had savoured and shared the sheer joy of a physical and all-consuming love and passion, and her body ached with need.

Mrs Mortimer and Ralph were already seated in Marcus Blythe's first floor, panelled library where he conducted his affairs. They had taken the chairs on the opposite side of the desk to Mr Blythe and he brought a chair for Annie and placed it at the side nearest him.

'I hope I'm not late?' she began, then stopped as she heard a clock in the hall strike ten.

He smiled at her. 'Punctual to the minute, Mrs Hope. Please, make yourself comfortable.'

Mrs Mortimer glared at her and Annie knew by the look on her face that she was wondering why she should even be there at the reading of Mr Sampson's will.

Why *am* I here? Annie wondered. Mr Blythe did request it. Perhaps after all Mr Sampson wanted me to run the shop – I wouldn't mind as long as Mrs Mortimer wasn't there, but oh, Ralph! No. I don't think I could. But how desperate am I? I need to work.

Her thoughts were interrupted by Mr Blythe's mellow voice beginning to read '*The last Will and Testament of me, Aaron Joseph Sampson, resident of the City of York.*' She watched Mrs Mortimer's mouth working beneath her veil and saw Ralph turn to look first at his mother and then at her, his mouth opening slightly.

What? What was he saying? I wasn't concentrating. Something about Henry and the shop and getting married. She was only aware of Mrs Mortimer's face getting pinker in spite of her powder and her cheeks quivering.

'*And to you, my sister, Mrs Charlotte Mortimer, to be given each year for five years, the cloth of your choosing from the said drapery premises to the value of thirty pounds each year. To my nephew Ralph Mortimer one gift of cloth to the value of twenty pounds to be made into a suit by Mr Denby the tailor, payment of which has already been made.*'

'That concludes the instructions.' Mr Blythe moved the parchment from which he had been reading to one side. 'Is there anything that needs to be explained further, or that you don't understand?'

His question was directed at Annie but it was Mrs Mortimer who spoke, her face livid and her tongue waspish as she vehemently spoke. 'I shall challenge that will. This woman has insinuated herself into my brother's favour. That business should be mine by rights, mine or my son's!'

Mr Blythe nodded his head and picked up another sheet of paper. 'Mr Sampson foresaw that you might well challenge it, Mrs Mortimer, and left me a letter to this effect. His will has been made for some time now, in fact about two years after your son Henry was born, Mrs Hope.'

He peered down his nose at the letter. 'The date of this is approximately six months ago, and states; "my sister Mrs Charlotte Mortimer may feel slighted that the drapery businesss has not been left to her or her son, Ralph. I feel, however, that they are not in need financially of extra income, and therefore my intentions should be made perfectly clear, as outlined in my will, that Mrs Hope and her son Henry will be the beneficiaries, and I trust that my relatives will accept my wishes with good Christian charity."'

'I must add,' said Mr Blythe firmly, 'that the only alterations which were made in the will were at my suggestion and that was that it would be fitting for him to leave Mrs Mortimer a small gift as a remembrance; and so he chose to leave you and Mr Ralph the gift of cloth, a suitable gift, he thought, for a draper to leave.'

'But, I don't understand.' Annie was bewildered. 'Are you telling me that Mr Sampson has left Henry his shop?'

'Legal jargon is very complicated I know,' Mr Blythe said patiently. 'But what it amounts to in general terms is that the shop premises of the drapery which Mr Sampson owned outright, will be yours, unless you should marry within three years of the pronouncement of the will, in which case it will revert to your infant son Henry; this is an obvious procedure to safeguard the inheritance, as otherwise if you should marry again, the property would automatically become your husband's and not your son's. But,' he added with a genial smile, 'the profit from the business is yours outright, to do with whatever you wish.'

Annie sat stunned. She had a business of her own. That dear man had left it to her. An inkling of conversation she had had with Aaron came back to her which she had almost forgotten. *'Even if you won't marry me, Annie, I intend to leave the business to you and Henry'.*

'Thank you so much for coming, Mrs Mortimer, Master Ralph,' Mr Blythe rose to his feet. 'I'll wish you goodday.'

Annie in a trance also rose but Mr Blythe stayed her with a movement of his hand. 'Perhaps you would be good enough to stay, Mrs Hope, I—'

'Please,' Annie interrupted him. 'I have something to say.' I'll have to tell them, she thought. I'll have to tell them that I am married. It's best that they know.

She sat down again and pondered where to begin. 'When Aaron asked me to marry him, he knew of my feelings towards Henry's father, and that because of a misunderstanding we were apart. I told him that after I returned from my journey to find Robin – Mr Deane, I would give him my answer.' She turned appealingly to Mr Blythe. 'He had been so kind to me and I didn't want to hurt his feelings, but I had already decided that I couldn't marry him, that the only man I would ever marry would be my son's father.'

Ralph Mortimer assumed a bored expression and sat leaning on his elbow with one finger against his cheek.

'But the strangest thing happened. Whilst I was in Hull, I met again with Henry's father, and we were married immediately. When I came back to York, Aaron was so ill that I couldn't tell him. He would have been so pleased for me.' She bowed her head and thought of the old man with tenderness and sorrow.

'And who is this man who decided to marry you at such short notice?' Mrs Mortimer snorted. 'And why isn't he here?'

'He's Captain Matthias Linton.' Annie stared at the woman. This would give her something to think about. 'And he left immediately after our marriage to fight for His

Majesty's navy in the war with the French.' Mentally she crossed her fingers. No need, she thought, to tell her that he had been pressed into service with members of the rabble. Sufficient to tell her only what she needed to know.

'Well, good gracious.' Marcus Blythe leaned across his desk. 'You don't mean to tell me that it's Henry Linton's son? Squire Linton from Staveley Park up on the Wolds?'

Annie nodded. 'The same.'

'Well, well well. Who would have thought—! I know the family well of course. I've looked after Henry Linton's affairs for years.' Marcus Blythe rubbed his hands together as if he was well pleased.

Mrs Mortimer's attitude changed. Her nostrils quivered and she pursed her lips and then rose to her feet. 'Well, of course, Mrs Linton, had we known—! You must call, we should be so pleased—.' Her voice trailed away, Ralph had also risen to his feet and stood hesitating behind his mother.

'I don't think we have anything to say to each other, Mrs Mortimer, that we haven't said before.' Annie's voice was cutting. How the woman would gossip and drop the name of Linton into every conversation. 'Except that I would prefer to use my business name of Hope while I am in York. That is how I am known. There is no need for public interest in my private concerns.'

'I quite agree,' broke in Marcus Blythe. 'And of course I don't need to remind anyone that what has passed here today is private and confidential.' He glanced pointedly at Ralph and then Mrs Mortimer. 'It goes without saying, of course. Good-day then.' He rose again from his desk and crossed the room to open the door. 'Thank you so much, Mrs Mortimer. Take care in that curricle, young man. Repairs are costly as are broken limbs. Good-day.'

'Well now, Mrs Linton. What news!' He fairly rushed back to his desk. 'But I think there is more to tell? But first we must have a little celebration.' He went to a corner cupboard and opening it brought out two crystal glasses.

'We must have a glass of wine to celebrate your acquisition of a business and what is more, your marriage to a fine young man!'

'You know Matt?' She took the glass with trembling fingers. The revelation of the morning's events was just sinking in.

'Since he was a boy – and Tobias. I knew them both. Sad, very sad, about Tobias,' he sighed, his jubilation sinking for a moment, but then rising again. 'But here's to you and your husband; when he returns may you have a long life together.'

As Annie raised her glass to his she realized that this was the first toast to her marriage. Tears started to scold her eyes and she couldn't hold them back. 'Mr Blythe,' she cried huskily. 'Can I confide in you?'

37

She tried to keep a straight face as she approached the shop and not let the joy she felt bubble over. She had told Mr Blythe about Matt being pressed into the navy and he advised that she go to his father at the earliest opportunity. It was possible, he'd said, that once Matt had returned to these shores, his father could use his authority to bring him home.

'I can't understand,' he'd pondered. 'Why he didn't use his own influence. The navy doesn't usually impress gentlemen into the service, though they might well have tried to persuade him to join them, especially with his experience in ships.'

Annie, too, was puzzled. She well knew that the navy badly needed men in the war against France. A bounty was offered to volunteers, but transportees and criminals who knew nothing of ships or sailing often had their sentences commuted to service on board ship. But Matt owned his own ship which was used in overseas trade, and he could, she thought, have demanded protection against impressment.

Except for Bernard Roxton, she mused. He would have had him, one way or another. Yet it wasn't that, she felt sure. She recalled what Sergeant Collins had said to them. 'You're playing a game,' he'd said. Toby had paid for his life with his game, and Matt too, she was certain, had finished playing games and had decided to repay society for his part in smuggling raids; and what better way than in service to the King?

She rattled on the door to be let into the shop. Rose was dusting the shelves and Robin was ticking off numbers on a list. They both looked at her expectantly as she entered.

'Where's Henry?' she asked.

'He's playing upstairs. He's all right, Annie, I keep checking.'

'Will you fetch him down, Rose? I've something to tell you all.'

They looked at her curiously, but Rose hurried up and brought a protesting Henry downstairs. He put his arms out when he saw Annie and ran to give her a hug.

She sat down on a chair and lifted him onto her knee. 'I have to tell you that from today there is a new owner of the shop,' she said solemnly. 'She will take over immediately and the new landlord of the property will no doubt want to speak of what he intends to do in the future.'

Robin groaned and banged his fist on the counter. 'God's teeth! I don't believe it. Not Mrs Mortimer? She'll drive all 'customers away! And Mr Ralph Mortimer? There'll be no holding him. He'll be arriving here in another fancy carriage and team, lording it over everybody, mark my words!'

Annie felt her mouth twitch and she drew in her cheeks to stop herself laughing out loud.

'I don't think we'll stay, Annie.' Rose whispered. 'I don't feel safe with that Mr Ralph, and if Fayther gives us some money we can maybe set up somewhere else, maybe have a stall in the market.'

Annie burst out laughing. 'It's all right,' she hooted. 'It's going to be all right. I'm teasing. It's *mine*. Mine and Henry's. Mr Sampson left it all to us!'

They decided that it would be seemly to have a small celebration, that Mr Sampson, being the man he was, wouldn't mind; so Robin went out to get a meat pie and a jug of ale, and Rose and Annie set out a table in the back room.

'I've brought pig's trotters, a meat pie, a pair of freshly cooked pigeon, some bread and an apple tart.' Robin had borrowed a wicker basket from the baker. 'That'll keep us going until supper. Oh yes, and—,' he dived to the bottom of the basket and brought out a bag of sticky marshmallow. 'Some confection for the young master. Have to keep him sweet.'

Henry took it from Robin but instead of eating the sugary sweets, said with careful consideration. 'Now that I haven't got an Uncle Sampson, I think I'd like to go and see my grandfayther, please, Mamma.'

Annie stroked his head. 'Yes, Henry. We will go. Not yet, but soon.'

Marcus Blythe had advised her to change the name of the shop as soon as possible. 'Do it immediately,' he'd said. 'So that there is no speculation or gossip.'

'But I don't want to change the name,' she'd protested. 'It's been Sampson's draper for such a long time. It doesn't seem right.'

'Then don't change it.' He'd looked at her from under his beetling brows. 'Just add your own.'

They watched a few days later, she and Robin, from the edge of the road as the sign writer put the finishing touches to *Sampson & Hope, Draper.*

'I can't believe it, Robin. It just seems impossible when I think about my past.'

'I allus knew tha'd make summat of tha self, Annie.' Robin smiled at her and squeezed her arm. 'I allus said tha was a lady.' Then he drew back in mock alarm. 'I beg your pardon, ma'am. I was forgetting myself. I must remember to call you by your proper name now.' He gave her a small bow and she laughed. He looked quite handsome these days and he still had a twinkle in his eye: he would pull the ladies into the shop, young or old.

'Don't call me Mrs Linton, Robin. Not here.' Her face fell. 'Not until Matt returns. Until then I'm Mrs Hope.'

'But if you go to see Squire Linton? Surely then?'

'Yes. Then I'll be Mrs Linton, whether he likes it or not.'

He raised his eyebrows curiously. He didn't know all

the facts and she had no intention of discussing them. She had never told him of the time when she had slept in Squire Linton's barn, or of the time when she and Matt had play-acted that she was a foreign widow. There were some things she would keep to herself.

A carriage drew up beside them and they moved aside so that a lady and her maid could descend.

'Quick,' Annie murmured. 'Customer.'

Robin moved forward, a greeting on his lips as the imposing lady entered the shop, and Annie spent a moment longer gazing at her name above the window. She gave a half smile and was about to turn away when she saw a reflection in the window. The waiting carriage had thrown a dark shadow and in this shadow from across the road she saw the image of a girl.

For just a second she felt dizzy, for it was as if she was looking into her past. The girl's hair was long and unkempt about her shoulders and her feet were bare, and she was staring across at the shop, as Annie had so many times done the same, when she had wished for new clothes for her back or food for her belly.

Slowly she turned. If the girl had gone, then it was some kind of premonition. I've come up from the scrap heap, she reflected. I must be careful not to fall back in to it.

The girl had gone! But wait; no, there she was, running away. It was Polly! 'Polly!' Unheeding of who was watching or listening Annie picked up her skirts and ran after her. 'Polly! Come back. You can come back.'

The girl slowed, looking over her shoulder, and then hesitatingly, she stopped.

Annie beckoned to her. 'Come here. I want to talk to you.'

Polly slowly shuffled towards her. Annie knew instantly that she had been sleeping rough. Her clothes were crumpled and dirty, she had no shawl and below her sleeves there were bruises on her forearms.

'What happened, Polly? I mean after the Mortimers told you to leave?'

The girl bit her lip and looked at Annie with frightened eyes. 'Me Da turned me out. 'Said if I couldn't earn any wages then he wasn't going to keep me. He said I could sleep in t'street for all he cared. So that's what I've been doing.' She stifled a sob. 'I wasn't doing no harm, Mrs Hope. I was only looking at what t'painter was doing, and wishing that I'd listened to thee when tha was telling me my letters and numbers, and then I'd have known what it said.'

'It says, Polly,' Annie said gently. 'It says, Sampson and Hope. Did you know that Mr Sampson had died?'

'Aye, I did.' Polly sniffled. 'I followed funeral carriage to church, though I didn't go in. He was a fine gentleman, allus kind to me.'

'Polly? Would you like to come back? The shop is mine now. I own it. I shall need someone to look after Henry.'

Polly's face took on an aura of disbelief. 'Oh, Mrs Hope. Yes please!' Then she hesitated. 'But, Mr Mortimer? Will he be there? I don't want to come if—,' she paused again. 'But, I suppose I would come even if he was. I'm that hungry, Mrs Hope. I'd do anything now.'

Annie put her hands to her mouth and shuddered. Nothing changes, she thought bitterly. Life is the same as it ever was. If you're in the gutter there's always someone willing to stand on you as they pass by to better things.

'He's not there, Polly. I told you, it's my shop now. I can do what ever I want. I have two nice people working for me, they'll be kind to you. Come,' she put out her hand and Polly put her dirty one in it. 'But first of all,' she grimaced. 'We'll have to get you clean!'

She sent her around the back of the shop and let her into the yard. 'Take all of your clothes off,' she said. 'It's all right, no-one will see you. I can't risk taking fleas and bugs into my lovely cloth.'

'What are you going to do?' Polly asked suspiciously, although she started to unbutton her bodice.

'You'll see in a minute. Wait there.' Annie went inside. Robin was still chatting to the customer and Rose was showing the maid some ribbons, they didn't notice her as she slipped upstairs. Polly won't stay if she thinks I'm going to dowse her, she mused as she took off her muslin dress and wrapped herself completely in an old smock which she used when she and Mrs Cook dusted the shop.

'Right Polly.' Polly was standing in the middle of the yard, her arms crossed about her pubescent body. 'First we draw the water.' Annie took the handle of the pump and drew off a bucket of water. 'You can draw the next one.'

Annie threw the whole bucket full over the naked girl before she realized what was happening and she stood there gasping, a cascade of water running down her face and hair.

'It's not fair, Mrs Hope,' she spluttered. 'Having it thrown at me is bad enough, but having to pump another bucket full as well!'

'It's good for your soul, Polly and bad for the fleas. You'll feel different again by the time I've finished with you.'

Annie too was soaked through by the time she had pushed Polly's head under the pump for a final rinse down. Polly shivered and her teeth chattered and Annie wrapped her up in a large fustian sheet. 'Upstairs you go, and try not to let any customers see you. There's a fire lit and you'll soon get warm.'

The shop was empty of customers and Robin and Rose both turned and stared as Annie and Polly put their heads around the door and ran, dripping water on to the polished floor, up the stairs to Annie's room.

'Shall I start work now, Mrs Hope? I'll take Henry to the park.' Polly buttoned herself into one of Rose's old gowns which Annie had begged from her, being nearer in size to Polly than she was herself.

'No. Today you can eat and sleep.' Annie turned her around and tightened up the strings on her skirt. 'I'll make you a bed downstairs for now until I decide where to put you. Tomorrow we will talk about your duties. You shall have a proper job and a proper wage.'

Polly looked at her with bright trusting eyes. Dear God, Annie pleaded; if I look after this child, will You let somebody look after my poor bairn – my Lizzie?

*   *   *

They hadn't realized how the time was passing. They had a profitable first six months, when people who hadn't shopped at Sampson's before, curious to see the new owner, came to look and stayed to buy. Annie put in new fixtures and shelves and fitted out alcoves with wax dummies to drape material in the latest style of London fashion, and displayed them with fashion magazines opened at the appropriate page. She put comfortable chairs by the display so that customers could sit and browse and whet their appetites with the finery sketched within the pages.

'If only we had more room, Annie, we could sell more trimmings, and fans and reticules and bandeaux for the hair as well.' Robin was always coming up with ideas for improvement and expansion. 'Rose has some suggestions for trimmings to complement the material.'

'I know she has, Robin. But we are drapers not haberdashers, and the haberdashers in the town wouldn't be very pleased if we poached their customers.'

'True,' he admitted. 'We wouldn't like it if they started selling cloth and I suppose we couldn't do both successfully. Still it's a pity, Rose does have a way with trimmings.'

Annie smiled indulgently, he was so besotted with Rose. She saw the touch of hands as they brushed by each other behind the counter, and she knew that some of the customers saw it too for they would catch Annie's eye and gave a small knowing smile, while the young ladies or maids would gaze at Robin with yearning eyes.

It was during the early months of summer and they had the door open to let in some air for the heat was quite intense; but then the dust from the road, as the horses and carriages clattered by, rose up in clouds and blew in through the door and settled on the floor and the shelves.

'We'll have to close the door, Rose, the cloth is going to get dirty.' Annie watched Rose as she moved slowly to the door and stood with her hand on her hip taking in a deep breath. She was large with pregnancy but looked well and healthy and Robin was taking great care of her.

'Mamma!'

Annie turned as Henry called her. He was standing halfway down the stairs, half dressed in his pantaloons with his jacket buttons fastened all wrong and Annie's crocheted net purse in his hand.

'I'm going to see my grandfayther,' he announced. 'You said I can go soon, and it was soon a long time ago. When Polly comes back from shopping we shall go.'

'Indeed!' Annie raised her eyebrows. 'And don't you want me to go with you?'

'Oh, but you're always so busy.' He dismissed the idea with a wave of his hand. 'So I decided I would take Polly instead, and Charlie,' he added.

'And do you know the way?' she enquired humorously. 'How will you travel?'

He pulled a face as he considered. 'I haven't worked that out yet, but I'll tell Polly that she must find out.'

Annie sat on the stairs and pulled him down beside her. 'It's true I did promise you, and I hadn't wholly forgotten, but I also explained how important it was that we made a success of the shop, so that we had money for food and clothes and the toys that you always want from the toy shop.'

'But you don't always let me have them,' he complained.

'No, we can't always have everything we want, I'm afraid. Not straight away. Sometimes we have to wait for what we want.'

He pursed his lip. 'Is that why I've had to wait to see my grandfayther? It seems like a long long time.'

'It is a long time,' she admitted. 'And perhaps we've

waited long enough. Could you perhaps be patient for a few more days until I prepare for our journey? And then we'll go, and we'll take Polly and Charlie too.'

She first visited Mr Blythe to tell him of her intentions. 'How do you think Squire Linton will react to my calling? Should I write first and advise him that he has a grandson?'

'Mmm,' he mused. 'I think that perhaps you should just arrive. It is possible of course, that he won't be at home, in which case you will have had a wasted journey, but on the other hand, if he once sees the boy—!'

'But he's not very fond of children, so I understand.' Annie thought of what Matt had told her of his own restricted childhood.

'I have thought that he has changed over the last few years.' Marcus Blythe leaned back in his chair as he spoke and tapped his finger tips together. 'He's lonely in that great house with only a couple of servants to talk to; he may welcome the company of his own flesh and blood. And if he doesn't, then you will have to turn around and come back again. Tiresome, I know but – how will you travel by the way?'

'I thought I'd hire a chaise and driver, it's too awkward a journey to travel post, especially if we're not welcome and have to come back. Can I afford it, do you think?' she asked anxiously.

'Bless you, my dear, of course you can. But I have a better idea. You can take my chaise, and Lowson, he'll take care of you; better than some driver you don't know.'

'Oh, but,' she protested. 'What will you do? Have you another carriage?'

'A landaulette that I never use! The weather is good, I'll use that for my business around York, I don't intend to travel any distance. And don't hurry back on my account, Mrs Linton. Take your time, and enjoy a change of scenery.'

Mrs Linton! Mrs Linton! How strange it feels to be called by that name. A shiver ran up her spine as she thought of the journey in front of her. This journey, she meditated, was more of a venture than any she had undertaken. A visit to a man who had once ordered her off his land, and the same man who had kissed her hand and wistfully desired that his son didn't let her slip through his fingers.

'Polly,' she called as she ran upstairs to her room. 'Pack our bags.'

Polly was sitting on the floor playing with Henry. They both looked up and Henry scrambled to his feet. Annie picked him up and swung him around. How heavy he was getting, too big now to be called a babby.

'Henry Matthias Linton,' she smiled down at him. 'In two days time we are going to see your grandfather – Henry Linton.'

38

Polly complained of feeling ill for most of the journey and Annie had implored her not to be sick on any account on the fabric seats or moroccan cushions in Mr Blythe's stately carriage. Henry was curled up in a corner, his box of lead soldiers on his knee and Charlie at his feet, watching the world go by as casually as if he regularly travelled in such a fashion. Annie gazing at the shimmering heat haze across the tranquil hills, worried about leaving the shop, even though she had arranged for two more assistants to come in and help Robin, for Rose was getting near her time of confinement and was becoming very slow and ponderous as her weight increased.

So, too, as they drew nearer to Staveley Park did her anxiety increase. She felt her confidence falter and apprehension over her position return. Then mentally she drew back her shoulders and lifted her chin. Tha'll not get 'best of me, Squire Linton, she thought, even if I am a nobody. I'll tail it back to York, me and my son, if tha as much says a word out of place.

Then she laughed at herself. There was no reason why he should treat her disdainfully, he was perfectly charming the last time she had met him. She fingered her pearls as she pondered, then smoothed down her gown and shook out the creases and saw the glint of gold on her third finger.

She twisted it around, until the seam, where she had had an extra piece of gold inserted into the earring by the goldsmith, came to the front. Matt's father doesn't know, of course, she brooded, that his only son had married a woman without rank or distinction, a woman of no worth who could never be a lady —

and had married her in a dockside ceremony by a reprobate priest.

Lowson slowed the horses as they entered the iron gates to the long sweep of drive which led to the handsome house at the end of it. Annie peeped out of the window. Strange how she hadn't really looked at it the last time. She'd been so anxious for food and a bed that she had gone straight to the back door of the kitchen, with barely a glance at the once imposing entrance, where now the paint was peeling from the long windows and the stone steps were chipped, with weeds growing in between the cracks. The windows, as before, were shrouded by heavy concealing blinds as if the occupant had neither desire to look out nor a welcoming invitation for a visitor to look in.

The horses stamped their feet and blew whinnying gusts of breath as Lowson lowered the steps and helped her down, and as she thanked him, one door of the double doors opened and Mrs Rogerson was standing there, a look of incredulity on her face as she took in first Annie and then Henry as he jumped down from the carriage.

She bobbed her knee. 'Good afternoon, ma'am. I'm afraid t'master is away at present, though he'll be back in an hour or so.' She hesitated and screwed her hands together and looked into the distance over Annie's shoulder. 'He didn't say as he was expecting—'

'No.' Annie interrupted. 'I didn't write. I was in the district and thought I would call.' I could get back in the carriage and be gone in minutes, she thought, and all Mrs Rogerson would tell him was that a visitor called and declined to stay.

The housekeeper seemed to be keenly observing her, her eyebrows raised. 'Ma'am? You're very welcome to wait and take some refreshment.'

Annie blinked and realized that the woman had asked her a question. 'Oh, yes. Thank you; if you're sure that Squire Linton won't object?'

'There's no knowing, ma'am.' Mrs Rogerson opened the

door wider and muttered, half to herself. 'We'll have to see what humour he's in when he gets home.'

Jed appeared from a doorway beneath the stairs and touched his forehead. 'Shall I help t'coachie with luggage, ma'am?'

'No,' Annie decided after a second's hesitation. 'We may not stay. I – erm, I have another call to make. If Squire Linton is a long time I may have to go on.' And if he decides he doesn't want us, she mused, I don't want to give him the satisfaction of throwing our luggage down the steps after us.

Mrs Rogerson led them through an inner hall and into a small dark sitting-room on the left of the entrance. 'If you'd like to wait in here ma'am.' She went to the window and pulling on a cord drew up the blinds. The late afternoon sun poured in, filling the room with warmth and lighting up the polished floorboards and highlighting the colours of the Persian carpet.

'Ah.' The housekeeper took a breath of satisfaction. 'This room allus is good in the afternoon and early evening. This was the late Mrs Linton's sewing-room.' She swept off the sheets which were covering the chairs and folded them under her arms.

'Have you been here long?'

'Aye, I have ma'am. A long time. There's onny Jed and me left of the old staff.' Annie felt uncomfortable under her probing gaze. 'Will I bring wine, or tea or chocolate?'

'I'll take tea,' Annie said firmly, 'and my son will have chocolate. Polly, what will you have?'

Polly dragged her awestruck gaze away from the gilded frames of the watercolours on the wall and the Chinese vases on either side of the French clock above the carved fireplace. She stroked the striped damask covering on the chairs. 'Chocolate please, Mrs Hope, but I hope I don't spill.'

Mrs Rogerson glanced at Annie. 'She can come with me into the kitchen, ma'am. She'll be more comfortable there. Young master too,' she added, 'if he wants.'

Annie smiled. 'Off you go, Polly – but you can stay with me,' she said, drawing Henry towards her as he was about to move off after Mrs Rogerson. Polly only knew her as Mrs Hope and Annie knew that she would be dumbstruck in front of strangers, but Henry she was sure, would give the game away to those in the kitchen by telling them that Henry Linton was his grandfather.

She took a chair by the long side window which looked out over parkland and beyond towards a thick copse. She sipped her tea when Mrs Rogerson brought it and watched as cock pheasants, their irridescent feathers glinting, strutted around the grass followed by a string of plainer female birds, while from a meadow around the back of the house she could hear the low of cattle and a gentle bleat of sheep.

'Isn't it lovely here, Henry?' she said, glancing down at him as he stretched out on the floor placing his toy soldiers into marching order. 'It's so peaceful.'

'But is there anyone to play with?' He looked up. 'What do boys do?'

She shook her head and answered quite honestly that she didn't know. 'When Squire Linton comes in, I want you to stand up immediately,' she said. 'And don't speak unless you're spoken to. I have to explain a few things to him first.'

'About my father?' he asked, looking at her with blue eyes so like Matt's that she could have cried.

She nodded, not trusting herself to speak, then she drew in a breath. She had heard the sound of boots on the gravel and the sound of a man's voice roughly calling for Jed.

'Who's called?' she heard him say. 'There's been a carriage here by the look of it. Was it Blythe?'

There was an inaudible reply and then silence. She heard the swish of Mrs Rogerson's skirt across the stone-flagged hall and the sound of the outer door being opened and a soft murmur of voices.

'Master will be down directly, ma'am. He's just changing.' Mrs Rogerson brought in a tray and removed the crockery. She nodded her head and gave a tight little smile. 'He's had quite a good day, I reckon.'

Annie sank back on the chair and closed her eyes. She didn't know how to approach him. All the planning she had done, the things she had decided to say to him, the explanations, simply vanished and her mind was a blank. She got up from the chair and went to the window and stood with her back to the room looking out.

The door opened quietly and she heard a sharp exclamation, an intake of breath, and she turned to see Henry Linton standing by the door, one hand on the door knob, the other pressed to his lips, and her own Henry, his eyes wide, rising from the floor.

'Oh. Mrs Hope!' Henry Linton recovered his composure. 'They said it was a Mrs Hope, but I didn't expect – didn't dare to think that it was you.'

'I startled you. I beg your pardon,' Annie began.

'No, no, it was nothing.' He dismissed the idea; then: 'yes, but only for a moment. My late wife used to use this room and for a moment I thought – it was stupid – seeing you by the window – you know how the mind can play tricks! Please, won't you be seated?'

He glanced down at Henry and observed him for a moment, fingering his neck stock as he did so. Then he put out his hand and Henry with barely a glance at his mother put out his own to shake.

'Mrs Hope.' Henry Linton leaned towards her as he eased his long frame into a chair. 'Forgive me if I don't immediately conduct formalities and ask how you are, for I can see that you are very well indeed; but have you news of my son? I have had no word from him for nearly twelve months, and although he doesn't visit as regularly as I would wish, he doesn't as a rule leave it so long. I've not had so much as a letter or a message, and with this war—'

'Yes.' Annie's voice was husky with nerves and emotion. 'I have. It isn't good I'm afraid. He's been pressed into the navy. I don't know which ship or where in the world he will be, but he was waiting to be put aboard a tender in Hull the last time I saw him.'

'What!' He rose to his feet. 'A son of mine? Good God! Why didn't he contact me or Blythe?'

Annie said nothing but watched him as he paced the room, his face florid. Henry came and stood next to her and she put her arm comfortingly around him.

'He'll be holed up with criminals and convicts and drunkards. The scum of the earth! This is all because he wanted to be a seafarer and have his own ship, you know.' His voice rose. 'He should have gone into the navy as an officer if he was so damned fond of the sea!'

He stopped his pacing and ranting and looked at them as if he had suddenly become aware that they were there. 'I'm so sorry. Forgive me. It's come as a shock you see. I've lost one son. Now it seems as if I might lose another.'

Annie saw Henry open his mouth as if about to speak and she lifted a finger to silence him. 'Perhaps it would still be possible to have him exempted, sir. If you could speak to the magistrates at some of the ports?'

'Indeed I will.' He sat down again. 'I'll do even better. I'll write to the Admiralty immediately. Did they have a warrant do you know?'

Annie almost laughed. If he had seen, as she had, how the gangs of press-men took their victims, he would know that regardless of whether the lieutenants had a warrant, there were always bands of lawless tyrants ready to round up any man, sound or not, in the name of the king and the price of a bribe.

'I don't know, sir. I only know that his ship was taken on a false charge by the Customs at the same time as he was caught by the navy. Some of his men were caught also.'

'Thank you, Mrs Hope. I'm much obliged for your information.' He looked at her keenly and stroked his beard. 'Did you see much of Matthias, er, before his impressment I mean?' He glanced at Henry who was still standing by her chair. 'I wondered how you came by this knowledge?'

She took a deep breath. 'I came across him by chance when I was visiting Hull again. We – we'd lost touch. My fault I have to say.'

'Hmm. I said he'd let you slip through his fingers didn't I?'

She gave a weak smile, now he would start to remember.

He put his head on one side and then shook a finger. 'I've got it! I knew there was something different about you!'

Annie waited, a slow flush suffusing her cheeks.

'Your accent! You can speak English now. You had hardly a word when Matthias brought you to Mrs Burnby's place.' He glanced again at Henry. 'I can't recall him saying you had a child though, but then—.' He seemed to do a mental calculation. 'Perhaps you hadn't?'

Annie turned to Henry. 'Go and wait outside the door please. Don't wander around but stay where I can find you. I want to talk privately to Squire Linton.'

Henry obediently went to the door, but turned and said, 'I might get lost, Mamma. It's a very big house.'

'So it is, young man.' Henry Linton followed him and went into the hall and bellowed. 'Rogerson! Mrs Rogerson. Ah, there you are. Take this young fellow with you and give him some cake, and bring him back in ten minutes.'

He returned and sat down again so that he was facing her. 'Yes. Annaliese, wasn't it? I remember thinking what a delightful name. You were a widow if I recall?'

Annie stared down at her lap and twisted the small gold ring round and round her finger, then she looked up and stared into Henry Linton's eyes. 'No, sir. Not a Dutch widow. A widow, yes. But not Dutch. It was a jape, sir.'

'A jape! Oh, good heavens; my sons were always playing games and jokes. You'd think they would have grown out of it by the time they were adults.' He sounded quite humorous, she thought. Not angry. Not yet.

'But why? Was it because of that damned silly masquerade? Thought you'd go a bit further did you?'

'Before I explain that, sir, I'd like to tell you something

else first. You might not be very pleased, but it's done now.'

She tipped up her chin and gazed defiantly at him. Where she came from it was no sin to be pregnant out of wedlock. But she knew that the rules were different for his class. A lady, no matter how high born, would be turned out of her home and deprived of any possessions if she should fall in such a manner with no man willing to marry her.

'Your son and I were lovers.' She hadn't meant the statement to be delivered so tersely; she had wanted it to be soft and gentle and emotional. But, he had a twinkle in his eye. He wasn't shocked.

'I was caught with a child,' she said softly. 'I didn't think Matt would want me, and I ran away. I ran to York and have been living there ever since.'

He stared at her and she couldn't tell now what he was thinking.

'I went back to Hull on a business visit for my employer, taking my son with me, and there I saw Matt again.' She bowed her head and felt the tears flow. 'He was waiting at the dockside; waiting to be transferred to the naval tender. I think it was my fault that he was pressed. He would have tried to get away if he hadn't been so unhappy.'

She lifted a tear streaked face to Henry Linton. 'He'd been searching for me ever since I ran away.' She brushed away her tears and cleared her throat. 'There was a priest with him, he'd been pressed too and he offered to marry us before they sailed. Matt wanted to marry me in case he didn't come back.' She paused, then uttered in a breathless whisper, 'He wanted to give Henry his name.'

'Henry?' Squire Linton's face was inscrutable.

She nodded. 'Henry Matthias. Those were the names I had given my bairn.'

He narrowed his eyes. 'Your bairn?'

'Aye, sir. The reason I didn't speak at Mrs Burnby's party was because of my accent. My English accent, sir, not a Dutch one.'

'And so – the boy—?' He indicated towards the door.

'Yes, sir. Is Matt's son. Your grandson.'

Outside the window a song thrush was singing, repeating its clear refrain again and again, while inside the room the silence was broken only by the ticking of the clock on the mantelshelf.

Henry Linton cleared his throat. 'Why have you waited so long before coming? Before bringing the boy?'

'I wouldn't have come at all, sir,' she said. 'But Matt asked me to, and I promised Henry – he's always asking when can he come and see his grandfather.'

He frowned. 'You wouldn't have come? Why not?'

'I wouldn't have wanted you to think that—,' she broke off; how to explain that she didn't want him to feel he was committed to acknowledge them in any way?

'You felt that I might consider you were wanting money or position? Is that it?' His eyes seemed to pierce into her.

'Yes sir.'

A gentle knock on the door disturbed them and he called to come in. 'You said to come back in ten minutes, sir.' Mrs Rogerson waited at the door with Henry and a curious Polly hovering behind them.

'Come here boy.' Henry Linton beckoned. 'And bring some tea, Mrs Rogerson.'

'Stay with Mrs Rogerson please, Polly. I'll call you when I'm ready.' Annie made a point of speaking politely to Polly, unlike Henry Linton who bellowed at his servants.

He drew Henry towards him and took hold of both of his hands. 'Now, young man.' His voice was gruff as the door closed behind Mrs Rogerson and Polly. 'Do you know who I am?'

'Yes, sir.' Henry shuffled uncomfortably.

'Well, and who am I?'

'I think you're my grandfayther, sir.'

'Only think? Don't you know?'

'Well.' Henry hesitated. 'Mamma says that you are, but

my friend James has a grandfayther and he's not like you, and he doesn't live in such a big house.'

A ghost of a smile played around Squire Linton's mouth. 'How isn't he like me? Apart from the big house?'

'He doesn't shout as much as you, sir, and he plays games with James, and with me sometimes.'

'And you think that I wouldn't play games with you? Well, I never did play games with my sons,' he mused. 'Children were meant to be kept quiet and out of my way, not for playing with. Anyway, there was never time for games.'

He glanced at Annie sitting quietly watching them. 'But sometimes when we get older,' he faltered, 'we have regrets and wish things had been different and that we could start all over again.'

He stroked the top of Henry's fair head. 'You are so much like your father and grandmother.' His voice became low and husky. 'I would have known you anywhere. When I came into the room and saw you on the floor playing with your toys, and your mother standing by the window, it was as if the years had rolled back and life was as before.'

He stood up and swung Henry into his arms and stood in front of Annie. 'Perhaps this is my chance to make amends. Perhaps – but please God it isn't so, I may have lost another son—, but I have gained a daughter and a grandson.'

Annie grasped the hand which he proffered. 'Sir, I—'

'Annaliese. Will you stay?' There was a pleading in his eyes though his voice was now firm and steady. 'At least for a little while, so that we can get to know each other?'

'Sir, I haven't told you everything.' She got up from the chair and faced him, ready for flight. 'There's much more.'

'It can wait. We have plenty of time.'

'But I'm not Annaliese,' she insisted. 'I'm Annie; just plain Annie.'

He shook his head and put Henry down. 'I don't care for that so much. A common name.' He pursed his lips. 'Anna. Anna is better I think. That's what I'll call you. If you have no objection, that is,' he added as an afterthought. 'May I call you Anna?'

It wouldn't harm to give in this once, Annie thought. It's gone better than I expected. I've caught him on a good day. He's feeling mellow and sentimental and he seems to be genuinely pleased about Henry. But then a man in his position wants a lineage. The trouble is, she pondered wryly, that I know more about him than he knows about me, and when he finds out, as he will, then there are going to be some sparks flying.

'Very well, Mr Linton,' she said appeasingly. 'If Anna suits you, I have no dislike of the name, and I've found in my experience that any name will serve as well as another.'

'Good.' He nodded as if satisfied with the arrangement. 'Then that's settled; you'll stay. Now, what should you call me? Henry will call me grandfather, *not* grandfayther I hasten to add. And you Anna, what name will you know me by? I can't imagine beautiful young women calling me father,' he said with a roguish smile, 'but I suppose it has to be.'

'*Father*,' she exclaimed. 'You want me to call you father!'

'Why not,' he said briskly. 'Or would your own father object?'

She shook her head and covered her face with her hands. To break down now over a simple word when she had kept her emotions in check for so long, was painful and intolerable. 'I have no fayther.' Her voice was muffled and he leaned closer to hear. 'I have no fayther or mother, never have had, or none that I remember.'

'Anna! Please don't cry.' He bent over her and diffidently grasped her about the shoulders. 'Please Anna. I can't bear it when women weep.'

39

A week passed and in that time she told him of living in York; of the drapery business she owned with Henry; of Marcus Blythe, Henry Linton's own lawyer who was also hers and whose carriage was now sheltering beneath the coach house walls here at Staveley Park.

She told him of her meeting with Toby and Matt in Hessle; but not of the smuggling. Nor yet did she tell him of her own life before that. Not of her existence beneath the wharves of the Humber, nor of her children of her marriage to Alan. These, she decided, could wait until she knew him better, until such time as he was sufficiently fond of her and Henry, not to mind.

He brought out his dusty carriage which he said he never used, as he preferred to ride his horse, and took them around the estate. He showed them the farms and the cottages in the hamlet, and she remembered them from her last visit, when the cottagers had closed the door on her, when they hadn't wanted to know the stranger on that cold snowy night.

He showed them too the vast meadow lands which were dotted with grazing sheep and told her of the damn fool idea that Matt had of turning it over to the plough.

'But wouldn't it give the cottagers work?' she'd ventured. 'It surely would be better than them sitting idly at home?'

'And more work for me. And what's the point when there's no-one else interested? No son to take over after me.'

He'd glanced at Henry then who was looking out of the

carriage window counting sheep, and had then fallen silent as they made their way back home.

They ate in his book-lined study at a small table. He couldn't be bothered with the fuss of eating in the dining-room, he said. 'Can't be bothered with all of that, laying out the silver and glass; not worth it just for me. Besides, I'd have to get extra staff, Mrs Rogerson couldn't manage otherwise.'

'It seems a pity,' Annie said. 'It's such a lovely room.'

She had been quite overwhelmed by the interior of the house when Mrs Rogerson had shown her around, for although it was less grand, and not so large a mansion as Mrs Burnby's where she had been to the masquerade, it had a modest elegance, displayed in its classical plasterworked ceilings, in intricate carved cornices, in richly carved fireplaces and panelled walls.

Mrs Rogerson had pulled off the covers from the furniture in the drawing-room with a sigh. 'These have been covered over for nearly twenty years ever since 'mistress died; and then each year since Masters Matthias and Tobias finally left, Master has shut off a room. Said there was no point in having rooms with nobody to admire them.'

Annie admired them. They were the most beautiful rooms she had ever seen, and the gilded furniture though old and the fabric faded, was exquisitely handsome.

'It's a French style, ma'am, so I understand. Mrs Linton was a great connoisseur of what was right for each room. And a collector too. We've boxes of Chinese porcelain and Italian glass that she acquired, some of it she brought with her when she married 'Squire. It's been put away in case of breakage, and it needs careful handling, and I just don't have time to spare.'

She told Annie that she was housekeeper and cook. That the squire had given the cook notice because he wasn't fussy about eating, and had said that Mrs Rogerson could prepare him something simple on a tray.

'I've got a girl in the kitchen and another one for cleaning and then I bring women in from the village twice a year so's we can bottom everywhere. It's bad enough for me,' she'd said, 'but old Jed is at Master's beck and call all day long. He even got rid of coachie 'cos he said he didn't need him, and he's just got a stable-lad to look after hosses.'

Annie sensed the woman assessing her, though she didn't look at her directly. She hadn't recognized her, she was sure, but then how could she? She was quite different in her simple, though fashionable, gowns from the roughly spoken ragged girl with the donkey-cart, that she had been all those years ago.

'Maybe now, ma'am, we'll be able to open up some of the rooms again, if you and young master are staying?'

It was a direct question as to the length of time they were staying, though asked obliquely. And only this morning Mrs Rogerson had come with a list in her hand and asked Annie about supper.

'I don't know, Mrs Rogerson,' she'd replied firmly. 'I'm only a guest. You must consult with your master as usual.'

'Would young Henry like a pony?' Henry Linton poured her a brandy as they lingered after supper. The question was sudden, quite unexpected.

'I've been thinking about it for a day or two. And we've a curricle in one of the coach houses. I could teach you how to drive it.'

She sat stunned for a moment. Was he expecting them to stay for a long period – or indefinitely? Matt had said, wait there until I come back, but she hadn't told his father of his words.

'You're very generous to suggest such things, sir' she said quietly, 'but we can stay only a few more days. I shall be so sorry to leave, but I mustn't impose on you any longer. You've been very kind, but I must get back to York – to my business, and Mr Blythe will want his carriage.'

For a second she thought she saw a fleeting dismay in his eyes but it was instantly followed by a flash of anger.

'What! What do you mean get back to your business?'

'I told you, sir, of us having a drapery—,'

He guffawed. 'You surely don't think you can go on with that? Not now. It's not possible. You'll have to sell.'

'I don't understand, sir.' She was confused as to his meaning, why wasn't it possible?

'I can't have any daughter-in-law of mine in *trade*, you must surely understand that. Great Heavens, it's just not done!'

'Why not? It's a very good shop, all the ladies of York come to buy from me.'

'Well that's just it, isn't it? We'd be the laughing stock of the county if it got out.'

'If it got out?' she whispered. So there were divisions, not just between rich and poor, but between sections in between. The ladies who patronized the shop had usually been very pleasant towards her; or were they simply being gracious as befitted their status? Oh, Annie, she pondered. You've still a lot to learn.

'Why, they'd come in just to have a look at you, to see what kind of woman Matt had married. I don't care for myself, but think of Matt when he gets home – his wife serving behind a shop counter! And Henry. Think of when he goes to school. He'd get bullied and ragged no end.'

She laughed in amazement. What a fool she was. She thought she'd bettered herself, dragged herself out of the gutter and here she was, still not good enough.

'Matt knows what kind of woman I am,' she attacked back. 'He knew me when I had less than I have now, and as for Henry, I'm his mother no matter what.' Was that true, she wondered as a niggle of doubt crept in, or would Matt be different in his old home? She couldn't imagine Henry changing towards her, but under other influences, he might.

She suddenly felt frightened and insecure and all her old terrors came flooding back. She couldn't bear it if Matt and Henry should turn against her, she would die rather than suffer that.

'Ah, but did he?' He leaned forward and shook an

admonishing finger. 'Did Matthias know? It's all right falling for a pretty face, I've done it myself many times, but did he know your background? Did you tell him you had no family and that you worked in a shop? Or did you twist him round your little finger so that he wanted you, come what may. I know you women, how you tease.'

Her anger flared. 'You know nothing about women, sir. How could you? Not women like me anyway – women of your own class maybe – but not my kind.'

'Ho, ho.' He leaned back in his chair and laughed. 'I do believe the little lady has a temper. And tell me, my dear,' he said sardonically. 'How are *you* different from any other woman. I've known all types of women in my life and I know how they entrap men.'

'Not my sort, mayster.' She dropped her voice to a husky whine. 'Tha can't be teasing menfolk when tha's starving and searching for a crust o' bread.'

His smile faded and he narrowed his eyes, then he gave a nervous laugh. 'That's very good, Anna. Where did you learn to mimic like that? Why you sound like—. You sound like—. You've been visiting the villagers, haven't you?' he added sharply.

She shook her head. He'd paled as if understanding was seeping through. But he still didn't know who she was. 'Them folks have a better life than I ever had, sir, even though they're living in broken down hovels, with a mayster who doesn't care if they live or dee.'

'That's enough.' Abruptly he got to his feet. 'Enough of this foolishness.'

'Nay, mayster,' she persisted. 'It's not foolishness. They have a roof of sorts over their head, even though 'thatch is ragged and let's in 'rain. Not like 'likes of me who spent their childhood with their feet in river water sheltering beneath 'wharves, or scavenging for leftovers in rich men's yards.'

'Stop. Stop it at once.' He was angry now and raised his voice.

'Now sir, do you believe what I say?' She spoke now in

her ordinary voice. 'That you wouldn't know about women like me? Your class of gentleman couldn't begin to know, not unless they were really searching amongst the dregs for a woman of a different kind, and thank God I never did stoop so low, though I was tempted many times.'

There was a quiet knock on the door and Mrs Rogerson entered. 'Can I clear the supper things, sir?'

'No, you can't,' he bellowed at the startled woman. 'Get out. I'll call you when I need you.'

She fled, but not before she cast an anxious glance at Annie.

'There's no need to shout at Mrs Rogerson,' Annie began. 'She's done nothing.'

'Don't tell me what I can or cannot do in my own house. You're not mistress yet, nor likely to be.'

'You're too hard on your servants.' Annie thought she had nothing more to lose. He'd tell her to go now. 'Mrs Rogerson works so hard and you don't give her as much as a thank you.'

'She gets food, a bed and a wage. Why should I thank her? She should be grateful to be here.' His face was red as he glared at her. 'Ah, I see it all now. You don't know how to behave towards the servants, and no wonder. You have no maid to help you dress, and you speak to that chit of a girl who can't string more than three words together, who looks after Henry—, as if she's an equal instead of the servant she is!'

'She's only a child. I speak kindly to her,' she shouted back. 'She reminds me of my own daughter.' The words slipped out by accident, she hadn't intended telling him yet about Lizzie and the boys. Slowly she added. 'She also reminds me of me; of how I used to be.'

He said nothing but simply stared at her. Then he went back to the table and poured himself another brandy. He didn't offer another to Annie and she wished that he had as she felt her passion evaporate to be replaced by a black melancholy.

'You have a daughter?' His words were low and he sat down as if weary.

'Yes, sir, and two sons. I was a widow before I married Matt.'

He nodded his head in a resigned fashion as if there was nothing more that would surprise him. 'I think, madam,' he said in a crabbed, bitter voice. 'That you had better leave this house. We shall not get along. I am unused to females behaving in the way that you do. However, you may leave Henry with me. I'm willing to educate him in a manner befitting my grandson.'

'What!' Was the man mad? Leave Henry? 'How could I leave Henry?' she cried. 'You had no love for your own sons, you will have even less for a grandson.'

He stared sourly at her. 'Of course I loved my sons, but it doesn't do to show it. Makes them soft; like women. But I don't wish to discuss it with you. You may leave him if you wish.'

'I don't wish it.' She stormed to the door and grasped the door knob. 'We'll leave first thing in the morning.' She gave him a superior smile though her mouth trembled and she was close to tears. 'You won't remember Mr Linton, but this is the second time you have turned me off your property.'

'What do you mean? You haven't been here before.' He looked at her from dull eyes and she saw, or thought she saw, grief.

'Yes, I have. The first time I walked away, my feet deep in snow, after spending the night in your barn. This time at least I can drive away in a carriage, even though a borrowed one. I said then I hoped you would never have to stretch out a hand for charity and find none.'

She opened the door and paused before leaving. 'I'll bid you goodbye, sir. We won't be coming back here again. Not even if you were to go on your bended knees.' She gave a half laugh, half cry. 'Which you never will of course. Not you. I'm sorry for you, for you have no warmth, no pity. I'm really sorry.'

She was halfway up the wide curved staircase when she bethought herself. She didn't want to meet him again in the morning. They wouldn't take breakfast she decided. They would move off at first light and stop at an inn for refreshment. She turned and went back down and going below stairs to the kitchen she sought out Mrs Rogerson.

As Mrs Rogerson opened the inner kitchen door Annie glanced beyond the woman's shoulder. Jed was sitting with his elbow on the kitchen table, his chin in his hand and the young maid was pouring him ale from a jug. They both looked up at her and she felt as if she was re-living her past. Only this time she was inside the house, not waiting at the outer door.

'Mrs Rogerson.' She whispered so that the girl wouldn't hear. 'We will be leaving first thing in the morning. We won't require breakfast. Will you ask Jed to tell Lowson to have the carriage ready at the door by seven o'clock.'

'Oh, ma'am.' There was genuine dismay on the woman's face. 'I'd hoped you were staying longer.'

Annie shook her head. 'No. Have Jed collect our bags first thing.' She gathered up her skirt and fled from those sympathetic eyes and ran upstairs to her room.

She packed her belongings into her travelling case and then looked in on Henry. He was sleeping soundly, his hands tucked beneath his round cheeks and next to him on a day-bed Polly slept, her hand stretched out limply towards him as if in reassurance. Annie lifted up her hand and tucked it under the covers and gently stroked her face. Polly had changed so much since coming to live with them, she was more attentive to her duties now that she was secure and no longer frightened.

Mrs Rogerson had given Annie a room which she'd said was next door to Master Matthias's. She'd opened the interconnecting door and showed her in. The old high mahogany bed and furnishings had been shrouded in sheets, just like the other unused rooms. Annie looked in now and wondered with a deep sadness which bit deep into her, if the bed would ever be slept in again.

On impulse she ran back into her own room and pulled off the deep soft pillows and the feather quilt from her bed and took them back into Matt's room. She tore the dust sheets from his bed and the mirror and the polished wooden chest of drawers, and left them in a heap on the floor.

She drew back the damask embroidered cover and lay her pillows and quilt on the mattress and standing on the stool at the side of the bed climbed in.

Her sleep, what little she had, was disturbed by images of Matt and Henry, somehow superimposed one into another. She saw Matt as a boy living lonely in this great house. In her dream he gave her a sad smile and spoke to her, but they were Henry's eyes that were looking at her. There was a ship with its sails on fire and men jumping into a foaming sea, and there, too, was Toby with a dark stain on his coat, clutching Matt and Henry by their hands.

She thought in her dream that she could hear footsteps along the corridor, a pencil of light showing beneath the door as if someone with a candle was wandering around in the dead of night and she slid further below the quilt and hid her head.

When she awoke dawn was breaking and she climbed out of bed and went to the window and opened it. The sky was streaked with red and gold and a young thrush was clearing its throat for the first song of the day. The notes soared through the silence of the morning waking other creatures, enticing them to join the chorus, the blackbirds and robins, the tiny wren and the deep *koo koo* of the collared doves above the stables. From the meadows she could hear the bleat of sheep and the barking of a dog, and the distant cry of a lonely shepherd.

With a sigh she turned away. Such a pity. It was so lovely and appeared so peaceful; yet she knew that down in the dale, in the hamlets and villages, there were people there, who, like the poor people of the towns were more intent on feeding themselves and their children and escaping from the poverty which trapped them, than admiring a pleasant view.

So, Matt, she mused sadly as she gazed around the room. I've come to your home as your wife. I've slept alone in your bed. I've come as far as I can and now I must go back. I'm not wanted here. But I felt you here with me. I had my arms around you, even though only in my dreams. God bless you, my darling. Come to me soon.

She went to her own room and dressed and thought wryly of Squire Linton's remark of her not having a maid to help her dress. Sometimes it might be an advantage, she thought as she lifted her arms to fasten the buttons at the back of her dress. She tied her hair in a double knot at the nape of her neck and then went to waken Henry and Polly telling them to hurry, not to ask questions, but that they were going home to York.

Jed knocked on the door at a-quarter-to-seven and handed her a letter which he said had just been delivered. 'I'll tek these bags down now, ma'am, and come back for young master's.' He picked up her cases which were strapped and ready and went back out into the corridor. The door was open and she glanced up as she tore open the envelope, wondering curiously who would write to her here. Perhaps it was Marcus Blythe wanting his carriage back.

She saw Jed put down the cases and then hesitate, scratching his head. 'What is it, Jed?' she asked vaguely. 'Is something wrong?'

'No, nowt's wrong, ma'am. But we was wondering, me and Mrs Rogerson.' He rubbed his chin and glanced at her from beneath his brows. 'We was wondering what tha wanted us to do about the cart?'

The letter was from Robin, written a week ago. She looked up at Jed. 'Sorry, Jed. What did you say? The cart? Which cart?'

As she asked the question she looked into Jed's eyes and saw awareness, and something else also – compassion. Her cheeks flushed. The cart! The cart which she had left here so long ago and had forgotten about!

So they had known ever since she had arrived. Jed and

Mrs Rogerson had known all along who she was, yet had never given her so much as an inkling that they knew; not by a word, a look or a gesture. They had treated her as they would have any other guest in the house. No – more than that. They had treated her, and Henry, as if they belonged here, as if they were wife and son of the heir to Staveley Park.

She sat down on the chair by the bed and stared at Jed still waiting by the door. She gave him a sudden smile, there was some hope for mankind after all if there were good honest people like Jed and Mrs Rogerson around.

'Keep it, Jed, if you want it, or sell it, or chop it up for firewood. I don't mind. It was replaced long ago, as was the donkey.'

He gave her a grin, the first she had ever seen on his craggy face, nodded and touched his forelock and picked up the bags and left.

She sat for a minute musing in some amazement that they should behave in the way they did, without taking advantage of her. She glanced down at the letter in her lap. Then she gasped and sat upright and re-read the laboured writing.

'*Please come back, Annie,*' Robin had written. '*I'm at my wits end. Rose is so ill and I'm fearful for her life and the babby's, and my own if anything happens to her.*'

Then that's settled, she thought as she hurried into Henry's room. We'd have to go anyway. Poor Rose. Poor Robin. We must leave immediately.

Charlie was waiting at the bottom of the stairs, his tail wagging as he saw them. Mrs Rogerson was there with a blanket in case the morning was chilly, and through the open door Jed was loading their bags into the waiting carriage.

'I'm right sorry you're going, Mrs Linton,' she said in a low voice. 'I hope as you'll come back soon.'

Annie gave a slight shrug and then added. 'I have to go now, Mrs Rogerson. I'm needed in York. A very dear friend is in trouble.'

There was a sound from behind them and the study door opened. Henry Linton came out. His clothes were dishevelled, his neck stock undone and he looked as if he hadn't been to bed.

'Grandfather!' Henry ran to him. 'I'm sorry but we have to go back to York. Rose is very ill and Mamma must go and look after her.'

Henry Linton looked pale and drawn as he placed his hand on his grandson's head. 'And must you go too, Henry? Or can you stay?'

Annie caught her breath. How dare he say that? After all the harsh words which had passed between them. She looked Henry Linton straight in the eyes and opened her mouth to speak. Then she stopped. His eyes were bloodshot as if he had been weeping.

'Mrs Rogerson.' Henry Linton cleared his throat. 'Would you be good enough to take Henry outside for a moment while I speak to Mrs Linton?'

Mrs Rogerson stared at Mr Linton, a look of amazement on her face at the sound of his polite words; then she blinked and gathered up Henry and Polly and a skittish Charlie and hurried them outside and closed the doors.

'What is this, sir?' Annie began immediately on the defensive. 'We must leave. I have received troubling news, I must leave at once.'

'Anna.' He took a deep breath and closed his eyes. 'Anna,' he repeated, opening them wide, and she saw pain there. 'You are right. I am a tyrant. I didn't give my sons the affection they wanted. And my wife, my beautiful wife,' he put his head down and sighed deeply. 'She deserved better than me, but she didn't really care for me, we married because it was expected of us, not because there was any love between us. We could perhaps have grown to care for each other but I found affection elsewhere, and she found it with our sons, and then it was too late.'

He looks like an old man, she contemplated. His handsome face was haggard, his hair unbrushed.

'But you must try to understand, Anna. We are what our

425

fathers make us. My father beat me every day to make me strong.' He must have seen the dismay on her face for he hastened to add, 'I swear I didn't do the same to mine, but nevertheless I insisted on discipline. It might have seemed harsh,' he muttered, 'their mother said it was. But I never listened to her and she accepted what I said as being right.'

A thin smile crossed his face. 'Not as you would, Anna. The tigress defending her cubs.'

If only you knew, sir, she thought bitterly, how I have defended my young, and lived with my conscience ever since.

'If she had been more like you, with your spirit, maybe things would have been different.'

'I am as I am, because I had to survive, sir,' her voice was cutting. 'We are from different worlds.'

He nodded. 'I know. I understand now, and I'm sorry. I'm sorry that I spoke the way I did. I am no gentleman. I am lower than the lowest.'

This was no man that she knew; not the rough-tongued squire who had turned her off his land, not the handsome, bantering charmer who had amused her at the masquerade, nor the father who had escorted her about his estate. This was a man who had sunk as low in misery and self-esteem as it was possible for anyone to do.

'Will you stay?' His manner was appealing, his voice low. 'I will be different with my grandson. And though I can't promise that you and I won't fight or have our differences, we could perhaps come to some understanding.'

She shook her head, she'd vowed she wouldn't set foot in this house again. 'No, sir. I would be an embarrassment to you. It's no longer a game pretending to be different from who I am. I'm a nobody; no family, no background. I could never be a lady.'

'But your son, yours and Matthias', he can be different,' he pleaded. 'Which would you rather he was, a draper, or the owner of all this,' he swept around his arm, encompassing the house, the land, the whole estate.

'You still don't understand, do you?' she reproached him. 'It doesn't matter which. As long as he's able to hold his head up and know who he is, that's what matters.'

'He's my grandson, that is who he is.' His voice became sharp again. 'Whether or not you like it, one day he will inherit this estate. Isn't it better that he grows up knowing it, growing to love this land, as I do, rather than coming to it and not knowing where to begin?'

She was caught off guard. She hadn't thought of that. She'd assumed that he would simply cut them off, have nothing more to do with them. He must have done some hard thinking all the night. She remembered her dream of footsteps prowling the corridor last night, and was convinced that it had been Henry Linton, unable to sleep for his troubled conscience.

'I said that I wouldn't set foot in this house again.' She uttered the words firmly, though her determination was wavering.

He smiled. 'I remember. Not even if I went down on my bended knees!'

He put out his hand and grasped the bannister and lowered himself onto one knee. 'It's a long time since I did this to a young woman, and for an entirely different motive. But I'm begging you, Anna. Will you stay? For Matthias's sake and Henry's, if not for your own?'

She couldn't believe her eyes and she wanted to laugh if it hadn't been such a serious question. Then she saw the humorous twinkle in his blue eyes and she drew herself up straight.

'Only, for Heaven's sake,' he groaned. 'Do be quick and make up your mind. I've got the most fearful cramp.'

She laughed aloud. How ridiculous he was. But if he was prepared to look ridiculous, then it surely must prove that the man had some qualities after all?

'We can't stay now. I must go back to York.' She indicated the letter in her hand and said with some forethought. 'But perhaps after all, we might come back.'

'Let Henry stay,' he entreated as grimacing he stood

upright. 'Please. And if you must go then come back when you can. I did enjoy your company, Anna, before our quarrel.'

Still she shook her head, she dare not leave Henry. Suppose he was unhappy?

'I swear I'll take care of him,' he pleaded yet again. 'On my life.' He put his hand on his heart. 'And that of my son's, I'll take care of him.'

She gazed at him for a long moment as she considered. Then she made up her mind. 'We'd better ask him then, hadn't we? If he wants to stay, and *only* if he does, then he can, but only if Polly stays too,' she added.

They went to the door together. Outside, Mrs Rogerson, Lowson and Jed were standing by the carriage talking in low voices and Polly was watching as Henry threw twigs for Charlie to chase.

'Henry. Come here a moment, please.'

The child stood in front of her and with a grin lifted dirty hands for her to see.

'Henry. Your grandfather has asked if you would like to stay with him for a while. I must return to York as Rose is ill. But if you want to you can stay.'

She tried to keep her voice impartial, not to persuade him one way or another, and if she was surprised or disappointed in his answer then she didn't show it.

'Can Polly and Charlie stay too?'

She nodded, a lump forming in her throat as her son made his first decision.

'*Ye—es*. Please.' Exuberantly he threw a stick up in the air and Charlie tore off after it. 'Charlie likes it here. He used to live here, you know, when he was a pup. Jed told me. Someone called Tobias took him away. Yes please, grandfather. I'd like to stay.'

40

She wept most of the way back to York, shaken and jolted in the empty carriage as Lowson urged on the team along the rutted roads, and wondered what comfort or happiness her new status had brought her. I've lost my son, she sobbed, just as I lost the others. Not one did I lose at childbed but I've lost them all now. If I give Henry a new life with his grandfather, I'll lose him, he'll never wholly belong to me again.

After a while her good sense took over and she began to consider. If we both lived at Staveley Park, Henry would still be mine, his grandfather wouldn't get all his own way, that he wouldn't! But do I want to live there with Henry Linton? Do I want to see that lovely house opened up so that when Matt comes home it is a home to him as it never was before. Heavens Annie, what is happening to you? To live in a house as grand as that! And think. You could maybe persuade Mr Linton to do up the cottages down in the valley, or at least mend the thatch. But slowly, slowly, she chastized herself, don't run so fast.

And the shop. Robin could run the shop. That would please Henry Linton and it would bring in my own income, I wouldn't have to ask him for money. She'd revelled in her independence, she wouldn't give it up easily.

Robin opened the shop door as Lowson handed her down and lifted down her baggage. She thanked him and asked him to tell Mr Blythe that she would call and thank him personally for the carriage. Robin looked worried and drawn as he ushered her in.

'She's had a terrible time, Annie. I had to send for you.'

'It's all right, Robin,' she reassured him, taking off her hat and shaking down her hair. 'I was coming back anyway.'

'She's lost 'babby, Annie.' Robin sat down on a shop stool and sank his head wearily into his hands. 'My poor little Rosie. She's heartbroken. I can't console her.'

'I'm so sorry, Robin. It's hard, I know, to lose a child, especially the first. It'll take time to get over, but there'll be other bairns.'

'That's what 'doctor said. He said it would be easier next time.' He shook his head and wept. 'How can I put her through that again. It's not fair.'

'She's young, Robin. Next time will be easier. First time is always the worst.'

Robin said he hoped she didn't mind but they'd used her room upstairs. 'I wanted her near me when she started in labour, and we were that busy in the shop, I daren't leave it.'

Annie ran upstairs to her room and found Rose lying in her bed. She looks so beautiful, Annie thought, her face pale and sad and her hair draped around her shoulders like a dark cloud.

'I want to get up now, Annie. Robin says I must stay in bed, but I do nothing but fret when I'm alone up here. If I get up I won't think so much of my poor babby.' Tears filled her eyes. 'He was so lovely, Annie, so lovely, but so still.'

Annie comforted her as best she could and agreed with her that she should get up. 'Sit in the chair today, and tomorrow come downstairs. It'll take your mind off your loss. But Rose,' she said gently. 'Tha'll not forget him.' She slipped without realizing into her old dialect. 'Tha'll have other bairns and they'll mean just as much to thee, but tha won't forget the one you lost.'

'I've a lot to talk about, Robin,' she said as she went downstairs again.

'Aye, and so have I. If it hadn't been that I was so worried about Rose, I would have told you in my letter.'

'Told me? What? Has something happened?'

'The shop next door is coming vacant. Mr Thompson came in to tell me. He's giving up his business and going to live with his daughter.'

'Isn't he selling the business?' The confectioner's shop was usually busy, though she had noticed recently that the old proprietor was often standing on his doorstep idly watching the traffic and passers-by.

'He says nobody wants to buy it, he's had it on the market for some time, but the price of sugar and flour has gone sky high and nobody will pay the prices any more.'

'So? What are you saying Robin?' she teased. 'That we buy it and go in for spun sugar creations?'

'What I'm saying, Annie, is that we take the lease and use it for haberdashery.' His face became animated, wiping away the misery she had seen when she'd arrived back only an hour ago. 'Rose's father said he would give us a dowry, we could use it to set up.'

'But what about here. What am I to do without you?' Her own plans seemed to be dashed. She couldn't leave the shop in any other hands but Robin's.

'No, no.' He hastened to reassure her. 'I shall stay here and Rosie will run next door. We could even,' he added enthusiastically, 'knock down a wall later and make a way through.'

'You'd have to buy the building before you could do that,' she said practically.

'I know, I know. My mind is running on. But what do you think, Annie? Is it a good idea?'

He gazed at her, his face expectant and eager. If anyone could make the idea work and succeed, it was Robin, she decided.

She smiled back at him. 'I think it's a wonderful idea, Robin. It's just the tonic that you and Rose need. We'll go to see Marcus Blythe in the morning and put it to him.'

Mr Blythe thought it an excellent idea, though he advised that they musn't expect to make a profit immediately. 'You have the expense of fitting it out, carpenters don't do the

431

work for nothing, Mr Deane, and you will need shelves and counters and such, I expect.'

'There are shelves and counters already,' Robin said. 'I've had a good look at the interior and we could manage with what there is, for a year or two anyway.'

Marcus Blythe nodded approvingly. 'And staff of course. You must get extra staff, Mrs Deane couldn't run it single-handed, and you will be running the drapery for Mrs Linton. But yes,' he agreed. 'I think it will work very well.'

He offered them refreshment. Robin declined and hurried back to the shop, but Annie stayed on, there were several things she wanted to discuss with Marcus Blythe.

She told him that she had left Henry behind at Staveley Park. He nodded. 'You were wise. Linton is not an unkind man, though he might appear unfeeling. He has mellowed, I've noticed, over the last few years, and I think too that he has been very unhappy and lonely in that great house of his. So, will you go back and wait there for your husband?'

'I think that I might, though sometimes I feel that he'll never come back.' She felt that she could talk to this kindly, wise man. 'He seems to have disappeared out of my life.'

'We will do all we can, my dear.' He shuffled amongst the papers on his desk. 'I have here a letter from Henry Linton asking me to add my name to his in the appeal to the Admiralty. If it is a case of unjustified pressing – and Captain Linton should have had genuine protection and therefore been exempt from impressment, then we can threaten legal proceedings. I will send a letter off today.'

She felt a great weight lifted off her mind. What it was to have influence! She thought of the press-gangs that she had seen in her youth, who roamed the streets and inns of Hull, taking by force or 'persuasion' drunk or sober members of the public.

She remembered the riots of the mob who tried to break down the doors of the rendezvous, held in a dank alehouse cellar or gaol, in their attempt to release the men who were held there. No clever lawyer to help them escape the navy. They were cursed to sail the seas whether or not they had a mind for it, be they tailor or butcher, drunkard or pauper, they were all thrown into the same stinking, barred hold of the receiving ship. She knew. She had seen for herself.

*　　*　　*

Robin wrote to Mr Sutcliff telling him of his proposal about the haberdashery and of Rose losing her baby. He had a letter back from him immediately to say that he approved of the plan and would come over to discuss it, and a note from Joan to Rosie telling her how sorry she was and that Lily was expecting Mr Collins' child. 'Meg also has a suitor,' she wrote, 'a farm lad from the next village, it seems as if I am doomed to be the old maid of the family, and I am so miserable.'

'I think, now, I can safely go back to see Henry,' Annie said about three weeks later. 'Everything is running smoothly here and when your new staff arrive for the haberdashery you won't need me.'

'You go, Annie.' Robin gave her a hug. 'We'll send for you if you're needed. I know where your heart is. Go to see Henry, I know how you're missing him.' He grinned. 'And go and play the lady, you'll be good at it. I always said you were a real lady, didn't I?'

She smiled gratefully. Dear Robin. He had always been so faithful and had an implicit belief in her.

As she made her plans to leave, Marcus Blythe advised that she borrow his carriage again. 'No sense in buying your own when there's one standing unused in the coach house at Staveley.'

'There's a curricle too,' she ventured. 'The squire said he'd teach me to drive it. And he wants to get Henry a pony.' He'd like that, she mused; so would she. She thought of the times she had ridden on Sorrel. Of her first attempts to mount him at Toby's insistence, and of the susequent thrill she had had when chasing away from the river-bank and the revenue men, of Sorrel's hooves pounding and her own heart beating in unison.

'Sorrel!' she exclaimed.

'I beg your pardon?' Mr Blythe questioned.

'Oh, I was thinking of the horse I used to ride. He belonged to Toby. I brought him to York but had to sell him. I couldn't afford to keep him. I see him sometimes,' she said, 'he pulls a gig.' She thought with affection of the powerful yet gentle animal; whenever she saw him she always stopped to stroke his nose.

'You could perhaps buy him back. If you offer a good price, that is,' he added. 'There are few people sentimental about their work-horses, I'm sure you could get him if you wanted.'

She left his rooms feeling much happier. He had advised her on her monetary position and she couldn't believe how much money she had. There was a real possibility of Matt coming home, she would find Sorrel and take him back to the grasslands of Staveley Park, and in just a few days she would see her darling Henry.

*   *   *

She had written to say that she was coming and as the carriage drew up outside the house, they were all waiting on the steps to greet her. An exuberant Henry, a relieved-looking Polly, a polite and cordial Henry Linton and a beaming Mrs Rogerson standing in the doorway behind them.

Jed took off his hat and touched his forehead as she stepped down from the carriage and then moved back as Henry propelled himself down the steps to greet her.

'Oh, Mamma. I'm so glad you're here at last. I want to show you my pony that grandfather bought for me, and he said that when I know how to handle her he'll get me

434

a little trap.' He paused for breath. 'I call her Whisper and I'm having a splendid time; and I've been very good like you said, and so has Polly, haven't you Polly.'

He turned to Polly standing shyly behind him. Polly, to her surprise gave her a small curtsey. My word, Annie thought wryly. Mr Linton has been busy.

'I hope you don't mind my buying Henry a pony,' Mr Linton murmured as he came to greet her. 'I wasn't trying to gain favour, but I saw just the one, so suitable for a child.'

She gazed at him frankly. He wasn't the type of man to offer or advance a gift as a persuasion or enticement, she realized that well enough. He had given the animal to Henry because he wanted to.

'You're very kind, sir,' she smiled. 'Henry will be delighted. And,' she added. 'Whisper shall have a companion. I've traced Sorrel, Toby's horse. He'll be coming next week.'

Her words had such an effect on Henry Linton that she wished that she had waited before mentioning Sorrel. His eyes immediately filled with grief and he put his hand to his mouth and quickly excused himself and hurried indoors ahead of them.

Jed nodded to her and whispered. 'Mayster was fond of that hoss. Master Toby used to ride up here on him whenever he came to visit.'

'Yes, Jed, I know,' she said, full of remorse. 'I remember.'

She had changed out of her travelling clothes and was resting on the day bed in her room when she heard the sound of a bell being rung.

Henry knocked and came in. He was washed and changed into another suit and his hair neatly brushed. 'Come along, Mamma. That's the supper bell ringing. We have to go down.'

In some surprise she got to her feet and laughingly followed him down the stairs. There had been no such formality when she had stayed last time, Mrs Rogerson had simply knocked on her door and told her supper was ready.

Now however, Henry led her by the hand towards the dining-room, the beautiful, panelled dining-room which was never used. He opened the door and then looked up at her gleefully. 'There, Mamma. What do you think of that? Grandfather and I planned it as a surprise for you.'

A candelabra was set at each end of the long polished table which was now covered in a white damask cloth. Ivory handled cutlery was set in three places and there was a blue and white service of plates and tureens with matching finger bowls. Sparkling glassware and silver serving-dishes glinted from the flame of the fire and the candles, and Annie looked in awe and delight and then turned to Henry Linton who bowed formally to greet her.

'Sir, there was no need,' she began.

'I know,' he smiled as he interrupted her. He looked very handsome in his velvet coat and knee breeches and frilled stock around his neck. 'But I thought that as today was rather special – we were looking forward to you coming back, weren't we Harry – that we planned this as a surprise for you. I remember that you said how much you admired it.'

He looked directly at her. He was trying very hard, she thought. He was making such an effort to welcome her here. He was for the moment anyway, discarding his old habits and proposing to conform.

'So, Anna. Will you stay? Will you make this your home, yours and Harry's?'

She was honest. 'You realize, sir, that I am not used to splendour such as this? As I explained, I am from a much simpler background than yours. It may take me some time to adapt.'

He nodded and motioning her to sit down at the table, drew out a chair for her. Young Henry stood waiting, his eyes alight, watching to see if his mother was pleased with their preparations.

'I do realize.' The squire took his place opposite her.

'We both have to adapt – to each other – as well as to changed circumstances.' He smiled a wide smile and for the first time she saw that he too had a narrow gap between his teeth like Toby and Matt. 'But I'm sure we shall manage, although I don't imagine that it will be easy for either of us. We are both, I think,' he said wryly, 'a little short on patience. We are not long-suffering or submissive and we won't see eye to eye. But we must learn from each other.'

He poured her a glass of wine and lifted his in a toast. 'So can I propose a toast?'

She lifted her glass and nodded in acquiescence.

'To us both, then.' He reached to touch her glass with his, '—and forbearance.'

'And me, and me.' Henry lifted his glass of watered wine towards theirs. 'Don't forget me.'

'How could I possibly?' Henry Linton turned to his grandson and raised his glass. He smiled at Annie and she knew he was won over. His grandson had already found a place in his heart. 'To you, Harry, and to your father, and to Staveley Park.'

41

She heard the pounding of hooves on the drive early the next morning and rose from her bed to see who it was. A rider had dismounted and was talking to Jed. She saw him hand over a letter and then mount again and canter away.

She threw a shawl over her bedgown and hurried downstairs. Her heart hammered. Could it be a message from Matt?

'Is it a message for me, Jed?'

'No, ma'am,' Jed pulled off his shabby hat. 'It's urgent for mayster. I'm to tek it to him straight away, but I've not seen him about yet.'

Probably because he was late to bed, Annie mused. We shared three bottles of wine as he reminisced about his life and I told him a little, but only a little of mine, and then I left him nursing a bottle of brandy. He might well be feeling a little groggy this morning.

But he wasn't. He appeared at the top of the stairs dressed in his working clothes, his heavy breeches and sturdy boots and plain coat.

He wished Annie good morning, and took the message from Jed. She watched his face as he read, trying to glean whether it was good or bad news.

'Tell Kent to prepare the carriage.' He spoke briskly to Jed. 'I'm leaving for London immediately.'

'London?' Annie asked incredulously as Jed hurried away. 'It's about Matt isn't it?' She clung to the bannister rail. 'There's news?'

'Yes, my dear.' He handed her the letter. 'But we mustn't yet build up hope. They've located which ship he's on, the *Glory*, but it's somewhere off the coast of Spain and they

438

cannot possibly contact him until it returns to England; however, they have invited me to discuss the issue with them. God damn it,' he burst out. 'They know they're in the wrong – I shall challenge the legality. Somebody will answer for this.'

She sat down on the bottom step of the stair as he went back up again to change for his journey and mused that if Matt was as far away as Spain then it could be many months before she saw him again. Then the thought crossed her mind that the navy only knew that the *Glory* was the ship he had sailed on, they wouldn't know if he was still on it.

Henry called down to her from the long-galleried landing. 'I'm sorry to have to leave you so soon, Anna. Mrs Rogerson will help you all she can. Do what you wish, and I'll be back as soon as I can.'

He was gone within the hour and Annie wandered around the house, opening doors to rooms which were closed up and shuttered, mounting the stairs to the top floors where the servants would have slept had there been any. Mrs Rogerson slept on a bed in a room beyond the kitchen and the kitchen maid went home to the village every night at ten o'clock and came back every morning at five. She didn't find where Jed slept but guessed that it was above the stable along with the groom Kent.

I'll speak to Mrs Rogerson about it, she thought as she came down again. It's so pointless having all these rooms and her sleeping down stairs. Though it's probably warmer near the kitchen; the rooms at the top of the house had a musty chill about them and she guessed that the young maid wouldn't want to sleep alone up there.

There was a rattle of wheels on the drive and she lifted her head, another carriage was approaching. She went into the sitting-room off the inner hall and waited for Mrs Rogerson to open the door.

'Mrs Burnby, ma'am. Are you at home?'

She gazed nonplussed at the housekeeper. Of course she was at home. Wasn't she here staring her in the face?

'Are you receiving visitors, ma'am?'

Annie swallowed. 'Oh. Er, yes, certainly. Show Mrs Burnby in please.'

Not by a flicker of an eyelash did Mrs Rogerson show that she guessed Annie was ill at ease. She opened the door wide to bring in the visitor and said, 'Tea and chocolate, did you say, ma'am?'

'Thank you Mrs Rogerson, if you would please.'

'My word, you'll have her eating out of your hand. The servants in this house are not used to such pleasantries.' Mrs Burnby swept in and extended her hand. 'How pleased I am to see you again, Mrs Linton, it has been such a long time. So good of you to see me. Henry left a message yesterday that you were here at last and would I call, and now I hear that he has gone off somewhere.'

'He's had to go to London on rather urgent business.' Annie dropped the name of London as casually as if it was a commonplace city for visiting instead of the capital of the kingdom which she only knew by repute.

'Indeed!' Mrs Burnby arched an eyebrow. 'Has he word of Matthias?'

It seems that Mrs Burnby is a confidant of Henry Linton if she is so well informed, Annie thought. I wonder what he has told her of me?

'We've received news of Matt's ship and Mr Linton has gone to the Admiralty to discuss certain issues with them.'

'That's excellent news.' Mrs Burnby nodded, then looked with some satisfaction around the sunny room. 'I am so glad that you have at last decided to come and live here, Mrs Linton, instead of your house in York. Henry needs the company, he was becoming quite morose.' She unbuttoned her greatcoat and Annie took it from her and indicated that she should be seated. 'Yes, I've noticed the difference in him already since he has had your dear little Harry with him. It will do them both good. A child like Harry needs a man around, and until Matthias returns—'

'If he returns.' Annie sank into a chair. 'Sometimes Mrs

Burnby, I feel so miserable. It has been so long.' She hung her head. 'To find Matt and then to lose him again.'

Mrs Burnby leaned forward and grasped her hand. 'I do understand, my dear. Henry has told me something of your difficulties; that you have had no training in formal or social accomplishments, and having no family to turn to it can't be easy for you. But,' she said briskly, 'that is why I am here. I shall help you.'

Annie looked at her in surprise. What did she mean? And her amazement increased as Mrs Burnby went on.

'Now. Whilst Matthias is away we must busy ourselves and prepare for him.' Mrs Burnby drew herself upright and Annie saw only good intentions. 'This place needs a mistress – has done for years. We shall make sure it gets one.'

Mrs Rogerson knocked and brought in the tray laid with china cups and saucers and two silver pots with tea and chocolate.

'You will enjoy having a mistress about the place, won't you, Mrs Rogerson? And some more help?'

Mrs Rogerson's face creased into a smile. 'Oh, yes, ma'am. That I would.' She gave Mrs Burnby a curtsey and left the room.

Annie poured chocolate for Mrs Burnby and tea for herself and handed her a plate of biscuits, fresh from the oven. There's been a conspiracy, she thought. I rather think Mrs Rogerson was expecting visitors. She sipped her tea thoughtfully. 'But *I* can't authorize bringing in servants,' she began. 'Mr Linton will be annoyed, he likes things as they are.'

'No, he won't. Not if we do it gradually. After a while he will start to enjoy the extra comforts. He always used to anyway,' she said with a hint of a smile. 'In the old days, I mean.'

'Have you known Mr Linton a long time?'

'Oh, indeed. Since we were children. There isn't anything I don't know about Henry Linton, so if you are ever in doubt, you only have to ask me. I know the old rascal inside out.'

She sipped her chocolate and then placed the cup back onto the table. 'But the first thing we must arrange is a companion for you. Now who do we know?'

'But why should I need a companion? I have Henry – or Harry as he seems to prefer, and when Sorrel comes we shall ride every day. And when Mr Linton comes back I shall ask him if I might go with him around the estate.'

'But, don't you see—? Oh, of course, this is what Henry meant when he said you hadn't any idea of what was right and proper.'

Annie bristled. What else had he been saying about her.

The frayed feathers on Mrs Burnby's hat nodded as she emphatically gave her opinion, and Annie made a mental note that when next she visited York she would bring back some new trimmings for Mrs Burnby.

'You can't stay here alone without a husband, especially when Henry is away.' She lowerered her voice though there was no-one to hear them. 'You must have a female companion. You must realize that?'

How very strange these people were. Annie was baffled. Mrs Burnby presumably knew or guessed that Harry was born out of wedlock and that her marriage to Matt had come later. Yet now she was trying to protect her reputation. 'I don't know anyone I could ask,' she said. 'I have no female friend who could possibly come.'

'Then we must advertise for someone,' she mused. 'I'll tell you what we'll do,' she sat back with a smile. 'You can have my Danielle until we find someone. I can manage without her, I think, just for a short time.'

Annie was filled with dismay. To have a female here, a servant who was probably higher born than she was. She'd want to dress her hair and help her dress and would expect her to behave in a ladylike manner! No, she couldn't. She wouldn't!

She shook her head and said firmly. 'No, Mrs Burnby. You're very kind to suggest it but I couldn't deprive you, I—.' A thought struck her; she knew just the person. 'I've thought of someone who would, I'm almost sure, be glad to come.'

Joan Sutcliff. She's so miserable at home with Lily happy with Sergeant Collins, and young Meg with a beau. They can manage without her, I'm sure she'll come, and I can be myself with her, I shan't have to worry about saying or doing the wrong thing.

She beamed at Mrs Burnby. 'I'll write straight away and ask her. More chocolate, Mrs Burnby?'

* * *

Joan Sutcliff didn't write back but simply arrived a week later in a hired chaise. She jumped down from the steps and hauled out six pieces of luggage and flung her arms around Annie's neck. 'Tha's saved my life, Annie. I thought I would go mad at home with Lily and Stuart and now Meg, all mooning around lovesick.'

'I can't promise that it will be very exciting,' Annie laughed, 'but it will be different.'

Joan looked up at the house. 'Oh, it's so grand, Annie.' She clapped her hand to her mouth. 'Mrs Linton, I mean. I'm sorry, I might forget sometimes at first, tha'll have to forgive me?'

'It doesn't matter Joan – Miss Sutcliff, I mean,' Annie answered with a laugh. 'We'll just have to try and remember when there's anyone else about. But this will be a friendly household. I've already decided that. I couldn't live here otherwise.'

Henry Linton arrived back a few days later and expressed no surprise to find another female in the house. He greeted Joan pleasantly enough and asked polite questions about trade on learning that her father was an innkeeper.

'Well, Anna. I know that you are anxious to know the news,' he said as he poured the two ladies wine at supper.

Joan rose from the table. 'Would you like me to leave, sir? You have matters to discuss with Mrs Linton.'

He shook his head. 'Not unless Mrs Linton wishes it.'

She said she didn't and Joan sat down again, casting a hesitant glance at Annie. It was going to work, Annie thought with relief. I'm so glad that she came.

'Well, as I told you, they've located the ship he is sailing on. Located – Pah! What they mean is that it's somewhere between the Atlantic and the English Channel. The seas are full of ships and it is apparent to me that these powdered big-wigs who are supposedly running the war, don't know the difference between a man-o'-war and a cork in a tub! There's news of mutiny on our ships. The men are sick of poor food and conditions on board, not to mention the fact that most of them would rather be home minding their shops.' He poured himself another glass of wine and stared into it and Annie waited patiently for him to continue.

'Anyway. I got them to agree that Matthias shouldn't have been pressed. It was a liberty to do so; not only as a gentleman, but also that he was exempt as a captain of a merchant ship. I told them that I would bring an action in the courts if necessary. They'll talk to their law officers. It's only a matter of procedure now.'

Annie felt her eyes fill with tears. 'So – so, then he can come home?'

He nodded. 'He can come home.' His voice was husky. 'God willing that he is alive and well and not in a watery grave alongside his brother.'

Annie saw in his face the great strain Henry Linton was under. Not only was he full of regrets for what had happened in the past, but now he must feel that he was in danger of losing Matt as well as Toby. She reached out a hand towards him. 'We musn't lose hope.' Her voice choked. 'He's strong and vigorous, he'll not let a few Frenchies stop him from coming home to us.'

*   *   *

Though they seemed to have reached a mutual understanding of each other, both Henry Linton and Annie knew that life together wouldn't be easy and there were times when their tempers frayed and they could not hold in their emotions any longer. Then either Henry would object to her 'mollycoddling' the servants as he called it, or she would call him a tyrant for the way he treated them, and they would slam doors or shout at each other, and that in turn would lead him to roar that she was no better than a street urchin and she would screech that that was exactly what she was.

Then she would pack a bag and go off to York and stay with Robin and Rose, who greeted her with delight, but who, she realized, no longer needed her there for the business. The accounts were always up to date and the cloth from the merchants always ordered in good time for the next season; and after a week or so, she would bid them goodbye and return to Staveley Park.

But Henry Linton was protective towards her and though he insisted that she accompany him to social activities, he made sure that he was always at her side in case awkward questions about her background should be asked. She detached herself from the idle chatter of the ladies, and towards Clara and Jane, who occasionally came to stay with their aunt, Mrs Burnby, she remained aloof. And these two qualities which she maintained merely because of nervousness and what she thought of as her inadequacies, somehow added to her mystery.

And in spite of their differences she and Henry Linton began to realize that they were very alike, and Annie recalled the verbal fights that she and Matt used to have and the names he used to call her, before they realized that the emotion they felt wasn't hate, but love. And in remembering this, Annie's ragings at Henry Linton became tinged with humour and they would start with anger and finish with laughter.

The servants, and now there were more, seemed to

breathe a sigh of relief at this change of atmosphere, and Jed one day touched his forehead and said, 'Don't thee worry about me and Mayster over much, ma'am. I'd be powerful bothered if he didn't rant and rave at me – I'd think I'd done summat really wrong,' and Annie began to realize that there was a different order of things in this society; that sometimes people were more comfortable knowing their place and what was expected of them.

She had asked Henry Linton if Mrs Rogerson could have more help and he'd shrugged and said she should do as she wished. Another girl was brought from the village and a youth to bring in the wood and clean the boots and to do the heavy work, instead of Jed. And Polly looked brighter for the addition of younger company to talk to, though Annie noticed that she gave herself a few airs and seemed to consider herself a step above the kitchen staff, being nursemaid and companion to Harry.

The first winter was cold and a thick layer of snow covered the ground and Annie ordered fires in all of the rooms, including the top floor where the two young maids now slept. She allocated a room for Mrs Rogerson too and though she was reluctant at first, she eventually moved up and Jed shifted himself into her old room behind the kitchen.

There was still no news of Matt though they had an official letter from the Admiralty saying that after due consideration they had decided that he might be released from the service with the navy, though they would be pleased if he would agree to stay.

As the thaw came she started to ride again on Sorrel, sometimes with Harry who had become very proficient on his little pony, sometimes with her father-in-law and Jed around the estate, and she noticed that he listened more to Jed's suggestions about ploughing and crop-growing, and agreed that the sheep were not as profitable as they once were.

'We've plenty of land, sir,' Jed said one day as they stood at the top of a valley. The snow was slowly melting and green patches were showing through. 'We could try a few acres just to see how it worked. There's men and hosses enough to do it and if we got started soon we could get in a spring crop.'

Henry Linton grunted and looked down the valley. 'All right. We'll do it. Get the men started and I'll have your hide if it doesn't work.'

Jed grinned and tightened the reins of his mount. 'Aye sir, I'll go right away and get them set on,' and Annie gave him a smile at his look of triumph as he rode away.

But, often, as the spring slowly began, as the smell of new grass and chalkland flora, the bleat of young lambs and the *peewit* call of the lapwing opened up an impelling instinct in her, she took off her boots or shoes and put on an old dress and her gold-lined cloak, and rode barefoot and bareback to the edge of Staveley Park land and gazed down. She narrowed her eyes and looked down, down into the steep-sided valleys, beyond the dips and curves of the narrow roads and tracks, on past the farms and copses which surrounded them, towards the villages of North and South Cave and beyond them to the ribbon of glinting water which was the river.

Her river. The Humber. The vast estuary which ran to the sea, the sea which carried the ships where Matt might be. And then she remembered her dream. The dream of the ship with sails blazing, and of Toby and Matt and Harry holding hands together and smiling at her. And she would turn away, sobs shaking her body, and ride back, back to the great house of Staveley Park to Henry Linton and Harry, who were waiting for her there and she would know that it wasn't enough, that she was still very much alone.

*   *   *

There came one night when she couldn't sleep, when she tossed restlessly in her bed and then got up and went into Matt's room and laid wide-eyed on his bed. Dawn was still an hour away and she could hear the lonely call of an owl and an answer from its mate.

She went to the window and looked out. The garden was streaked by moonlight – the trees touched by its silver were sending long shadows across the grass, and the rosebeds in the lawn were deep, pitch dark pools. She gazed out, her arms clasped about her and knew that sleep had finally deserted her.

Quickly she dressed. She put on a warm dress and a shawl and over that her old cloak and padded silently downstairs. The door of the inner hall creaked as she gently eased back the bolt and opened it, and then again the outer heavy wooden doors slowly opened to let in the cool air. She closed the door behind her and sped away, feeling the sharpness of the gravel on her feet as she ran to the stables.

There was no sound from the hayloft where Kent, the groom, or Jennings the new youth, had their beds, and stroking Sorrel gently to soothe him she led him outside. She mounted him on the grass in the paddock so that no-one would hear them as they cantered away and she set off once more to the head of the valley where she could watch the dawn break over the Humber.

She tied Sorrel to a tree and with her heavy cloak wrapped around her she sat on the edge of a bank at the top of a hill and waited. The dimness of the mystical time which hangs between night and day, hovered over her like a dark cloud, enveloping her in its shroud. Then the darkness began to disperse, bedewing her with moist grey vapour. Droplets of water gathered about her face and hair but, as the sun rose and the warmth increased, dried on her skin making her feel as if she had freshly bathed.

The light rose like a curtain in the east, opening to bring forth a natal dawn. A dawn of such dazzling splendour it almost took her breath away. A flush of rose, a glory of gold, a light of a million candles lit the sky to herald a new day, and with it a fresh hope that today might be the day when she would hear that Matt was safe.

She saw then the glint of the river as the light in the sky mirrored on the water. She gazed in wonder. This wasn't her river; not the deep muddy waters that she knew so well, not the rushing river of childhood nor the eddying vortex of hidden secrets and fears. And although she couldn't see its movement from this great distance, she knew that this was a cleansing, flowing, springtime flood with an irridescent rainbow staining its opal surface.

She rose to her feet and let her eyes follow its course until the curve of the land hid it from her view, then she rove back again to its glistening centre and once more into the awakening valley. A horse and plough were moving infinitesimally slowly, so it seemed, across a dark field; a flock of geese calling intermittently flew across the valley, and a kestrel hung suspended above her, while from the copses and woods came the waking cry of a thousand birds.

How awesome it is, she wondered. A new beginning. I've never seen the day begin so, even though I've seen many dawns. She stood a moment longer unable to take her eyes from the panorama in front of her. This has to be an omen for something very special. She felt within her a renewed hope, a bright and fervent expectation.

She stretched her arms to the sky and remembered that other time when she had done the same, down by the river in Hessle, and Matt had appeared. She smiled sadly; such dreams, Annie – yet life would be nothing without them – and cast her eyes nearer. The track from the lower village was clearer now, the chalk surface was bright in the clear morning light and showed the dark figure of a horseman riding towards her.

He must have set out in the middle of the night from somewhere, she mused as she watched. The horse was a bay she saw as they came nearer, the man of upright bearing in white breeches and dark coat with high white stock and cocked hat. She put her hand to her forehead. He was wearing a sword and the lapels of his coat were white like the sea officers wore.

She became breathless as her pulses raced. Could it be? It had to be. Please God, let it be him. She picked up her skirts and ran down the hill and stopped again to take another look. She couldn't see his face for the shadow of his headwear, yet there was something, some shape of his shoulders, the tilt of his head. It was!

'Ma – a – tt.' She stretched out his name in an imploring syllabic note which echoed down the dale. He looked up and around and she realized that he couldn't see her, that she was in shadow with the hill behind her. She took off her cloak and turned it inside out and waved it and called again.

It was him! It was him! He saw her and she heard his cry as he urged on his mount and galloped towards her, and she ran, crying and stumbling over the grassy hummocks, jumping ditches and crevices to reach the chalk road.

He flung himself off his horse and ran the last few yards towards her, his arms outstretched to catch her as she flew down the hill to be held close and safe and loved.

42

'I can't believe that you are here, after all this time. I must be dreaming again.'

Matt kissed her lips again and again. 'I'm here,' he whispered. 'Though it seems like a dream to me too. And yet it's as if we have never been apart. You look just the same – your hair hanging down your back – your feet bare. You're just as I have imagined you to be every time I've thought of you.'

She laughed and rolled over in the grass to hold him close again. 'What a blessing I came out here to watch the dawn. You might have arrived back at the house and not known me dressed in my finery!'

The sun was warm on them as they lay on the hillside. The smell of the disturbed grass was rich and fragrant and the tracery of new leaves on the tree branches above them etched a dappled pattern across their faces.

'You haven't become a lady, Annie? Don't tell me that father has been trying to convert you?'

'I told him that he would be wasting his time. I can't change. I am what I am, though I do try. I don't want to embarrass him in front of his friends – or yours,' she added anxiously. 'I don't want you to be ashamed of me.'

'I'd never be that.' He got up and pulled her to her feet and held her close. 'Never. Those who want my friendship must accept me for what I am, and my wife.'

He reached for his shirt which was lying on the grass and she saw his weather-brown back and the scars running across it. She touched his back gently and he flinched. 'What are these, Matt? Who did this?'

'Practically every seaman has a scar to show for his life

at sea!' He shrugged off her questions as he tucked his shirt into his breeches.

'Tell me!'

He looked down the peaceful green valley towards the direction of the Humber. 'It started when we were put in the tender at the quayside. There must have been a hundred men, maybe more, packed into that stinking hell hole. There was a grating across the hold and it was padlocked, and some of the men had been there for days. We couldn't see daylight, there was no air and no room to exercise. So I complained! Loud and long, and then others did too, and I was brought out and accused of causing an affray and endangering the ship.'

She saw a sudden anger on his face. 'Me!' His voice was harsh and bitter. 'Endangering the ship! When I only ever took true seamen on the *Breeze*, and here were these men telling *me*! Men who had hardly ever tasted water, let alone sailed on it!'

'Ssh.' Gently she calmed him.

'Twelve strokes of the cat!' He grimaced. 'I could have borne the pain, but the injustice will always rankle.'

They started to walk up the hill to collect the grazing horses. 'And of course my reputation preceded me. I was marked down as a trouble-maker. It seemed that everything that went wrong on that first voyage was of my doing, and if I objected, which I usually did, I was given the lash. I would have jumped ship if I could but I was confined to the hold whenever we were in port.'

His face suddenly brightened. 'Then I was transferred to another man-o'-war, the *Glory*, and found my old friend Greg Sheppard in command. He'd volunteered and been given a commission. I persuaded him to apply for Parson White to be transferred and then the three of us took an oath that we'd fight the French and their allies instead of our own navy, and we'd scuttle old Boney's ships.'

'I used to dream,' Annie said slowly. 'I dreamt that you were on board a burning ship and that Harry and Toby were with you. I was so frightened.'

452

'The ship did burn. On this last voyage we ran into a major sea battle, which made all the others seem like skirmishes. The British ships were surrounded by the big French gunships and we sailed up right behind them. They must have felt like bears with a snapping dog at their heels, but our gunner crew were magnificent and raked several of the French ships. Then it seemed as if all hell broke loose, even the sea and the sky seemed to be alight, and we were hit several times.'

He gave a deep sigh and his face was etched with pain.

'Don't say any more, Matt,' she pleaded. 'Not now. Leave it.'

'No. It's best if it's out, then I can forget it.' As they reached the horses he put his hand on Sorrel's neck and gently stroked him. 'Cannon shot brought down a blazing mast. I was beneath it, but Parson White pushed me away. It hit him and knocked him clean into the water.' He closed his eyes for a second as if remembering. 'He was a brave man, Annie, as was Greg Sheppard. The country should be proud of such men. I'll never forget them.'

Annie felt her eyes fill with tears at the sadness Matt must feel for the loss of his friends, they had paid back tenfold for their previous misdemeanours, and she gave thanks that Matt at least had come safely home.

He turned and reached out to take her once more in his arms. He smoothed her hair and smiled and she saw the creases of pain that only time would eradicate. 'I love you so much Annie. It has been so long since I held you like this – kissed you,' he kissed her on each wet cheek, 'made love to you. I was beginning to feel that you were lost to me forever.'

He looked up beyond the hillside, beyond the woods, towards Staveley Park. 'And now I want to see my son. He will have forgotten me, won't he?' he asked with anguish written in his eyes. 'He met me only once. He won't know this stranger.'

She shook her head. 'Your father and I speak of you every day, and I remind him constantly of the day we saw you at the quayside; the day we were married.'

Jed had been sent out to look for her. They'd been anxious when they couldn't find her, he said, as he rode towards them. He touched his hat to Matt and said. 'Good day, Mayster Matt. Tha's back, I see.'

Matt laughed and put out his hand to shake the servant's. 'Yes, Jed. I'm back, as long ago you said I would be.'

The old man nodded, his voice was gruff. 'Aye. I was reet about thee, but wrong about Mayster Toby.' He blinked his watery eyes, then raised his whip and pointed. 'They're sending out another search party, ma'am. Here's Squire and Mayster Harry come looking.'

At the top of the dale Henry Linton on his horse with Harry by his side on his pony, were riding towards them.

'He's old enough to ride?' Matt gasped. 'My son!'

Annie wiped her eyes on her shawl. 'He's seven, Matt. Go on, go on. You've a lot of catching up to do.'

She watched from Sorrel's back, as Matt cantered towards the two riders and then saw Henry Linton as he recognized his son, suddenly goad his horse forward. They both leapt from their mounts as they reached the other and with swift steps flung their arms around each other.

Harry watched the two men and then pulling on Whisper cantered towards Annie who was riding to meet him. 'Mamma. Who—? Is that—? Is that my father come home at last?'

Annie jumped down from Sorrel and lifted him down. 'Yes, my darling. It is.'

Conclusion

Before a final curtain can be drawn over Annie's life, it is necessary to pass swiftly over intervening years; the years in which her happiness with Matt was almost complete. Almost, but not quite, for when a life is happy, time passes without awareness; but for Annie, at the birth of each of her sons, Tobias, Edward and Joshua, she was aware of a small pocket of emptiness deep inside her which never went away. As Matt gazed proudly and lovingly at each of these small beings, she thought each time of her other children.

Of her lost sons the memory faded, they became shadowy and distant as she was surrounded by her growing boys, but Lizzie's pale timid face and large blue eyes, were still as bright in her memory as ever. And she would lie in her bed and listen to the slow tick of the clock and sense the dark shadow of a dead man descend on her. Only when Matt was there could she be comforted, when he held her in his arms and whispered that Lizzie would understand.

When Bonaparte turned his gaze on the shores of England, Matt took a commission as a lieutenant in the Sea Fencibles under the command of Lord Keith. This force was to be a last line of defence against invasion and made up of volunteers, mainly naval men and fishermen who would be protected against unjustified impressment.

'I'm not needed here, Annie, not whilst Father is still master; but I can be useful along this coastline. Nelson favours this scheme though others are against it. And,' he said, taking her hand in an effort to convince her, 'it means that I shan't be far away from you.' He smiled and kissed her tenderly, 'I know too, that you are safe here with Father and Harry and the boys. And by the time this war is over, Father will be ready to hand over the reins to me.'

So she had to let him go to Nelson, who it seemed needed him more than she did, and they exchanged a secret smile when Matt was told that one of his duties was to assist the coastal signal officers and the revenue men, and wondered if he would come across his old enemy Roxton.

It was at this time that Annie realized that she was no longer needed at the drapery shop in York, that her commitment to the running of the business was so small as to be neglible and that Robin and Rose would dearly like to buy it for themselves.

'You deserve to have it, Robin, you have done so well here. I kept it on all these years as an act of defiance, because it was something which belonged to Harry and me that couldn't be taken from us, and I knew that Henry Linton didn't approve.' She gave a warm smile. 'But he and I have both changed and neither of us have to prove our worth to each other any more. And Harry! Why he's not in the least bit interested in fashion or cloth; he'd rather be knee-deep in barley or sheep wash! I'll write to Mr Blythe and ask him to draw up the necessary papers and you can take down the name of Hope.'

But Robin insisted on keeping the name. 'Without hope, Annie, life isn't worth a button. We'll keep it to remind us of how things used to be.' And so the sign above the renowned drapery and haberdashery establishment became Sampson, Hope and Deane.

The disbandment of the Fencibles, Henry Linton's mild stroke and yet another pregnancy came within the same year. Matt would now be home for good, to run the estate with Harry while Henry Linton contentedly watched his grandchildren at play.

Matt ran his hands gently over her swelling abdomen.

'If this is another son, Annie, we shall scare the wits from our enemies. We can start our own army or navy with the manpower we have here. Four sons,' he whispered in the darkness, 'yet, I would dearly love a daughter to spoil.'

And so she gave him a daughter. Elizabeth. But she would let no-one call her Lizzie. 'You can call her Elizabeth or Eliza or Beth,' she said softly as she lay exhausted with the tiny baby in her arms. 'But not Lizzie, for I have one Lizzie already.'

And she whispered to the child when they were alone. 'I'm happy, Elizabeth, but only as happy as I can ever be, for whenever I feel a joy welling up, like today, something always reminds me that I'm not allowed complete happiness. That I don't deserve it.'

*　　*　　*

'I've decided to go to Hull tomorrow, Matt.' She had made up her mind, calmly and deliberately. Elizabeth was two, she and the other children could be left with the nursery maid, the governess and with Polly in over all charge. She would take Joan with her for company and Grigson would drive them.

'But, I wanted to come with you, Annie, and you know that we've arranged for old Blythe to come tomorrow. Harry and I must both be here.' Matt looked at her in dismay. 'Leave it a while longer. You mustn't go alone.'

She shook her head. 'I must, Matt. I have to.'

He was anxious, agitated, and she stretched out her hand to him. 'I must face this alone, Matt, and if I don't go now, my love, I'll never go.'

He took both her hands in his and kissed them, and held them against his lips. 'I don't want you to go. I'm so afraid, Annie. So afraid that you won't come back.'

'What? Matt! Not come back? Why would I not come back?' It was her turn now to be afraid. 'Matt? You don't think—?' She started to shake. 'The law won't be waiting—, will it? Not after all this time?'

457

He shook his head and soothed her. 'No. No. Not that. There'll be no-one who will remember. No, it's just—! I am selfish I know, but, it's just that I have a terrible foreboding that if you find your other family, then you'll stay with them and won't come back to us—, to me.'

She stared aghast. How could he think such a thing? How could she leave her children, her home, her husband whom she loved? She saw pain in his eyes and sorrow, but something more—, could she see doubt?

Comprehension hit her like a blow and she understood the reason for his distress. Had he always been unsure of her? Had this lack of faith been constantly hovering within his mind? Twice in her life she had run away. Once from circumstances which even now she hardly dare contemplate, and had left her young family behind. And once she had run away from Matt, taking away from him the opportunity of deciding himself about the role of fatherhood and depriving him of Harry's early years.

'You have to trust me, Matt,' she whispered. She reached to touch his face and saw a few silver strands in his sideburns and beard. 'What can I say to convince you? I can only tell you that I love you. With my dying breath I will love you, and my children. I will come back to you.' She shuddered as the black shadow descended on her once more. 'Unless Fate takes a hand and keeps me from my promise.'

*   *   *

At the last minute she decided to take Tobias with her too, he was a mischeivous ten year old, with eyes as dark as the uncle he was named after, and as much exuberance, and was quite likely to cause complete havoc without her watchful eye on him.

She gave him strict instructions now as she left him at the Cross Keys inn with Joan, that provided he was on his best behaviour, then he could visit the quayside to look at the ships until she came back from her errand.

She had made enquiries from the landlord of the inn to ascertain if the shipping firm of Masterson was still there. If Will Foster still lived in Hull, then his old company might know of his whereabouts. *If I find him, then I'll find Lizzie and my lads.*

The town looked different, she thought, as she made her way across to the High Street. There were new streets and buidings, although some of the old landmarks were still there. *King Billy's still here;* she looked back down the Market Place and caught the gleam of gold from the equestrian statue, *they haven't got rid of him.*

Her steps slowed as she reached the narrow High Street, so many memories came flooding back and she wasn't sure if she could cope with the answers which her questions might bring.

This old street hadn't changed at all, unlike the rest of the town, except that some of the merchants' houses had been converted into business premises. *The residents have moved away from the stink,* she thought. *It's still there,* the clinging, odorous smell of boiling blubber.

There was a sign up at the front door, *Masterson and Rayner,* but after a moment's hesitation, she turned away and walked down the side of the building, down the staith which led to the river Hull.

'Can I help thee, ma'am?' A youth came out of the yard gate. 'Are you lost?'

'Lost?' she answered vaguely. 'I'm not sure. I think I might be.'

'Well, this lane leads to 'Old Harbour, tha'll not want to be down here. Where does tha want to be?'

'I'm looking for Mr Masterson or Mr Rayner.' Her words came out automatically. *There, it's done,* she thought dully, *the die is cast. Let Fate do what it will.*

The youth nodded. 'There's only Mr Rayner now. Mr Masterson died a while back. If you'll come with me,' he politely doffed his cap. 'I'll ask if he's free.'

She followed him through the yard and waited in a small room just inside the door. She felt as if she was trapped in time as she waited while he went in search of John Rayner. Along with the stench of blubber and seed oil and the acrid smoke of the charnel houses, she could smell the Humber and with it a faint tang of the sea. Gulls screeched over the river Hull, which ran alongside the High Street, and which she noticed, the boy still called by its old name, the Old Harbour, which once had been the only harbour for the whalers and trading ships of the world and which even now, she had seen, was crowded with shipping unloading onto the staith side.

'Can I help you? I understand you are looking for me.'

Annie swung round at the voice. It was John Rayner, Masterson's nephew. Gone was the good-looking young man that she remembered from long ago and a mature, handsome man stood in his place. He stroked his fair curly beard thoughtfully as he observed her.

'Mr Rayner, you won't remember me,' she began nervously. 'My name is Mrs Linton. My husband is Captain Linton of Staveley Park.'

Don't give too much away too soon, Annie. She began to feel sick with apprehension. I shouldn't have come alone. I should have waited for Matt.

He gave her a courteous bow and extended his hand for her to come inside and led her up a flight of stairs, through a room with a desk, and into a small sitting-room. He indicated that she should be seated and reached for the bell rope. 'You'll take a dish of tea, Mrs Linton?'

'Thank you, no.' She sat down apprehensively. She felt nervous and like the old Annie Swinburn she used to be, awkward and full of fear, now that she was back in the town where she had been born.

He sat down opposite her in a matching leather chair; there was a small dying fire in the grate and he bent to put on more coal.

'What can I do for you, Mrs Linton?' He dusted his hands together and she thought that his blue eyes narrowed for a second as he observed her.

Annie drew in a deep breath. 'You won't remember me, Mr Rayner, but I once lived in this town. My husband – my first husband that is—' How I hate to even think of his name, she thought, he onny ever brought me misery and pain. 'Alan Swinburn – he worked as boatsteerer and linesman with this company.'

John Rayner sat forward with a sudden exclamation. 'I do remember you. I know who you are. You're Lizzie's mother!'

*   *   *

At first his questions had been sharp and direct. Accusing almost. But as she related her life, omitting her crime, telling him only that she had once been in mortal fear for her life, and had to flee, he became more compassionate and his face took on a sympathetic expression.

But when she asked how did he know her Lizzie, he smiled softly and said, 'I have known her almost the whole of her life.'

'And my lads? Do you know them too?'

He shook his head. 'I regret, Mrs Linton, that your sons are dead. Your eldest boy died not long after you left, and Jimmy was lost at sea.'

She sat silently as he explained the circumstances. She had known in her heart that her sons were gone from her. Ted had been a sickly child, she always knew that he wouldn't make old bones. And now Jimmy lay beneath the Arctic waters with his father. 'May they rest in peace,' she whispered.

'Amen to that,' John Rayner spoke softly as if not to disturb her thoughts.

She stared at him. He knows Lizzie! How does he know? 'You know my Lizzie?' She spoke the words out loud. 'You know where she is?'

'Yes.'

A deep silence gathered in the room as she waited for him to continue, although she could hear the voices of men in the yard and the rattle of wheels on the road outside.

'How is it that you know all of this, Mr Rayner?' She was puzzled as to this gentleman's involvement with her family. 'And you know of my daughter? How is that? Is she in your employ?'

A flicker of a smile touched his lips and he shook his head. 'No, she is not. But as I said, I have known Lizzie for most of her life. She went with the Fosters and their children to a place called Monkston on the Holderness coast, where they were in my uncle's employment. Mrs Linton, – your daughter Lizzie married Tom Foster, who is now a miller; and I married the Foster's youngest daughter, Sarah. Lizzie is my sister-in-law.'

She felt tears flood her eyes again and she could hardly breathe she was so choked with emotion. After so many long worrying years, to know that Lizzie was alive and well and cared for. And she would be cared for, for she remembered young Tom Foster and what a grand lad he had been.

And she was a miller's wife; not living in poverty as she had always imagined, but with status in a community! Annie's heart almost burst. Lizzie had resiliance after all, she wasn't now the nervous, frightened child she had once been. She had risen above the wretchedness she had known and she had done it without her mother's help.

She took out her handkerchief again and wiped her eyes and saw John Rayner watching her. His face looked troubled.

'I suppose you want to meet her?' He spoke quietly, an anxious note in his voice.

'Why, yes!' She looked at him in surprise. 'That is why I have come.'

'Is that wise?' He held her gaze. 'It has been a long time. She is not the child she was; perhaps not the child that you are expecting her to be?'

'I know that she is now a grown woman, of course. Perhaps she even has childre' of her own?'

He nodded. 'They have two sons, both healthy. She and Tom have a settled life.'

A great depression began to envelope her. It stole into her mind and body weighing her down with its heaviness. What was he trying to say?

'Lizzie never speaks of her childhood in Hull, Mrs Linton. Not that I am aware of at any rate, though I have heard her and Tom speak of the games that they used to play at Monkston when they were children. For those who don't know of her background, it would appear that she had spent the whole of her life at Monkston.'

Annie felt faint. 'You're not saying that she would deny me, her own mother?'

John Rayner took hold of her hand as if she was a child in need of comfort. 'I'm not saying that. Lizzie is a kind, caring woman. She has found fulfilment with Tom and her family and is no longer the nervous child that she once was.'

It was as if he was repeating her own thoughts. 'What are you trying to tell me?' she whispered. 'That I shouldn't see her now that I've at last found her?'

'It isn't my place to tell you what you should or shouldn't do, Mrs Linton. I am only telling you how things are.' He looked down at her hand which he still held. 'Do you think Lizzie knew why you went away? And if she did know, does she remember? Or is it locked away in the furthest reaches of her mind?'

She felt the blood drain from her face. 'Do you know why I went, Mr Rayner? Does everyone know?'

He shook his head. 'I know because Will Foster told me. He's dead now, is Will. He was a good friend of mine, and he told me in confidence many years ago, when I asked why Lizzie's mother had gone.' He patted her hand and strangely she felt relieved that he did know. 'I have told no-one. This is the first time anyone has asked me.'

Her thoughts were jumbled. Her resolve to at last seek out Lizzie was crumbling. Would she indeed be welcomed back, or would Lizzie despise her for leaving her? But what else could I have done, she thought desperately? What had been the alternative? I never wanted her to know that I had killed a man, no matter that he deserved it. And if she didn't know, should she tell her now?

She raised her head and her words came out thick and slowly. 'You think it would be best if I went away without seeing her?'

'If you care for Lizzie, and I'm sure you do, then it would be the wisest, most loving thing you could do.'

*   *   *

She refused his offer of refreshments but accepted his insistence that she should be escorted back to the inn. He called for the youth, Bob Hardwick, who had spoken to her earlier and as they waited for him to appear, he assured her that he would contact her if ever he felt Lizzie was troubled and needed her.

Annie felt weak, yet calm. It was the right decision; and though she was saddened, within her pain lay a tenderness, a small spot of joy which came from knowing that Lizzie was happy. I wouldn't spoil that happiness, she thought as she looked back at John Rayner, still standing watching her from his door. I know now that she is loved and cared for. She doesn't need me, I was the one who needed her. She stifled a sob as she took Hardwick's proffered arm. It's the price I must pay.

The market vendors beneath their canvas stalls were shouting to attract custom from the crowds of people who were milling in the Market Place. They held up squawking chickens, wriggling rabbits and ripe cheeses as they passed.

Annie permitted herself a smile. There was good natured bantering with the customers haggling for a cheaper price; young children chasing one another between the stalls, and a group of militia men were idling their time away ogling young women and getting a lipful of cheek from them.

She gave a deep sigh. She felt curiously disburdened.

464

Her fears had passed. She could look forward to the future. Tomorrow she would go home. There was nothing for her here. She was a stranger.

Across on the other side of the Market Place she could hear the voice of a preacher. He was imploring all to follow in the way of the Lord and to be saved from damnation as he had been. Each time he finished preaching a judgement, someone rattled on a drum.

'Hey!' A shout came from behind her. 'Hey!'

Annie walked on towards the Cross Keys. Bob Hardwick turned around.

'Hey! I know thee!'

All her old instincts returned. She knew better than to turn around. To turn around was to invite confrontation, or to invoke a request from a beggar. Or to be confused by a jostling pair who would apologize for mistaken identity and then make off with a purse or baggage. Young Hardwick should surely know better than that.

'Annie Swinburn!'

Bob Hardwick slowed his step and glanced doubtfully at Annie, then he turned again. 'Be off with thee,' he shouted. 'Don't be bothering us. Go on, clear off.'

Annie's temples started to pound and she felt a flush mounting her cheeks which rapidly disappeared, leaving her white faced as an old woman confronted her.

'I knew it was thee. I knew one day tha'd come back. I've been waiting on this day!'

Annie with frightened hammering heart, stared mesmerized into the malevolent glaring face of Mrs Morton, Francis Morton's mother.

'Be off with thee, woman.' Bob Hardwick made to turn the old woman away, but with a surprising strength she lashed out, taking him unawares and making him stagger backwards.

Mrs Morton pressed her bloated face towards Annie, her eyes were hidden beneath pads of swollen flesh and her breath was rancid. She lifted her arm and Annie warding off what she thought to be a blow, knocked off her own velvet hat; her pins came out and her long hair tumbled down.

'Hah. It's thee all right. I'd know those locks and innocent blue eyes anywhere. I've dreamt of meeting thee again for twenty years.'

'You're making a mistake. I'm not who you think I am.' Annie's voice was tight and nervous.

The woman screwed up her eyes. 'Huh. Fancy talk and fancy clothes. Tha allus did think tha was a cut above everybody else.'

'Get away.' Bob Hardwick seemed to recover his senses. 'You don't know this lady. Be off or I'll call 'constable.'

Annie shuddered. So this was it at last. She should have known. Should have guessed that Mrs Morton would wait to avenge her precious son. Like a spider in its web she had been waiting all these years.

'Don't know her? Don't know her? 'Course I knows her.' She pointed an accusing finger at Annie and she shrank back against a shop window.

The shopkeeper came out, wiping his hands on a white apron. 'Clear off, Meg Morton. Tha's nowt but a troublemaker. Leave 'lady alone.'

A jostling throng started to gather around them and Annie began to shake. Some of the onlookers had come for sport, but she remembered how quickly their laughter could turn to violence. If they should believe Mrs Morton! She turned to Bob Hardwick. He was a stocky fellow – if they could elbow their way out of the press.

He'd gone! Wildly she looked around but all she could see was grinning faces. Then she saw him. He was running up the Market Place. She saw him stop and grab a boy and point a finger and then set off running again.

There was a sudden shout from further up the street and the crowd as one turned their heads, necks craned to see what was happening elsewhere. 'It's sodgers,' came a cry. 'Now there'll be trouble.'

Annie saw from the corner of her eye a flash of colour,

466

the clatter of hooves and rumble of cart wheels. She felt the grip of a hand on her arm.

'Don't think tha'll get away, dearie.' Mrs Morton hissed in her face. 'I'm off to fetch 'law. There's nowhere for thee to hide in this town. I know all 'places, all inns and hidey-holes, and I'll find thee, don't think that I won't.'

'Now then, Ma. What you up to? Come on, leave 'lady be.' A fair-haired man pushed his way through the dwindling crowd who were leaving for excitement elsewhere. Annie thought she would faint. Her breath came short and shallow and she gasped. It could have been Francis Morton risen from the dead. The same fair hair, laughing blue eyes and full sensual mouth.

'Sorry ma'am.' He touched his forehead. 'Me ma here is allus looking for somebody she used to know. She's forever stopping young women, thinking they look like 'one she wants.' He smiled at her, his eyes appraising her. 'I'll take her home, she'll not bother thee again.'

Mrs Morton lashed out at him and he caught her in a tight grip. 'Tha'll not take me anywhere 'till I've fetched 'law. This is her, I'm telling thee. She's come back like I allus said she would.'

'Aye, Ma, we know,' he humoured her and turned to Annie. 'She allus blamed a woman for my brother Francis's death. She's been looking for her for years.'

Mrs Morton had been watching him as he spoke, her eyes darting from him to Annie. She gave him a sudden shove which sent him off balance releasing her from his grasp and she tore off up the street. 'I'm fetching 'law,' she shouted as she scurried away. 'Keep hod of her, Ralph, don't let her get away.'

Another shout erupted from up the street; there came the sound of a pistol shot followed by a woman's scream. Both Annie and Ralph Morton looked up. A mob were swarming around a company of soldiers, she could see their red uniforms and the plunging heads of horses.

Bob Hardwick came running back. 'I've sent for 'constable and Mr Rayner,' he said, breathing hard.

Another great shout erupted from the crowd. The three of them turned as the crashing of carts and the frightened whinnying of horses rent the air. They saw the flash of steel as soldiers drew their swords and the arms of the rabble reaching up to drag them down from the backs of their mounts.

'Look out! Look out!'

A pair of greys, pulling on a gun carriage, their reins hanging free as their driver fought for his life beneath a melee of flailing fists and battering boots, threshed their forelegs in the air and tore away down the street towards them, the gun carriage and its cannon swaying and rattling behind them.

The crowd scattered, stalls were overturned as the mass of people fell back, trampling on one another in an effort to get out of the way. Bob Hardwick grabbed Annie and drew her back into the shelter of the shop doorway.

Morton scanned the street towards his mother's retreating figure. 'Ma! Ma! Watch out!'

Mrs Morton's black swaying shape was alone in the middle of the road as she scurried on in determined purpose.

'Ma!' Morton's voice rose to a scream and he sprinted towards her as the horses, in their mad bolt for freedom, gained on her.

Annie turned her head and closed her eyes, but not before she had seen the black robed figure of Mrs Morton tossed and hurled beneath the flying hooves and heavy wheels of the lumbering gun transport, like a bundle of bloody rags.

Someone ushered Annie into the shop and gave her a chair. She bent over and put her head on her knees and the shopkeeper fetched her a cup of water.

He shook his head. 'What a dreadful thing to happen! She's been a hazard for years, wandering around 'town, causing trouble, but even so!' He looked down on Annie, he'd been watching and listening to all that happened. 'Don't blame thaself, ma'am. Her family shouldn't have let her out on her own. There's enough of 'em to look after her.'

Annie took a deep breath. Her last adversary. She was surely dead. No longer able to accuse her. But she felt no joy, no relief; only remorse that the old woman should be trampled down in the way she had been. Was Mrs Morton any worse, she wondered, in her addled determination to bring her son's killer to justice, than she had been in protecting her own daughter from him?

A shadow fell over her. It was Morton. He looked down on her and she felt a sickening fear. His face was white, there was a coldness in his eyes and a slight tic twitching on his upper lip.

'She's dead. Never stood a chance. It's as if she never heard owt, she was that determined to get to 'magistrate.' His stare was accusing. 'There's more to this than meets 'eye. She said she knew thee.'

It's no good. I'm finished. Annie felt a great weight pulling her down. He'll be so bitter about his mother, he'll be prepared to believe anything she's ever said. I can't go on. I can't keep on running any more. When the constable comes, I'll tell him.

A figure blocked the doorway obscuring the light. She lifted dull eyes and prepared to stand. It wasn't the constable, it was John Rayner. He was holding Annie's hat in his hand. He glanced at the figures grouped around Annie, his eyes lingering momentarily on Morton, and then came towards her.

'Such trouble. I'm so sorry. I came as quickly as I could.' He gave her her hat and with trembling fingers she put it on and tucked her hair into it. 'I'd better take you back to the inn. You're very shaken I can see.'

'Just a minute, sir.' Morton blocked his path. 'Beggin' tha pardon, Mr Rayner, but there's questions to be asked of this lady. My ma—afore she was just run over, said she knew her from a long time back.'

John Rayner expressed his sympathy. 'I'm so sorry about your mother, Morton. So very tragic. There are people out there who have a lot to answer for if they listen to their consciences. There's a soldier dead too, people injured. A bad day all told.'

He shook his head in commiseration. 'Your mother was mistaken, I fear. Mrs Linton is a relative of mine, here on a visit. It is highly unlikely that your mother knew her.' He put his hand on the young man's shoulder as he bent his head and started to weep. 'Take her home. Let her rest in peace.'

*　　*　　*

She told Joan and Tobias that she had witnessed an accident which had shaken her. She would go straight to bed and tomorrow they would go home. Home, she thought. I'm going home.

'Did you find news of your family, Annie?' Joan looked at her anxiously. 'Was Mr Rayner able to help you?'

'Oh, yes. He did. He helped me in more ways than I could ever thank him for. He was able to tell me all I wanted to know.'

The next morning she was awakened by the insistent banging of a drum. The preacher was back in the Market Place, lecturing and cajoling. We all find our happiness in different ways, she thought, as she looked out of the window on to the street below. This unknown preacher has found his in the way of the Lord, and mine is waiting for me up on the hillside. She was leaving the past behind, the spectral shadows of the Morton family which had been hovering over her were gradually disappearing; only the future was important now.

'Mamma, Mamma. I want to show you something before we go home.' Tobias pulled on her skirt as they climbed into the carriage. 'Yesterday, Joan took me to see the ships in the dock, and then we saw the Humber. Mamma!' His eyes were shining. 'I don't want to be a farmer like Grandpa and Harry. I want to be a sea captain, like Papa used to be. I want to go to Trinity House School.'

She had given one son to the sea. Her eyes filled with tears when she thought of Jimmy, lost from a whaling ship. How could she risk giving another?

'Please, Mamma, can we drive that way so that I can show you where it is?'

'Of course we can, though I do remember. You forget Tobias, that once I lived here.' She smiled down at her eager young son and felt a sudden thrill of achievement. A son of hers going to the finest naval school in the land, and right here in Hull, where her own humble beginnings had been? Why, this town might be proud of her yet. Goodness. Tobias might even become an Admiral! Anything was possible!

Annie leaned her head against the leather seat as the carriage moved off and thought of Matt. She couldn't wait to see him, to share with him the joys and the sorrows. They would be up on the Wolds before dusk, home at last. Home, how sweet the word.

She opened her eyes as she heard again the sound of the preacher. She put her head to the window. She could see his black-coated figure and an incongruous red waistcoat, his large hat and beneath it some kind of spotted bandana. Beside him stood a woman with a drum.

'Stop!' She pulled down the window to call to Grigson. 'I want to get out.'

She jumped down from the slowing coach. 'I'll be a moment only. I must speak to the preacher.'

'Annie – Mrs Linton, please.' Joan was agitated at the picture of her mistress dashing across a public place.

'I'll go with her, I'll look after her. Don't worry.' Tobias, in search of fun was out of the coach in a flash.

Annie took hold of Tobias's hand as they approached the preacher. He had his head lifted to the sky and one eye closed in supplication. The other was covered by a black eye-patch.

'Parson White,' she breathed. 'You're alive!'

He opened his eye and closed his mouth and stared at her. 'Mrs Linton? Can it be?'

'Parson White,' she repeated. 'You're not dead!'

He shook his head. 'As I live and breathe, I'm not dead! The good Lord wasn't ready for me and here I am.' He put out his hands and grasped hers. 'Tell me that the Captain is alive and well!' He glanced at Tobias. 'Tell me that this is another of his sons!'

She nodded, too choked to speak. When she was able to continue she said huskily. 'But Matt said you were dead. He said you had saved his life and that you had been knocked into the sea and were drowned.'

'Indeed I was knocked into the sea and I thought that my last moment had come. I was down in the depths as deep as could be. But something or someone called me back, and I rose to the surface.'

He clasped his hands together and closed his eye again. When he opened it he looked down at Tobias. 'I was saved, young sir, to serve my fellow man. My fellow man saved me and I will give my life to serve him—, them!'

'But what happened, you old rogue?' Annie couldn't help but laugh. 'Matt will be so delighted when I tell him.'

Parson White raised a finger. 'Tell him by all means that his fellow mariner is alive and well and sends his humble regards. But don't reveal the manner of my escape, I beg you. It would upset him greatly.' He dropped his voice to a whisper so that Tobias couldn't hear.

'I was in the sea and drawing my last breath. I knew that I couldn't possibly survive. The ships were on fire. It seemed that even the sea was alight there was so much conflagration, and I was ready to meet my maker. Suddenly I felt something nudging me. I thought at first it was a spar or piece of floating timber, and I grabbed it. It turned over. It was a man's body. A body so blown apart that it was barely recognizable.'

He put his hand across his face. 'But I did recognize

him. Hadn't I shared his grog? Hadn't he and I and Captain Linton fought the same enemy?'

'Greg Sheppard!' she whispered. She had never met Matt's sea captain friend but he spoke so often of him, that she felt she knew him.

'Aye. It was he. There was no doubt in my mind. And he held me there above the water – didn't leave me once. It was as if it was his last act, even though he was well and truly gone from this world, to save me for some purpose.'

He blew his nose, loud and long. 'So don't tell the captain how he was, only that he died a hero's death.'

'You can tell him yourself,' she smiled. 'For he'll want to come and see you when I tell him that I found you.'

'Tell him, too, that I have got me a good woman.' He pointed to the small woman in a brown bonnet and cloak who was sitting on a stool holding a drum.

'Aye, she set me on the right path. She feeds me and takes care of me.' He winked his eye. 'Aye, and gives me a good deal more besides.'

'So, you're a respectable married landsman now? You've given up the sea for good?' Annie nodded amiably at the woman.

'Ah, well.' He shuffled his feet. 'The sea has given me up, I fear. I'm too old now for such a life, but the good Lord is happy to employ me. As for marriage,' he dropped his voice to a whisper. 'I was once married, ma'am, sanctified by church and law.' He cleared his throat. 'That good lady is still alive, but—,' he raised his hands to the heavens. 'We,' he indicated the woman, 'we have God's blessing on us until such time that the first Mrs White departs this life. Which won't be for some considerable time, I fear,' he added in an undertone, 'for she was very much my junior.'

Annie laughed and shook her head. 'You are, I think, a hopeless case, Parson White. But I am so pleased, so *very* pleased to see you again.' She grasped his hand and squeezed it.

'And I you, dear lady, and your son. Your other son?' he remembered. 'He is well, I trust?'

'Matt gave me five children,' she said, drawing Tobias to her. 'All healthy, and this one wants to be a seaman like his father.'

Parson White scrutinized Tobias. 'He has the look of his father and the eyes of his uncle. He'll make a good sailor, I'll be bound.' He drew closer. 'Tell me, Mrs Linton, and then I will detain you no longer, for I see your coachie getting anxious in this melee. Captain Linton and yourself,—erm, though you were of course married in the sight of God and witnesses right there on the waterside, were you, that is to say, did you ever wed again in church to conform with society's rules?'

She stared and stared, then slowly shook her head. She had always thought that she was a respectable married woman. Was this reformed reprobate parson telling her she wasn't? She had never once questioned her married state and neither, as far as she knew, had Matt.

It was too ridiculous for words. She started to laugh. She laughed and laughed until her sides ached and tears ran down her face.

She was still laughing when she stepped into the carriage, and she waved to Parson White as they bowled away, and his wife, in God's eyes, gave a rattling tattoo on her drum.

* * *

They climbed and dipped over the chalky downland and fell silent as they viewed the steep-sided grassy dales and the wooded dells. They could hear the rattling cacophony of pheasants and saw their bright plumage as they pecked in the ploughed earth. An owl, up early, called from the woods and Annie listened intently for an answering cry from its mate. There. The reply came clear and strong echoing over the valley.

Soon they would be home. They were almost on the

edge of their own land, and the old house, hidden in a fold of the hill, would be waiting, waiting with a houseful of children, a father and a husband.

Annie pulled down the window and called to Grigson to stop. Joan gave a deep sigh and glanced significantly at Tobias.

'I'm going to walk,' Annie said. She took off her hat and threw it onto the seat and then bent down and unfastened her boots and slipped them off. She rolled down her stockings and took those off too and tucked them inside her boots. 'I want you to drive on.' She smiled at the relieved look on Joan's face, she had never been over-fond of walking, 'and tell Captain Linton where I am.'

'Shall I walk with you, Mamma? There might be wild animals or robbers waiting to jump out at you!' Tobias watched her anxiously.

She patted his cheek. 'Wild animals and robbers are no match for your mother, didn't you know that? No. You go on home and tell the others that I'm coming, and tell Cook we'll have a celebratory supper tonight, and you can all stay up late.'

She watched as the carriage rattled away and waved her hand to Tobias's outstretched arm hanging from the window. She put her hand to her head and pulled out her hairpins and combs and put them in her pocket. Her hair dropped long and free, lifting in the slight breeze. She walked on feeling the sharpness of the chalk road beneath her bare feet, not minding it, but enduring the self-imposed discomfort as it sharpened and intensified her thoughts.

This walk she had wanted to take alone. She needed a quiet time to consider her past as well as the future which lay in front of her; to try to recognize the person she had once been and had now become, and to know if they were one and the same.

At the top of a rise she took a rest; her heart was hammering from the uphill climb and her breathing was rapid. She undid the buttons on her tight wool jacket and let her gown beneath it flow free without restraint.

'That's better,' she breathed, 'now I can go on.' But she paused a while longer to look back. She was overlooking a deep valley; to the right of the track she had walked up was a wood of mature trees. The leaves had turned to autumn gold; oak and ash glowed as the sun dipped, red and fiery behind her, and sycamore shed their crisp large leaves creating a yellow-brown carpet.

To the left of the track was a steep incline where the pasture land was cropped short by bleating sheep and scurrying rabbits. She narrowed her eyes as she saw the flash of a red bushy tail as a fox pounced on its supper and sped off with a screaming rabbit between its jaws.

But the view she was searching for lay in the far distance on the road she had just travelled. The scene which had always brought her comfort, even in the depths of her worst despair. The Humber, a brown river, flowing deep and strong and carrying the waters of other, lesser rivers, surged on without her, sweeping on in its inevitable rush to the sea.

'If ever I come this way again,' she whispered. 'I shall not be alone.' She took one more glance, the sky was darkening, the river was almost a trembling pencil line merging with the shores of Lincolnshire.

She turned away and looked up the valley towards the next rise. That was the place where she had waited once before, when Matt had come home. When she reached it this time it would be too dark to see the river again.

A figure sat on horseback atop the rise. It had to be Matt, come to fetch her home. She waved her hand and he waved back and urged his mount towards her.

He looked down on her from his horse's back. 'So, Mrs Linton. You came home after all?' He joked, but she saw anxiety on his face.

'Is all well at home?' she asked. 'Father? The childre'?' Her old dialect slipped out and he smiled, and dismounted.

'All's well,' he said. 'Did you find what you were seeking?'

She nodded and felt a fleeting shadow of pain. He put out his arms. 'We've missed you, Annie.'

She didn't move into the shelter of his arms as she might have done, but stood back and studied him seriously. 'Captain Linton! Wilt tha marry me?'

He gave a short laugh and his eyes crinkled at the corners. 'What? How can I marry you? I'm married already. I have a beautiful wife, five handsome children, so how could I possibly marry you? Besides who would ever marry such a creature? Look at you – why, you're no lady, with your hair hanging down your back and your coat undone and your feet bare!'

'I've come up from 'gutter, Mayster,' she croaked. 'Take pity on me!'

He took one large stride towards her and enfolded her close in his arms. 'Oh Annie, never leave again. I've missed you so much.'

She could no longer smell the sea or the river on him. She could smell the aroma of land, of hedgerow and meadow grass and the smoky fires of home.

With her arms wrapped tight around him she kissed him. 'Wilt tha marry me, Captain Linton? How many times do I have to ask?'

He laughed and returned her kiss. 'All right, you scarecrow. I'll marry you.' He leapt onto his horse and put out his hand for her to come up. 'Only tell me when we've had one marriage ceremony, why we should want another?'

She put her arms around his waist as they broke into a canter and whispered into his ear. 'Well, it's like this, Captain. When I was returning home from Hull, I met an old preacher – he'd once been a seaman and a smuggler—!'

His laughter and then hers resounded around the valley. It was echoed by the screeching of a barn owl which flew on silent wings across the hedges; was caught and repeated by the raucous cry of the pheasants, and the evocative bark of a fox. And where the chalk valleys descended gently into open flatlands and muddy shore, the mighty river Humber flowed ever onwards towards its destination.

THE END

A SELECTED LIST OF FINE NOVELS
AVAILABLE FROM CORGI BOOKS

THE PRICES SHOWN BELOW WERE CORRECT AT THE TIME OF
GOING TO PRESS. HOWEVER TRANSWORLD PUBLISHERS
RESERVE THE RIGHT TO SHOW NEW RETAIL PRICES ON COVERS
WHICH MAY DIFFER FROM THOSE PREVIOUSLY ADVERTISED IN
THE TEXT OR ELSEWHERE.

All Transworld titles are available by post from:

Bookpost, P.O. Box 29, Douglas, Isle of Man IM99 1BQ

Credit cards accepted. Please telephone +44(0)1624 836000,
fax +44(0)1624 837033, Internet http://www.bookpost co uk or
e-mail: bookshop@enterprise net for details

Free postage and packing in the UK.
Overseas customers allow £2 per book (paperbacks) and £3 per book (hardbacks)

CHILDREN OF THE TIDE
by Valerie Wood

It was a long walk from Hull to Anlaby, and the woman holding the newborn baby was tired when she arrived at the grand home of the powerful Rayner family. She was shabby but refused to be intimidated, and when young James Rayner appeared at the door she thrust the child into his arms. The mother had died, she said, the father was 'young Mr Rayner' – and then the woman vanished, leaving the respectable shipping family of Hull shattered.

No-one wanted to be responsible for the child. No-one thought to ask *which* 'young Mr Rayner' was the father – for surely it could not be Gilbert, who was about to make an excellent marriage? It was left to Sammi, James's young girl cousin, to take the baby back to her parents' home on the Holderness coast, rather than see it raised in the misery of one of Hull's orphanages.

Her arrival home with the unwanted child was to signal the beginning of a family furore. James was banished to London, and disaster began to beset the three branches of the Rayners.

By the bestselling author of *The Doorstep Girls*, *Far from Home* and *The Hungry Tide*, winner of the Catherine Cookson Prize for Fiction.

0 552 14476 2